INTO THE DARK,
WE GO

D. G. WOODS

Title: Into the Dark, We Go
Author: D. G. Woods

Summary: Nellie, a 23-year-old college dropout, is scrambling to rebuild her life two years after her boyfriend went missing. Now at a standstill, she's preparing to move back in with her mother, a prospect that fills her with dread. When two strangers approach her, claiming their sister vanished under similar circumstances, Nellie grasps a last connection to the love she once knew and a chance to find answers. She joins their search, following a fragile trail of clues into the heart of the Appalachian wilderness.

The further these desperate allies venture, the more the lines between reality and the unexplainable blur. The same shadows that stalked those before them now track their every step. The woods are hungry, and this time, Nellie could be next.

As they become entangled in generations of buried small-town secrets, Nellie questions whether they are closing in on the truth or being lured deeper into the dark.

Published in the United States of America by Cabins Press LLC.
ISBN: 979-8-9920445-4-6
This book is intended for adult readers (18 and up).
First Edition: October 6, 2025

For Wes

Content Warning

This book contains mature themes and graphic content that may be disturbing to some readers. Please be aware that the following topics are addressed within the story:

- Grief and loss
- Substance use
- Murder and graphic violence
- Gore and disturbing descriptions
- Retrospective mentions of domestic violence and sexual abuse
- References to suicidal thoughts or behaviors
- Depictions of torture

Reader discretion is advised. If you are sensitive to these themes or have experienced trauma related to any of these topics, please consider your own emotional well-being before proceeding.

Chapter One

May, 2017

"ARE YOU SCARED?" he asked.

I'd gone camping with my parents a couple of times as a kid during our trips to Florida, but we always stayed on campgrounds with other tourists. Even though the grass was slick and spotted with pits deep enough to swallow me whole, and my mother had warned me about alligators, I wasn't scared. I knew I was safe.

But now, alone with only darkness surrounding us, every sound made me flinch.

I stiffened by the embers of our dying fire. Ghostly fingers walked up my spine and brushed my lips. I felt like I was being watched. I wasn't sure what I feared—some kind of Blair Witch presence hungry for blood or a human lurking in the trees, watching and waiting for us to fall asleep in our flimsy tent.

We smoked a joint, and Lucas laughed while I grew increasingly paranoid, constantly listening for footsteps and cracking twigs.

He tried to distract me. "Look at the stars, Nell," he'd say, raising his face towards the dark abyss above us. "Amazing, right? It's like the sky is breathing."

But all I could see were the looming trees, monstrous giants with bare branches clawing for their next feast.

He told me stories of camping with his buddies back home, always emphasizing that rule number one in Appalachia was to stay out of the woods at night. When I asked him why he'd ventured in, he claimed he wasn't scared of anything in life and that fearlessness was its own kind of protection. But I was terrified, praying for dawn to come. Yet, the darkness only deepened.

Eventually, it was time to retreat to the tent. Lucas quickly fell asleep, but I lay awake, panicked, as the woods stirred with sharp cracks and tinny echoes and howls that shook the roots beneath us. I listened intently, rigid and ready to flee at the first sign of danger.

That was the only time I'd gone camping with Lucas.

September, 2020

MY PHONE BUZZED, interrupting the bleakness of my morning routine. The caller's ID showed a Missouri area code, so I declined and blocked the contact. The constant barrage of unwanted calls and messages had numbed me—usually spam or, worse, journalists and podcasters seeking to dredge up memories of Lucas. Some had even tried their luck for a confession, picking over my wilted heart like swollen maggots.

Yet, I never bothered to change my number. At first, I held onto the hope that Lucas might try to reach out from wherever he was, but as time passed, that hope faded. The unwanted calls, and even those from friends who were avoiding me, became fewer and farther between.

I couldn't blame them. In one of my psychology lectures, our professor shared a theory that people are more likely to believe the worst about others. "It's a means of self-preservation," he said. "If you suspect someone close to you is capable of something terrible, like murder, wouldn't you instinctively try to protect yourself by keeping a safe distance, even without concrete evidence?"

I never imagined that, of all the psychological theories, I'd have to implement this one in my life.

Just as I declined one call, another came in.

"How's the packing going?" My mother didn't bother with small talk, always getting straight to the point.

"It's going, Mom." I sighed and activated the loudspeaker, knowing she'd keep pushing until she got the answers she coveted.

"Everything okay with the landlord? You're arriving on Saturday, right?"

"Yeah, I'll be there next Saturday evening or Sunday afternoon at the latest."

"I'll get your room ready."

"Thanks, Mom. Just leave everything as it is, okay?"

I knew it was a lost cause, but I tried anyway. My mom couldn't resist the urge to control everything. She was very particular about her tastes. If something was not to her liking, the experience of everyone involved became miserable. I recalled one Thanksgiving when I'd presented her with a handprint turkey garland we'd crafted in kindergarten. I thought she'd hang it above the dining table—pride of place. But while Dad and the guests praised my masterpiece, Mom removed it from sight, saying it was too whimsical for her elegant decor.

"For goodness' sake. This is meant to be a party, not a museum exhibit." Dad retrieved my art from the spare room, untangling the stringy mess Mom had made. He was loud enough for the guests to grow uneasy, but they tried to laugh it off as he re-hung the bobbing turkeys and patted my head. "There. What do you think, Nell?"

I nodded, nestling into his palm to avoid Mom's cold stare. She was sour throughout the evening.

"Now, about that job at the hospital," she continued, "I can put in a good word for you in the finance department."

I counted to five before responding, trying to remain calm. "Thanks. I'll think about it when I get back."

"Think about it?" Her disapproving tone seeped through the phone like a cold mist. "You've been waiting around long enough, don't you think?"

"Mom, I have a job. I pay my bills. I'm not waiting around."

"It's your life, but I can't watch you squander your potential. You're so smart, and it's going to waste."

"Mom!" My voice betrayed me with a childish whine. She had a way of making me feel like a scolded seven-year-old again. "I have to go. My shift starts in half an hour."

"I always knew that boy was trouble," she continued against my protests. "Now look at yourself! Waiting for him to show up, getting yourself in trouble."

"Mom, stop. Please."

"You're just wasting your life, waiting for someone who's clearly not worth it."

The familiar knot in my stomach tightened.

"I'm not waiting for anyone."

"If you think you're respecting his memory by putting your life on hold, you're wrong."

My mom had a knack for recycling the same guilt trips, and somehow, it worked every time. We exchanged terse goodbyes, and I hung up, feeling utterly depleted. A photo of Lucas and me at the stadium after a game was still my phone's wallpaper: his face flushed with victory, his sweat-drenched jersey clinging to his broad shoulders as he leaned in to kiss me, the wind blowing my red hair against him. I loved us like that.

Lucas had lived and breathed football, and his dream of going pro right out of college consumed him. He had wanted it more than anything in life.

Now, the team had a new receiver, and I hadn't brought myself to follow football since, nor could I muster the courage to change the photo yet.

IT WAS early September in Minneapolis, but summer showed no signs of giving up. The heat was relentless. Even in the mornings, it was so warm that I wore jeans and T-shirts, adding a light shirt on top. The first few months after Lucas's disappearance, when it became clear he wasn't coming back, and it wasn't a stupid prank, I wore his hoodie everywhere. I left the rest of his things untouched in his gym bag, trying to preserve his scent.

The "North Point" cafe was a short walk from my house, across the river over a pedestrian bridge and to the left towards the North Loop, where the sun spilt like an egg yolk over the water.

It was the one place I felt at ease, and I hated myself for admitting it, but it was because Lucas and I never visited together. There were no memories of him—of us—pressed against the old oak walls, stealing kisses and daring touches. No secret moments in a shaded leather booth, laughing over a cold brew. It was a blank canvas. Something of my own, a job, and nothing more. For four mornings and two evenings a week, I could forget.

Two more nights a week, I worked as a waitress at a pub. The tips were good, and the place wasn't popular among students. However, there were times when I did get recognized. I could sense it right away. That gaze was unmistakable. At first, they would stare at me, then excitedly talk to each other, occasionally glancing in my direction.

Bingo! You've hit the jackpot. You've found the best bar in town where they serve an amazing Jucy Lucy, and your waitress is the one who supposedly committed the perfect murder and got away with it. Let's talk about how they never found the body. Just don't stare too much, and be sure to leave a good tip, or she might finish you off, too!

September, 2018

THE STADIUM WAS FILLED with the scent of fresh turf and buttery popcorn. The aroma clung to me as I weaved through the throng of eager fans, the air heavy with a brewing storm. Or maybe it was just my nerves. I'd been jittery all evening. The scoreboard flickered, flashing with a frenetic red glow before darkening again.

"Have you seen Lucas?" I asked a stocky defensive lineman from the team. He either didn't hear me or deliberately ignored me, still deep in conversation with two girls who barely looked of age. They giggled and tossed their hair as he leaned down to laugh with them.

"Jonas!" I snapped my fingers, and his bulk turned to me. He waved in a general direction, and I followed his lead, pushing my way through clusters of jerseys and painted faces.

It had been nearly a week since our fight, and I hadn't seen him since. Someone told me he'd gone to visit his family in Black Water, which seemed strange, given that the semester had just started. But in that time, I had ample opportunity to reflect on our relationship. I missed him deeply and wanted him back.

I could have waited until the game was over to catch up, but it felt necessary to talk to him sooner. My anxiety was eating away at me, and giving it more time felt like I'd lose him forever.

I struggled to keep my nerves under control and fidgeted

with the bracelet on my wrist. It had been a gift for our first anniversary and featured two charms—a tiny football and a running sneaker—symbols of our combined interests.

I frantically scanned the crowd, rhythmically knocking the sneaker into the ball to calm my angst. My breath caught in my throat when I spotted him emerging from the sea of people ahead, tall and handsome, his uniform making him look like a warrior ready for battle. He was entertaining a short blonde girl, his attention fully absorbed by her as she spoke. I could only assume she was trying her luck. Had rumors about our fight spread already?

I stood to the side and waited until they finished, lest I look the jealous type and make things worse. She glanced at me with a curious expression before nodding and, finally, walking away. I swallowed my jealousy, and with it, the desire to ask him who that was. Instead, I greeted him with a timid, "Hey."

"Hey," he repeated neutrally, crossing his arms over his chest. I tried not to squirm under his scrutiny.

"I've been searching everywhere for you."

"You found me." His one-sided responses annoyed me, but I ignored this one. We needed to move forward. My stomach churned as I struggled to keep my composure.

"I just wanted to talk," I continued.

"I don't have much time. The game's about to start." It felt like an excuse to brush me off. There were still a good ten minutes left.

"I know. I just wanted to tell you that I love you. I needed you to know."

His expression softened, and he reached out to brush a strand of hair behind my ear.

"I love you too." He smiled and glanced above my head at something in the distance. He seemed more distracted than usual. "Let's talk later, okay? After the game."

"Okay," I forced a smile despite my worry. "Go get 'em."

"Always do," he replied, and the wink he gave me when he turned away stirred butterflies in my stomach.

And then I noticed—

"Hey, where're your lucky socks?" They were his talisman, his charm; he wore them religiously.

"Don't need 'em!" He smiled, and confidence rolled off him like the wind over the field as he disappeared into the locker room.

It was weird. He always wore them during games. And although he told me he loved me, the tension in my stomach wouldn't ease.

The crowd vibrated with anticipation. My friends were already seated on the bleachers, chatting eagerly before the game started. I desperately wanted to join in their carefree conversation, to shake off the horrible feeling that it was already too late, but I couldn't.

Sarah noticed my awkwardness and stood to greet me with a peck on the cheek. "How did it go?"

I nodded slightly without going into much detail. My best hope was to see Lucas after the game.

By the second half, the opposing team was struggling. With three injuries and two substitutes, they were dead on their feet. Sarah nudged me, pointing towards my boyfriend. At least, I hoped he still was.

"What's up with that?"

Lucas was awkwardly stretching his arm around, and his face contorted in a wince. Every twist and turn of his torso seeming to cause him pain. He favored his left side, as if his shoulder blade was bruised or worse.

My body stiffened at the sight. I feared he'd been injured and was pushing through it. He was notorious for that. But then he brushed it off, dodging a tackle, turning a short pass into a long gain, and breaking free for a 40-yard dash. He was unstoppable.

The other team never stood a chance.

I lingered for a while after the game to spend time with the girls. The team was most likely celebrating, and I wanted to give Lucas some space to enjoy himself, to show him I understood he had other priorities, and to let him know I was okay with that.

THE STADIUM SLOWLY EMPTIED, the crowd dispersing like a cloud of spores. I watched the team exit the field, a knot of dread tightening with every disappearing player. Lucas was nowhere to be seen. The sound of celebrations in the distance suddenly felt hollow. Had he left already? Was he trying to avoid me? Was he with that girl from earlier?

No, he wouldn't do that. We had a ritual we'd stuck to for the past two years: I'd attend every one of Lucas's games, and afterwards, we'd meet up at the old concession stand by the east exit. It didn't matter if he had plans or commitments.

I pulled out my phone and dialed his number. It went straight to voicemail.

I hurried along the sidelines, where players often celebrated their wins. My eyes darted back and forth, searching for his silhouette.

"Did you see where number twelve went?" I asked a water boy collecting bottles from the bench.

He pointed half-heartedly at the entrance. "No idea. He was here just a second ago." Without waiting for my response, he turned back to picking up trash.

There was no way I'd missed Lucas. I'd watched the team leave.

The stadium lights started to dim, gradually plunging the field into heavy darkness. I headed toward the still-illuminated entrance, feeling the vast, empty space draw close as a lover.

The fluorescent lamps flickered out, and the tunnel vanished. Cold air seemed to move of its own accord, a chill sweeping down and then up. I stilled and strained my ears for any other sound—a locker slamming, a muttered curse, anything. I tried Lucas's phone again, but it remained stubbornly off.

Then it came: a movement from the dark, a quiet rustle like dead leaves. My breath hitched.

"Lucas?"

No answer.

I forged ahead, illuminating the way with my phone. My footsteps resonated like cold, wet slaps against the walls. The stale air grew thick and musky, carrying a hint of unturned soil and something else, something richer and unsettling. Decay.

Finally, I reached the locker room and pried the door open. Most of the lockers were ajar, and the phone light stumbled over them with my frantic breaths. The rustling was near. I could hear it much clearer now, lurking in the shadows with my unsteady heart.

I pressed on the overheads and looked up to see a plastic ribbon tied to the air vent. Its loose ends fluttered in the airflow, whispering and coaxing like silver tongues.

Under it, by an open locker, lay a gray sports bag, its contents spilt out. All the guys had the same generic gear, but I recognized the worn strap and the faded logo on these too well. They were Lucas's. His water bottle and a towel were nearby, with a couple of textbooks and his change of clothes and shoes. His phone was missing, though. I hoped that meant he had it with him.

"Lucas?" I called out, knowing there was no other exit. He wouldn't have left without his things, half undressed in the dead of night.

The hope that it was all a stupid prank faded at that moment.

Lucas had vanished.

2

Chapter Two

September, 2020

IT WAS BARELY 8 AM, but when I opened the door, a small crowd had gathered outside the cafe, glancing at their watches and phone screens as though I'd done them a personal injustice.

I'd served a dozen customers before Anna, the second barista, arrived. She was breathless and unkempt as she adjusted her apron, diving in to work on the coffee machine. In my nearly full year working here, she'd never been on time. I didn't comment on that. As long as she didn't pry into my life, I was willing to overlook her tardiness.

Together, we barely managed the morning rush, but by lunchtime, the chaos had subsided enough for one of us to leave the counter. Anna cleaned and reset the tables while I wiped down the machines. We both looked up when the little bell above the door jingled. A young couple walked in: an emo-looking girl wearing a black fedora and a Ghostface T-shirt, and a guy with a buzzcut and a military bearing. The girl scanned the semi-empty café before spotting me, then nudged the guy and tilted her head toward me. He followed her gaze, his blue eyes meeting mine.

I froze. This was the typical reaction when people recognized me. Thanks to the careless media and my former best friend, Sarah, finding me wasn't hard.

The guy approached the counter with a calm smile. "Nellie? Nellie Foster?"

"Who are you?" My ears began ringing as familiar pressure flooded my head.

Seeing my tension, he stepped back and raised his hands in a conciliatory gesture. "I'm Mitchell. This is my sister, June." He motioned to the girl in black. She didn't look friendly.

I fidgeted, my eyes darting toward the door and then around to see if anyone else could hear us. Anna remained focused on the tables.

"What do you want?" I whispered.

"We're looking for our sister," June said abruptly. "It might have something to do with your boyfriend's disappearance."

Mitchell smiled apologetically and turned to her. "June, please, let me handle this."

My knees grew weak. I couldn't do it. Not again. I clenched the counter so tight my knuckles turned white.

"Please leave." Tears pricked at the corners of my eyes, and I was terrified to blink, fearing they'd spill down my cheeks and betray my despair. "I have nothing to do with anything."

"We know," Mitchell assured me with a soft smile. "We're just trying to find out what happened to our sister."

"I don't understand. What does she have to do with my boyfriend? Did your sister go missing here, in Minneapolis?"

June huffed, rolling her eyes and turning away. "No, she went missing back in Kansas City."

"That's where we're from," her brother advised. "We—"

The door swung open with a chiming exclamation. The lunchtime crowd filed in behind the siblings, growing impatient after a minute. I barely noticed how they tapped their feet or shot annoyed glances my way, too fixated with June and Mitchell and their news of another missing person.

"Please, give us ten minutes," Mitchell pleaded. "I'll explain everything, and if you tell us to leave, we will. We don't want trouble. We're just trying to find our sister." He studied my face earnestly. "Ten minutes," he repeated. "And we'll go."

June glared beneath her tilted hat.

I wanted to tell them to leave now, but something about them held my tongue. Despite June's hostility, their presence felt sincere. They didn't seem like the usual roaches who sought to feed off tragedy. It had been two years—two whole years of silence, wondering, and aching—but if there was a chance they knew something about Lucas, I couldn't let it go.

"I'll get my colleague to cover," I said, apologizing to the punters. "Anna?"

WE SETTLED AT AN OUTSIDE TABLE. The sun beat down like a furious God, and I winced beneath its fist. Across from me, Mitchell sat ramrod straight, his tall, broad frame casting a shadow that I ducked into. His sister slouched beside him. I wrapped my arms around myself, despite the warmth.

"Ten minutes," I clarified.

Mitchell began without hesitation, "Our sister, Amanda, went missing last September. No one knows what happened to her."

"She was heading home late that night. We saw the CCTV footage. The streetlamp flickered, then everything went dark. And then... she was just gone," June said, almost reluctantly.

"That's why we wanted to talk to you. It's kind of like what we read about your boyfriend—how he just disappeared," Mitchell added.

A chill coursed through me. Theories about Lucas's disappearance abounded, including some that ventured into the supernatural, but that didn't necessarily mean their sister was linked to it.

June pushed her phone toward me. I took it gingerly, studying the photo of a young woman in her late twenties. Her shy smile and blonde hair shared an unmistakable likeness to her siblings.

But I didn't recognize this face. All I knew was that thousands of people vanished every year, some by choice. It was a hard pill to swallow, but anyone who'd ever had to deal with a missing loved one had to accept it at some point. I kept those thoughts to myself.

"I've never seen her, sorry," I said, empathetic.

Mitchell shook his head, with a faint, sorrowful smile. *No worries,* it said. And then, with a glimmer of hope, "Do you think your guy could've known her? Has he ever mentioned an Amanda?"

I thought about it for a second.

"Not that I remember. Sorry, but your sister went missing half a thousand miles away from here. I don't think they've met." I started picking at my bracelet but forced myself to stop, not wanting to give away my nervousness or any personal information.

Mitchell hesitated. "We're not sure if there's a connection, but—"

"We found an article about your boyfriend when we were looking for Amanda," his sister interjected, "about people vanishing without a trace from public places. We thought it might be something. His case was kinda big."

She gave me a challenging glare, as if trying to elicit a reaction. I didn't bite.

Mitchell let his sister finish her thought and said, "And there's more: Amanda went missing around the same time, a year later. September of last year. I know how stupid it sounds now that I'm saying it out loud—" He trailed off.

The sun ducked behind a cloud, and we all visibly chilled. Their motivation for speaking with me was questionable. They could've gone anywhere in the country and spoken to anyone with a missing loved one, but why here? How the hell did they come to the conclusion that I, of all people, was the one they had to speak to?

I swiped through more photos of Amanda until one caught my eye: a picture of a tree. But it wasn't the tree itself that drew me in. It was the carving on its trunk. The symbol resembled an eye in a circle, intricately detailed and eerily occult. It looked like something straight out of a horror movie. As Sarah would say, it had a "very dark vibe." Yet, the carving felt strangely familiar.

"What is this?" I asked, turning the phone to Mitchell.

"I don't know. It was just there." He looked between me and the screen. "Do you know what it is?"

"No, but I think I've seen it before."

"Where?" he asked.

"In Lucas's things, drawn on a Post-It note." I recalled the wide, observant eye, the press of pencil so hard it had nearly pierced the paper. "I thought they were just scribbles. I'm not entirely sure."

I studied the carvings closer, but the more I looked, the more I doubted if it was the same. "They kinda look similar. Might be nothing, though."

"Or might be something." June's tone was pushy. She looked very young, barely eighteen. The same age I was when I met Lucas. Probably just as naive. And she was eager to find connections, even where none existed.

"Sorry, guys, I'm not sure what you want from me. I really don't know anything. Is there anything else?" Something was unsettling about this entire thing. Lucas's obsession with his talismans was cute and quirky, but this made me deeply uncomfortable.

"Yes, actually. That's why we came here to talk to you in the first place." Mitchell raised his head as if he just remembered an important detail. "The police took Amanda's belongings and laptop when the investigation started, and we only got them back a month ago. She had been corresponding with a psychic online and had made a few purchases from their online store. It's here."

"A psychic?" I asked, incredulous.

"Yes, a medium or something," Mitchell replied. "It's our only lead, so—"

My head was spinning. A second ago, they were asking me about Lucas, and now there was a psychic.

"And this psychic is here? In Minneapolis?" I asked, utterly confused. "Did Amanda come here?"

June chimed in, clarifying, "We found the online shop in Duluth. But we figured it was close enough. Same state."

"Why don't you go to this psychic then?"

"We will," replied Mitchell, "but we thought you might want to come with us."

I almost choked on a breath. "Why?"

"Just to check it out? We're trying to understand if these two disappearances are connected."

"What if we find them there? Isn't that something you'd want?" June interjected. She was trying to guilt trip me.

I paused, weighing the thought. Duluth was roughly a two-hour drive, a route I'd taken with Lucas many times for hiking or skiing. But none of that mattered now. It had been two long years, and he was gone. I was about to leave this city behind. There were no revelations in this conversation, and I'd been down this path too many times, especially in the first months after Lucas's disappearance, when I was desperate to cling to every detail and memory, searching for hints that weren't there. He didn't leave a trail of breadcrumbs for me to find him. He just vanished. And he wasn't coming back.

"Shouldn't the police be handling this?" I asked, trying to deflect their expectations.

June smirked but remained silent. Mitchell shook his head and pursed his lips.

After a beat, I stood up. I couldn't take any more of this. "I gotta get back to work."

Mitchell impulsively grabbed my hand, his grip brief but unexpected.

I hesitated, taken aback by the sudden touch. Mitchell quickly realized his mistake and released my hand, his face flushing with embarrassment.

"Sorry, I...I didn't mean to."

I sat back down, still feeling the surprise of his gesture. "It's okay," I said, trying to ease the tension.

"Whatever you tell us will stay between us. I promise. We're in the same boat here."

I had serious doubts that the boat was truly the same unless they, too, were scapegoated by a mob thirsty for blood and drama, blamed for their sister's disappearance.

Nonetheless, I asked, "What do you want to know?"

June handed me her phone again, the screen displaying notes:

Mary Flynn, 34 River Road, Duluth, Minnesota. Mystic Wonders

There was a website link below.

June pulled up a poor-quality image on her phone. I assumed it was a photo of a photo, grainy and soft, like a sketch rubbed by angry fingers. I examined the woman. She appeared to be in her forties, with black hair framing her pale skin and thin lips painted a deep red. She wasn't beautiful, but something about her face —her hollow cheeks and eyes too big for her head — made her intriguing. I didn't recognize her either.

"Is this the psychic?" I asked.

"Did Lucas ever see psychics?" Mitchell ignored my question. "Or talk to any on the Internet?"

I raised an eyebrow. "Doubt it. He was superstitious, but...I mean, who isn't in football, right?"

June nodded. "So maybe he shopped online?"

I shook my head. "He had his lucky grandpa's socks and a few other weird things, but that was about it. He was more into studying these things than buying knickknacks."

Mitchell slumped back, disappointed. "Do you have access to his computer or phone?" he asked, dejected.

I shook my head no. Lucas's phone disappeared with him. Apparently, the police tried to track it, but there were no pings from masts to suggest it was on or changing locations. The rest of his things were taken by his parents. I didn't have much, only his gym bag, which I brought home with me the night he disappeared. The police never asked about it. There were also a few belongings he'd left in my room. Without those, I might have wondered if he'd ever really been part of my life.

"When did you say Amanda disappeared?" I asked.

"September thirteenth last year," Mitchell replied.

Lucas had gone missing a full year prior, on September twenty-fourth, the day of the game. I was still stumbling to find any connections.

"If you're not coming with us, do you mind sending us a picture of his... scribbles?" Mitchell asked.

"Sure, if I can find them."

Disappointment etched itself on June's face. She reclaimed her device without making eye contact with me.

"Sorry, I couldn't help more."

Mitchell and I exchanged numbers, and he sent me screenshots of everything they had on the psychic. I didn't want them, but he insisted.

"Just in case you remember something," he advised. "I still

think you should come to Duluth with us. Even if we don't find anything, at least it's a new place to visit."

I didn't tell them I'd been to Duluth many times. "I'll think about it."

"You know what you're gonna do with this info?"

"Haven't decided yet. I might go to the police and see what they say."

June looked up from her phone with a skeptical smirk. "Good luck with that."

I smiled wryly. "It feels like the right thing to do."

Mitchell, on the other hand, encouraged me, "You can use our names, mention Amanda if it'll help." He slipped on a pair of sunglasses he'd kept in his shirt pocket. "We're headed out tomorrow morning. Let us know if you change your mind."

January, 2017

SOME FIGHTS ARE like explosions that sling shrapnel into your heart. They burrow in the thick, dark silence for years, squirming closer to that sensitive spot that could break even a fated romance. The scars heal, and the pain fades, but the memories stain your soul like a roadmap of tragedies.

That's how it felt after our first big fight.

Lucas's room had been cluttered with textbooks, clothes, and all sorts of trinkets that he swore brought him good luck—a gris-gris, a few bones that I *refused* to touch, and a stag skull he claimed to have shot himself on a hunting trip with his dad. I wasn't thrilled about his hunting—I'd always found it violent, but I kept that to myself.

In my attempt to support him, I'd decided to help with his laundry, a task that he, a nineteen-year-old college student, often neglected.

His dorm room was heavy with the smell of sweat and dirty

clothes, but he didn't notice any of that. He was glued to the screen: a football game, during the playoffs, chips and chocolate spread on his bed. The rest of the world ceased to exist.

I held up a pair of clean, weathered socks. "Where do you want these?"

Lucas was too focused on the stream to pay much attention and gestured vaguely towards the dresser. Only when a streak of tartan green glided past did he shoot me a side glance and snap with horror.

"What the fuck did you do?"

I'd never heard such rage from him. He shoved his laptop aside, the screen flashing the final seconds of the game, but he didn't care anymore.

"What?" I stammered, holding the socks like wilted flowers.

Never had anyone yelled at me like this. My father had always been gentle with me, even when I was a teenager pushing boundaries. Unlike in many families, my dad was the good cop, always on my side, even when it meant siding against Mom. My high school boyfriend never spoke to me so harshly, either. To be fair, we never even fought. After my father's death, we drifted apart and broke up almost amicably.

"You washed the socks!" His roar choked the room.

"Yeah." I hated how weak and feeble I sounded. "So?"

"They were my great-grandfather's lucky socks! You've washed all the luck out of them!"

"I'm sorry–" I said, trying to diffuse the tension as he snatched them from my quivering hands. "I didn't know."

"You ruined them!"

I would later learn that those socks were a treasured family heirloom: a peculiar good luck charm believed to have saved his great-grandfather from a collapsed mine shaft.

Initially, I tried to apologize, but Lucas kept yelling, his accusations snowballing from the socks to my perceived lack of support for his football aspirations. I ended up leaving in tears.

Two days later, Lucas apologized, admitting he had overreacted. He even joked that the socks perhaps worked their magic even better now that they were clean, and his practice had gone exceptionally well.

I swore to never touch his laundry again and even made amends with a small gift—a little green good luck crystal from a local magic trinkets store. He'd laughed and pocketed it, a sign that we were okay again.

Chapter Three

September, 2020

MY MOTHER WAS CONVINCED I'd move back in with her in Cleveland, even though I never actually agreed. My apartment and my job were in Minneapolis. I couldn't just abandon everything. Still, over time, I'd started giving in, easing myself into the idea of coming home. Most of my things were already tucked away in my childhood bedroom at Mom's tidy '90s-style suburban house. Now, the rest of my clothes were strewn across my Minneapolis room, waiting to be loaded into the car.

But one question remained: what should I do with Lucas's things?

His gym bag and a few leftover items were buried in the back of the closet, a haunting reminder. It seemed strange to take them with me to Cleveland. We'd been together almost two years when he vanished, and now another two had passed. I thought I had said goodbye to the hope of seeing him again, but getting rid of his things seemed sacrilegious.

I hesitated for a moment, then pulled his bag out of the closet. I could recite its contents: the battered boots with a skull-shaped hole on the right heel, the deodorant only half-used, the white towel with a green hair dye stain on one corner from a Halloween costume gone wrong. But I'd rarely touched them. The memories hurt, and I wanted to preserve them. I pushed aside the 'lucky' mine shaft socks, grazing the green stone I'd gifted. And there, pressed between the crumpled pages of a textbook, was the Post-It note. I studied the photo Amanda had taken and compared it to the other. Lucas's symbol was less detailed, just the main shape. But it was close enough to make me wonder if they depicted the same image.

I placed the talismans back in the bag, except for the Post-It note, which I kept aside. I would go to the police and share this newfound information about Amanda and the psychic, but nothing more. I wouldn't pursue the investigation. I wouldn't mention the occult symbols. This way, I could assuage my conscience and not lose myself again.

THE POLICE STATION was quiet and stained with the sterile, institutional scent of disinfectant. It took me a few minutes to approach an officer. The whole ordeal with Lucas suddenly felt like an open wound to be feasted on again, and I had barely recovered from the last ravage. When he went missing, they *invited* me as a witness, and I fell for it, foolishly unaware of their intentions. After hours of intense interrogation, they finally disclosed that they had footage of me during the time of Lucas's disappearance.

Surprisingly, they were already aware of this information before bringing me in for questioning but as I was informed later, they were simply trying to tire me out and extract a confession. An attorney explained that I had the right to leave at any point, but clearly, the police had never informed me of this.

I slipped a pre-printed document containing the information Mitchell and his sister had shared with me onto the counter. But as I recounted their story to the young man, I realized how implausible it was.

"And how are these people connected?" he asked, visibly bored.

"I don't know, but I thought you could look into that."

The duty officer raised an eyebrow. "Ma'am, what's your relationship with the missing person?"

"I'm his girlfriend."

He jotted something on a piece of paper. "Do you have any identification with you?" I handed him my driver's license. He placed it down with a weary expression and tapped the keyboard.

"I see that the missing person's report was not filled out by you."

"That's correct. His parents filed it. I was a witness in the case."

"I understand; however, I'm not authorized to share case details with non-family members," he said, returning my license.

"I'm not asking you to disclose anything," I said, trying to suppress my frustration and annoyance. "I just want you to consider this new lead and investigate it."

His eyes rolled ever so slightly, and he said in a 'I am not paid enough for this' tone, "Ma'am, I'm sure the detectives have everything they need for this case."

I pushed the paper further across the counter. "Please, just look into it."

The officer took it, skeptically turning it in his hands before handing it back to me.

"Ma'am, I don't see any connection."

"I just told you what the connection might be!" I said, exasperated.

Footsteps echoed down the hallway, and a woman in uniform scrutinized the scene. I must have been louder than I'd thought. "What's the matter, Officer?"

The duty officer gestured towards me. "Miss Foster is asking about a missing person case, but she's not a relative."

I let out a frustrated sigh.

The woman was quick to pass judgment after a thorough examination of my person. I probably looked more composed than most who ended up in her office—clean jeans, smooth hair, unblemished skin. I wasn't any more of a threat than a perturbed cat. Even so, I still shrank a little under her gaze.

"I'll take it from here, Officer." She had a cloud of red curls that bounced as she took the vacated seat. I hoped mine didn't look as unforgiving. "Please, start from the beginning."

I recounted the events while she listened attentively, her pale eyes never leaving mine. After examining the printout with equal focus, she typed the name into the database at a deliberate pace.

"Mary Flynn... nothing found," she murmured, scanning the screen. "Let me try another approach."

I held my breath as she clicked away, fearing any movement might disrupt our progress. The previous officer's skepticism had been suffocating, but this sergeant's demeanor was refreshingly different.

"The name is too common for a nationwide search," she explained, drawing to a halt, "and even if this is her real name, there won't be any records if she's never had any violations."

Disappointment settled like a stone in my stomach. But the sergeant continued, "However, I'll keep the printout and ensure it's attached to the case. Leave your contact information, and I'll reach out if anything develops."

"Thank you."

She led me to the door. "Miss Foster, I'm inclined to remind you that this may take time. It's possible these women aren't connected to the case at all."

. . .

I STEPPED out into the dust and exhaust fumes of downtown Minneapolis, less relieved than I'd expected. I hoped that leaving Lucas's disappearance in the presumably capable hands of law enforcement would ease my guilt about not going to Duluth, but instead, a growing sense of unease gnawed at me.

For a while, I sat in the car, hands resting on the steering wheel, unmoving. The sun was inching towards the horizon, and clouds gathered from the west. On the other side of the street from the police station, a massive billboard advertised a rehabilitation facility, urging passersby to "Take the first step towards a fresh start before it's too late!"

My mind was empty.

As much as I hated to admit it, my mom was right. Returning to Cleveland was the only sensible choice. There, in a place where nothing reminded me of Lucas, I could focus on myself and my life. I could find a job, continue my education, or try something new. I'd have a chance at a normal life, free from the constant reminders of the tragedy. And I wouldn't have to stay forever. Once back on my feet, I could start fresh somewhere else, where no one knew me or my past.

But I couldn't silence the feeling that I was being heartless and selfish for wanting to leave and move on, no matter how hard I tried to justify it. Would I be able to live with myself if I didn't at least try to find out what happened to Lucas? This lead, slim as it was, offered a chance at answers. The worst that could happen was I'd hit another dead end, sending Mitchell, June, and me right back to square one.

I needed someone to confide in, someone to help me untangle my thoughts and hopefully silence the guilt. But I had no one to turn to. My college friends were gone, and I hadn't formed new connections. All I had was my mom.

She answered my call right away as if she'd been waiting for it.

"Hi, Mom," my voice trembled. Something warm slipped down my cheek. I hadn't even noticed I was crying.

"Nellie, what happened?"

"I wanted to bounce some ideas off of you. It's about Lucas."

Her irritation flooded through the speaker. "Nellie." Her voice was cold as a tomb.

"I've met some people looking for their sister. She's missing... like Lucas. I thought maybe we might be able to find new information together. But—"

"You called me to say you won't be coming? So typical."

"Mom..."

"Can't you just leave well enough alone and avoid more drama?"

"Mom..."

"Was the police investigation not enough for you? And the attack on that poor girl?"

"Mom!"

After venting, she fell silent for a beat before adding, "I'm not going to enable this decision. It's yours to make. Just don't say I didn't warn you."

I hung up, slamming the phone onto the seat with such force it bounced off and fell to the floor. I cursed under my breath as I bent down for it. Duluth was just a short distance away. I wondered if it would be a bigger mistake to pass up the chance to uncover something, even if it turned out to be nothing. Besides, I clung to the hope that getting some kind of closure could potentially save me from the uncertainty of moving back home and relying on my mom indefinitely.

With that thought in mind, I sent Mitchell a text with the picture of Lucas's Post-It note:

"I'm coming with you. What time should we meet?"

September, 2016

HE GAVE OFF A 'FUCK BOY' vibe. And he could get away with it, too.

Beside the enormous bowl, where bottles of beer and cider bobbed in a sea of semi-melted ice, he spoke to me for the first time.

Tall, with wheat-blonde hair that he casually tossed back with a flick of his hand, he exuded a confidence that permeated the room. He was undeniably attractive, but it was his gentle assertiveness that truly commanded the space. The boys I went to school with weren't like that. Lucas was laid-back and effortlessly cool.

"Need a hand?" He nodded towards the bottle I was struggling to open against the corner of the kitchen table. He pulled keys from his pocket and applied them to the bottle's neck.

"I'm told the secret to a killer party is bein' able to open a bottle with whatever's lyin' around. Luckily for you, I can open a bottle with just about anything."

"I was getting desperate. Thanks." I eagerly embraced the role of the distressed damsel. The cap jumped up with a click, almost hitting me in the face.

"Sorry!" He seemed genuinely embarrassed, quickly picked up the fallen cap, and twirled it in his hand. "This one's got a little attitude, huh?"

The joke was silly, but I laughed. "Now that we've narrowly avoided a Prohibition-level disaster..." I was about to leave, not sure if he was willing to continue the conversation.

"Wait," he said, tilting his head. "Who'd you come with?"

"Just the girls from the track team."

"Track? No way! I would've pegged you as a cheerleader, hands down." He noticed my puzzled expression and flushed slightly. "Sorry, that's... uh, not what I meant. You have really beautiful hair... And, ah, the rest of you, too."

I almost laughed again, observing his charming struggles with eloquence.

Turns out first impressions can be wrong.

WE SETTLED onto the blanket in the yard of the house, where the party buzzed. The thumping beat of music surrounded us, and in the distance, cheers and laughter erupted from a game of beer pong. In mid-September, the nights were cool. Lucas draped his jacket over my shoulders.

He had this cocky country-boy look, and the way he talked, prolonging vowels in words, turning 'cat' into 'caet,' and sprinkling in that 'aw' sound here and there, added to his overall charm.

Through the tattered clouds, the moon appeared. Lucas pointed to it. "You know, they say moonshine is best brewed durin' the wanin' moon."

I chuckled. "Family business or a hobby?"

"Neither, unfortunately."

"So, you haven't tested it yourself?"

"Personally—no." His frown was all disappointment. "But my high school chemistry teacher conducted experiments."

"Breaking Bad style?"

"Somethin' like that."

"And what were the conclusions of their research?" I asked.

Lucas looked sideways, slightly wrinkling his nose as if trying not to laugh, and replied, "If you brew moonshine in the school lab, you'll get fired."

"Maybe they just brewed it during the wrong moon phase?"

Lucas laughed and leaned in, placing his hands on the back of my head, and my breath hitched as his lips pressed against mine.

4

Chapter Four

September, 2020

WE SKIPPED the morning traffic and sped along the modest two-lane i-35, winding its way between sprawling forests on both sides.

When I picked up Mitchell and June from the hotel, they were already waiting for me at the entrance. Mitchell effortlessly carried a compact suitcase in one hand and a gray backpack on his shoulder. June, on the other hand, had a huge, bloated tote bag stuffed with her things and an enormous black backpack. I didn't judge. Whenever I traveled by car, I packed all the necessities in a blue Ikea bag. My mother argued with me about its practicality, but honestly, things get just as messy in a suitcase, and it's harder to access them.

Today, June wore a long, lace skirt paired with a "Nightmare on Elm Street" T-shirt, her fingers adorned with several silver rings. Her fedora, the same one she wore the day before, topped off her outfit. When I arrived to pick them up, she gave me a menacing glance. Or at least, what I assumed was a menacing glance. It was so over-the-top that it almost made me chuckle.

Mitchell entertained me with chatter, telling me about his time in the military and somehow avoiding discussing the true purpose of our voyage. It almost felt like we were on an exciting road trip.

In the rearview mirror, I saw June alternating between poking at her phone and pensively gazing out the window, watching the small towns pass by—one indistinguishable from the next.

"Picture this: we're settling in for the night at camp, guys getting some rest. Then, out of nowhere, a wild goat comes tearing past the guards and into the tent, nipping at our chow packets." Mitchell's accent thickened as he spoke, hands flying with excitement. "It was like a dadgum tornado on hooves, sending us all scrambling! We're talking a dozen dudes stumbling around, tripping over each other, getting all banged up, and that stupid goat don't get a scratch on it!" He chuckled, shaking his head at the memory.

I forced a smile, feeling a little too tense to fully enjoy the tale. I caught a glimpse of June in the rearview, and her expression said she'd heard this story before, perhaps quite a few times.

"So, you made it to sergeant?" I asked after he'd stopped laughing.

"Yes, last year," he confirmed, keeping it reserved.

"What's next?"

"Usually, a staff sergeant," he made a slight pause, "But not for me. I recently demobilized." He rubbed his neck and then checked the time.

"Oh," was all I could say, "Because of your sister? Because of Amanda?"

"Yeah," he started, hesitant, then his voice firmed up. "Nah, I just needed a change. But Amanda going missing—that definitely played a part in my decision."

"How so?"

"I figured I'd give being a cop a shot."

"In Kansas City?"

"Of course, where else?"

"You could go anywhere," June chimed in. "Yet you chose that dump."

"Why is it a dump?" Mitchell's surprise was genuine.

"Because it's lousy! Nowhere else has as much crap happening."

"So you want to move?" I asked June.

"As soon as I save up enough money," she said defiantly.

"Where you gonna go?" her brother turned to her, leaning his left arm on the back of my seat. "Who's gonna have your back? We stick together; that's what we do."

His sister didn't respond, turning away from him and staring out the window. I felt uncomfortable, so I chose to focus on the road, pretending nothing had happened.

I didn't have brothers or sisters, but I had a mother I wanted to escape. Remembering that the distance between us would soon be reduced to an uncomfortable minimum made me feel dizzy.

"Did Amanda go missing at night, too?" I asked.

Mitch looked over at his sister as if checking whether she was okay with him sharing, then said, "Yeah. She was coming back from her support group. Someone said she stayed late, chatting. Seemed excited. Jittery."

They'd already told me there were no witnesses. Lucas also vanished at night from a crowded stadium, with no one seeing anything, so I knew it was possible.

"What kind of support group was it?" I asked.

"A domestic violence one," June said flatly.

"I'm sorry to ask, but if she was going to that group, could the person who caused her to be there be connected?"

"No," Mitchell's short answer seemed unusual for him.

"He's in jail," said June, looking me directly in the eye through the rearview mirror.

"I see." I didn't know what else to say.

My phone lit up with a photo of Lucas and me, a message from my mother appearing beneath it. Mitchell's eyes followed mine.

"Tell me about him, about Lucas," he said, nodding towards my phone.

I hesitated. I'd shared plenty with Sarah, and she'd leaked it all, letting it distort and spread from one person to the next.

My mother hated it when I talked about Lucas. The rest of my friends turned their backs on me after what happened between Sarah and me. So I kept it all bottled up, carrying it inside me like a precious vial of poison that I had no choice but to swallow again and again.

However, something in Mitchell's expression put me at ease. He'd also lost a loved one, and I felt a thin thread of connection with him and with June. Something I hadn't felt in a while.

But I still didn't know what to tell him. What we had with Lucas had unraveled slowly, morphing from a promising start into a nightmare that remained suspended the moment he vanished.

"What do you want to know?" I turned to Mitch, taking my eyes off the road for a second.

"Well, for instance, how long were you together?"

"Almost two years."

"What's your take on what happened to him? Did he mention anything weird before he disappeared? Maybe his behavior changed?"

"I'm not sure." It had been so long, sometimes I doubted if I had ever really known him at all.

June chimed in from the back, "They say you murdered him." She grinned, seemingly pleased with the reaction—my uncomfortable silence and her brother's disapproving glance, and then added, "But we kinda ruled that out. So, the mystery remains."

"Well, maybe this psychic lady will shed some light on the story."

"Ever been to one?" Mitch asked.

"A psychic? No, never," I mused, and then added with a forced laugh, "If she starts talking to the dead, I'm so outta there!"

"Don't believe in the supernatural?" he said with a chuckle.

"I guess not."

"Me neither. Although," Mitchell scratched his head thoughtfully, "I have seen some weird shit."

"What do you mean?"

June leaned forward, interested, and grabbed our headrests. Clearly, this was a story she hadn't heard before.

"Shit went down at night when we were on patrol. We were moving through the desert, and then suddenly everything just... stopped."

"What do you mean *everything stopped?*" his sister interrupted.

"Froze up. Dead silence. No nothing. But it was different from the usual nighttime quiet, you know? And the weirdest thing, I saw something on the horizon." He took on an expression of far-off wonderment. "It was like a bright light, but it was off, you know? I'd never seen anything like it before."

"Like a UFO?" I offered.

He shrugged and continued, "I was watching it, and then it just vanished. Like it never even was there. And then, everything went back to normal."

June asked, "And what do you think it was?"

"No idea," Mitchell replied honestly. "But it was really fucking strange. Pardon the language."

I waved it off. *No big deal.*

"Did anyone else see it besides you?" June asked from the backseat.

"No, it all ended before I thought to call any of the guys."

I smiled slightly, and Mitchell noticed, seeming a bit embarrassed.

"What?"

"Nothing, really. Sorry."

"Speak!" he laughed. "Tell me honestly, what's my diagnosis?"

"It's nothing! It's normal for a person to try to find a supernatural explanation for things."

"Really?"

"Yes. We're wired to make sense of the inexplicable. It's just a way of reassuring ourselves that the world still makes sense, even if the explanations we come up with are far-fetched. So, don't beat yourself up over doubting the rational world. It's in our nature."

"Thanks, Doc. For a second there, I thought you were gonna tell me I'd lost my mind or something."

"No, not at all," I grinned. "One session would be too little for a diagnosis."

Our fun was interrupted by June nervously fidgeting with the wooden beads on her wrist. I'd thought they were bracelets, but they turned out to be a rosary wrapped tight as an angry serpent around her hand. "Enough flirting. We didn't come here for that."

Mitchell and I exchanged a glance, slightly embarrassed, even though there was nothing overtly flirty in our conversation, at least not to my knowledge. A hush fell between us, not because we were obediently following a teenager's command but because June had skillfully brought back the tense atmosphere that our chatter was dispelling. Soon, she asked to stop for coffee, and when we got our drinks, she sat without a word in the front seat next to me, throwing over her shoulder, "Mitch, sit in the back. I'm getting a little queasy."

Her brother didn't argue with her, but when I caught his

reflection in the rearview mirror, he playfully made a face as if to say, "I see you, little sister."

I smiled politely in response. June gave me a stern, "Don't you dare" glance, her expression clearly conveying, "My brother is off-limits".

I didn't mind. I wasn't interested.

September, 2017

HE SAID I couldn't come with them.

When I arrived at Lucas's dorm, he was frantically stuffing items into his hiking backpack. It seemed like he had completely forgotten about our plans but wouldn't admit it, and my presence only irritated him further. This camping trip came out of nowhere, and when I started asking questions, he became defensive quickly.

"It's a guys' trip. We just wanna hang out."

"You didn't say anything about it before!"

"So what? What's your problem?"

"What's *your* problem?" I retorted, getting angry. "You're acting weird, and now you're going on this trip I've never heard about!"

"I *did* tell you about it. You just didn't listen, like always!"

"When will you be back?"

"Would you just stop trying to control everything?"

"It's a simple question!"

"I'll be back Monday, okay?"

I didn't anticipate getting into an argument, but I could swear on my life Lucas hadn't mentioned this trip before. Everything about it was odd, the timing, the secrecy.

Suddenly, he changed his tone, once again becoming loving and caring. "Babe, it's just a boys' camping trip. Nothing more.

We can hang out next weekend, okay?" He kissed me. "Just go have a girls' night out or something."

I wasn't going to, but Sarah called and asked me to hang out with her at a bar because her Tinder date stood her up. By the time I got there, she was already flirting with some guys from the football team—the same guys Lucas had told me he was going camping with. My heart sank.

"Hey girl, why the long face?" she asked, tipsy.

I didn't respond before taking a shot of Fireball and feeling it burn my insides.

"Lucas went camping with Matt and Jacob."

"But Jacob's here," she said, looking at me like I was a silly goose and had it all wrong.

"I know."

"Wait, you don't think he's—?" She didn't finish, but I knew what she was going to say.

"I don't know."

My first thought was to call him, but Sarah stopped me.

"No! Wait till he's back and ask how it went, and then you can catch him in the lie."

But we didn't follow through with this plan. Instead, we ended up getting drunk and sending Lucas pictures of us with his friends. He never responded to any of my texts.

He did get back on Monday but mentioned nothing. He acted normal, and I convinced myself it was all in my head.

Chapter Five

September, 2020

WE DROVE through a tiny downtown and continued uphill, moving away from the lake. The uniform residential neighbourhoods gradually gave way to older, sturdier houses, many of which were in visible need of repair—peeling paint, sagging porches, and overgrown yards.

Finally, Mitchell pointed out a driveway leading to one of the hilltop houses, which had no signs or numbers. I slowly drove into the yard, the gravel crunching beneath the wheels, my heart racing with every turn. I kept telling myself *Lucas isn't here*, but my mind played tricks on me, making me panic. What if I saw him now? What would I tell him? My palms grew sweaty on the steering wheel as anxiety gripped me.

The house loomed before us, a Colonial Revival-style home with classical white siding that had faded to a dull sheen. Its dark windows stared like cold, empty eyes, daring us to approach.

June and Mitchell stepped out, but I stayed in my seat, nausea churning in my stomach. I took a few deep breaths and forced myself to follow the siblings.

My hands trembled. I dropped the keys, and their metallic jingle sliced through the silence. When I bent to pick them up, my phone slipped from my grip. I winced and glanced at the others, hoping they weren't annoyed by my nervous clumsiness. June looked calm, but her posture was stiff, and her knuckles were white around the phone in her hand.

Mitchell scanned the yard, his gaze settling on a shiny new Tacoma parked by the garage. It seemed like an odd choice for a fortune-teller. The truck looked out of place, its spotless surface clashing with the house's worn, weathered siding. Mitch clicked his tongue in approval.

"Are you sure this is the right address?" June asked her brother, dubious.

Mitchell answered, "Yes." He hesitated, then finally started walking towards the house. "Come on."

He knocked on the door before I was ready.

"Maybe she's not home," I ventured, hopeful. But it was quickly doused by a pang of guilt. This was my chance to uncover something about Lucas, and I was faltering.

Footsteps approached. My heart hammered in my chest, loud enough that I was sure everyone around me could hear it. The inner door creaked open.

Through the fine mesh of the screen door, a figure appeared the same height and build as Lucas. My dry mouth seemed to suck all the moisture from my lips. I stood paralyzed behind Mitchell and June. *Oh God*, I kept repeating in my head, *Oh God, this can't be real*. Grateful that they couldn't see my face, I swatted tears from my eyes.

The man stepped closer to the door, and the light fell on him, pushing his silhouette from the darkness. Dark-haired and dark-eyed, it was most definitely not Lucas.

I swallowed hard, unsure whether I felt relief or disappointment, and hastily wiped my face again with my sleeve.

Mitchell took a decisive step forward, politely introduced himself, and delved straight into why we were there. "Sorry to bother you. We're looking for our missing relatives. Mind taking a look at their photos, see if you've seen them?"

I envied how composed and confident he sounded. The man hesitated, contemplating this suggestion. But then, he opened the screen door, stepping onto the squeaky porch.

He was older than me, probably in his early thirties, dressed in simple blue jeans, a muscle-fit gray T-shirt, and a plaid shirt with rolled-up sleeves, looking nothing like the psychic we had expected. Perhaps we did have the wrong address, after all.

He cleared his throat and asked, "Photos?"

I quickly unlocked my phone and handed it to him. But instead of looking at it, he stared at me as if surprised by my presence. I wasn't sure if it was an "Is this the girl who got away with murder?" look or if I was just being paranoid.

While he studied the photos, Mitchell continued, "We're actually up in Duluth tracking a lead. We're looking for someone named Mary Flynn. She owns a business, supposedly registered to this address."

We had agreed on our story beforehand, stating that both Amanda and Lucas had placed orders at an online store to avoid confusing the psychic. Even if Lucas had no connection to this place, it was better to keep our narrative consistent and straightforward. We also decided to keep the odd carvings on the tree, as well as Lucas's scribbles, to ourselves, at least until we established a good rapport.

The resident of the house looked up at Mitchell and slowly shook his head. "No one here by that name, I'm afraid." Then he turned to me and added, "I'm Nick, by the way."

"Do you happen to know where she moved to?" Mitchell asked.

"No."

"And the people in the photos?" Mitchell continued regardless. "Have you seen them?"

"No." He gave me another quizzical look as he handed back my phone.

June impatiently pushed her own toward him. "Are you sure? Take another look."

He stared at the screen for a couple of seconds, then peered at me again. I turned the phone back to him, showing Lucas's photo.

"I'm really sorry about your relatives, but I've never seen them," he said.

As we got ready to leave, Mitchell insisted we give him our contact information in case he remembered something important later. I didn't expect much, but I went along with it. Nick took our names and numbers, though it was clear he wasn't thrilled about it.

June didn't wait for us and headed to the car, disappointment evident in her long, irritated strides. Mitchell and I didn't linger; we quickly thanked Nick for his time.

It was unusual to be on the other side of the investigation, the one inquiring rather than the one being questioned. Refreshing, even.

On our short drive back to the downtown area, Mitchell, who'd done most of the talking until now, seemed lost in thought.

Before entering the central street that intersected the highway, he finally spoke. "Let's stop somewhere and grab a bite. I'm starving."

We chose a small brewpub restaurant. After we had taken a table and placed our orders, Mitchell turned to me. "What are your plans for the near future?"

I gave a half-shrug. Nothing specific. Just moving in with my mom and wallowing in misery.

"How about you?"

"I'd like to stick around for a couple of days, talk to the locals, see if anyone heard of this Mary woman. Someone's gotta know something."

"And what if you don't find her?" I asked.

"Then we'll look elsewhere. We have one more lead we're checking out next."

"Where?"

"West Virginia. Amanda was on a trip there shortly before her disappearance."

"Why didn't you say anything earlier?" I asked in surprise.

"We figured we'd start with you, see if your guy's tied to this mess. Plus, the psychic. Now that this lead's gone cold, we're gonna fly out there, see what's what."

I was certain they hadn't mentioned anything earlier because they didn't trust me. They wanted to meet me first and make sure I wasn't some creepy, jealous-girlfriend-turned-killer type. Even though they had their reasons, I was still offended.

"And precisely where did Amanda go?" I couldn't keep the coldness from my tone.

"We ain't sure. Her credit card was used at a gas station in Ridgewood County last before she turned home."

I choked on my cola and coughed. While Mitchell sympathetically patted my back, I desperately tried to convey something important to him. June stared straight at me, calmly dipping her fries into ketchup, waiting for me to either suffocate or stop coughing with the imperturbability of a cat watching a glass teeter off the edge of a table.

I was starting to think that maybe Lucas and Amanda's disappearances weren't so separate after all.

"I think I know where to look in West Virginia." I finally managed.

"What are you talking about?" Mitchell sat straighter.

"You didn't know? Lucas is from Black Water, Ridgewood County."

"What? No way!" The siblings spoke over each other.

"We thought he was local," June added, meaning Minnesota.

"No, and like your sister, he'd just returned from visiting his parents a couple of days before." The memory of my last fight with Lucas flashed through my mind, leaving one more scratch on my heart.

"This is insane!" June almost screamed.

The waitress frowned with disapproval. Mitchell signaled his sister to keep her voice down. Unlike her, he quickly regained his composure and adopted a businesslike tone akin to that of a seasoned police officer. After what I'd been through with the police, it gave me the ick.

"Have you been there? You said you met his parents."

June immediately started searching for the mentioned city on the map, forgetting about her food.

I continued, "No, never. We only met once. At the police station in Minneapolis after Lucas disappeared."

Lucas never officially introduced me to his parents, which, to be fair, always bothered me. Whenever I brought it up, he'd brush it off with a promise that it would happen soon. It never did.

When I finally met his parents, we barely exchanged two words. They were withdrawn, likely due to their grief and shock. There were no attempts at further communication on either end. I didn't want to bother them, and they never reached out.

Mitchell bombarded me with questions about Lucas, hoping to uncover more coincidences, but unfortunately, there were none. Unlike Amanda, Lucas wasn't part of any support groups or societies. He was a typical American student and a talented football player with big dreams of making it to the NFL. In contrast, Amanda led a quiet life in Kansas City, living alone after her sister rented a room and moved out to start her own life. Though they didn't explicitly mention it, I sensed a fallout between June and Amanda shortly before the youngest moved out.

Mitchell fell into thought, chewing on the cold remnants of his fries. After a moment, he looked up, eyes narrowed. "Something must have happened there. I knew we gotta go there. My training doesn't start for another three weeks, so I've got time."

"I don't care about work. I can just not go back at all," June said with a careless toss of her head, earning a disapproving glance from her brother.

Mitchell turned to me. "You gotta come with us."

I had commitments in Minneapolis, but I caught myself already making mental notes to cancel my shifts at the café and the bar. Then, there was Ohio and the paper-shuffling job at the VA hospital waiting for me under my mother's wing. She expected me home by next Sunday, leaving us with a tight deadline. If I wasn't back by then, she'd be furious. Though they were fading, I clung to these concerns out of habit, the fragile threads connecting me to normalcy unraveling. The hope of inserting something between me and the life waiting for me at my mom's was winning out.

"Can we take my car?" I asked. It made sense to do so, allowing me to drive straight to Ohio afterward.

"Sure thing." Mitchell's expression softened into a nod.

"Ride in that old bucket again? It smells like moldy chips." June shook her head. Her brother nudged her under the table, and she rolled her eyes theatrically.

Mitchell booked two rooms at the motel, one for June and me and another for himself. This might have been a nod to the old-fashioned practice of segregating accommodations by gender, or perhaps he just wanted his sister and me to bond before our road trip. Either way, when I entered the room, June was already heading out to join her brother, leaving me alone with my thoughts. I sat on the second bed, smoothing the worn bedspread.

I finally admitted to myself that I felt excited and alive—perhaps for the first time in a long while. My mother was right. I had locked myself out from the rest of the world. But setting off with people I'd only met two days ago to search for Lucas wasn't exactly what she meant by "living up to my potential." On the other hand, I was done justifying myself to her. And I could still make it home on time. Our trip would likely take less than a week.

I lay on the creaky bed. The pungent scent of old fabric, dust, and disinfectant enveloped me, filling my nostrils and exacerbating my headache. My stomach twisted with slow-building anxiety, like a tiny whisper in my ear warning me of upcoming danger. In my head, I ran through all the worst-case scenarios, but none seemed catastrophic. Yet, I couldn't quite put my finger on what was making me feel so unsettled. Was it the fear of confirming that Lucas was really dead? This knowledge had always lingered in the back of my mind. But what would I do if he came back into my life after all this time? Would I be wracked entirely by it?

Hoping to smother the headache, I took two ibuprofen and surrendered to a restless sleep.

My dreams were dark and tangled. I was either chasing Lucas through a crowded space, desperate to reach him, or running through the woods, calling out his name. Scary symbols from Amanda's photo were carved into the trees, staring and unblinking.

When I woke up two hours later, darkness had settled outside. My heart raced, and it took a moment to recall my surroundings. June hadn't returned yet.

My phone was buzzing. I picked it up and saw an unfamiliar number from Minnesota. I decided to take my chances and answered.

"It's Nick. You came by my house today," said the familiar voice. "Can we meet? I have something to share with you."

Chapter Six

September, 2020

I THOUGHT he'd want me to come by his house again, but he suggested a bar downtown. I was relieved. I didn't need to be a horror movie fan to know the risks of going to a stranger's house alone at night.

I stepped out of the motel room, about to knock on the door next to mine when I lapsed in judgment. Nick had both my number and Mitchell's but chose to call me. Perhaps it was something to do with Lucas rather than Amanda. I trusted Mitchell and June, but I worried that Mitchell's assertiveness and June's lack of patience might intimidate the guy, so I decided to talk to him alone to increase my chances of actually finding something out. And I fully intended to fill them in later, once I knew what Nick had to say.

The bar was mostly empty, with just a few people hunched over drinks at scattered tables. It smelled just like the bar I worked at—fries and beer. However, this one seemed a bit more upscale, with candles on each table. I ordered a hard apple cider and sat down at a table by the window, waiting for Nick. A couple in the corner interrupted a long kiss and fell into quiet conversation, smiling at each other.

I forced myself to stop picking at my bracelet.

Seated facing the entrance, I watched the door intently and caught sight of Nick's arrival the moment he strode in, still disheveled and wearing the same checkered shirt. He looked nothing like Lucas, but their height was nearly the same, around six foot two. That resemblance alone made me uncomfortable, triggering something visceral, as if my body remembered Lucas before my mind could suppress the thought.

Nick recognized me, too, and headed straight for my table.

"Where are your friends?" he asked, settling into the uncomfortable wooden chair.

"I wasn't sure if you wanted to see all of us or just me."

I couldn't tell whether he approved.

"You guys came asking about Mary and caught me off guard. I got lost for a minute. Wasn't sure what it was about."

"Okay?" I was growing impatient.

"And it wasn't until you left that I realized I should have told you."

"Told us what?"

He fell silent, collecting his thoughts before responding. Throughout this time, I held my breath.

"May I ask why you thought your relatives had any connection to her beyond her store?"

I let out a small sigh, "It's all we had."

"So, you have something else now?" he pressed, catching onto the past tense.

He still wasn't saying why he'd called to meet. I pressed my palms down on the table, weary of the cat-and-mouse game. Maybe I had made a mistake coming here alone and not letting Mitchell handle it.

"We might. Look, can we stop playing this 'no, you tell me first' game? Why did you call me here?"

I handed him the crinkled Post-It note with Lucas's scribbles on it. "That's all we've got. Plus, a photo with a similar symbol on a tree. See, I've nothing to hide."

He looked amused by my agitated tone, but his brow furrowed as soon as he saw the note. "Slow down a bit. What is this?"

"I've no idea," I replied. "It was in Lucas's things. And Mitch and June's sister had a picture on her phone of something similar but carved into a tree. Do you know what it is?"

He slowly shook his head, tracing the lines on the paper. "No. Do you have the photo?"

"Yes. But seriously, your turn."

He paused, then revealed, "Mary Flynn was my mother."

"Oh," I exhaled in surprise. "Why didn't you... Wait, 'was'?"

"She passed away. Two years ago"

"Passed away? Not missing?" I clarified, ensuring I gathered as much information as possible from him.

He gave a tight nod and then pointed at my empty glass. "You want another one?"

I thought for a second, then agreed. While Nick ordered, I finally had the chance to take a good look at him. When we visited his house, I was too nervous and distracted, but now I could see him clearly. He appeared younger than I had initially thought, likely in his late twenties rather than early thirties. From behind the blurry glass door, he had looked like Lucas for a second due to his height and similar build. But that was where the resemblance ended. Lucas had blond hair and gray eyes. Nick's hair and eyes were dark brown. Lucas had no tattoos, while this guy's right arm was covered in ink, intricate, intertwining patterns that crawled upward and disappeared beneath his rolled-up sleeve. I forced myself not to stare too long, so I didn't get a chance to decipher the designs.

He set our drinks down and changed the subject without warning, tipping his chin toward my university hoodie.

"What do you study?"

"Psychology," I said, caught off guard by the sudden shift. "But I dropped out last year."

"How come?" He took a long swig of beer.

It felt like the reason for our meeting was making him nervous, despite his relaxed demeanor. Maybe that was why he kept falling back on small talk instead of getting to the point of why he'd called me. His calm exterior was betrayed only by the subtle tapping of his fingers against the glass.

"The whole boyfriend disappearance thing, mostly," I said, trying to downplay it. "What about you?"

"Biology," he replied, then added for some reason, "I went to school in Oregon. Practically grew up there."

"I thought your mom lived here."

"She did for as long as I can remember. But she sent me to boarding school in Oregon, and I stayed there until a couple of years ago."

"What made you move back home?"

"Different reasons. My mom's death. And things didn't work out with my ex, so I thought I needed a change."

"Did it help?"

"Kind of. I didn't plan on staying here that long, though."

"I'm sorry to ask, but what happened to your mom?" I asked, trying to steer the conversation back on track. After all, that's why we were here.

"She was hit by a car."

"Here, in Duluth?"

"No." He looked at me a little too closely as if weighing whether he wanted to say more. Then he added, "It happened on some small country road in West Virginia, not far from where she grew up. Black Water, if that means anything to you."

I nearly choked for the second time that day. My brain struggled to process another connection leading us to the same place. It seemed impossible, and yet, it was happening. Nick noticed my widened eyes and raised his eyebrows.

"Lucas was from Black Water, West Virginia," I said.

"Strange coincidence." He shrugged as if he didn't quite know how to react or perhaps didn't think it was a fascinating piece of information.

"You're kidding me, right?"

The more of these overlaps surfaced, the less I believed they were accidental. Amanda knew Mary. Mary might not have known Lucas, but they were from the same place. The connections were still hazy, but they were beginning to take shape.

"So all three—Mary, Amanda, and Lucas—are somehow tied to this town, Black Water, and you're calling it a coincidence?"

To be fair, Amanda wasn't definitively tied to Black Water, but it was close enough that I left it out to keep him talking. His mother, psychic or not, had to be involved in these disappearances. Or was I swayed by Mitchell and June's contagious conviction, tumbling into a spiral of cognitive bias, drawing meaning from nothing more than chance?

Nick shrugged again, his evasiveness as apparent as the ink on his skin. God, I wanted to strangle him.

I exhaled, closed my eyes briefly, and then said, "We're going to Black Water to see if we can find whatever makes people disappear."

"Or kills them," he suggested.

I looked up at him, once again facing the possibility that Lucas might be dead. Each time the thought made me shudder. I still spoke of him in the present tense, but reluctantly, I nodded and said, "Or kills them." Then it hit me. He wasn't talking about Lucas. "Wait, killed? I thought you said your mom was hit by a car!"

"She was. Kind of. A car ran her over," he paused. "Three times."

"Holy shit!"

"Yeah," he exhaled, confirming that my reaction was justified.

"Do they know who did it?"

"Nope."

It couldn't have been an accident. Hit-and-run is one thing, but hitting a person with a car, backing up, and then deciding to take their chances and flee the crime scene, running the victim over yet again, was a horrifyingly conscious choice.

"And you never thought to look into it?"

"Not until you guys showed up," he raised his eyebrows. "Homicide is not that common, statistically speaking. There are always higher chances that you'll die being hit by a car than be murdered. And that's what the police report said, too, anyways."

"The police thought it was an accident?"

"Yep."

"So we have two people missing and one dead, all allegedly linked to the same place," I recounted the facts. "Don't you think that is more than just odd?"

"I think it's something to take into account."

I looked at him again with a heavy sigh. He was making mental notes, but he was cautious about what he shared.

"We're leaving in the morning. We'll go to Black Water and see what's going on there."

"Are you inviting me to come?"

"I'm just saying that we're leaving in the morning, so you can take that into account as well."

He looked at me, offered a small, inward smile, and shook his head.

"You could find out what happened to your mom," I baited. We needed him. His mother could be the missing link that would ultimately tie everything together.

"Alright," he agreed too easily. "You friends won't mind?"

"Why would they?"

. . .

"ABSOLUTELY NOT," Mitchell cut me off the next morning when I met them to tell them about my night's adventures. "And seriously, Foster, what the fuck were you thinking, going to meet with a stranger alone? He could've murdered you!"

I gave a noncommittal wave of my hand, imagining he'd freak out if I told him how dating apps work. We all crammed into Mitchell's hotel room, which was surprisingly tidy. He had even made his own bed while June and I left ours messy, our clothes and toiletries scattered all over.

"And he lied to us," June chimed in, immediately siding with her brother against me.

"He didn't know who we were! All he knew was that his mom was killed, and then random strangers came knocking on his door. How would you feel in his shoes?" Frustrated with Mitchell's sudden reluctance, I resorted to my mother's guilt-tripping techniques. "And, by the way, we weren't exactly forthcoming with him from the start."

"Wait, did you tell him anything else?"

"Yeah, everything." I flashed my palms up at their dropped jaws. "I know, I know, I will never make it as a spy."

Mitch rolled his eyes. "Good grief, Foster."

"How do we know he didn't kill his mother himself?" June asked, playing with the trim on her Psycho T-shirt. "What if he's a serial killer?"

I was running out of arguments, but deep down, I felt that Mitchell was just upset because I hadn't included him when I went to talk to Nick, and June had simply sided with her brother out of loyalty.

To be fair, I had asked myself all the same questions, but Nick didn't give off a serial killer vibe. And, for once, I trusted my instincts.

I sighed. "Well, if it helps, there are three of us and one of him. I'm pretty sure we can overpower him if it comes to that." I turned to Mitchell. "And didn't you say that the more coincidences, the better our chances of solving this?"

June raised an eyebrow, taking on a judicial air. "You did say that."

"Alright," Mitchell reluctantly agreed, "But no more wandering off before checking with the team. This applies to everyone. Got it?"

I gave him a mock salute and sent a text to Nick, letting him know what time we'd pick him up.

June, however, wasn't done. "But just to be clear, I don't like him." The look she gave me was all-knowing.

"You don't like me, either," I blurted, immediately regretting it.

But somehow, she seemed flattered and gave me a smile.

"At least we've now established you're not a serial killer," she said.

"How can you tell?"

She cocked an eyebrow. "Well, for one, serial killers are organized, and you travel with an Ikea bag."

Chapter Seven

September, 2018

WE WERE at my place after spending a lazy day together in bed, getting dressed to go out for dinner, when I asked Lucas, "When will you be back?"

Something had been bugging me about his camping trips, even though there hadn't been any issues since the last incident. We had been together for two years, longer than most couples we knew. But lately, I was scared he was slipping away. He'd had one bad game a while back, and ever since, he hadn't quite been himself. He was distant and evasive, disappearing on random weekends.

"I don't know." He didn't even turn to face me.

I frowned. "How can you not know?"

"I'm just visiting my parents, so I'll be back when I'm back. You ready?"

My head spun, and my ears rang. He lied. Again. With a brazenness that was almost insulting. Not only had he failed to maintain a consistent story, but he had also shown a staggering lack of creativity. Just a week ago, he had told me he was going camping. When I asked him who would be joining him, he sidestepped the question with ease. And now, he claimed he was visiting his family, completely forgetting what he'd told me before. His lie was pathetic, too. He'd just been home, and now he was going again? In September, right after the summer holidays and during the football season? I almost wished he had mustered the effort to come up with a more convincing story, like a sick grandmother, to garner some sympathy.

"A week ago, you told me you were going camping," I said, trying to keep my voice down so my roommate wouldn't hear.

"What?" Lucas turned to face me, confusion etched on his face and then looked away. "Oh, I changed my mind."

I took a step closer, my voice trembling with emotion. "What's going on, Lucas? Why are you lying to me?"

He rolled his eyes. "Would you just let it go? I'm so sick and tired of your suspicions."

I felt a sting from his dismissive tone. I wasn't being paranoid. *He* was being deceitful. And possibly unfaithful.

"You are fucking lying to me!" I shouted, breaking into angry tears.

Lucas turned defensive. "What's the big deal? I need a break, okay?"

I felt lightheaded. "A break from what? From me?" I glanced nervously at the closed bedroom door, hoping Sarah was in the bathroom and couldn't hear us.

He yelled, "What's wrong with you? For once, can't it be something *not* about you?"

I was desperate and heartbroken, my emotions raw. Through tears, I pleaded, "Tell me where you're going. Are you seeing someone else?"

Lucas's voice boomed in a furious pitch, "Why would I cheat on you? I've already got my hands full with your bullshit!"

His words slapped me hard. I stood there, tears streaming down my face, my world crumbling. He looked at me, then kicked the chair and said, "I'm out of here," before slamming the door behind him.

Sobbing, I dropped to my knees, holding my mouth with one hand and my stomach with the other.

That was our very last fight.

September, 2020

WE RETURNED to Minneapolis in the afternoon. Nick was already waiting when we pulled up to his house, a duffel bag slung over his shoulder, ready to go.

Our first stop was my apartment. I wasn't sure how long the trip would take, but with only a couple of weeks left on my lease, there was no reason to come back. So, I decided to gather the rest of my belongings and move out.

I tried to usher all three of them out so I could pack in peace. There wasn't much left to do, but it would still take a solid hour, and I preferred to do it without three pairs of eyes on me. Mitchell and June went to grab a bite nearby, but Nick lingered, ignoring my not-so-subtle hints to leave.

Thankfully, my roommates weren't home. The last thing I needed was their curious glances at me and some guy I was bringing in—a situation that had never happened before. I moved off-campus after dropping out, so they'd never seen me with anyone. I didn't care what they thought, but I was still relieved to avoid their judgmental stares. Plus, no one was around for awkward goodbyes. We weren't friends. We just coexisted.

"You can wait here if you want," I said, pointing to the couch in the common area shared with the kitchen. "My roommates aren't home. I just need to make a few calls and rearrange plans."

He didn't sit. I went into my room and started packing, apologising to my bosses over the phone for the short notice leave.

"Sorry for the mess," I called out to Nick once I hung up.

"Moving?" Nick guessed, and through the doorway, I saw him survey the room.

"Something like that." He made me feel like an insect under a microscope as I sat on the floor, struggling to focus. I secured one of the bags shut.

"Where are you going?"

"Home, to Ohio," I paused to tape up a box.

"You have family there?" Nick continued quizzing me about my personal life.

"Just my mom."

"No siblings?" he pressed, his tone neutral, making it hard to gauge whether he was genuinely interested or just filling the silence.

"It's just my mom and I."

"What about your dad? He around?"

"Jeez, what's up with the third degree?" I shot him a wry grin, amused by his serious tone.

"Just making small talk."

"Choose a lighter topic. My dad passed away."

"Sorry," he said, finally peeling himself away from the door and moving closer.

"You mind giving me a hand?" I pointed at the three boxes, a suitcase, and another Ikea bag full of stuff. Lucas's gym bag was there, too.

He slung the blue bag over his shoulder and grabbed one of the boxes. I took the gym bag and the other box and then fished out a baseball bat from the corner. We'd have to make one last return.

"What's up with that?" he asked as we headed down to the car.

The bat seemed out of place among the boxes and bags, sitting there without explanation. I'd never been a fan of baseball, but my father was. When I was a kid, he took me to practices and games, which I agonised through, too bored and uninterested to commit. After he died, my mom got rid of most of his belongings—she hated clutter—but I managed to snatch his baseball bat and kept it ever since.

"It was my dad's," I said simply, sparing him the pitying details.

"Are you looking forward to going home?" Nick asked on our way back up to collect the last of my things.

"Not really," I confessed, scanning the room one last time to make sure I hadn't forgotten anything.

Nick hadn't mentioned his father, and since we were already getting personal, I had the green light to ask. "Where's *your* dad?"

"Don't know, never met him." He was nonchalant.

Lucas would have made a terrible joke about Nick's dad being a ghost, given that his mom was a psychic. I smiled to myself but didn't say anything. The joke was stupid anyway.

We removed the last of my belongings from the apartment and loaded them into the car. And then, with deliberate slowness, I placed the key on the kitchen counter and gave the apartment a last withering look.

All ties to Minneapolis were officially cut.

MITCHELL SET STRICT RULES: everyone took turns driving, and drivers switched every four hours, following a clockwise rotation. The driver had complete control of the music, while the passenger was responsible for navigation. No one dared argue with the former military man.

I drove first. Next to me, Mitchell was recounting a story about the goat to our extended audience. In the rearview mirror, Nick was reading something on his phone while June cast sidelong glances at him, which he ignored.

As we approached Chicago, traffic thickened. Local drivers

weaved recklessly through lanes, disrupting the flow. Tired of both the dull scenery and my eclectic playlist, which mostly featured Skrillex, Nicki Minaj, and Taylor Swift, the group perked up at the first glimpse of the city. But the skyline soon vanished, swallowed by the industrial outskirts.

June's tense silence lingered, taut and ready, like a bowstring pulled too far, ever since Nick settled into the back seat near her. She'd managed to keep it in check for a while, but now, four hours later, that restraint cracked. She turned to Nick with an almost confrontational directness.

"So you just… moved back into your mom's house after she died?" she asked bluntly, without attempting to smooth out the conversation.

"Around then, yeah, why?"

"It's just weird that you're only telling us now. Did you, like, go through your mom's things?"

"I did." Nick ignored the first part of her sentence.

"And was there anything?"

"Like what?"

"I don't know, you tell me," she goaded.

"There wasn't anything related to your sister or Nell's guy."

"Maybe anything weird or creepy that caught your eye?" June squinted.

Mitchell listened, not saying anything. I thought he'd interfere, considering how he tried to smooth things over between me and his sister. But this courtesy apparently didn't extend to Nick.

"What, like a self-moving Ouija board? Or videotapes of my mom summoning the devil?"

"You said it."

"For fuck's sake!" Nick exclaimed, covering his eyes with his hand. "No, there wasn't anything suspicious. Just stupid books on manifestation and shit, and that's about it."

But June kept pushing despite his outburst. "Why didn't you just toss everything and leave?"

"Cause I was trying to do the right thing and make sense out of her paperwork, online store, and orders," he said, trying to keep his voice steady.

"The website's still live," June said, her voice inquisitorial, like she was trying to catch him in a lie.

"I'm managing it now."

"What, now *you're* the psychic?" she taunted.

"June!" warned Mitchell, but she didn't react.

"I'm just handling her online orders, okay? I was going to shut everything down, but I didn't. And she was no more a psychic than I am. So I was just being careful when you came around. Can we drop it?"

"Why, Nick, we're just trying to get to know you." In the rearview mirror, I saw how June leaned back in her seat, arms crossed, and a smirk on her face. Somehow, she really got to him.

Nick sat diagonally behind me in the rear passenger seat, and I could practically feel waves of irritation radiating off him. "I didn't sign up for a full-blown interrogation. So cut the crap."

Mitchell turned back, trying to protect his sister. "We just want to understand what we're dealing with here."

"Can you try doing it without prying into every detail of my life?" Nick retorted and then added without changing his tone, "I haven't asked you why you were kicked out of the military because I know it's irrelevant."

Mitchell exploded, turning to face Nick. "What the fuck did you just say?"

Uh-oh. Mitchell never mentioned anything like that, and from what he told me, I understood that he simply resigned. Was Nick more informed, or was he just shooting in the dark? And if so, was this actually true?

"Guys," I interjected softly. However, no one seemed to notice or care.

For a second, I thought they might start a fight, but Mitchell locked eyes with him, sat back in his seat, and muttered, "Fucking asshole."

Cars were honking outside, adding chaos to the city's noise. I was struggling to focus on the heavy traffic, trying to maneuver the Dodge out of it without causing any damage. Still, on the inside, I felt like throwing open the door and jumping into the frenzy of vehicles, ready to take my chances.

When I was six, my parents and I drove to Fort Myers, where my dad's friend rented us a small boathouse for the week. Somewhere along the way, my parents started bickering over something my dad had done wrong or forgotten to do. After a heated exchange, they plunged into a sullen silence that lingered for hours.

This trip felt like a bad rerun, only now there were more people and even more tension. The acrid smell of exhaust seeped through the weak A/C, mingling with the silence and thickening the air. We were only a few hours into the drive, and I already dreaded what might come next.

I felt like a kid, listening to my parents' endless arguments. I wasn't willing to sit through it anymore.

Without saying another word, I took the nearest exit and pulled onto a quiet street with no traffic, stopped the car, and switched on the hazard lights.

Everyone looked at me. Mitchell asked, "What's going on? Why did we stop?"

"We're not going anywhere until you all stop bickering and start acting like adults." I crossed my arms over my chest and gave each of them a stern look. June looked away, but Nick held steady.

Mitchell took the liberty of breaking the tension, "Let's grab a bite. It's a crime to be in Chicago and not try deep-dish pizza. Heard so much about it."

"I agree with you on this one," Nick concurred, smoothing things over.

"Whatever, *mommy*," June muttered sarcastically.

Mitchell stifled a quiet laugh with a cough. I, secretly relieved, shook my head, catching Nick's faint smile out of the corner of my eye.

Chapter Eight

June, 2016

FOR AS LONG AS I can remember, my mother had a strong aversion to processed foods. The sight of pizza at kids' parties made her face pinch with distaste, while at home, we always had a hot, homemade dinner. As a first-generation immigrant, she treasured her mother's old handwritten recipe book, frequently consulting it when cooking or baking. Our pantry was a testament to her culinary traditions, lined with labeled jars of marinated goods and homemade jams. Every Thanksgiving, she'd proudly place her cranberry jam alongside the turkey, only for my father to sneak in a can of jellied cranberry sauce, teasing that "the bad stuff" was better for the soul. My mother would frown but never protested.

Whenever my dad and I went to an arcade or theme park, she'd pack me a healthy lunch, complete with carrot sticks, and warn him not to let me indulge in "those places." But every time, he'd disobey, and I'd end up enjoying pizza, hot dogs, ice cream, and cookies.

When I was a child, their constant tug-of-war felt like a

game. But as I got older, it became exhausting. My mother was all about rules and expectations, while my dad was just about having fun.

After he died, my mother stopped cooking as much. She picked up more shifts at the hospital and was home less often, leaving me money to order pizza—something once banished from our house. She started making trays of lasagna and freezing them to save time. To my seventeen-year-old self, it felt like all her nutrition rules had only existed to challenge my dad. With him gone, so was the discipline. It seemed like she'd been pushing him away all along. And my teenage brain couldn't forgive her for that.

September, 2020

THE NEARBY VINTAGE diner we settled into screamed retro: red leather booths lined one side of the restaurant, and a long, shiny counter with spinning stools stretched along the other. The walls were plastered with posters from classic 80s movies. As we were flipping through the laminated menus filled with greasy goodness, I took charge of the conversation.

"I think we can push through and make it to Ohio before stopping for the night. From there, it's only about four to five hours to Black Water."

Mitchell gave a thumbs-up. "I like the way you think, Foster. Let's do it. June, your turn to drive."

"I know," June grumbled.

"Tomorrow, we'll get up early and have a few hours of daylight to look around," her brother decided.

"What are we going to do in Black Water?" Nick asked.

"Good question, Boyd. That's why..." Mitchell eagerly cleared a space, pushing the condiments and water glasses aside. He reached under the table, pulled out his backpack, and extracted a folded paper map of the United States, a notepad, and a mechanical pen, carefully laying them out.

June, used to her brother's methods, watched with a detached expression, sipping her Coke through a straw. Nick maintained a deliberately neutral face. Mitchell's enthusiasm felt slightly over the top, like that of a child absorbed in a game.

He spread the map across the table, taking up a significant portion of the surface. "So," he said, clicking his pen, "What do we know?"

"Lucas's parents are here," I said, pointing at Black Water on the map. The town was too small to be marked, but I'd studied it so much on Google Maps that I'd memorized the area. Mitchell circled the spot.

"When Amanda went to West Virginia, her last known location was here." He placed another mark not too far from where Lucas's parents were. "Do you recall where your mother was found?" Mitchell asked Nick.

Nick turned the map and quickly scanned the surrounding areas before pointing to a spot near Black Water. The fact that the three locations were all close to each other didn't surprise me.

"But they didn't go missing in Black Water. Lucas disappeared in Minneapolis, and Amanda in Kansas City." I voiced the obvious, just to keep track of everything.

Mitchell nodded and marked them on the map. Now, the area was too vast, the connections too tenuous.

June raised an eyebrow. "This doesn't add up."

"Perhaps we should focus on Black Water and not other places. At least for now," Nick suggested.

The waitress brought our order, and the aroma of tangy tomato sauce, sweet caramelized onions, and rich melted mozzarella instantly shifted our priorities to the most basic one: hunger.

Mitchell swiftly folded the map with practiced motions, clearing space on the table.

"Maybe it's not about where they went missing. Maybe these are just symptoms, and the main cause is there," Nick continued, slipping a slice of pizza onto his plate. Cheese strings trailed from the tray with a gooey, melty resistance.

Mitchell shifted his jaw, then gave a small grunt of agreement. "Alright. We're going there anyway. Let's just concentrate on these," he said, tapping his finger on the folded map under his hand. "I agree, Black Water might be our best bet."

Nick finished his first slice of pizza, and as his initial hunger was sated, he turned and said, "Can you show me the sign Lucas and Amanda kept again?"

June looked at her brother, who nodded his consent. She slid the phone to Nick.

"So, what do you think?" she asked after he examined the photos for a few seconds.

"I'm not sure."

"Come on, you're not gonna tell me you don't know anything? Your mom was, like, a psychic."

I wasn't sure why June was clinging to Nick's mother so much. My mother was a nurse, and I didn't know the first thing about CPR or anything else medically sound.

Whatever Nick felt, he kept it to himself this time. "What does that have to do with anything?"

June snorted, but I interjected once again to diffuse her. "How about we talk to Lucas's parents first and see where that leads us?"

"What about this sign, then?" June insisted, tapping her phone screen.

"Alright, let's play it smart," her brother said. "We can ask around about this symbol, but let's not go waving it in Lucas's folks' faces. Might spook them. You know what his folks do for a living, by the way?"

The last question was addressed directly to me.

"I think his father owns a business," I paused as I racked my brain. "A sawmill, maybe? Or was it a lumberyard? Something with wood, anyway." I snapped my fingers, trying to conjure up the memory. "And his mom is a stay-at-home mom, I'm pretty sure."

Whatever we had was very sparse, but it was something.

At the very least, the pizza was good.

WE ARRIVED at the rundown motel, the neon sign creaking in the wind. June shot her brother a disapproving look.

"What the hell did you book?"

"I booked whatever had room for four people! It looked fine in the pictures! And it's just for one night, anyway."

While Mitchell was checking us in, June browsed Google for reviews, her brow furrowed with concern. I shared her unease but decided not to say anything. Mitchell paid out of his own pocket for all of us, and I didn't want to upset him. Nick kept to himself, seemingly trying to avoid any further confrontation with June.

She gasped at her phone. "Look at this! Someone wrote there were bloodstains on the sheets!"

The tired clerk gave her a blank stare as if to say, *'Yeah, yeah, heard this one before,'* and then turned to Mitchell. "Anything else?"

June kept pushing, "Do you sell plastic sheets and Clorox?"

"No, but you can try Dollar General, about half a mile from here," the clerk replied, handing us the keys.

As soon as we entered the room, June pulled back the covers to check if her sheets were clean. They appeared to be fine.

"You should also check for bedbugs behind the headboard," I suggested. "I mean, if you want to be really thorough."

June scrunched her nose, visibly repulsed. "Eww."

She tried to push the entire bed set away from the wall to no avail.

I chuckled and checked my sheets and mattress for suspicious stains as well. I'm not a germaphobe, but sleeping where someone might have been killed wasn't something I could easily dismiss.

June grumbled for a little longer and finally settled down in bed, having inspected it once again with her phone flashlight.

Just as we were getting ready to sleep, she suddenly asked, "Do you think they're still alive?"

I hesitated. "I don't know."

I'd never navigated a situation like that before. When Lucas went missing, I was alone in my grief. Now, I was struggling to find words to console June. I felt like a trapezist, walking the fine line between offering comfort and overstepping the fragile connection we'd established. Nothing I could say would ease her pain.

June's silence stretched a beat before she added, "Do you think we'll find Lucas in Black Water?"

I shook my head. "No... I don't think so."

"Then why are you even here?"

I took a deep breath. "I couldn't forgive myself if I didn't try."

June's voice cracked in the darkness. "I want Amanda to come back."

My heart went out to her. "Me too."

She choked back a sob and whispered, "I don't think she will, though."

. . .

THAT NIGHT, I had a dream about Lucas. He stood alone in the empty stadium, impassiveness dulling his features. I expected to feel happiness, or at least relief, at seeing him. God knew I wanted to run to him, wrap my arms around his waist, and rest my head beneath his chin.

I was rooted to the spot, paralyzed with fear. I couldn't move or look away.

My legs felt rooted, deeper than the trees that grew through the bleachers, as if nature had claimed the place long ago. Lucas slipped backward, vanishing into their shadows. Silent, menacing, like a ghoul.

I tried to flee, but my limbs were lead, pulling me to my hands and knees. Grass shifted beneath my fingers, rolling into a damp, mossy floor speckled with stones and twigs and foetid animal carcasses.

I tried to crawl away, to writhe with the worms spilling from the dull eyes and open mouths of deer, but my body was heavy and unresponsive.

Help!

Every time I looked away, the trees crept closer.

I hid my face in the collar of my shirt. Another presence shifted nearby, heavy as a storm, but I was too afraid to look up.

My mouth moved to form words. *Please. Leave me alone. Go away.* But they stayed trapped in my head, a whisper dying in my arid throat.

And then, I heard his voice.

"Nell."

I looked up.

Symbols were burned into the trunks of trees around us. Crows perched on their wiry branches, watching with unforgiving eyes.

"Lucas?"

He emerged from the dark all at once, his eyes staring past me as he came closer, but his feet barely moved. He was gliding, a puppet suspended in the air. It looked like him, but he was all angles and blurred edges. Skin turned to moss and bone.

I willed myself to wake up, certain this was a nightmare, but my eyes locked onto the figure standing over me. Lucas's image was frozen, unyielding, like a photograph. It seared into my mind like a branding iron. His gray, unblinking eyes wouldn't release me. I tried to scream, but only air rushed out.

A crushing weight pinned me down, making every breath a struggle. I squirmed beneath him, slapping and kicking for freedom. My throat was on fire, and my vision flashed.

Then, as suddenly as it began, the pressure lifted, and I choked on the scent of wet wood and mulch and the muskiness of old sheets. I bolted upright in bed, drenched with sweat, my heart racing like a wild animal.

I frantically scanned the room, but Lucas wasn't there. June slept peacefully in her bed. She'd thrown the covers off. Her T-shirt had ridden up, exposing her pierced belly button. Her gentle breathing was accompanied by soft, quiet snores.

The room was stifling and heavy with heat, and the air conditioning busted. I tossed aside the tangled sheets and stumbled to the window, gulping down a rush of cool air.

I remained awake until dawn.

Chapter Nine

September, 2020

JUNE WAS SUPPOSED to be helping Nick using her phone's map, but instead, she was glued to the window. The rolling hills grew taller, taking us up into the mountains.

With her attention elsewhere, Nick relied on road signs to navigate, a skill he seemed to excel at. I envied him. I was lost without GPS unless I knew the route well.

Beside me in the back seat, Mitchell followed his paper map, cross-checking against passing signs as if compensating for his sister's navigational neglect. That, or he couldn't bear to relinquish full control.

"Getting close," he announced.

My stomach clenched. I caught myself playing with my bracelet again, one charm already loose. I tucked it into my pocket to save it from any more wear, and tried to calm down. Without warning, Nick switched to the far-right lane, pulled into a deserted rest stop, and put the car in park.

"Nell should take the wheel when we go into town," he said.

"Why?" Mitchell and I asked in unison.

"Just a gut feeling."

"No, you've only been driving for an hour." Mitchell sounded frustrated.

"It's okay, I'll drive," I said. Though Nick's reasoning seemed weak, I didn't want to stir up another argument, so agreeing was easier.

Mitchell wasn't happy, but he didn't say anything as Nick and I switched seats.

I grabbed the steering wheel, still warm from Nick's hands. We exited the highway and turned onto a narrow, single-lane road marked with a sign for "Black Water." It wound between hills thick with forest, and I slowed to traverse the sharp turns. The road seemed newly renovated—the asphalt smooth, the markings crisp.

After half an hour, the trees thinned out, revealing scattered houses. The forest receded, and the narrow country road became a street.

"Turn right there," Mitchell instructed, checking the map.

A short honk from a police car tore me from reacting. A sturdy cruiser with a faded gold star on its side pulled up behind us. I hastily glanced at the dashboard to see if I was speeding. I wasn't.

Once we'd pulled over, the Sheriff, a stout man with a short, fiery red beard, emerged from the vehicle.

"Stay calm. Everything's fine," Mitchell said, abruptly putting away his phone and map and folding his hands on his knees.

I'd never been pulled over by a cop before, and I was immediately nervous. However, my father covered this scenario when he taught me to drive, so I was familiar with the drill. I pulled the keys from the ignition and placed them on the dashboard, lowered the window, and then returned my hands to the wheel.

"License and registration, ma'am," the Sheriff said in a flat, detached tone. He peered into the car, scanning every detail.

"Everything all right, officer?" I handed him the documents.

He didn't acknowledge my question. His brow furrowed as he scrutinised my papers. Only after a few long seconds did he say, without looking at me, "Routine check. Just arrived in town?"

"Yes, sir," I said, forcing a friendly smile, though my hands were turning clammy on the wheel.

The Sheriff returned to his SUV, probably to run my license and registration. I stared at the three others in the car, but no one said a word.

I shot Nick and Mitch a sideways look that clearly asked, *What's going on?*

Nick raised his hands slightly, palms up in a helpless little shrug.

Mitchell, on the other hand, sat ramrod straight, like he'd swallowed a broomstick. For someone who talked about becoming a cop, he looked deeply uncomfortable around this one.

The Sheriff came back with a heavy gait and leaned in, scanning the interior once more. For a few seconds, his face felt uncomfortably close to mine. I could smell the pungent mix of sweat, stale cigarettes, and a hint of something metallic on him. It was unnerving, and I fought the urge to recoil, but stayed put, eyes fixed ahead. Everyone remained quiet; even June sat rigidly beside me, silent for once.

"You folks aren't from around here," he stated the obvious, having already seen the out-of-state license plate. "Just sightseein' or...?"

"Just passing through. Decided to do some hiking," I replied.

"Be careful hikin' in these woods. You know it can be dangerous, with the wildlife and all."

"Thanks, officer. We'll be careful," Mitchell chimed in.

"I was talkin' to the driver, son," the Sheriff said, his expression turning stern. "Anythin' in the car that shouldn't be here? Firearms? Drugs?"

I shook my head. "N-no."

The Sheriff's focus shifted to the backseat, locking onto Nick and Mitch. "What about you two? Carry anythin' to liven up a party?"

I didn't want to know what he was implying.

"No," Nick answered firmly.

"Just traveling with my sister and friends," Mitchell said.

"Young lady?" The Sheriff addressed June, taking in her black outfit and messy blonde hair. She shook her head, eyes wide with repressed fear. It was the first time I'd seen her look spooked. I wondered if she picked up on the same creepy vibe I did.

"What's in the trunk? Mind if I take a look?"

Mitchell shifted uncomfortably.

"Just our luggage," I answered, reaching under the seat to release the latch.

The Sheriff walked to the back of the car, my papers still in hand. He shifted a few bags, found nothing suspicious, and finally closed the trunk.

"Alright, everythin' seems to be in order," he said, handing me back my papers. "You folks be careful hikin', ya hear?"

"Thank you," I said, swallowing hard as he walked away from the car.

I tried to put my driver's license back in my wallet, but my hands were shaking, and I dropped the card somewhere under the seat.

"What the hell was that? Why did he stop us? Did he threaten us?" June erupted into a barrage of questions while I tried to retrieve my license.

"Just some small-town Sheriff bullshit," Mitchell said, trying to downplay the situation. Then he turned to me, annoyance clear in his voice. "Just so you know, for future reference, you can say no to a car search if they don't have a warrant."

"Why would a Sheriff be doing road patrol?" Nick muttered, mostly to himself.

And I couldn't shake the feeling that it was to keep tabs on newcomers.

THE HOTEL TURNED out to be an enormous resort, complete with a golf course and outdoor pool, all surrounded by green mountains. Compared to the rundown motel we'd stayed at before, it felt almost luxurious. I didn't think Mitchell fully realized what he'd booked until we pulled in. Still, there were benefits. In a larger hotel, it would be easier to pass as just a group of tourists here for a relaxing weekend.

But as we wound through the grounds, it became clear we'd arrived in the off-season. The place was nearly deserted. A lone golfer moved across the course, a couple lounged by the pool, and a single staff member tidied an empty patio.

The majority of the rooms were situated inside small, white, antebellum-style cottages, each one divided into four separate units. They had charming names like Magnolia, Hydrangea, and Dogwood, which suited their picturesque, garden-like surroundings.

When June and I reached our room, we were met with outdated decor and evident signs of wear and tear. The space was small, with a tiny entryway leading into a cramped living area that held a worn-out sofa and two armchairs. The bedroom was equally compact, with two queen beds, but the bathroom was surprisingly spacious, featuring a large, albeit slightly rundown, bathtub.

In the unit next door, where the guys were staying, Mitchell gathered us in the confined living room for what he called a "briefing."

"Now, listen up." His accent softened his stern command as he spoke. "First rule: we watch out for each other. That's why we're doing the buddy system."

He scanned the room, making sure we were all paying close attention.

June slumped in the armchair, half-reclined with her legs stretched out, idly fiddling with her rosary. Now and then, she'd look up at her brother, indicating she had been listening.

"We're gonna pair up," Mitch continued. "Two teams of two. You're responsible for your partner's back, and they've got yours. Nobody gets left behind and nobody's left standing around with nothing to do."

That's how I became June's buddy.

"Why can't I be *your* buddy?" June complained to her brother.

"Because you and Nell are rooming together," Mitch explained with extreme patience. "I want you two to be glued at the hip. Whether you're grabbing a soda or taking a walk, you go together. Nick and I will do the same. We'll swap partners if needed, but nobody goes solo. Period."

"Even to the bathroom?" June muttered, but Mitchell had already moved on.

"It's about staying safe, staying alert, and keeping each other in the loop if things go sideways. You got that?"

June leaned back in her chair, crossing her arms over her chest and let out an exaggerated sigh, a perfect picture of teenage discontent.

"Okay, everyone dismissed. I mean, that's it. Any questions?" Mitchell concluded, spreading his hands.

Nick shot me a quick look, but I chose to ignore it. Perhaps Mitch was laying it on a bit thick with the military jargon, but everything he said made sense to me. Plus, he was the only one with tactical and combat experience, so I wasn't overly concerned about his presentation style. In fact, it was a little thrilling, like we were part of an interactive game where we played as soldiers on a mission.

THE NEXT STEP was emotionally daunting, at least for me. With only one lead to pursue, we decided to act quickly and visit Lucas's parents, not wanting to waste any time.

After some pouting on June's part, it was decided that Mitchell and I would meet with the Whitmans alone, acting as advocates for Lucas and Amanda, while June and Nick explored downtown to gather whatever insights they could.

"You keep a close eye on her," Mitch told Nick. He'd pulled him to one side, a slither of space gasping between their chests. His expression said, *If anything happens to her, you'll answer to me*.

Despite Mitch's concern, I wasn't worried for them. Nick's intimidating height, combined with June's graphic Hellraiser T-shirt and unfriendly face, made them a formidable pair few would dare approach.

Chapter Ten

September, 2020

TO MY EMBARRASSMENT, I got nervous at the last minute, and it showed: I couldn't stop fidgeting, my hands trembled, and I kept dropping things. Then again, I started to make that something of a habit.

"What if they secretly think I had something to do with their son's disappearance?" I asked Mitch when we were together in the car.

Mitchell looked at me, puzzled. "Why would they blame you?"

"Isn't that what people usually do? Look to place blame?"

"It's going to be okay, Foster. Deep breaths."

I saved their address after Lucas asked me to mail something to them one time—a birthday card, or anniversary note I'd encouraged him to gift, trying to get on their good side before we officially met.

Now, as I nearly fell out of the car, my only hope was that they hadn't moved.

. . .

THE OLD FARMHOUSE-STYLE home had been lovingly restored, its classic lines refreshed by a recent makeover. Lucas mentioned that his parents had lived there since they got married. His father renovated the house himself, pouring his heart and soul into it. The scent of fresh-cut grass wafted through the air, the lawn perfectly manicured. On the porch, with its newly painted railings, an old-fashioned radio softly sang Willie Nelson tunes. We seemed to have slipped through the decades, landing squarely in the past.

Lucas's father was sitting on the wooden stairs, carving a bird-shaped figurine from a piece of basswood, the shavings curling softly at his feet. He looked the same, albeit more faded than when I last saw him at the Minneapolis police station. His face had grown even thinner, accentuating the defined angles of his bone structure, with more lines and wrinkles etched into his skin.

Mr. Whitman's movements were precise and straightforward, the knife in his hand fluttering around the wood like a butterfly over a flower. When he noticed us, he set the tools down and stood up. His height, the same as Lucas's, made him appear younger. When he had been sitting on the porch, I'd mistaken him for a scrawny man in his sixties. But now, standing, he appeared tall, with good posture and a strong frame.

"What can I do for ya?" he said in a low, rumbling baritone.

"Mister Whitman, I'm not sure if you remember me. We met in Minneapolis," I began, hoping to jog his memory. "I'm Lucas's girlfriend."

"Oh yes, Natalie, was it?" the old man said, adjusting his eyeglasses.

"Nellie," I corrected, unoffended. "And this is my friend, Mitchell."

"My apologies," he smiled, his eyes crinkling at the corners. "What brings you here?"

Mitchell interjected, "We're here about your son's disappearance."

Lucas's dad grew serious, his expression clouding over. "Do you have any news? The police never contacted us."

"We're not sure, sir. Maybe it's best if we sit down to talk."

"You're not from around here," he narrowed his eyes at Mitchell, turning the volume of the radio down.

"No, sir. I'm from Missouri."

"Missouri, huh… Quite a distance," he nodded to himself. "You Lucas's friend?"

"No, sir. I am here 'bout my sister. She disappeared. Just like your son, sir."

Mr. Whitman squinted as if trying to see where this conversation was going.

"I'm sorry to hear that. Did *she* know Lucas?"

"Not sure, sir. But before she disappeared, she took a trip here, to Black Water. Maybe you've seen her? Do you mind looking at her picture?"

I was slightly annoyed at Mitchell for talking over me and dragging the conversation to his sister.

The old man removed his thick-framed glasses, rubbed his tired eyes with a worn thumb and index finger, and then fished out a crumpled napkin from his pocket. He meticulously wiped the lenses before putting them back on.

"Reckon you're right. Maybe we should step inside. Where's my manners at?"

He held the door as we walked in, then called out from behind us, his voice booming through the house and making me wince. "Emily, we've got company!"

We stepped into a light-filled foyer, its creamy yellow walls glowing in the setting sun. The dark wood floors creaked under our feet. To the left, a staircase with elegantly turned balusters and a curved handrail led upstairs. The wall beside it was lined with family photos, a quiet and poignant reminder of happier times. Somewhere up there was Lucas's room. Unless his parents had repurposed it to avoid the weight of painful memories. But I had a feeling they'd left it untouched.

I reached out to the old wooden coat rack, my fingers tracing its worn surface. The air smelled faintly of lemon polish, layered over something older—dust in the vents, dry paper, a hint of medicinal cream.

This was the house where Lucas grew up. Strange to think of him racing up and down these stairs.

Mr. Whitman led us to the living room, adorned with rustic touches, including a few sets of antlers—probably souvenirs from his hunting adventures—mounted on the walls. I tried to envision Lucas living here, watching TV and playing video games. His school trophies from football games were on display, alongside framed photos on the walls and mantelpiece.

We settled into the worn, plush couch while Mr. Whitman took the chair across from us.

"How about you start from the beginning so my old head can follow?" he said.

"My sister went missing last year, under similar circumstances to your son. She'd been out here visiting before she disappeared. You might've seen her? Mind taking a look?" He pulled out his phone as I restrained my growing frustration.

Mitchell was driving the conversation further away from what we had planned: concentrating on asking Mr. Whitman about Lucas's recent visit home.

Mr. Whitman adjusted his glasses, took the phone, and scrutinized the image.

"Don't rightly look familiar, but my eyes ain't what they used to be," he said. "Emily, take a look at this," he called out to his wife.

Lucas's mother, a quiet woman with a measured expression, entered the living room with drinks. She reservedly greeted us, her face betraying not even a hint of recognition, then carefully examined the photo, scanning it with her faded gray eyes. Lucas took after his dad in height and build, but his hair and eye color were unmistakably his mother's. Now, her hair was gray, but she still dyed it the same light shade I'd seen in photos of her younger self.

She avoided our eyes, her movements tense and hesitant. It was clear that our presence made her uncomfortable.

"Who is this?" she asked, taking a seat after arranging the drinks on the coffee table.

"It's my sister, Amanda. She's missing, like Lucas," Mitch said.

"She's a mite too old for Lucas, don't you reckon?" She kept studying the picture.

"They weren't dating, honey," her husband advised, nodding toward me. "He was dating Natalie."

I hesitated to correct him again.

She regarded me as if seeing me for the first time. "I see." Then she returned the phone. "Never seen her. What's that gotsta do with Lucas?"

"We're trying to figure that out, ma'am."

"Alright then."

Her face suddenly contorted in a grimace that she hid behind her hands.

"Excuse me," she said and hurried out of the room.

Mitchell's face fell. "We're terribly sorry," he offered, sounding genuinely apologetic. "We didn't mean to upset you."

"Excuse me for a spell, would ya?" Mr. Whitman trailed after his wife.

A large grandfather clock ticked loudly, its steady rhythm filling the silence. Mitchell took a sip of his iced tea. I stood up, too anxious to stay seated, and began pacing the room. I was mad at him. We had upset Lucas's parents and found nothing useful.

I studied the photographs of my boyfriend in mismatched

frames, following the visual story of his life—childhood photos on the left, gradually giving way to more recent ones towards the right. In one photo, likely taken before prom, he stood with a girl. A sharp pang of jealousy struck me, and my thoughts wandered to rumors of him cheating—maybe with his high school ex.

I quickly pushed the idea away.

In a couple of photographs, he was pictured with a friend at different ages. The most recent snapshot showed them on a backpacking trip. They were deep in the woods, grinning at the camera with their gear slung over their shoulders. The friend's darker hair and sharper features made him appear slightly older than Lucas. I picked up the frame and flipped it over. On the back of the photo, a message was written in neat cursive: *Lucas and Duane, senior year.*

Mitchell stepped up beside me, sensing that something had caught my attention. I pointed to the picture without a word.

"We should talk to this Duane guy," he said, taking the photo from my hands and examining it briefly before returning it to the shelf. I adjusted it slightly, restoring it to its original position before noting the football trophies from his school days.

"Lucas was as talented a receiver as I ever did see, God rest his soul."

I hadn't noticed Mr. Whitman return, and his sudden presence made me jump. Then the gravity of his last words hit me, and I fought a wave of nausea. Lucas's own father deemed him dead.

"He got himself a football scholarship, did ya know? My boy, he was somethin' else." He approached the shelf, picked up one of the awards, and studied it with a sense of pride.

"He earned this one after that game against Oakdale High." He grew quiet, lost in a rush of memories. "I was so proud, I could've burst when they presented it to him in front of the whole school." He gently placed the plaque back on the shelf, his hands trembling slightly.

"I miss him, too," was all I could say.

WE TRIED ASKING a few more questions about Lucas's whereabouts during his last visit, but his father struggled to recall much of it. He said everything seemed normal. Lucas spent time with family and caught up with friends before heading back to Minneapolis.

Disappointed, we didn't want to tax their hospitality or stir any more sorrow and made our way out. I felt weirdly hollow. I hadn't expected to uncover any major revelations, but the complete absence of new leads was more frustrating than I'd anticipated. Of course, I could still try to talk to Lucas's friend, Duane, before wrapping up here and heading to my mother's.

Thankfully, Mr. Whitman had Duane's old residence and phone number scribbled in his address book.

"Used to pick Lucas up there when they were young'uns," he explained. "He's probably still there. Didn't leave like Lucas did. When his daddy passed on, he got the house."

He held open the door for us to exit. "I appreciate y'all tryin' to do somethin'. We're gettin' on in years and have learned to accept what we can't change."

"We'll make sure to give you an update if we find something, sir," Mitchell said, his posture straight as a soldier.

"Bless you, son," Mr. Whitman replied, as he gave Mitchell a firm handshake and me a warm hug.

His wife didn't come out to say goodbye, but I saw a curtain twitch as though she were watching.

"SEE, IT WASN'T SO BAD," Mitchell said, starting the car and pulling away from the Whitmans' house.

I gazed out the window, watching Mr. Whitman wave from the porch before settling back into his chair, picking up his unfinished figurine and carving knife. Responding to Mitchell or pretending to stay calm felt like too much effort, so I remained quiet and tried to let it go. It wasn't his fault the Whitmans couldn't tell us anything.

I was holding a piece of paper on which Lucas's father had written Duane's address.

"Shall we go, just the two of us?" I asked Mitchell.

He thought for a moment, then squinted like he was picturing something unpleasant and shook his head. "Nah, those two are going to go at each other if we leave them alone any longer, so I wouldn't risk it."

But he couldn't have been more wrong. Left to their own devices, Nick and June stood on the museum stairs, looking surprisingly relaxed and engaged. June's eyes sparkled with excitement. She looked overstimulated, as if she'd had too much caffeine, and immediately spilled her newfound information without even asking how things went with Lucas's parents.

"This town is crazy! Did you know it was founded by a witch coven?"

I vaguely recalled Lucas mentioning something like that in the past.

"I thought this was a mining town," Mitchell queried.

"The city was founded by people who got kicked out of the original settlements," June said, brushing off his question. "They were accused of practicing magic or Satanism, or whatever."

The church, bathed in the warm hues of the setting sun, boasted its newly painted sides in pristine white, as if trying to wash away the dark past June had just mentioned. Sunlight reflected off the church windows, casting a harsh glare in our direction, like a disapproving finger warning outsiders not to disturb the fragile balance of the place.

"So, everyone in town is a descendant of witches?" I

muttered, still struggling to make sense of the information June had dumped on us.

"Not everyone," Nick corrected, his tone matter-of-fact. "Also, the coven died out a few decades after its founding."

June's enthusiasm was palpable. "Yes, there was a massacre! Can you freaking believe it?"

Mitchell grew curious. "Was the entire museum about witchcraft?"

His sister launched into a detailed explanation, tripping over history as though it were trying to pull her back. "No, there was still a lot of boring stuff about the settlers and migration routes or whatever. But the witchcraft was the only part that didn't make me snore. They worshipped the devil, and that's how they stayed alive. But then they had a fallout, fought over their grimoire, and that's all."

My mind reeled. It all seemed so irrelevant, yet my curiosity was piqued. "Kind of like the Salem witch trials?"

June dismissed the comparison. "Nah, they pretty much killed each other."

"The coven disappeared, and the town lived happily ever after," Nick wrapped up the conversation. "How about you? Any leads?"

"Oh yeah!" June finally remembered our absence. "What did you find out?"

"Not a lot," Mitchell responded for both of us. "But we got Lucas's friend's address. We should follow up on that and see if he knows anything."

"Are you sure he still lives here?" June asked skeptically.

"You'll be surprised," Nick said, "not a lot of people leave towns like this one. Most stay forever."

But the hope of catching Duane that night was fading. No one answered his landline, and Lucas's dad didn't have a cell number for him, and it was getting too late to show up unannounced.

"Let's pay him a visit tomorrow," Mitchell suggested. "It's a Sunday, he'll likely be at home."

"Do you think Amanda really came here?" June asked her brother.

"I don't know, Junie. But we've come here to find her, so we're staying till we figure something out."

Mitchell gave June a gentle pat on the back, and although she was always so prickly, she didn't push his hand away. It was the first time he called her 'Junie' in front of us as well.

I didn't have any siblings, but at that moment, I regretted being an only child. Having an older brother must be nice. I caught Nick looking at me, probably thinking the same.

Just then, the museum's front door creaked open on its own, the sound resounding like a groan through the square. The sudden noise made me flinch. We all turned, but it slammed shut just as quickly.

I felt a light pressure on my back. It was Nick trying to console me.

"You okay?" he asked, his voice low and concerned. "You seem a little on edge."

I gave a subtle shrug, and he guided me away from the square, following the siblings, who were walking ahead towards the car.

"This town gives me the creeps," I confessed.

"Every town has a dark story. This one just happens to be about witchcraft and mass deaths."

A THUNDERSTORM WAS BREWING. The sky rumbled like an upset stomach. Nick and I sat on a small hotel balcony, gazing aimlessly at the greenery, unable to leave each other's sight— Mitchell's orders. He and June had gone to pick up some food, and the buddy system ensured that no one was alone.

The food we had at the resort earlier was appalling. Every

dish was drenched in a sickly, greasy sheen, the meat was tough and dubious, and even the humblest comfort food, mac and cheese, had been transformed into a rubbery, carb-loaded monstrosity. With no other options, Mitchell and June ventured out to find something—anything!—better.

"May I ask a personal question?" Nick lifted his eyes to mine.

I put my phone down, already on alert. "Shoot."

"You holding up?"

I snorted, more out of reflex than humor. That was the personal question?

"Did you look me up?" I asked, cutting straight through it, though I knew the answer. The way he asked, the way he looked at me, it wasn't just curiosity.

"Yeah," he said without blinking. "Wanted to know who I was working with."

He gave a small smile, softening the joke, but I didn't return it.

"Then you know enough."

"Not really. Headlines don't tell the whole story."

"And I'm not about to fill in the blanks. Sorry."

He nodded like he expected that. "Fair."

There was a pause, just long enough to make it feel like something was shifting.

"It won't suck forever," he said, "No one here thinks anything bad of you. Even June."

I let out a bitter laugh. "Well, she's the first."

"No, she isn't."

"Oh yeah? Who else thinks I'm not a serial killer?"

"Sergeant Mitch, for sure." That elicited a laugh from me. Then, with a hint of a smile, he added, "Me."

I wanted to tell him he didn't need to reassure me. I wasn't looking for comfort. I just didn't know what to do with it. But something in me loosened. His words weren't anything special, but they landed. For the first time in a while, I felt a sense of safety.

He continued after a pause. "Lucas liked you, too, I think. He'd have been a fool not to."

"What makes you say that?"

He hesitated, clearly having revealed more than he intended. "I'm trying to say that even if a fraction of whatever's on the internet is true, you deserve better."

"Don't," I warned. I wasn't sure if he was hinting at Lucas's cheating or our fights, but I had no intention of discussing it with him, and I certainly wasn't seeking his validation.

"Sorry."

We sat in silence, our conversation still continuing in my head.

"I loved him," I said abruptly, speaking of Lucas in the past tense for the first time.

Regardless of his whereabouts, a two-year absence was a long time for feelings to last.

Nick was quiet, waiting for me to continue, but I didn't say anything else. The truth was, when Lucas vanished, a part of me disappeared, too.

Chapter Eleven

November, 2018

LUCAS HAD BEEN MISSING for over a month. I tried calling him every day, sending messages like, "Where are you?"—"Lucas, please, answer me!"—"Lucas, the police are looking for you!"

But not a single response came back. The texts weren't even marked as delivered.

The longer he was gone, the harder it got. Every day, I stared at his name in my contacts, my heart racing, willing myself to press the call button.

What if he answered? What would I even say?

I stood outside the University of Minnesota's main building, too restless with anxiety to sit on the cold stone benches. Students bustled to and fro, hurrying from class to class. I felt like everyone was staring at me. I had ditched track practice for the first time ever, and was now waiting for my soon-to-be-ex-best-friend, Sarah, my mind racing with thoughts of the podcast episode I'd heard earlier. Some crappy local true crime show that somehow had actual listeners.

"The Vanishing" was the title of the episode. The specificity of the content left me reeling; the fights that I had only shared with my closest friend over tears and stuffed animals. The hosts quoted things I'd thrown out in rage, like "I hate him" and "I'm so done with him," and even quoted intimate texts. They claimed Lucas had been cheating on me, which I was already aware of, but no one else knew about my fights with him in such detail. Only Sarah.

She snaked out into the brisk fall air, tugging her collar up over her mouth like it could hold her tongue. With her was another girl, someone I didn't know but had seen around, with long black hair twisted into a messy bun. They were talking and laughing, distracted, like they didn't have a care in the world. It made my blood boil.

"Hey!" My voice was thick with venom as I strode toward her. I hadn't planned what to say, hoping my gut was wrong and this was all a big misunderstanding. Her deer-eyes told me it wasn't.

"What the fuck, Sarah?"

Sarah jumped, hand flying to her chest. "Nell, jeez, you scared the daylight out of me. What's wrong?"

I was rattled by her feigned innocence. Every movement, every gesture, every blink seemed insincere. *Faker. Liar.*

"What did you tell people about me and Lucas?"

"What are you talking about? I didn't tell anybody anything!"

"You're a fucking liar!" If people hadn't been staring before, they were now.

Her friend took a small step back, eyeing me with exaggerated concern as if I were holding a bloodied knife. She gently tugged at Sarah's elbow in a silent *let's go* gesture.

Sarah folded her arms. "You need to calm down."

"You need to stop telling people lies about me!" The finger I pointed at her could have pierced the ether.

"You're a fucking nutcase, and you need to back away from me!" Sarah spat.

Before I knew it, my fist connected with her face. I'd always been a good runner, but apparently, I also had a pretty powerful right hook. And, as it turned out, low impulse control.

Sarah stumbled back, clutching her bloody nose. I winced when she landed on her butt with a panicked wail. People began to gather around, drawn in by the commotion.

"Sarah, I'm so sorry!" I offered a hand to help her up, but she shoved me away.

"Don't touch me! Everything they say about you is true."

September, 2020

THIS PART of town seemed neglected, with houses that were little more than weathered trailers pressed like corpses into tiny graves.

Duane's house, a dingy green structure that sagged on one side, stood at the end of the street, alongside a similarly rundown piss-yellow house with a tarp-covered roof. The address was spray-painted onto a scrap of drywall leaning against the flimsy fence.

As always, Mitchell stepped onto the porch first. We waited with bated breath when he rapped on the door, but there was no response. From the place next door, a dog yapped, children yelled, and a woman shouted over the hum of a TV, but Duane's house remained quiet.

Dead quiet.

"Maybe he's sleeping?" June suggested.

Mitchell knocked louder.

The neighbor's door swung open, and a disheveled woman wearing a dirty, worn bathrobe peered outside.

"What's all this racket, for cryin' out loud?" Her voice was a rusty gate. "Can't you see he ain't home?"

"Excuse us, ma'am, we're looking for Duane Conley. Does he live here?"

"Prob'ly down at the bar, gettin' liquored up like his old man. Apple don't fall far from the tree, and them two's as alike as peas in a pod." She slammed the door shut, and the yelling continued.

Mitchell looked slightly annoyed, but remained composed, and immediately began issuing instructions. "June, get on your phone and find out what bars are in town."

"A bit early for a bar, isn't it?" Nick asked, wincing at the pale sun still burning our retinas between breaks in the clouds.

"Early bird gets the worm," Mitchell said, and we all walked back to the car.

It started to rain, and I studied how the windshield gathered tiny drops of water, like small scratches on the glass. Nick turned the wipers on. I loved September, but the weather could never seem to make up its mind.

After striking out with Lucas's parents and missing Duane at home, it felt like nothing was going our way. I couldn't shake the feeling that no matter how much we pushed, it would all lead to the same dead end, that maybe there weren't any deeper layers to this disappearance. Maybe we were just wasting time, avoiding reality.

Mitchell turned to face me and June in the backseat.

"Do you want to sit this one out?" he asked, making eye contact with me. The slight nod of his head told me he was asking me to play along for his sister's safety. June was only nineteen, and he didn't want her in a bar. "We can drop you and June off somewhere."

I frowned. Mitchell's command to stay behind without consulting me grated on my nerves. I understood that his priority was protecting June, but I wished he'd considered my perspective. Thankfully, his sister interfered, freeing me of the need to construct a polite argument for why I had to come too. After all, Duane was *Lucas's* friend.

"I'm coming with you," June insisted, and wouldn't take no for an answer.

THERE WAS ONLY one bar in town. Back in Minneapolis, I'd wear makeup and dress up to go out. Here, though, jeans, a tank top, and a plaid shirt over it seemed to make me fit right in.

The "Borehole Tavern" was a worn, wooden building that seemed to lean inward, as if withholding a secret. The parking lot in front of it was unpaved, with only dust and mud covering the ground, but the cars were plentiful. The neon "Open" sign blinked above the door. As we entered, we were met with a thick weave of smells: stale beer, sweat, and smoke.

It was barely noon, but the place was already packed. Our quartet drew some surprised looks, but patrons quickly lost interest. I noticed, though, that June and I were getting some attention from the locals, and I promised myself not to let her go to the bathroom alone.

I was a bit worried Duane might not be there, but I quickly recognized him sitting at the bar.

I signaled everyone to stay behind and sat next to him.

He looked even shorter in person, perhaps because of his slouched shoulders. His face was bloated and weary, with dark circles under his eyes. His clothes were grimy, as if he'd been wearing them for days without a second thought.

"Duane?" I said softly, and briefly, he looked startled, his eyes wide with a flash of fear, as if he'd been expecting someone else, someone who might bring harm. But when his bleary eyes finally focused on me, his tense expression softened, though not into warmth or recognition, but into a faint, guarded relief that it was only me sitting there, and not the person he'd been dreading.

His breath hit me before he spoke, sour and thick.

"Who the hell are you?" he asked, slurring his words, and then took a sip of whatever cheap bourbon he was drinking. He swayed slightly, his movements sluggish.

"My name is Nellie. I'm Lucas's girlfriend."

With a struggle, his eyes landed on my face again. "What do you want?"

"I need to talk to you about Lucas." I didn't bother with small talk—Duane was in no shape for it—and cut straight to the point. "He went home before he disappeared. Did you see him then? Did he say anything?"

Duane laughed, but it wasn't a funny laugh. It was a scary one, threatening. He wasn't tall, and his build was quite skinny, so he didn't seem dangerous. But something about Duane felt off. His laugh grew slower and eventually ended with a sob that he hid with a loud snort. He took another sip of his drink, spilling some of it on the counter.

"Duane?" I tried getting him to focus again.

He ignored me and waved for another round.

The bartender glanced at me warily, then turned back to Duane. "Pay for this one first."

"I'll cover it," I said, intervening. "How much does he owe?"

A check appeared in front of me. I glanced down, shrugged, and handed over my card. Duane didn't even acknowledge me. The bartender served him another drink, which he promptly downed.

I tried again. "It's not just about Lucas. We think more people might have disappeared in the same way."

"We?" he asked.

"My friends," I shot a careful look towards them. They sat at one of the tables, staring at us. "They're looking for their sister, Amanda. Please, talk to us."

Duane sadly shook his head, slamming the glass on the counter. Then, he got up from the stool, underestimated how drunk he was, and immediately fell. I jumped and tried to get him up. Mitchell and Nick came over and hooked Duane's limp arms over their shoulders to walk him out.

"Who are ya, and what're ya doin' with this poor sumbitch?"

The guy who approached us was a tall, muscular man in his late twenties. His dark hair was buzzed short, revealing a prominent forehead and a chiseled jawline that seemed set in a perpetual scowl.

"We're his friends," Mitchell stepped in, his tone brooking no argument. "We're taking him home."

"Ain't seen you around," the guy said.

I swallowed, noticing a few more men sizing us up from different sides of the bar. We may have stepped into something we didn't expect.

Mitchell, still holding Duane up, spoke. "Listen, man, we're not here to stir trouble. She's Duane's old friend," he gestured toward me, "and we've just come to visit, but didn't expect him to be like this. If you want to take care of him, fine. It's not like he cares who puts him to bed right now."

The guy chuckled but stepped aside, seeming to relent. But when I glanced over my shoulder, he was still watching—calmly, from under his brows, like a predator biding its time.

We helped Duane, who was barely able to move his legs, out of the bar and into my car. I wasn't sure if he had driven there, but he definitely wasn't in any shape to drive back. He would have to retrieve his car later when he sobered up.

Nick drove while I tried to keep Duane upright, but he hung in the seatbelt like someone slumped after a car crash. He was completely out, mouth open, head lolling with every turn we took. I didn't want to touch him, but I kept one hand near his head, trying to steady it, half amazed he hadn't snapped his neck yet.

Duane didn't have any keys on him. The bartender must've taken them. Luckily for us, the side door to his house was unlocked. We stepped into a dingy, outdated kitchen that reeked of stale grease, rotting food, and a faint undercurrent of mildew. Flies buzzed thick in the air, landing on sticky countertops and crusted-over dishes stacked in the sink. The dusty blinds were pulled shut, dimming the already dreary room. We moved through the clutter, our feet bumping into empty bottles, sending them across the floor like billiard balls scattering after a break.

We brought Duane into what must have once been the living room, dominated by a sagging brown couch so dulled with grime it was impossible to tell its original color. The carpet beneath our feet was a chaotic patchwork of stains, burns, and unidentifiable blotches. An old, bulky TV in a worn wooden stand supported a newer, sleek model, its screen dark and lifeless. Papers were scattered everywhere, but the worst part was the state of the walls. Strange symbols were scrawled across the paint in a shaky ballpoint pen. Whether he had been dabbling in some bizarre occult stuff or simply losing his grip on reality, I couldn't say.

Above the TV, a stag skull hung crookedly. Its hollow eye sockets seemed to stare straight through us. I shuddered. In the dim light, it looked disturbingly alive.

We eased Duane down onto the couch. His eyes were already fluttering shut as he slumped into the filthy cushions.

"Duane?" I called softly, taking a step forward.

He didn't even twitch. I shook his shoulder, but there was no response.

"Is he alive?" June asked.

I gestured weakly toward his chest, where the faint rise and fall of his breathing was the only sign of life.

"Should we leave him be?" I asked, feeling frustrated. "I have no idea how to talk to him right now."

June let out a dismissive snort and stalked out of the room. Mitchell approached Duane and gave him a firm shake, commanding, "Wake up! Rise and shine, Duane!"

The guy mumbled something incoherent, his hand flailing weakly as he tried to swat Mitchell away like an annoying fly.

"Move," June said from behind, and Mitchell barely had time to jump away before she threw a whole bucket of water over him.

"What the fuck!" Duane jolted upright, water dripping from his hair and clothes. Then his hand darted under the couch and retrieved a pistol.

Mitch immediately tucked June behind his back. Nick pulled me by the arm toward the door.

Duane held the weapon shakily, sweeping it from one person to another, his gaze wild. "Who the fuck are you?"

Worried, Mitchell looked around. The neighboring houses were quite close, and we didn't want anyone to call the police.

"Here we go again," June rolled her eyes, unimpressed and seemingly not even spooked by the firearm.

"Duane, we met at the bar, remember? I'm Nellie, Lucas's girlfriend." I was gripping the doorframe now, ready to dive into the kitchen.

"Lucas?" he repeated, his voice groggy.

"Lucas Whitman, your friend?"

"So?"

Mitchell stepped forward, palms splayed in a calming gesture. "Hey, hey, we're friends. Lucas is missing, and so is my sister. We're looking for them. We want to help."

Duane finally lowered the piece and leaned over to grab another bottle of Jim Beam from somewhere behind the couch. It still had some liquor at the bottom. He finished it and threw the bottle on the floor.

"Help," he repeated with a laugh. Then bitterly to himself, "They think they can help."

"What do you mean?"

"I mean you're so dumb," his voice slurred. "Lucas's gone."

"Gone where?" Mitchell leaned in and took Duane's shoulder.

Duane twitched, flickering fear or an unpleasant memory crossing his face. "A scary place."

"What scary place? Do you know what could have happened to him?"

Duane suddenly covered his eyes with his palms and started sobbing like a child. "I don't know, I don't know anything! Get away from me! Don't touch me!"

Mitchell seized the opportunity, using Duane's confusion to carefully remove the firearm from his lap. He passed it to Nick, who immediately stepped away, taking the weapon out of harm's reach.

"Duane, you're not in danger. Everything is fine. You're safe."

The alcohol he'd consumed that morning finally caught up with him, and his body began to revolt. He lurched forward, vomiting onto the carpet with a miserable groan. June kicked the empty bucket she'd brought the water in towards him, but Duane ignored it, too far gone.

I looked helplessly at Mitchell. He waved us off. As we turned to leave, Duane suddenly croaked from the couch, "I told him it was a bad idea, I told him not to go..."

"Go where?"

Duane's head lolled to the side, his eyes closing as he muttered, "Trees with eyes..."

"What trees with eyes?" I asked, but he was already out cold.

"Duane! Duane?" I shook his shoulder, trying to rouse him, but there was no response, just the stench of his vomit on the carpet.

"Leave him be." Nick touched my elbow and motioned for us to follow him out. "We'll talk to him when he's sober."

Chapter Twelve

September, 2020

"I HATE DRUNKS," June muttered, disgust written all over her face. Her brother gave her a gentle pat on the shoulder.

We stood on Duane's lawn, shaken but not ready to throw in the towel.

"What about those 'trees with eyes'? You think it means anything?" Mitch asked June.

When they talked to each other, it sometimes felt like Nick and I weren't even there.

"I'm more concerned about the symbols he had on the walls," Nick said.

"What symbols?" Mitch turned to him. "I thought those were just kids' drawings."

"Maybe. Maybe not."

To me, they looked more deliberate than a child's scribbles, and I regretted not taking pictures. But we were too distracted by Duane, especially once he started aiming at us.

"I can go back and snap some photos," I offered, ready to

take the bullet—figuratively—if it helped us move forward in our search.

A curtain twitched in the neighbor's window. The woman from before peered out, her eyes tracking us like we didn't belong. Mitch noticed her too and hurried us toward the car.

"What's the point? He's dead drunk. We'll come back when he's sober and compare them to Amanda's photo."

I nearly rolled my eyes. Mitch only cared about Amanda.

But as much as I hated to admit it, he was right. There was no reason to go back now. With that, we loaded up and headed back to the downtown area.

"They were best friends with Lucas. Duane should know something," I said once we were on the road, leaning forward so Nick and Mitchell could hear me. "I'm still not sure how it relates to Amanda or Mary, though."

"And we should definitely look into these 'trees with eyes,'" Nick agreed, making eye contact with me in the rearview mirror before focusing on the road again. "I want to know what it is."

"We should show him Lucas's scribbles. Maybe this is what he meant? Maybe it's the same thing?" I suggested.

"Uh, hello? How about you include everyone in the conversation?" June interrupted, sounding offended, even though she'd done the exact same thing not even ten minutes ago.

"Sorry, thought you were listening," I said, turning to her. "Do you have a suggestion?"

"Yes." June pointed to a two-story building. The sign read, "Arcane Blackwood: Tarot, Divination, & Mystical Arts," and the neon "Open" sign glowed invitingly. "How about we ask there? I mean, Nick's mom was a psychic. Maybe they knew each other?" she said, as if sensing the group's skepticism. "Or at least we could ask her about the symbol."

"That's… not a bad idea," her brother admitted.

Nick obediently parked the car by the shop.

· · ·

THE DOORBELL CHIMED SOFTLY as we entered. Mitchell sneezed, immediately enveloped by the intense scent of incense sticks, sage, and a medley of other aromatics. I pinched the base of my nose as I slipped around a standing amethyst geode.

The space was a treasure trove, overflowing with an assortment of esoteric relics: shelves, racks, and cabinets were packed to the brim with books, essential oils, herbs, magical texts, amulets, crystals, figurines, Tibetan bowls, and much more. Behind a screen, a table and two chairs faced each other, probably a nook for tarot readings and personal consultations. Soft, ambient music played in the background, enhancing the mystical ambiance. The setup felt almost too perfect, like a deliberate attempt to embody every witchcraft cliché—a façade rather than anything genuine.

The store owner was nowhere to be seen. We dispersed, each of us drawn to a different curiosity. June browsed books and figurines, while I went to the table where different-colored and sized stones were displayed in wooden boxes. I picked one up. A smooth, black orb quickly warmed in my palm. Mitch sneezed again somewhere on the other side of the store.

"Bless you!" a rich, velvety voice responded, and I almost jumped, turning to face the source of it.

My gaze immediately sank into her deep scooped neckline. Forcing my eyes upwards, I managed to take in the rest of her appearance. A woman in her late thirties to early forties, with a very feminine figure, was strapped into a tight black dress that reached her ankles. Her hair, dyed a vibrant red that made my natural color seem dull and insignificant, was curled and styled in loose, wavy locks. Though shorter than me, she wore high stilettos that made her appear my height.

When she stepped closer, warmth emanated from her, wrapping around me like a gentle hug. I pictured men entranced by her charm, longing to nuzzle their faces into her chest and absorb the intoxicating scent of her perfume.

"That's black amber," the woman said, looking at the crystal in my hand. "A powerful protective stone. Great for amulets."

Her voice was hypnotic, a sultry melody that made me feel like I was under some kind of spell. I imagined lying my head on her shoulder, feeling her hand stroke my hair, and letting her lull me to sleep.

I squeezed my eyes shut, willing the distracting thoughts to fade, unsure of where they even came from.

Clearly pleased with the effect she had, she took the stone from my hand and returned it to the box, alongside its counterparts. Then, she retrieved a light-pink stone, almost transparent, and held it up. "Rose quartz, for attractin' love." With a soft clink, she placed it back and picked up another stone, a brownish-red one. "And this is carnelian, for enhancin' sexual energy. I think this one would be perfect for you."

I almost choked when she placed the carnelian in my palm. Transfixed by her soft, flowing motions, I held the stone for a moment before returning it to the box, embarrassed by the feeling it left behind.

She turned to face my friends, and I was left with a tingling sensation running down my spine, an odd buzz in my teeth and gums. My companions were staring at her, likely as captivated by her demeanor as I was.

"Welcome to Arcana Blackwood. Let me know if I can assist you with anythin'."

Mitchell immediately approached her with his characteristic military stride, which felt out of place in the tiny store. He brushed the table displaying various magical trinkets, causing a chorus of dull clinks and thuds. None of them fell, but Mitchell's face flushed as he grasped the edge of the table, almost as if apologizing for the mishap.

"We'd like to ask you a few questions, if you don't mind," he said, his tone businesslike.

"Somethin' like an interview?" she asked coyly, scanning the rest of the group.

Noticing Nick, she narrowed her eyes slightly, then her full lips curved into a satisfied smile.

"Not at all, ma'am," Mitchell replied, trying to regain her attention. But her focus remained on Nick.

"My name is Mathilda Blackwood," she said, looking Nick up and down before extending her hand for a handshake. "But friends can call me Tilly."

"Nice to meet you, Miss Blackwood," Mitchell said, glancing back at Nick in confusion as if trying to figure out what had captivated the shop owner's attention.

Nick gingerly shook her hand and replied, "Miss Blackwood..."

"Please, Tilly," she insisted softly.

"Tilly, my friends are looking for some people who are missing," Nick said.

"I don't do search magic," she replied, crossing her arms under her chest. The movement accentuated her bust.

"We just wanted to know if you've seen them," Mitchell finally said. "Do you mind taking a look?"

Tilly turned her attention back to Mitchell, a faint smile playing on her lips. "Of course, let me see what you got."

"Do you recognize her?"

For what felt like the hundredth time, Mitchell swooped in, holding out his phone with a photo of Amanda open, relegating Lucas and me to the sidelines. My patience was wearing thin.

Mathilda took one quick look at the photo and nodded stiffly.

"Amanda was here?" June asked, voice trembling. She hastily set down the figurine she'd been toying with. It tumbled into a tray with a dull *thunk*.

"She was just askin' about the area," Mathilda replied. "We talked for a spell about the local stories and legends. You know." She made a languid gesture with her hand.

"And what did you tell her?" Mitchell asked.

The woman began moving around the store, drifting to the shelves like a deity.

"Nothin' special, just the usual warnings we give to outsiders: don't go whistlin' in the woods, don't be out after dark..." Her eyes drifted to the figurine June had dropped, and she walked over to pick it up, returning it to its shelf before continuing, "and if you hear any strange noises—crying, laughing, screaming—just pretend you didn't hear nothin'. Leave quietly; don't go running off. That's just good sense."

"Is that all?" Mitch asked, sounding slightly deflated.

"She bought an amulet from me," Mathilda said, pointing to a bundle of obsidian stones on leather straps on the table to her left. "This one."

"What is it for?"

"It has many uses: protection from negativity, cleansing, transformation, and working with the shadow aspects of the self..."

"She was here a year ago. How do you remember all that?" June asked skeptically.

Mathilda gently plucked the charred remains of the incense stick from the holder and replaced it with a new one. She struck a match and held it to the end of the stick until it caught flame. Then, she softly blew on it, her pursed, glossy red lips forming a little "O". The flame subsided, allowing the end of the stick to glow orange, and finally, scented smoke wafted up.

"Sweetheart, I have an excellent memory. In my profession," she made another grand gesture, sweeping her arm across the store behind her, leaving ambiguous whether she meant running a business or practicing witchcraft, "it's a necessity. And if you like, I can even find the receipt."

The brief pause that followed was my opportunity. I couldn't afford to miss it. I stepped closer to her, handing over my phone with photos of Lucas.

"And what about him?"

She began scrolling through photos, pausing at images of him in his football uniform, and snapshots of us smiling at the camera after a match.

"Definitely seen him before. A good-looking boy. He came in here with a friend and bought a rabbit's foot for good luck," she said, smiling and rolling her eyes to the ceiling, as if condemning his naivety. "Is he local?"

"Yes. Who was his friend?"

She looked at me with a sad smile and shook her head. "Sorry, dear. That's all I can tell you. He showed interest in occult literature, asked questions, but that's about it. What happened to him?"

"He went missing two years ago. We can't find him."

"The Whitmans' son?"

"Yes. Do you know them?" I asked, hopeful.

"Of course. It was a huge case, what with their son disappearin' and all. The Whitmans own the sawmill, and some of the folks from town work for 'em. When their boy vanished, the whole town was turned upside down. But it didn't happen here, did it?"

"No. He disappeared in Minnesota," I confirmed.

"That's right," she clicked her tongue, "Now I remember."

"Did she mention where she was headed?" Mitchell interrupted, steering the conversation back on track. I suppressed a sigh.

The store owner pondered for a moment, straightening out the figurines that June's hand had misplaced. "She asked me about the old cemetery," Mathilda said finally.

"Cemetery?" June looked up as though she'd been summoned by name.

"Our old settlers are buried there, God rest them. And there's this tale going 'round about some witch graves hiding in those woods, but honest to goodness, nobody can say for sure which ones are the real McCoy."

"Why would Amanda be interested in the old cemetery? What's up there?" Mitch asked, brow furrowed.

"Maybe she was fixing' to leave an offerin' for the witches," Mathilda said.

We all stared at the woman, trying to absorb her words. I was still processing what she had just said. *An offering for the witches.*

She continued, "In exchange for somethin'. People do that. You just have to find a witch's grave, leave what you're offering there, and make a wish. Tourists eat that stuff up. Locals too. And some of 'em, bless their hearts, think they might just dig out the grimoire."

"What?" June said, blinking, mouth agape.

"Do you know the town's story? Some believe the grimoire was buried with one of the witches."

"Why would they need it?" I asked, startled that someone would indulge in grave robbery over a local legend.

The woman lifted her chin. "Power. The kind people would do anythin' for. The witches used it for generations. It's said to hold all the secrets of the universe. And that it drives people insane."

I couldn't tell if she was being serious or joking. June and Mitchell exchanged skeptical glances.

"I'm having a hard time picturing Amanda doing something like that," Mitchell said, his voice doubtful as he looked to June for agreement. She nodded without hesitation.

"Yeah, she wasn't into this voodoo stuff."

"This ain't voodoo, sweetheart," Mathilda responded. "Sometimes, the closer we are to people, the less we truly know them. Blood ties don't preclude secrets."

The shopkeeper then approached Nick, smoothing the lace

on her neckline, her hand seemingly brushing against her breasts by accident.

"And you? What are you lookin' for?"

"I'm not looking for anything," Nick replied with haste, but I noticed his gaze wavered and briefly dropped.

"Oh, everyone is lookin' for somethin'." Tilly stepped closer to him, her stilettos elevating her a good three inches off the floor, but she was still a head shorter than Nick, so she tilted her face up to meet his eyes. "Either you don't know what it is yet, or..." She paused dramatically and smiled." You're hidin' it."

"And what exactly am I looking for?" Nick closed the distance between them, his eyes locking onto hers, and from the outside, they looked like they were about to kiss.

Mitchell and I watched them in muted surprise. The air between them was practically crackling, and the reason was... Nick. His energy shifted, his presence becoming more commanding, almost possessive, as if requesting something from the woman who was nearly pressed against him.

Watching them felt awkward, like we were intruding on a private moment. If I hadn't known better, I'd have thought they were former lovers who had suddenly crossed paths again, with old passions reignited. A flicker of jealousy hit me, seemingly out of nowhere.

Tilly held the pause. "I don't know." She stepped back slightly and swept her hand in front of her, as if brushing away an invisible thread connecting them. "I ain't no mind reader. Only tarot."

Nick frowned, apparently expecting a different answer.

Mitchell showed her another photo—the carving in the tree. "What about this? Have you seen anything like this around?"

"No," she said too quickly. "I'm sorry I couldn't be more helpful. But I'll give you some advice, and I want you to listen good. Them woods around here can be treacherous. Best you be careful."

"What do you mean?" I was tired of her vague warnings and theatrics. She was a textbook scam artist of a psychic—all mystery and warnings, with no real substance. Whatever mystical presence had mesmerized us earlier now looked like a costume, stitched together from scraps of charm and carefully crafted ambiance.

"I'll give you the same warnin's I gave your sister," Mathilda said, her expression grave. "If you hear or see somethin' strange, just let it be and get on outta there. If you stumble upon any symbols or objects that don't rightly belong in the woods, you best leave 'em be and get gone."

We thanked her awkwardly and headed for the door. Mitchell signaled June, who was still lingering near the shelves of trinkets.

"Take this, sweetheart." I didn't hear her approach, but Tilly was right in front of me, holding something in her closed hand. Caught off guard, I allowed her to place a small red stone into my palm. She continued with the same teasing tone, "It's a gift. It'll help clear out your sacral chakra. It's all blocked up, honey."

Whatever she meant by 'sacral' sounded suspiciously like something obscene, coming from her glossy plum lips. Unfortunately, my low levels of melanin, which gave my hair its natural red color, also meant that I had fair, sensitive skin that flushed easily when I was embarrassed. I felt the heat rise to my cheeks and forehead, and of course, everyone else saw it.

I bolted out of the store, shoving the ridiculous stone into my jeans pocket. June, laughing, caught up to me.

"She must not have liked me too much," I said, pressing the backs of my hands to my cheeks in a futile attempt to cool down and return to my normal color.

"But she sure liked you, Nick. I wonder why." June wagged her finger at him. He pretended not to notice.

"Yeah, man, what was that about?" Mitchell asked, almost

admiringly. "Elvira, Mistress of the Dark, practically threw herself at you!"

"How would I know?" Nick's face tightened briefly. "Strange woman."

"Felt like you knew her," Mitchell added, eyeing Nick curiously.

"Never seen her before." Nick walked ahead, cutting the debrief short.

"Or perhaps she knew him," June concluded.

Mitchell gave me an odd look I couldn't quite interpret, but I just shrugged in response.

"At least we know Amanda was definitely here," he said, "We're in the right place."

Chapter Thirteen

September, 2020

WE STOPPED for lunch at a quaint diner and sat outside to soak up the sun. The hills around the town still retained a deep green color, but if you looked closely, you could see they were slowly shifting to their autumn palette; yellow and brown leaves shuffled like a cluster of old wives under the umbrella of youth. Fall arrived here way later than it did back in Minnesota.

A sleepy waitress brought us menus and water.

"So, what do we have so far?" Mitchell asked.

"Witches, cemeteries, rituals, offerings. Digging up graves to find the grimoire," I said, counting them on my fingers.

Tilly hadn't exactly inspired confidence, and she hadn't told us anything new. Duane was still our only lead, and I wanted to get back to him as soon as possible, hoping he'd sobered up.

"Not quite what I'd expect we'd find," Mitchell said, rubbing his chin thoughtfully. "Ow." He winced, pressing a small cut on his otherwise smooth skin. Mitchell was the type to shave every day; his face was consistently hairless, fresh, and dewy. Nick, his polar opposite, was far less finicky. Dark stubble had begun to shadow his jaw, adding to the storminess in his thought-heavy eyes. I couldn't help but smile at the contrast. It showed in their behavior, too. While Mitchell was quick to speak and take charge, Nick preferred to stay in the background, holding his thoughts in until he was absolutely ready to share. Thinking out loud simply wasn't his style.

"But maybe it will lead us somewhere," Nick said, joining the conversation with a visibly more relaxed demeanor than earlier. "There could be some kind of cult operating here or—"

"Or a drug cartel," June said.

Nick seriously considered her words and then said, "It sounds plausible, but I don't know. Was Lucas into partying or something?" The last question was directed at me.

I shook my head and didn't offer any further explanation. Lucas might've smoked weed during the off-season, but only occasionally and in moderation. His sports career was his top priority. I didn't want them getting sidetracked and blaming his disappearance on drugs.

"A cult that somehow got to Lucas and Amanda. Hmm." Mitchell frowned, deep in thought. His gaze fell on his sister. She flipped nonchalantly through a book at the table, peering up at him as though she'd been caught with her hand in the cookie jar. "What are you reading there?"

She obliged and showed him the cover: *The Shadows of the Hills: Legends of Appalachia.*

"Where did you get that?"

June murmured something inaudible, her cheek resting on her fist. With her round face and light hair, she could pass for a sweet child if she wanted to, especially when she wasn't spitting sarcastic remarks.

"Did you steal the book from that store?" Mitchell guessed. "Have you lost your mind?"

"Just studying some useful literature. What else was I supposed to do?"

"Not steal!"

"I'm saving your money." June snapped the book shut and waved it in front of his reddening face. "Nellie didn't pay for that stone for... what's it called?... her chakra thing! And I got this."

"The stone was a gift," I intervened, grabbing the book from June.

I opened the table of contents, scanning the titles: "The Witch of Willow Creek", "The Raven's Peak Hills Werewolf", "The Guardian of the Woods"…

"Well," I sighed, handing the book back to her. "I hope you get more out of that than I will the stone."

"Juniper," Mitchell growled, his nostrils flaring. It was the first time he had used her full name, which meant he wasn't playing around.

"Mitchell," she replied calmly, unfazed by his irritation.

"Let's go have a little chat." He rose to his full height, and it was clear that a stern lecture was imminent. June reluctantly followed him, and they disappeared behind the building.

"I hope Sergeant Mitch isn't opting for corporal punishment," Nick quipped, watching them go with a raised brow.

I ignored his comment and turned to face him. "Do you know her? Mathilda? Tell the truth." I sensed this was my only opportunity to ask. He wouldn't talk in front of Mitchell or June, but maybe he'd open up to me.

Nick's expression turned defensive. "What? No!"

"Why didn't you ask her about your mother?"

He hesitated before confessing, "I don't know. I don't trust her. And honestly, she freaked me out a bit."

A weight lifted off my shoulders. "Yeah, she was a bit...odd."

June and Mitchell returned to the table just as our food arrived. They both seemed fine, with no visible signs of their earlier tension. I hoped that meant they'd worked things out.

June grabbed the book from the table and slipped it into her tote bag. Out of sight, out of mind.

"So, are we all *dying* to go check out that cemetery?" June asked, seemingly unbothered by the situation.

"Fucking Christ, Junie, don't." Mitchell winced as if he had a headache.

"Okay, okay, sorry, I'm just eager to *bury* myself in some research."

"Oh lord." Mitchell rolled his eyes but didn't say anything else, instead giving his full attention to the chicken sandwich in front of him.

Her dad jokes weren't that funny, but I still fought a smile.

THE CEMETERY WAS MORE expansive than we anticipated, with weathered headstones sprawling from the road's end up the hill's slope. A separate, "witchy" section was cordoned off, requiring a $5 admission fee per person. We paid up.

"The largest witch cemetery after Salem!" The grizzled caretaker, in his late sixties, sported a wild shock of white hair and a matching bushy beard. He waved for us to follow him on an unsolicited tour. His worn denim overalls were stained with dirt and what appeared to be engine grease. A faded name tag read "Gideon." He had been tinkering with a rusty old lawnmower before we entered, but seemed to have forgotten all about it now he had a chance to show off the attractions. He reminded me of a theatrical producer, revealing a circus of the dead.

He guided us through the area, past faded gravestones scattered with offerings: coins, bracelets, and other trinkets.

June nudged me with her elbow. "Told you."

When we asked about the "witchy" graves, Gideon tilted his head, a hint of skepticism in his voice. "Well, now, that's just an old tale. Ain't nobody knows if there's real witches buried around these parts or not. If you ask me, it's just a bunch of hooey. Folks around here spin stories like that to keep kids from wanderin' off at night."

"Why do they leave them here, then?" June pointed to the nearest grave, adorned with a plastic bracelet, as if she hadn't heard the story before.

Gideon's expression remained apathetic, but a hint of routine enthusiasm overcame his old bones. "Some folks believe leavin' somethin' like that'll persuade the spirits to grant 'em a wish or two."

June widened her eyes, encouraging him to continue. "What do you do with them after?"

The caretaker said this as if it were obvious, "I clean them out once a week or so, when I'm makin' my rounds."

"Is there ever anything valuable?" Mitchell asked.

Gideon rubbed his whiskers thoughtfully. "Ain't much else that comes to mind. But I do remember findin' a weddin' band here one time. Guessin' it was a mighty important wish they was makin'."

"Cool." June's interest waned as she began to decipher the faded letters on the gravestones. The caretaker began to prune dead flowers.

Mitchell picked up the conversation. "So, what's the story with this graveyard? Are these all supposed witches?"

Gideon knelt beside a nearby grave. "Don't know about every single one, but I reckon some of them was laid to rest here after that Black Water massacre."

June's head snapped up. "The what?"

Gideon set his tools down. "Do you know about the witch coven that controlled the city? They were havin' their gatherin's, doin' their devil worship and whatnot. But their leader, he got a might too full of himself. Thought he was above the law, he did."

"Wasn't it a woman?" I asked.

The caretaker playfully wagged his finger. "No, it was a fella.

And ain't that just the truth, men always stirrin' up trouble, one way or another." He addressed me and June with a sly grin.

June ignored the gesture and pressed on. "So, what happened?"

"They tried to take down the old man, but he had some tricks up his sleeve and some folks loyal to him. They went at each other, and a lot of 'em ended up dead. The rest high-tailed it outta here, didn't want no part of the trouble. That's what the story says, anyway."

"What about the main guy, the leader?" June asked.

"He was a preacher from Virginia who came to spread his weird ideas. He preached his way right into the woods, he did."

"Is he buried here?" Nick chimed in, gesturing at the cemetery.

"Naw, his body's never been found. Likely story is his followers, what was left of them anyway, buried him out in the woods somewhere. And that book of magic, it's gone missin' too."

We stood there, a little shaken. Hearing the tale in a museum was one thing, but having it confirmed was another. It turned out the story was true: the town had really witnessed a bloody witchcraft massacre.

"Someone told us the grimoire is buried in one of the graves," Nick said.

"Don't know 'bout that one."

"Interesting town you have here." Nick scratched the back of his head like he couldn't quite believe his ears.

"You should come for Halloween. It gets really crazy here."

"Have you ever noticed anything strange yourself?"

"What do you mean?" Gideon poked the side of his mouth with his tongue.

"I don't know, maybe someone took the story seriously?" Nick offered. "Tried to vandalize graves or maybe attempted some rituals or whatnot?"

"Ayuh, every now and again, for sure. But I've got it under control. I shoo 'em away for good. Whatcha wanna know for?"

"Just curious. A place like this must attract all sorts of people."

The caretaker shrugged. "We're a quiet town, mostly. Been that way for a spell now."

Mitch flipped out his phone. "Truth is, we're here on business. I'm looking for my sister; she's been missing since last year. Mind taking a look?"

"Sure thing." Gideon scooched closer with a hint of curiosity.

I pulled out my phone, too, ready to show him a photo of Lucas. It hadn't escaped my notice that Mitchell conveniently forgot to mention him. I shivered as I waited, a strange sense of déjà vu slipping over me like a ghost's embrace. I'd done this so many times before with little progress. It was starting to feel surreal. I'd looked at Lucas's pictures more in the past few days than I had in the last six months. But the more I stared at that once familiar face, that boyish smile, the more he felt like a stranger. Somehow, my memories of him no longer matched the person in the photos.

The caretaker shook his head at Amanda's picture, then pointed at my phone. "I know him—the Whitman boy! He's over there!" He gestured to the West of the graveyard.

I stumbled, the ground unsteady beneath me. "What do you mean he's over there?"

"His grave is over there. Want to see?"

I rushed towards the location, without waiting. By the time the others caught up, I was already standing before a plain stone plaque with Lucas's name and the engraving "Forever in our hearts, our dear son".

"This can't be right," Mitch said, stunned.

"There's a fucking date!" I almost yelled, my voice shaking.

"Oh my god, it's empty. It must be empty, right? Why did they do this?"

The shock short-circuited me. My feet were lead, and I couldn't tear my eyes away from the gleaming tombstone. Everything was foggy and far away, as if the world were moving in slow motion. There had to be some mistake. Lucas was missing, not dead. Nick's hand brushed my elbow gently, but I stayed numb.

"Okay, let's get out of here." Nick turned me away from the grave. I followed without resistance. It felt like all energy was suddenly sucked out of me, leaving me hollow and limp.

"Hey! I see you!" Gideon's angry shout slashed the air like a scythe.

We caught a glimpse of a small figure darting between the gravestones before getting lost in the bushes.

"Little dirtbag," the caretaker muttered. "Steals from the dead, for cryin' out loud."

"Why do you care?" June asked. "You throw it out anyway."

The caretaker licked his mouth again, tipped his hat and walked away, returning to his duties.

We started making our way out, but I kept looking back at Lucas's grave. Nick, walking ahead on the narrow pathways, turned back occasionally, as if to check I hadn't sprinted back and thrown myself, sobbing, on the grass. Mitchell and June, however, seemed to have already moved on, their attention diverted from the matter at hand.

"Come check this out!" June exclaimed.

We approached and saw that it read "Boyd."

"Isn't that your last name?" she asked Nick.

"It's a pretty common name," Nick explained. "My mom was from around here, so our family probably goes way back."

"Maybe you're a witch descendant," June suggested with a hint of excitement.

"Maybe," Nick replied deadpan. He turned to me. "You okay?"

Surprisingly, I felt better. The panic and despair had subsided, thanks to June's unintentional distraction. I'd heard Lucas's father refer to him as if he were dead, but seeing the grave was overwhelming.

"Why doesn't your mom have the same last name?" I asked Nick.

"She changed it. Said it made her sound more mysterious."

"Can we move on to something that actually matters?" Mitchell asked abruptly.

I wasn't sure why he was in such a bad mood, especially since it wasn't Amanda's grave we found. Maybe cemeteries made him uneasy. Or perhaps something else was bothering him, something he hadn't said out loud.

The cemetery bordered the woods. I turned toward the parking lot, eager to leave, but Nick changed direction, heading straight for the trees without a word.

"Where are you going?" I called after him.

"The boy went over there," Nick pointed to a parting in the trees.

I hesitated while Nick moved away and through the tall grass.

"So what?" Mitchell shouted. "Let's just go. There's nothing here."

"There must be something that interested him," Nick replied without looking back or slowing down. "We should at least check it out."

June rolled her eyes, but her curiosity got the better of her, and she followed him. Her brother tried to grab her hand, but she pulled away. Nick's sudden determination to follow the kid was baffling, but there wasn't much else to do except go along and hope no one called the police on us for chasing after a little boy.

"If I step on a snake, I'm going to kill you!" June hissed.

I assumed she meant Nick, not me.

Mitchell let out an audible sigh and trailed behind, bringing up the rear, his reluctance obvious. He didn't care for Nick, but he wasn't about to let his sister go unsupervised.

"Are you sure you saw him here?" I asked.

I was growing increasingly anxious that we'd become lost as we traipsed deeper into the growth.

Nick finally stopped and looked around. We clustered behind him, waiting to see what he'd do next.

"Maybe we should turn back," June said, brushing spiderwebs from her face.

Nick ignored her and pushed through the bushes. A moment later, he called us over. There it was—a massive stone, moss-covered and half-buried beneath the leaves. Scattered on top were bracelets, rings, and a neat pile of photographs, just like the offerings we'd seen on the graves.

"How on earth did you know it was here?" I gasped.

Nick looked just as shocked. "I didn't. I just wanted to see what he was doing there."

"So he steals them and brings them out here? But why?" June's fingers hovered above the objects.

"Don't touch anything!" Mitch pulled her back, grip firm.

"What's wrong, scared it's cursed or something?"

"No, we just have no idea what it is," her brother replied gravely. "Don't leave your fingerprints on it."

"We should at least check if there's anything useful to us," June insisted, meaning Amanda.

Mitch's response was flat. "At this point, I doubt we'll find anything useful."

He demonstratively stepped back, fixing his gaze on the surrounding trees with exaggerated interest, as if they were far more fascinating.

To say I was annoyed was an understatement. Even though everything at this cemetery and around it pointed to Lucas, somehow, we still focused solely on Amanda. It seemed my loss mattered less because I was one, and June and Mitchell were two.

I carefully picked up the photographs, damp from the rain. Some were still in decent condition, especially those that weren't on top. Heartfelt messages on the backs of some of them flickered in the dim light. And then I saw it. A photo of Lucas with Duane, similar to the one I'd seen at Lucas's parents' house. It was likely taken on the same trip, but with a different camera. The back read: "Sorry."

My heart, as if frozen until now, lurched to life with a jolting, painful beat as I came to realize what I was holding in my hands.

The handwriting on the photo wasn't Lucas's, which left only one other person who could have written this.

"We have to go back and talk to Duane," I said.

Chapter Fourteen

September, 2020

MY DECLARATION WAS UNHEARD.

I turned to find Mitchell squatting by a tree, clearly intrigued, while Nick and June stood beside him.

"What's that?" he pointed to a mark on the trunk. I approached, still clutching the photograph in my hand.

There was a small carving, not as intricate as the ones we'd seen in Amanda's photo and not as heavy as Lucas's drawing. It was a simple design—just a few lines and a circle—reminiscent of a child's handiwork. The mark was so low to the ground, barely reaching knee level, that it seemed whoever made it was sitting down at the time.

"I think it's a playground," Nick said, his finger tracing the carving. "The kid must have done it."

Mitch sprang to his feet, waves of anger radiating from him like palpable heat. His already tense posture stiffened further, his muscles corded with restraint. At first, I thought he was puzzled, but as the moments ticked by, his expression darkened. His face reddened with frustration. He struggled to unlock his phone, entering the passcode incorrectly several times before swearing under his breath.

June approached him like he was a skittish horse about to buck. "Jeez, let me—"

Stubbornly, he turned away from her and finally opened the phone's camera app. After snapping a few pictures, Mitch turned to Nick and me.

"Do you think he knew about this?"

"Who?" I asked, startled.

"The cemetery guy!"

Nick and I exchanged a moment of confusion. June stepped in once again, as if used to such outbursts. "Hey, that guy is a moron. He's probably never been here. Otherwise, he would have taken all this back to the cemetery or binned them."

She had a point: the treasures, collected and meticulously laid out on the stone by a child, were untouched.

"He's a fucking liar. He saw Amanda."

Mitchell's chest heaved, his face twisting into a harsh, bark-like scowl. He exploded into motion, his aggressive strides eating up the distance toward the cemetery.

June sprinted after him. "Mitch, wait!"

What was going on?

When we reached the cemetery, the sight stopped me cold. Mitchell had the caretaker by the shirt, his grip tight, shaking the man with enough force to make his knees buckle.

"You lied to us!" Mitch growled.

Gideon's eyes widened in shock.

June clung to her brother's arm, pleading with him to let go of the caretaker.

"Mitch, please! You're hurting him! He doesn't know anything!" Her voice shook with desperation.

"What the hell is wrong with you? Let him go!" Nick stepped forward, but Mitch didn't even acknowledge him. His focus was entirely on the caretaker.

He shoved a photo into Gideon's face. "I know my sister was here, and you saw her. Why are you lying?"

The caretaker shook his head, his mouth moving in protest, but Mitch wasn't having any of it.

"You'll kill him!" June yelped, her voice cracking.

Without warning, Mitchell blinked and released his grip. Gideon staggered backward, scrambling several feet away, his breath ragged and panicked.

"It's okay, it's okay," June whispered, her hand on her brother's arm.

The caretaker, still visibly shaken, moved further back, eyes wild. He spat on the ground. "What's wrong with you all? I'm callin' the Sheriff! Get outta here!"

Nick signaled for me to lead the way, stepping in behind us, likely to keep Mitchell from lashing out again. By the time we reached the car, Mitchell had gone quiet, as though the fight had drained out of him.

Nick opened the car door with an abrupt motion. "What the fuck, man? What was that?"

Mitchell didn't answer immediately. He turned away, his jaw clenched tight.

"Just let it go," June said quietly.

"No," Nick replied, stepping closer, his voice more clipped now. "We can't just let that go. We can't afford to attract that kind of attention."

Mitchell muttered under his breath, still avoiding looking at us. "I thought he knew something. He knows something. Amanda was definitely there. He lied to us."

"Maybe he did," Nick said, his tone cold but trying to stay rational. "Or maybe he really doesn't remember seeing her. Maybe he wasn't even working that day. Maybe she never went to that cemetery at all. But attacking the guy—that is the worst thing you could've done."

Mitch looked back at his sister. She sat in the back quietly, her lips pressed together. She knew he was in the wrong, and judging by her reaction back in the woods, it wasn't the first time he'd lashed out. Mitchell had anger issues, and she was trying to keep a rein on him. Having realized that, a wave of post-action fear washed over me. June could've been hurt. Getting close to someone who was deeply angry was dangerous.

My heart went out to the siblings. For the first time in two years, I felt a sense of connection with people who understood my pain. We were bound by shared trauma, and the lack of closure only deepened the grief. I still had my mother, strained relationship or not. June and Mitch had no one else to turn to.

Even so, it didn't excuse Mitch's behavior. It would be sheer luck if Gideon didn't report us to the police. And I was still angry at Mitchell for not mentioning Lucas. My boyfriend had been our primary link to this place, at least until we discovered Amanda had also come here.

The drive back to downtown was short and tense. I started fidgeting with my bracelet again, twisting it around my wrist to distract myself from the overwhelming urge to speak up and confront Mitch about everything I disagreed with. But I knew it was pointless, especially now. His shame was palpable.

June sat up straight and pressed her face against the window. "Wait, isn't that the little boy?" Her words tumbled over each other. "From the cemetery? I just saw him walking into the church!"

"You're right!" I leaned forward, gripping the door handle. "Pull over?"

THE CHURCHYARD WAS A MASTERPIECE, meticulously maintained with a flawless carpet of grass. Exquisite flower beds erupted with vibrant hues of velvety red roses and delicate pastel petunias.

A woman tending to an arrangement looked up. "Can I help you with somethin'?"

"We were just following—" June started, but Nick abruptly interrupted her, stepping forward.

"We were just passing through and saw how nice the church looked, so we thought we'd stop in. Who takes care of the grounds?"

I almost snorted at how unusual Nick sounded, being all polite. But it worked. The woman smiled graciously, deep-set wrinkles arranging themselves around her mouth and eyes.

"I take care of it myself. Been doin' it for years." Her pride was as radiant as the roses she nurtured. "The Reverend helps out when he's not busy. Nice man, the Reverend. Came to us from Richmond, you know."

I recalled something the cemetery caretaker had said about a preacher from Virginia who led the coven. Nick picked up on the same detail. He gave a small, deliberate nod of acknowledgment and leaned in slightly.

"Richmond, huh? We're actually heading there next. Do you happen to know which parish he worked at before coming here?"

The woman hesitated, her smile faltering for a moment. "Well, he was at St. Elwes Parish," she said slowly. "That was some time ago, though... before he came here."

"Must have been a nice change of pace for him," Nick said.

Her voice dropped, and she glanced away briefly, as if choosing her words carefully. "One could say that. There was... well, some trouble back then. But that was a long time ago." She quickly busied herself with the rosebush, pinching off a wilted bloom with more force than necessary, clearly eager to change the subject.

"The roses look beautiful," I chimed in, sensing she was uncomfortable with how much she'd shared with us, and added, "Is the church open? We'd love to take a look around."

"Come on in. The Reverend's inside."

Mitchell shifted, visibly uncomfortable with Nick taking the lead. "So, uh, is there anything... unusual going on in town?" he asked, trying to sound casual.

The woman's expression turned sour. "Unusual? Lord, have mercy, child! This town's been a might too lively for my taste, what with them motorcycles tearin' up and down the street day and night. I swear, it's enough to rattle the fillings right outta my teeth. Yesterday, one of 'em whizzed by my house so fast, I nearly flew outta my sandals! What's the world comin' to?"

For some reason, she directed her last question at me, and I couldn't tell if she was expecting an answer or just thinking out loud. I didn't know where the world was headed, either.

I gave a slow shake of my head, lips pressed together, hoping to convey a mix of sympathy and shared disapproval of the motorcyclists. It encouraged her, but not as I intended. She continued talking, having found attentive listeners in us.

"I'll tell you more," she lowered her voice. "Folks 'round here might say what they want, but I've got proof. Some right strange things been happenin' here." She glanced over her shoulder, then beckoned us closer with a finger. "I've been writing to some organizations, and they've confirmed it all. It's here, but nobody's talkin' about it."

Something about her demeanor had shifted, like a subtle crack in a grave. Ever since we arrived in Black Water, I sensed that something was off about this place. And now, we'd finally found someone willing to talk to us.

"I know it sounds plumb crazy, but it's the honest truth," she said, "I've seen it with my own two eyes! Microwaves explodin', glasses shatterin', shelves crumblin' down. And it ain't just things, neither! It's people, too. Everyone can feel it. Headaches, fatigue, and memory loss. They're messin' with our lives, and nobody's liftin' a finger to stop 'em. Cuz the government's behind it all, testing them direct energy weapons right in our own homes!"

She observed us, expecting a reaction. But we were too shocked to offer her one that would be acceptable or appropriate in this situation.

"Well, thank you kindly for your time," Mitchell said, edging away. "We'll go check out the church now."

Disappointed, she returned to tending the roses.

As soon as we walked a few yards away, June jokingly slapped Mitchell's arm. "Why'd you ask her about anything strange? She's clearly crazy herself."

"I didn't know that!"

"You love 'em crazy," June said, turning to Nick and me with a sly grin. "You should've seen his ex."

"Oh, shut up," Mitchell grumbled, but he said it playfully, swatting his sister away with a slight chuckle.

"I hope there's a second exit. I don't feel like talking to her again," June added.

Mitchell held the door for us, and we entered the elegant mid-size church. Inside was a haven of cream-colored walls and stunning stained-glass windows that filtered sunlight into kaleidoscopic patterns.

June scowled, slowly making her way through rows of polished wooden pews. "Ugh, I hate churches."

The scent of old hymnals, worn wood polish, stale air and aged carpet tickled my nose. I tried to recall the last time I'd been to church. Maybe when Grandma was still alive. I wasn't raised religiously, but my Dad's mom regularly attended church and sometimes took me along. The Reverend was a kind and friendly man. After the service, we would often stay and chat with him and the other ladies. They would give me candy and tell me what a good kid I was. I wouldn't have minded going, and had even entertained the idea of joining the choir, but my mother forbade it. Her rationale was that I was too young to be indoctrinated into religion. I sensed that her genuine concern was that I might find a sense of belonging there, one that didn't revolve around her.

The church was empty. No trace of the little boy, either.

"Hello? Anyone here?" June's voice echoed through the vast hall.

Mitchell hushed her to keep quiet, but it was too late. From the hallway to the left of the altar, a figure emerged. The black suit and white collar he wore identified him unmistakably as the Reverend.

He clasped his hands. "How may I be of assistance to you?"

"Hey, sorry to interrupt. Can we ask you a few questions, if that's alright?" Mitchell approached the stairs, looking back at us as if seeking confirmation that he should retake the lead. Or perhaps he was trying to show us he was keeping his cool after what had happened at the cemetery.

"I'm Reverend Carver," he introduced himself with a slight, somewhat condescending nod. Then he steepled his fingers briefly. "What brings you to our community?"

"We'd like to ask a few questions about the town."

"Oh?" Reverend Carver replied, his eyes narrowing slightly. "What seems to be of interest to you?"

"We're just trying to see if there's anything... unusual going on around here."

Reverend Carver pondered this, then shook his head. "I'm not aware of anything specific. Perhaps you could share some examples of what you're looking for?"

"Anything ritualistic? People gone missing? I'm not sure… Fights? Maiming?" Mitchell offered.

"Maiming? There's certainly no shortage of that."

"Oh, really?" June's sarcasm was as thick as the holy air.

"Addiction's a terrible thing," the Reverend nodded. "It's been a problem in our community for a long time, causing folks to do things they wouldn't normally do."

"Like what?" June asked.

"Take, for instance, a husband who, under the influence, raises a hand to his wife. Or young men fighting in alleyways. Black Water, I'm afraid, is not immune to these problems. But we're working tirelessly to address them."

"Yeah, but do you have anything else?" Mitch probed.

"Such as?"

June inserted herself abruptly. "Like, satanists? Or cults? Witches?"

Reverend Carver's gaze snapped to June's T-shirt, lingering on the image of a cat paired with a cheerful slogan, "Sometimes dead is better". His expression turned tense. "No, nothing of that nature. May I ask what prompted your question?"

Mitchell said, "We're just looking for some people."

We promptly produced our phones, displaying photos of Amanda—of course, she was first—and Lucas. The Reverend examined them without touching either one, then shook his head.

"So, nothing of that sort?" Mitchell asked again, his voice devoid of hope.

June threw a glance at Nick and added, "Or maybe unusual murders?"

"I'm not sure what you're getting at," Reverend Carver said with a stern expression, "but Black Water's a good town with good people. I don't appreciate any implication otherwise."

Mitchell cleared his throat. "Just one more thing. Did you happen to see a little boy come in?"

The Reverend shook his head curtly. "No, I didn't. Now, if you'll excuse me, I've parish business to attend to."

We didn't get a chance to say another word. It was just another dead end, unless we wanted to sit in the parking lot and wait for the little boy to eventually show up. However, that, combined with our pursuit of him around town, could result in the police being called on us. And after what had happened at the cemetery, we couldn't brush off another incident as a misunderstanding.

What surprised me was that Nick, who had just finished reprimanding Mitchell, now let him take the lead. He actually seemed to trust him not to lose control again. For once, I wished Nick would step up, but he kept deferring to Mitch. I couldn't understand why. Maybe he didn't want to spark more conflict with Mitch.

The Reverend's demeanor was curt and cold, like someone who would quietly sweep scandals under the rug and smile benignly for the cameras. He was eager to get rid of us, the outsiders with too many questions. He and his answers were as welcoming as a brick wall.

With no new leads at the church, we had no choice but to move on. I was still hopeful of catching up with Duane.

Chapter Fifteen

September, 2020

"WE NEED TO TALK TO DUANE," I said again, but Mitch was busy scolding his sister, and Nick didn't contribute his support.

"Why the hell did you mention murders to the Reverend?" Mitch asked June.

June folded her arms across her chest. "Because I'm sick of you all tiptoeing around with your photos. Someone murdered Nick's mother. Why not start with that?"

Nick ran a hand through his hair, clearly uneasy. "Because I'm not about to throw around the word murder and shut people down. You want them to talk, right?"

I also found Nick's reluctance to ask about his mother puzzling, but I agreed with him. Going around asking about a murder that had been ruled accidental manslaughter with no witnesses and no suspects felt as risky as walking a tightrope over a pit of vipers, especially knowing the killer could still be local.

Before anyone could speak again, Nick patted his pockets

and said, "I think I dropped the keys in the church. I'll be right back."

June and Mitchell were still bickering, so I followed him, keeping the buddy system in mind but mostly trying to get away from Mitch before I lost my temper. Someone had to act like an adult.

We walked back to the church, and as we opened the door, I recognized the muffled tread of someone trying to tiptoe. I peered up. The little boy—the one the Reverend claimed wasn't there—was fiddling with something by the altar. The door creaked closed, and he scrambled to his feet, his small body instinctively shrinking away from view as he darted behind the altar.

"Wait, please!" I called out as he fled and gestured for Nick to stay back, not wanting to scare the little boy any more.

I stepped closer, slowly and carefully. The kid looked to be about seven or eight, with skinny limbs and unruly hair. His nails were long and caked with dirt, and his oversized clothes fluttered around him like sails. There was a faint scent of grime and neglect in the air.

"Hi," he said, pausing before me, his eyes wide with a mixture of hesitant interest and caution, like a stray animal sizing up a stranger—curious but ready to bolt.

"Hey, I'm Nellie." I crouched to his level. "What's your name?"

"Sammy." He smiled timidly, then corrected himself with a hint of bravado. "Sam."

I kept my distance, not wanting to scare him further. "We didn't mean to scare you, Sam," I said. "But I wanted to ask you a few questions."

The boy shot a look behind me at Nick, feet shifting. I could tell he was unsure about Nick's presence.

"This is my friend, Nick," I said. "He can stay over there or leave if you want him to."

Sammy looked at Nick again, his big blue eyes taking in every detail. "He can stay."

"We saw you at the cemetery today, Sam."

He edged away, gaze darting towards the door, as if searching for an escape.

"You didn't do anything wrong," I said, holding up my hands. "We wanted to ask you about it, if that's okay."

Sam blinked slowly, still wary. "Okay."

Questioning a child without his parents present didn't sit well with me. It was too reminiscent of how the police had treated me, and now we were putting a little kid through the same ordeal. But our intentions were different. We were seeking truth, not just closing a case.

"We found some things there," I continued, pulling out the photo from my pocket. "It's a friend of mine. Did you know him?"

The kid shook his head.

"Did you take this photo from a grave? It's okay if you did. Really."

Sammy mumbled, "I guess so."

I smiled, trying to put him at ease. "You've got a nice arrangement there in the woods."

Sammy kept quiet, waiting to see where I was going with this.

"It's really cool," Nick said, coming to stand beside me. He squatted down to our level. He moved so quietly, I hadn't even noticed him approaching. "Is it something you came up with?"

Sam's lower lip jutted out. "Yeah, why?"

Nick held up his hands, mirroring my earlier gesture. "Just curious. What's it for?"

"I dunno," Sam shrugged. "Just playin', I guess."

"Have you seen anything like this anywhere else? I mean, besides the cemetery?"

I immediately understood what Nick was hinting at. Just like he had with Sammy's secret spot, calling it a playground, he was now suggesting the playground mirrored someone else's creation. And yet, I still couldn't make sense of it.

Sam's shoulders rose and fell with a dismissive shrug. I needed to figure out how to steer the conversation and keep him talking.

"I'm sorry I took the photo," I said. "Can I keep it for a little bit? I promise I'll give it back once I find my friend. Is that okay?"

Sam kicked the carpet lightly. "I s'pose."

Nick moved to sit on the floor, legs folded. And just like that, the space felt more relaxed. He asked, "So, Sammy, you come here often? I mean, to this church?"

The boy bobbed his head. "Sometimes."

Nick read my face, and I knew he was thinking the same thing. If Sammy had been here regularly, the church staff would have known him. The Reverend must have known him.

I tried to build on the conversation. "You must have some friends here, huh?"

He shrugged again. "I guess so."

Nick pressed on. "And Reverend Carver, is he your friend too?"

The kid picked at his thumb nails. "He's alright."

"But he doesn't know about your secret place, does he?" Nick said. "It's okay. We won't tell him."

Sam shook his head and looked down, avoiding eye contact with Nick. But then he lifted his eyes to mine.

"You're not in any trouble," I added, tucking a strand of hair behind my ear.

We had made contact with the boy, and now I had to tread carefully to avoid spooking him. He saw something, even if he didn't fully understand it. If he was willing to share more, we could build on the details. Nick took the lead, and I didn't mind.

His tone and mannerisms were unexpectedly gentle, mirroring my own approach.

"So, can you tell us a little more about your secret place?" he asked. "It looks like a lot of work. Did you do it all by yourself, or did someone help you?"

Sam's face brightened. "I did it myself."

"So, no one else knows about it?"

"Just you, I reckon." He wiped his nose with the back of his hand.

"And how long have you had it?"

The boy paused, thinking. "A year, maybe."

Nick studied Sammy, his expression a careful balance of patience and urgency. "And you came up with it all on your own?"

The boy's face twitched, his expression sliding into something noncommittal. He needed more prompting. Nick, apparently, agreed.

"Or perhaps you saw someone else do something like that?"

Sammy's lips tightened, his discomfort evident.

Nick leaned in, softening his tone. "You're not in trouble. We just need your help to find our friends."

Sammy's voice dropped to a whisper. "I don't exactly know where it was."

I strained to hear, hanging on his every word. Nick's brow furrowed, and his voice came out too upbeat, as if trying to keep things light. "Where *what* was?"

Sammy's voice barely broke the silence. "It was like... a place in the woods. There were eyes on trees."

My heart hammered in my chest. All I wanted to do was scream, "Tell us more! Tell us about the trees with eyes!" But I bit my tongue, forcing out another smile instead.

Nick continued, "And you don't know where it was?"

Sammy shook his head. "My daddy got mad at me, and I got outta the truck and ran off. And then I was there."

"And what happened?"

Sammy's eyes dropped. "I dunno."

"Did something scare you there?"

The silence was palpable. Now, we were treading on very dangerous territory. Fear gripped the kid, just as it gripped Duane, the same haunted look in his eyes. One wrong word, and Sammy could slip away.

"It's okay, Sammy. You don't have to be afraid. We won't tell anybody," Nick promised and looked at me for reassurance to continue. I tapped my fingers against an invisible watch. *Wrap it up,* I mouthed. And Nick knew what to ask.

"Last few questions, I promise." Nick cupped his chin in his hand, offering nonchalance. "Were there other people at this place when you went there?"

Sam nodded, but that was all we could get out of him. Nick tried pushing, asking if Sammy knew any of these people, but the boy insisted he didn't.

"How did you find your way home?" I asked.

Sammy shrugged. "I dunno. I waited till mornin' and then just kept walkin' till I hit the road."

"Do you mind looking at photos of our friends to see if you recognize any of them? Maybe they were there in the woods?"

The boy hesitated briefly, neither confirming nor denying. I sensed he was desperate for the conversation to end.

I pulled out my phone and began swiping through photos, searching for the one I had of Amanda, when the door slammed shut behind us.

"What are you still doing here?" Reverend Carver's voice boomed.

We jumped to our feet. "We were just—" I glanced back at Sammy, but he was gone, having bolted the moment he spotted the Reverend. "—leaving."

The Reverend said nothing, just crossed his arms over his

chest and stood there as we made our way out. The door thudded shut, and the lock's bolt slid home, sealing us out.

"Did you find them?" June asked, rushing to meet us. To our blank expressions, she added, "The keys?"

"Oh. No." My stomach turned. I'd completely forgotten.

"I've got them," Nick said, jingling the keys. "Must've not checked my pockets properly. Nell, want to take the wheel?"

I DROVE through the streets of the small town, unsure where we were headed. We brought the siblings up to speed on our conversation with Sammy. Mitchell, distracted from his earlier embarrassment at the cemetery, slipped back into his usual commanding posture.

"So, you're saying there's something out in those woods that spooked this kid into building this weird shrine?" he asked.

"And there's more," I said, "We think it's where Amanda went, too. The boy said the exact same thing as Duane did— trees with eyes."

Mitchell took a deep, heavy breath. "Alright... I feel like we're getting somewhere, but it's still not adding up."

"It'll make sense once we talk to Duane again!"

But Mitchell vetoed the idea. "No."

"What? Why?"

"It's getting late, and we've put in a long day."

June rolled her eyes at him, as if saying "No kidding" to Mitchell.

"Yeah, but—"

"Duane's got a firearm and a drinking problem. And trust me, I've seen my share of guys like that. We should fall back to the hotel, grab some food, and reassess our situation. Then we can come up with a solid plan for tomorrow."

"But—"

"I agree, he's probably hiding something. But going there

now just doesn't make sense. We need to regroup and come up with a plan if we're going to find Amanda." He looked at my face, which said it all, then quickly added, "And Lucas."

I turned to Nick, expecting him to back me up, but to my surprise, he remained neutral.

"We might not get another chance to talk to him," I pleaded. "He was pretty agitated when we met him, and I got the sense he was spooked, too."

Mitchell folded his arms. He wasn't going to budge on this. "I've never met a drunk who's sober on the weekend. We'll have better luck tomorrow."

I could have screamed when Nick gave that poor excuse his silent approval.

With only a couple of days left before I faced my mother's scathing criticism in Ohio, my anger and frustration were simmering just below the surface. Mitch's condescending attitude was adding fuel to the fire. Who was he to tell me what to do? His military experience and tough-guy act no longer impressed me, not after a few days with him, and especially not after today. I knew he was just as lost as I was, but he was too proud to admit it. I was convinced that's why he'd shut me down. He was buying himself time.

Lucas, obsessed with football, would often geek out over various strategies when I'd join him in watching games. He loved explaining things, and I, head over heels in love, indulged him and pretended to be interested. He told me about situations where a receiver has to make a play when the quarterback is scrambling and throws the ball up for grabs, and the receiver must ditch the original play and make something happen on their own. That's how I felt, like I needed to seize the initiative. Facts were up in the air, dangling before us like carrots ripe for the taking, and yet we were hesitating.

It was time to take matters into my own hands and do what I thought was right.

Chapter Sixteen

September, 2020

MITCHELL HAD INSISTED on daily debriefs, where we shared every detail of our day, no matter how small. So, we gathered in the unit June and I shared to go over everything that had happened.

In his notebook, he jotted down bullet-pointed lists of what we'd learned and carefully marked the places we'd visited on the map. He stayed fully engaged, speaking with steady focus while the rest of us struggled to stay alert. I could tell he was pushing through, trying to recover from his outburst and prove he still had value. But honestly, I just wished he'd let us go to bed.

Weariness settled over the room like a thick blanket. Nick looked completely checked out. His vacant stare gnawed at my nerves, and I couldn't help but wonder if his mind was still on the odd woman from the store. *Tilly.*

"So, assuming Amanda did go to the cemetery, where does that lead us?" Mitchell spoke aloud, thinking.

I sat up straighter, hoping I would sound more authoritative. "Sammy saw the same symbol Amanda had photographed."

"Not exactly," Nick corrected. "He mentioned seeing some symbols, but we didn't get a chance to show him Amanda's photo before the Reverend kicked us out."

"Then we should find him again. And Duane—"

June's eyes narrowed. "That Reverend is shady. I think he lied about seeing that kid. He knows him."

Mitchell's expression turned wistful. "Mama used to say, 'Liars, cheaters, and thieves—'" He trailed off, his hand brushing across his face as if wiping away the memory.

June's lips curled into a nostalgic smile. "Yeah, she did."

The page in his notebook was titled "Amanda, Cemetery." I wanted to confront Mitch about how I felt, about how he was neglecting Lucas in our search, but the last thing I needed was an argument. I was too emotionally drained.

Or at least, that's what I told myself.

BACK IN OUR ROOM, June was glued to her phone. I sat on the bed, a decision brewing. The 'good girl' in me urged caution, suggesting I wait till tomorrow to approach Duane. After all, we were supposed to maintain the buddy system and confronting a madman with a gun was dangerous. Another part of me, the feral creature I squirmed to contain, snarled that enough was enough. It was time to take matters into my own hands.

Every detail from our encounters that day seemed off. The magic shop owner, the cemetery, the church, the little boy, the photograph. So disconnected. They were like loose threads, refusing to weave into a coherent tapestry.

I knew Duane held the key to unraveling this mess. Something had been going on between him and Lucas. And that's why I needed to talk to Duane *alone*.

I walked towards the door. June didn't look up from her phone when she asked in a sing-song voice, "Where are you going?"

"To get some air. I'll be right back."

"No, you're not." She was quick as a dart when she blocked the exit with folded arms. "You're driving somewhere." She eyed my fist where I held the car key like a secret. "You know you're not supposed to go anywhere alone. Is this about my brother?"

I hated lying, and I was terrible at it. My mother could always tell when I tried to deceive her, so I gave up instantly.

"I just want to check on something. It won't take long. Will you cover for me?"

"Tell me where you're going, and I'll think about it."

I cleared my throat and confessed, "To talk to Duane."

June's jaw flexed. "So it *is* about my brother."

"It's not. It's about Lucas."

June picked up her jacket from the bed. "I'm coming with you."

"If your brother finds out, he'll kill me before I can say 'over and out'."

"I'm my own person. So, what, you're just not going to go because I want to tag along?" She was calling my bluff.

I weighed my options. June might not have been old enough to drink, but she was old enough to make her own decisions. Even if Mitchell got mad at me, we were still following his orders, sticking together.

"Fine. But you say nothing about this. To anyone."

"If he's still drunk, I know how to get him to sober up," June said as we pulled out of the parking lot.

I raised an eyebrow. "Quite the expertise."

June's bucket of water trick had worked briefly, but almost got us shot. The confidence and quiet anger with which she executed the action last time made me wonder where she got that kind of experience.

"My dad was a drunk," she said, as though reading my thoughts.

"Did he quit?" My dad, a contractor, had worked with many AA members, so the story wasn't new to me.

"Kind of. He's in jail now."

I let the silence stretch out, sensing that June had already revealed more than she was comfortable with. But the few details she'd shared were already fitting into a troubling narrative. And a worrying thought began to take shape: the siblings' reluctance to talk about their family might be connected to Amanda's disappearance.

It was possible that Mitchell's obsession with finding Amanda wasn't just about duty or brotherly love. It was guilt. The same kind of guilt that drove me to search for Lucas, because for a while, I truly believed his disappearance had something to do with me.

THE NEIGHBORHOOD WAS PUNCTUATED by warm lights spilling from nearby houses, but Duane's house loomed ahead, its windows like empty eyes, foreboding and unwelcoming.

I knocked softly on the front door and waited in silence. No one answered.

June whispered, "Is he ever home? Or do we have to fish him out of that bar again?"

I shot her a look. I was already on edge, and her comments were more than I could handle right now. We waited a bit longer, then I tugged at the door to see if it would open. It was locked.

"Let's try the side door."

Like last time, it was open.

"What's the point of locking the front door if anyone can just walk in here?" June grumbled.

We stepped into the kitchen, but this time, it was pitch-black.

June wrinkled her nose. "What's that smell?"

A pungent, chemical stench hit me, unmistakable from the days I'd spent helping my dad with garage renovations. "Paint."

"That's weird."

It was. I seriously doubted Duane had woken up and decided to start a home project. More likely, he'd knocked over a jar of paint while stumbling around with a hangover. But the sharp, acrid reek still made my skin crawl. It didn't belong here.

"Duane?" I called, desperately groping along the wall for the light switch. "It's Nellie. We came by today. Can we talk?"

Finally, my fingers found the switch. A dim, grimy bulb flickered to life, casting a weak yellow glow that clung to the room like smoke.

"It's even worse than I remember," June said, surveying the mess.

"Duane?" I called again, hoping he wasn't the type to shoot intruders before asking questions.

We made our way into the living room, and as soon as we entered, I knew why paint fumes hung in the air. Duane had painted over all the symbols on the walls. The color didn't match. Sloppy patches of navy blue clashed with the original dingy off-white, stained by years of stale cigarette smoke.

"Why did he do it?" June asked.

There was something off about the room. "I don't know," I said. "Let's keep looking."

I hurried June out of there and made my way to the pantry. The door creaked open. Nothing but some cans of soup and an old, opened bag of rice, all covered in dust.

June flicked a grain. "What are we even trying to find?"

"Anything. Whatever doesn't feel right or seems connected to Lucas and Amanda."

"Nothing feels right here," June grimaced, then ventured into Duane's bedroom. I heard the soft click of the light switch, followed by the opening and closing of closet doors.

The second bedroom was crammed nearly to the ceiling with old furniture, boxes, and random knick-knacks, all cloaked in thick cobwebs and dust. I flipped the greasy light switch, but nothing happened. The bulb must have burned out.

Trying not to touch anything, I picked my way through the piles of junk, lighting my path with the faint glow of my phone's flashlight. Shadows stretched and recoiled with every movement, warping into shapes that looked ready to pounce. But when I turned the beam on them, they vanished, revealing only forgotten clutter.

The room wasn't small, but the chaos and clutter made it suffocating. Scattered possessions crowded every surface. A few steps into this hoarder's nest, and the exit stood impossibly far away. Surrounded by abandoned furniture, stacked chairs, empty bookshelves, and piles of clothes, I was trapped in a labyrinth of junk. If something jumped out from behind one of the cupboards or out of the closet, I wouldn't even manage to run through the mess. What a cliché horror scene that would be. June would get a kick out of it. Something gossamer brushed against my face, I jerked back, panicking and trying to swipe it away.

"Everything okay in there?" I called through to the girl, not so much to check on her but to remind myself I wasn't alone.

"Yeah, I'm good."

Her voice calmed my nerves a bit.

I tugged the sleeves of my hoodie down and began sifting through a few items, moving some books aside to see what lay beneath. Old detective novels, romance paperbacks, and stacks of newspapers. Nothing seemed to have been touched in a long time. There wasn't anything that would interest me in any way. No mysterious symbol carved or painted into the furniture, no books on the occult, nothing.

I opened a few drawers from the old, creaky chest by the wall, wincing at the foul stench of rotten rugs and decaying papers. Inside were school notebooks and stacks of correspondence, mostly junk mail.

Duane must not have been in this room for a long time.

"Nellie," June called, "can you help me?"

I hurried over, my eyes catching on old pictures that had fallen from the wall. If I hadn't been to the house before, I would have thought it was a crime scene.

June was crouched beside the bed, reaching under the mattress.

"There's something. Can you lift this?"

I grabbed the corner of the sagging mattress and heaved it up. June reached underneath and pulled out—

Several old porn magazines.

"Ew!" she flung them onto the bed, shaking her hand like it was contaminated.

"Can't believe someone still uses analog porn," I muttered, ignoring the quick thump of my heart.

She shot me a glare, but her expression quickly crumpled, like a child on the verge of tears.

"This is so disgusting," she said, still flicking her fingers as if trying to rid them of whatever she'd touched.

"Come on, let's wash it," I said, leading her to the bathroom and turning on the faucet.

The bathroom was as filthy as the rest of the house. Soap scum and grime encrusted the sink, and cigarette butts littered the floor. The air reeked of mold and stagnation. The toilet appeared not to have been cleaned in months. Or years. Beside it, a dusty beer can stood abandoned next to a grimy bottle of Clorox as if the two were keeping each other company. The bathtub sat hidden behind a mildewed, tattered curtain.

There was no towel in sight, only a filthy rug shoved behind the heater. June shook the water off her hands and wiped them on her jeans. I turned off the faucet.

Only then did we notice the dripping. A slow, steady rhythm, tapping on unseen water.

June and I exchanged glances. I exhaled, stretched out my arm, and yanked the curtain aside.

In the half-second it took to do so, gruesome images flashed through my mind—Duane, bloated and lifeless.

But the tub was empty. Just an inch of stagnant, yellowish water and a few soggy cigarette butts. I dragged out an uneven breath.

June's shoulders relaxed. "Can we go now?"

We made our way back through the kitchen, and I caught sight of something in passing. I turned the light toward the shelf lined with rows of mismatched jars.

One stood out. A red plastic container of instant coffee, nestled among the condiments and canned soups.

Lucas had used the same kind to stash his lucky nicknacks. He once confided that since childhood, it had been his go-to hiding spot for "treasures."

I stepped closer, pulled the jar from the shelf, and twisted the lid off. No coffee, just old paper and photographs.

June peered over my shoulder. "Jeez, is it more porn?"

"I don't think so," I said, spreading the contents across the table. Photos, printouts with MISSING stamped on them. A few newspaper clippings about disappearances. A cold knot twisted in my stomach.

June picked up a picture. "What's this?"

"I'm not sure." I flipped one over. October 12, 1986. June turned to another. October 1, 1998.

"They all have dates," she whispered.

The faces, some warped by grainy photocopies, and the stark lettering flickered before my eyes: 'MISSING', 'HAVE YOU SEEN THIS PERSON?', 'LAST SEEN WEARING...'.

There were so many.

"Grab them," I said, already stacking the papers in my arms. "And let's get out of here."

We switched off the lights and retraced our steps through the side door in the kitchen. Outside, the darkness had deepened, but a dim hue from the backyard light cast long shadows over the garage.

June suddenly halted. "The garage door is open."

The old overhead door was shut, but the side door hung ajar. There could have been plenty of reasons for that, but something about it felt wrong. A slow, creeping sense of finality settled in my bones.

"Stay here," I instructed June, and for once, she obliged.

I lifted my phone, using the flashlight to cut through the gloom. There were parts of an old car with no hood, gas cans and tools. I moved along the side, scanning the cluttered shelves. Then, out of nowhere, something brushed my shoulder. I shrieked, spinning around, the beam of light darting like a rabbit. An old bike dangled from the ceiling. I must have bumped into it.

"I think there's a light switch," June called from the doorway.

A second later, the garage flooded with light.

The first thing I saw was the wall smeared with splashes of red. Then, my gaze dropped to the ground. The pistol. The same one Duane had threatened us with.

And beside it—Duane.

He lay slumped on his side, face contorted and unrecognizable. A gaping hole consumed where his eye had been, flesh jagged and raw. The back of his head was a mess. Bone, hair, and blood indistinguishable. My stomach lurched. I stumbled back, my pulse hammering in my ears.

"Call 911!" I choked before doubling over and throwing up.

Duane was dead.

Chapter Seventeen

September, 2020

JUNE AND I GOT SEPARATED. With no concept of time, I was stuck in the small interrogation room. There were no clocks, no windows. My phone and belongings had been taken, and I'd already berated myself for not standing my ground. But when the Sheriff picked us up, I was too shaken to push back, too disoriented to track what was happening.

I wish my past experiences with cops had given me the nerve to say, *No, I'm keeping my stuff*, or refuse to talk without a lawyer. But I also knew that if I asked for one now, I'd be stuck here even longer, cut off from the outside world.

I considered asking to call my mother, one of only two numbers I knew by heart. The other was Lucas's. But my mother would lose her mind. I'd already missed a few calls from her over the past couple of days, and her increasingly frantic texts had forced me to respond, carefully, trying not to set her off. Lately, she'd been acting like I was some kind of fugitive, like she *knew* something was up.

I let out a listless sigh and looked around again, hoping to notice something new. The walls were a dull, institutional green, and the harsh fluorescent lights buzzed like dying insects. I felt trapped in a morgue.

A single table stood in the middle of the room, its lone drawer locked. Out of boredom, I tried to open it, but it wouldn't budge. The stale air only added to the foreboding atmosphere. It was all too familiar in the worst possible way.

Someone killed Duane. It had to be murder. Otherwise, why would I even be here?

The lock clicked, and the Sheriff, the same one who pulled us over on the way into town, stepped into the room. I straightened in my chair as if on cue.

"Miss me?" he smirked, shutting the door behind him.

"Not particularly," I said, annoyed—not at him, but at the whole situation. At being detained. At Mitchell. At myself.

He tossed a hefty folder onto the table. The thud echoed through the small room, making me flinch. But I knew the tactic too well. He was only trying to intimidate me.

He sat across from me, tilting the folder just out of my view, pretending to read. I didn't make a sound. After a few long minutes, he closed it, set it aside, and began tapping his fingers on the cover.

"I've already had a chat with your friend," he said, eyeing me steadily. "She spilled the whole story."

"Okay," I said, forcing a casual tone. He was bluffing. June wouldn't say anything to him. But even knowing that, I felt uneasy. The Sheriff's presence was dense and oppressive, like someone who knew he could do anything he wanted and face no consequences.

He wanted my version, so I dryly recounted how we found Duane's body, sticking to the story June and I agreed on.

We were just checking on him. The garage door was open, as was the back door to the house.

"Y'all take anything from the house?" The Sheriff asked.

"No," I lied, hoping he couldn't tell.

"You're mighty sure 'bout that?" His tone made my stomach drop. Did he know? Had he searched the car and found the photos and flyers hidden in the trunk, beneath the cargo liner? But then I remembered my attorney's previous advice and didn't take the bait. Besides, how could he be sure we took them? Were they even important?

"Yes," I said firmly, then added, "We didn't take anything. Am I being detained, or am I free to go?"

"You think you're so smart and sassy?" He leaned back in his chair, crossing his arms over his chest, his eyes narrowing.

I maintained a neutral expression, refusing to engage.

"What the devil were you two doin' out there, snoopin' around?"

"Just checking on a friend," I replied calmly.

"Good friend, then?" he pressed.

I held his gaze steadily. "He was my boyfriend's friend."

"Not yours?"

A commotion erupted outside the room. A man swore in a low, grumpy rumble, and then something hit the ground with a loud thud. A knock on the door followed instantly, and a woman peeked her head in without waiting for a response.

"We've got a two-four-five comin' in. Two males, aggressive. We need to separate them, and we need this room cleared."

The Sheriff cursed under his breath and stood up. "Follow me, Miss Foster."

He escorted me down the corridor, staying close behind, which made my skin prickle. I preferred him leading the way, rather than feeling his eyes on my back. He opened the door, and I stepped into a modest office, likely his own.

Unlike the sterile interrogation room, this space had a more lived-in feel, with beige walls, a small window, and memorabilia on the walls that tried to make the place look welcoming.

Despite the effort, it lacked a personal touch. All the decorations were strictly professional: badges, framed certificates, and photos of local landmarks or the Sheriff shaking hands with various people I didn't recognize.

His desk, in contrast to everything else in the building, looked expensive, made of solid wood, heavy and sturdy. It felt completely out of place. Across from it, on a small brown loveseat, June sat with her arms folded.

"Sit over there and don't you dare get up or move," the Sheriff instructed.

"I gotta use the bathroom!" June blurted, but he'd already left, slamming the door behind him. "Fine, I'll pee on your desk."

I was so glad to see her safe and sound, and in her usual snappy mood, that I immediately grew more at ease with the entire situation.

"Are you okay?" I asked. "I am so sorry I dragged you into this."

"Are you kidding? If it weren't for you, we wouldn't have found—"

I shushed her with a warning look, then shook my head, begging her not to say another word. I wasn't sure if the Sheriff had cameras or recording equipment hidden in his office.

"Yeah, finding a dead body was pretty traumatic," I said, emphasizing every word so she'd understand we needed to keep the other thing to ourselves.

I sat next to her and whispered, "You didn't say anything, did you?"

"Of course not!" She sounded offended. I tried to squeeze her hand in apology, but she wiggled out of my grip and went straight to the Sheriff's desk.

"What are you doing?" I whispered. "You're not really going to pee on it, are you?"

"I'm just checking what this creep is up to."

"What if he has cameras or surveillance here?"

"So what? We didn't do anything wrong."

"Apart from getting into his personal stuff, you mean?"

June shuffled all the papers and folders on the table. I got up and started arranging them back to their original state. Then she tried the drawers. The upper one was locked.

"Do you see a key anywhere?"

"No." I didn't bother to look.

She opened the other two drawers. One was filled with receipts, and another had a little calendar on top of some folders. The calendar had a date circled: October 1. A little over a week away. No other notes or dates were highlighted. She picked it up. "You think he has a date or something? Ew, who would go out with him?"

I grimaced.

We waited a little longer, and at one point, a woman came by to escort us to the bathroom. She was polite but distant and didn't answer any of our questions about how long we'd be kept, where the Sheriff was, or what was going on. We weren't even sure if we were officially being detained.

Eventually, the Sheriff's office held no more secrets. We counted every crack in the wall and got bored. June was reading some files on local criminal activities to entertain herself, but soon gave up on that too. We dozed off on the small couch, leaning on each other.

The sound of a throat clearing woke us. The Sheriff returned, seeming more tense than before. June moaned, stretching languidly. My neck ached from the uncomfortable position, and I was more worn out than before the nap. At that point, I didn't care if they threw me in jail. As long as there was a bed.

"You two are done here. Get your belongings and get outta my town. We don't need your kind around here."

"Why?" June drawled.

"Because I damn well said so!" His tired growl made us

move faster. "I'm sick of you people pokin' around, causin' a scene, making' my job harder."

"So, what happened to Duane?" I asked, suddenly finding some courage.

"Suicide. Now get on outta here."

DAWN HAD BROKEN when we came out of the station, and the gray light hurt my sleepless eyes. The sun hadn't risen yet, but the sky was stained with an ombre of warm pastels. I shivered in my shirt.

"Ah, the long-forgotten taste of freedom," June said, as I spotted Mitchell and Nick waiting outside. Part of me was relieved to see them. I'd left the keys in the car and texted Nick where they were before the Sheriff arrived.

Nick leaned on the Dodge, scrolling through his phone. Mitchell rushed straight to June.

"You're okay!" he exclaimed.

"Of course, I'm okay! Jeez, don't get all mushy on me," his sister said.

But Mitch kept going, fuming, "I swear to God, I'm gonna kill them! Why the hell did they keep you all night?"

I half-feared he was really going to storm into the station and attack the Sheriff, but instead, he turned to me, jaw clenched and eyes blazing with anger.

"What the hell, Foster?"

"I—"

"You put my sister in danger! What were you thinking?"

"I wasn't—

"I didn't expect that from you!"

With each shout, my frustration simmered. The sleepless night had left me raw, and the weight of everything that had been building up—anger, exhaustion, fear—finally broke through.

My temper snapped, and all my emotions came out with a tone of guttural rage.

"If you listened to me sometimes and actually drove the investigation, I wouldn't have needed to do it my-fucking-self!"

He seemed taken aback by my outburst. "What are you even talking about?"

"I'm talking about you only focusing on Amanda and ignoring anything related to Lucas!"

"No, listen, we're—" Mitchell started, but I interrupted him. It was his turn to swallow half-spoken words.

"No, you listen! I dropped everything to come here with you, and it would be nice to be considered for once! But all you do is ignore and disregard everyone else!"

"I'm just—"

"Oh my god, shut up!" June yelled. "She didn't drag me. I insisted. And don't say a fucking word until we show you what we've got."

"You found something?" Mitchell was astonished.

Nick, too, now looked interested. He put his phone away and took a step closer to us.

I was still angry, so I shot back, "Yeah, but you gotta stop yelling, and can we please get away from this station first?"

"You're the one yelling," Mitchell corrected, but obediently turned towards the car.

Nick crept up behind me, a smile tugging at his lips. "You're fun when you're angry."

"I'm not trying to be fun," I snapped. "I'm trying to do what we came here to do."

"I know, I'm sorry." He awkwardly patted my shoulder. "Hey, you're shaking. Here."

He pulled off his hoodie and handed it to me. I considered refusing, but changed my mind. Why not? I was cold, uncomfortable, and exhausted. Without even thanking him, I took it and slipped it on. It smelled like Nick—a warm, earthy scent with faded hints of cedarwood and a subtle muskiness that clung to the fabric. Spice and summer storms.

Something about that unsettled me, a strange tightness in my stomach I couldn't quite place. But I was too tired to overthink it.

It was just a hoodie.

"So, what happened?" Nick asked as we drove off.

I let out a long exhale and recounted. "We went to speak to Duane. I thought he might be more open with just me, or at least with me and June."

"You mean without us," Mitchell said bitterly.

June jumped to my defense. "Well, yeah, you kinda scare people a little, duh."

For the first time, she'd taken my side against her brother.

I recapped the events, feeling a surge of nausea as I recalled the state I'd found Duane in. As soon as we arrived at the hotel, I pulled out the stack of photos.

"He had it hidden," I explained. "We found it by accident. It looks like some of these are posters for missing people. And all the photos have dates on them."

With no large surface available, we spread the photos and printouts across the floor. I was so wiped out I nearly tipped over, but caught myself just in time.

"And you didn't disclose this to the Sheriff?" Mitchell clarified, scanning the spread.

"Of course not," June said.

"Good." He frowned, picking at the collection.

"Lucas or Amanda aren't there," I said. "We checked."

"Let's put them in chronological order," Mitchell suggested.

For a few minutes, everyone fell silent as we arranged the photos and papers. Some years were missing, but for the most part, we managed to put them in order. The earliest date was September 17, 1984. The latest was a year before Lucas's disappearance.

"I feel like we're onto something, but I don't know what that is," I said, hoping someone else would piece it together. All the dates were in the fall, mostly September, sometimes October. I buried my face in my palms and closed my eyes for a minute, hoping to refresh my mind without sleep.

"What are these dates?" June pointed to a selection.

"I'm not sure..." Mitchell replied.

I checked the time—7 a.m. The photo of Lucas and me still smiled back at me from my screen.

Nick, who had been on his phone for the past few minutes, suddenly announced, "These are Harvest Moons."

"What?"

"The Harvest Moon. Its date varies."

"And you think—" June started.

"Lucas and Amanda disappeared on Harvest Moons, too. I checked."

I lifted my face from my hands. We all looked at each other, stunned by the sudden discovery. It was too... easy. Too simple. But it explained nothing.

"When's the next one?"

Nick checked his phone. "October 1st."

"Wait, wasn't that the date on the Sheriff's calendar?" June asked.

I nodded.

"The Sheriff again, huh?" Nick muttered, still looking at his phone.

"Walk me through how you found Duane one more time. Every detail you can recall," Mitchell said, lifting his gaze, brow furrowed.

"I..." I winced at the memory. "He was on the floor, lying on his side. There was a hole in his head. And another one, in the back, where the bullet came out. Blood. A lot of blood. And other stuff." My stomach turned. "Why?"

"What about the gun you saw next to him? You're certain it was the same one he had before?"

"Yeah, I think so—"

"And there was a lot of blood? The back of his head blown open?"

"Yes and yes. It was a huge hole." The nausea rose again. "Can you tell me what this is all about?"

Mitchell's voice stayed steady, but his face tightened. "Thing is, if Duane had a .22—and the back of his head had a grapefruit-sized hole—he wasn't shot with his own gun. A .22 doesn't usually leave an exit wound."

"I know what I saw," I said. "Unless these guns look exactly alike."

"They don't. The mob used .22s for a reason. They'd walk up behind you, shoot behind the ear, and the bullet would bounce around inside your skull. Clean. Fast."

"How lovely," I muttered, swallowing hard.

Nick lifted his gaze from his phone, his brows drawn tight, jaw clenched. I could see the flare of barely restrained emotion tug at his shoulders, pulling at his chest, which heaved rapidly beneath his muscle-fit shirt. He looked like he wanted to interject, to shut Mitchell down, but then he looked at me, drawn by an involuntary shudder.

You ok? He mouthed the words, setting his phone aside.

I replied with a sly thumbs up and turned to Mitchell. "How would the Sheriff not know the difference between guns?"

"He *does* know, that's the thing. What you're talking about is a very poorly thought-out killing."

The Sheriff in a small town was a big deal. He was the authority. A chill crept up my spine. Not only had I stumbled upon a dead body tonight, but I might have crossed paths with the killer himself. I felt like we'd been toyed with, then released. Like a cat playing with its prey, letting the mouse think it's safe, before closing in for the kill.

And we were about to ignore his warning to leave town.

Chapter Eighteen

March, 2015

THE FUNERAL HOME'S viewing room was somber. Rows of gray chairs crowded the flower-choked space, my father's portrait barely visible. At the front, on a raised platform, sat a polished wooden coffin with its lid open.

My mother insisted on a viewing, despite knowing my dad wouldn't have liked it. Though he never said it outright, cremation seemed more his style, something quiet and private, with his ashes scattered on a remote beach or into Lake Erie. Mom had to do things her way, one final cheap shot at her husband, whom she seemed to have stopped loving a long time ago. Even now, she appeared to be avoiding him, circling around his body like the aesthetic was more important than him, even at his very last moments.

I wanted to scream. To throw the precious lilies that he was allergic to on the plush pink carpet and force her out. Out. OUT.

People kept arriving. Dad had known so many through work, AA and old friendships. He had a way of making people feel like they mattered. Mom greeted them all, but there was a distance in her demeanor, a cold, detached politeness. She barely nodded at their condolences, her smile brief and empty. She kept pacing in loops around the room, pretending to be busy and trying to minimize interactions.

Even as a child, I never understood why she and Dad had been together. In their old photos, their wedding pictures, they looked happy like any other couple just beginning their lives. When had that changed? When had they started drifting apart? When had Mom become this dull, unsmiling woman? And if things had been so bad for so long, why hadn't they just left each other?

I lingered at the back of the room, hesitant to approach the coffin. A part of me was afraid *she* would show up. The other woman. The thought alone twisted my stomach in knots. I had seen them together with my own eyes. Yet, it still felt unreal. But did it even matter anymore? He died soon after. I had mustered the courage to confront him about what I'd seen, and just two uneasy weeks later, he suffered a stroke.

A slow procession of relatives and friends filled the seats in a steady, mournful stream. The front row, reserved for Mom and me, remained empty. I had just been passed from one aunt to another, each wrapping me in a tight hug, murmuring soft condolences—"You can always count on us, dear".

Their kindness should have been comforting, but instead, it only deepened the isolation. Soon, they would all be gone, leaving Mom and me alone in a house that suddenly felt too empty.

I wanted someone to confide in, someone to tell me I was overthinking it, that I had misread the situation. That it wasn't my fault. I would have clung to their reassurance like a lifeline.

My mother detached herself from another group of newcomers with a flimsy excuse and began toward me. I didn't want to engage with her, didn't want to hear her agitated commands. So, I turned away and made my way to the front of the room, knowing she wouldn't scold me this time. Not next to my deceased father.

I looked down at his face, and for a moment, I saw the familiar features I had grown up with—the same long nose, soft mouth, gentle yet strong hands folded on his chest. The old scar on his right hand was just where it had always been, a pale line below the knuckles. He used to tell a different story every time I asked about it. A fight with a raccoon. Saving a kid from drowning. A shark attack. But Mom eventually told me the truth: he'd slammed it into something back when he was drinking. One of the many nights, way before I was born, that got swept under the rug.

His skin was pale and waxy, with sunken cheeks and a slack chest. The features were his, yet different, like a painting that had faded and warped with time. My mind struggled with the disconnect between this waxen figure and the father I once knew, the man he had been and the version I had loved.

Had I ever really seen him? Do we ever truly know anyone, even those closest to us? Or are we only given fragments, carefully selected and arranged, until we convince ourselves they form a complete picture?

September, 2020

NICK ASKED me several times if I was okay going to Duane's funeral. I checked in with myself and felt disturbingly numb, as if finding a dead body wasn't a big deal. I wasn't sure whether to be relieved or alarmed by that.

In the end, Mitch and I were the ones who went, leaving Nick and June behind. I had the closest connection to Duane, so it made sense. And while Mitch never said it out loud, I knew he wasn't about to leave June alone with me again. After what happened to Duane, he was already thinking about sending her home. The only things stopping him were her refusal and the fear that she'd be worse off without him.

I didn't interfere, letting them sort it out while Nick and I sat in the corner, pretending not to eavesdrop on their bickering. At least Mitch was off my back.

When we got into my car—though he insisted on driving—I was still mad at him and couldn't bring myself to start a conversation. June and I probably should have left a note for them that night, but I didn't regret going. I even wished I had done it sooner. Maybe it would have saved Duane's life.

The funeral felt like our last chance to learn something before we had to give up and follow the Sheriff's order to leave town. I hoped we'd run into someone from Lucas and Duane's past and get them to talk.

Then again, Mitchell was sure it was a sloppy cover-up, not a suicide, and that made asking questions a whole lot riskier. I didn't doubt his expertise in firearms, bullets, and exit holes, but it was hard to wrap my mind around the thought that a serial killer was walking around, let alone believe the killer might be the Sheriff.

ON OUR WAY to the funeral home, Mitchell was the first to break the silence.

"Listen, what you said yesterday. I get that. But you gotta understand, June is all the family I have left."

I turned to him, still sullen.

"She's a competent adult, and I will not take the blame for her decision to come with me. What was I supposed to do, go and snitch on her? Besides, I really needed to talk to Duane about Lucas, and you wouldn't listen to me. And now, it's too late."

He drew in a deep breath and let it out slowly, calming down. "It wouldn't have done any good if you went there earlier.

Could've gotten yourself killed, too. And I'd have another death on my conscience."

"I went because you only care about Amanda! But it's about me, too. It's about Lucas. And what do you mean, 'another death'?"

He didn't respond, his concentration on the road was exaggerated.

"If you keep hiding things from me, I swear, it's all over. I'm so sick of being disregarded, of not being told things."

I didn't just mean Mitch. I meant everyone, including my father and Lucas. Everyone wanted to keep their secrets, but in the end, it all only hurt more.

Mitch's response was a tight-lipped silence, his hands clenching the wheel. I could tell I was getting under his skin. Given his volatile temper, it was a risky move, but I pressed on anyway.

"It's not just about wanting to find out what happened to Amanda, is it? I know there's more to it. What did you do?"

He pulled the car over, put it in park with a measured movement, and then allowed himself to snap.

"I didn't stop it! I was just trying to get away! He'd been beating the crap out of me, and there wasn't a single thing I could do. And I left. And now Mom is dead. And Amanda... She didn't even want to see me. She blamed me for leaving. And I keep thinking that maybe, just maybe, if I'd stood up to him, if I'd done something... maybe she wouldn't have detached herself so much. Maybe she would talk to me, and maybe she wouldn't have gone missing!"

I didn't know what to say. Whatever had happened with his family ruined them, and for some reason, he took the blame. He was just as broken as I was.

"It's not your fault," I said, the words feeling inadequate, but the only thing I could think to offer. "And June is lucky to have you. I'm lucky to have met you, too.

We just need to be more open with each other, even when it's hard."

Mitchell took a deep breath, letting his grip on the wheel loosen. His face was still tense but softer. "I'll try to be better. Let's just get through this."

NEITHER OF US had anything close to proper funeral clothes. Mitch wore jeans, a gray T-shirt, and his usual denim jacket. I stuck with black jeans and a plain tee, and tied my hair back in a modest ponytail. It was the best we could do.

In the end, we'd been worried for nothing. The funeral had a thrown-together feel, like an obligation someone had remembered at the last minute. Most attendees wore clothes that bordered on careless. Two men had on matching work jackets with a septic company logo.

No one seemed heartbroken. We overheard someone complain about a broken truck. The whole thing felt less like a funeral and more like a coffee break at a run-down auto shop, the harsh fluorescent lighting casting a sickly pallor over everyone.

The urn was already on display, accompanied by a single flower in a vase and Duane's high school yearbook photo. I was relieved it wasn't an open-casket service.

But our hopes of blending in quickly faded. We didn't know anyone, and we stood out. Every so often, we caught cautious, suspicious glances in our direction. I felt so uncomfortable that it was as if I'd forgotten how to be human; every movement, from standing to sitting, felt awkward and unnatural.

Mitch and I sat in the back, but the room was small enough that we could still hear most of the conversations. Every single person seemed older than Duane and Lucas, so we didn't dare approach anyone. We had no idea who they were.

"...that bitch and her devil shop!" The words were loud enough to rise above the quiet murmur of voices.

Mitch nudged me. I was wondering the same thing he was: did they mean Mathilda?

"Shush, you," another man, face creased with age and irritation, responded. "Have some respect, for God's sake."

Mitch nudged me again, as if to say, *Go, talk to them*, and I mouthed, *No!*

Now that we had finally discussed him leading the investigation, he was leaving all the hard work, including talking to strangers, to me?

Our commotion didn't go unnoticed. An older man approached slowly, leaning heavily on his cane, his hand trembling.

"You're not from 'round here," he drawled loudly, drawing even more attention to us, "You Duane's friends? Didn't think he knew many out-of-towners."

I paused before answering, choosing my words carefully. "I knew Duane through a friend. Lucas Whitman?"

"Awfully sad. Both boys gone." He shook his head, a gravelly sigh slipping from cracked lips. "Like father, like son, I reckon. Duane... just like his daddy. Took the same way out. Must be somethin' in their blood."

Before I could ask what he meant, a sharp voice cut in, the same man who'd been talking about who we assumed was Mathilda.

"It's all that crap messin' with his head, I'm tellin' ya," the voice snapped. "And that woman, she just poured gas on the fire."

"Who, now?" Mitch asked.

"That witch runnin' that devil's den she calls a shop," the old man growled. "She's got folks' minds all twisted up, messin' around with things they oughtta leave be. Ain't no place for that kind of business in Black Water."

"Are you talking about the shop in town? Mathilda's?" Mitch cut in, seizing the opportunity.

"Who're you?" The man didn't bother waiting for an answer, barreling on with a scowl. "You're the ones pokin' around, askin' questions about the Whitman boy, ain't ya?"

My hands turned clammy in an instant. There was nothing wrong with searching for Lucas and Amanda, but knowing the locals were aware of our efforts made it feel ominous, like we were, in fact, doing something illegal. Two more men wandered over, drawn by the rising tension. We were starting to feel cornered, and I found myself looking around, searching for an exit.

"We're not—" Mitch started, but the man didn't let him finish.

"We got good folks in this town, and nobody was offin' themselves till you showed up!"

Statistically speaking, that was hard to believe, especially since they'd mentioned Duane's father had met the same fate. But we were in no position to prove who was right. Or so I thought, because Mitchell had a different opinion.

"Look, I'm just looking for my sister. She came here a year ago, here..." He pulled out his phone and showed them Amanda's photo.

"Ain't no whore sister of yours been here!" the guy snapped.

Oh no.

"What did you call her?" Mitch went nuclear in an instant, launching into a full-blown attack mode. I grabbed his arm. It didn't take much to rile him, but this was the worst possible time.

"Excuse us. We're leaving," I muttered, trying to drag Mitch away, but it was like trying to move a solid pillar—he was all muscle.

"So you come here, accusin' good people of some shit," the man spat.

Mitch tried to lunge at him, but I was holding him back with all my strength.

"We're not accusing anyone of anything," I pleaded. I thought of June clinging to Mitch's elbow, trying to stop him from hurting the cemetery caretaker. I hoped our earlier conversation had calmed him down, but now—this.

The few mourners began closing in on us, all men. They were cutting off our way out, and it was getting harder to breathe.

"What's going on here?" Reverend Carver's voice thundered through the room as he stepped inside.

Everyone fell silent and drew back, as though on command.

"These two have no business bein' here," someone said.

"Got no respect for the dead!" another chimed in.

The Reverend's eyes landed on us. "You came by the other day," he said.

I gave a meek little tilt of my head.

"I figured you were after something else. But this isn't the time or place for prying. The Whitmans' and the Conleys' need space to grieve. It's best if you respect that and leave now. Unless you'd prefer the Sheriff escort you out."

No one at the funeral looked like they were grieving, or even related to Duane, but the Reverend made it clear: we'd crossed a line just by showing up.

Mitch's arm slowly relaxed under my grip, and I eased my hand away, careful not to make any sudden move that might set him off again.

"We didn't mean to cause any trouble," he mumbled, the fight draining out of him.

The circle of onlookers begrudgingly parted, clearing a tense path to the exit. Outside, the Sheriff was climbing out of his cruiser. He gave us a grim look, and something in me flinched.

"That went well," I murmured, getting into the Dodge.

"That's an understatement," Mitchell muttered, starting the car. "And everyone seems to know why we're here."

I saw the Reverend and the Sheriff in the rearview mirror,

exchanging words and glancing our way. They seemed to know each other. Mitchell turned the corner, and they disappeared from view.

"Do you think he meant Mathilda?" I asked, mostly using the question as an excuse to talk to Mitch and make sure he wasn't about to explode on me again.

"Seems like it." Mitch was still tense, but not as wound up as he had been at the cemetery.

"We should have another chat with her."

"We will. But I want to check on June first."

That made sense to me. Now that people around town knew who we were and, more importantly, what we were doing, it was safer to stick together. The Sheriff's warning, combined with the Reverend's tight-lipped tension, did not bode well for us.

Mitchell continued, "You saw how the Sheriff and the Reverend were all buddy-buddy? Doesn't sit right with me."

Didn't sit right with me either.

IT WASN'T EVEN NOON, but the store greeted us with a "closed" sign. We knocked anyway.

"Closed, closed, I'm closed today!" Mathilda announced from behind the curtained door.

Mitchell took the lead, knocking again, more persistently this time.

"We need to talk."

The door opened just a crack, enough for the witch to peek out and see who was disturbing her peace. She looked more disheveled than before, her face etched with worry, hair twisted into a messy bun.

"Ain't nothing to discuss with you," she said, looking up at him as she blew her fringe off her forehead. "Folks 'round here didn't just up and die till you showed up."

I winced at hearing the same thing twice in one day.

"At all?" Nick didn't try to conceal the skepticism in his voice.

"Not like this," Tilly retorted.

"Wanna chat about how exactly he died?" Mitch suggested, pushing the door open and stepping inside. Mathilda moved reluctantly, letting us all in, then locked the door behind us.

"You jump into somethin' without knowin' what it is, then try to figure it out? Bless your heart, sugar." Her condescending tone didn't match her stern expression. "Listen up. You're strangers here. You don't know our ways or our land. I'm gonna give you some advice: get on outta here. Leave before things get any worse and somebody else gets hurt."

"Miss Blackwood… Tilly, we're not going anywhere until you tell us what you know. Someone has made negative comments about you. We think it would be in your best interest to talk to us." Mitchell sounded very formal.

She stubbornly shook her head. "Like I said, I don't know nothin'."

"How about we tell you what we know first?" Mitch offered, setting his backpack on one of the display tables and pulling out the photos from Duane's place. "Look at this. Who are these people? Why are all the dates during Harvest Moons? What was this doing at Duane's place?"

Mathilda folded her arms. "Seems like you're more full of questions than answers. But like I said, I ain't got nothin' for you. Whatever notion you got in your heads, I want no part of it."

"My mother was from around here." To my surprise, Nick stepped forward. He hadn't mentioned his mother to anyone before.

Tilly waited a second, as though deciding how to react. Then her eyes softened."I knew her."

Her response caught us all, including Nick, off guard.

"You did?" he asked in disbelief.

"Uh-huh."

"What happened to her?"

"I don't know. I'm sorry. She was a good person, just a might hot-headed at times."

"Help us. Please," he said, holding her cat-like gaze.

Mathilda hesitated.

"We just need to know what Duane and Lucas were asking you about. We know you talked to both of them," I said.

She tsked. "They were plumb foolish. Huntin' for that dadburn grimoire—"

"What does it have to do with anything? Isn't it just a tourist trap story?" Mitch still struggled to make sense of it.

Mathilda rolled her eyes. "I'm tellin' you what I know. Don't like it, then leave."

"No, please, continue," Mitchell pleaded.

"Like I said, whoever owns the grimoire has the power. And what to do with that power—well, that's up to each person."

June had had enough. "Cut the crap. What's up with the symbols? We saw one in Amanda's photos, that little punk Sammy carved one into a tree, and we saw some in Duane's house, but apparently, he decided to paint over them before someone offed him!"

Mathilda raised an eyebrow. "He painted over them?" She chewed on this. "Or perhaps someone didn't want him snoopin' around? Didn't want whoever else came to talk to him seeing anythin'?"

Until that moment, we had never seriously discussed the possibility that our publicly seeking Duane might be the reason he was dead. As much as I hated to admit it, it added up.

"What did you tell Duane and Lucas? Where did they go?" Mitchell wasn't playing games.

The witch chewed her lip, smearing her lipstick a little.

"There's a place in the woods. Just off the Black Water Creek trail. Turn into the woods by the Three Sisters."

"Three what? Never mind," Mitch said, "What's there?"

"Don't know. I've never been. But it's...there."

"What's 'it'?" Mitchell asked, annoyed with her vagueness.

"Don't know. Now go on, get."

Mathilda demonstratively unlocked the door.

"What's gonna happen if we go there? Is it safe?" Mitch asked as we were leaving.

The witch raised an eyebrow and remained silent. Clearly, our safety was of no concern to her.

We didn't say goodbye. But as we were walking out the door, Tilly spoke to our backs, "Obey the rules. The darkness often hides in plain sight. "

"What rules?" Mitchell asked.

But the store door had already shut. The "Closed" sign smacked onto the window.

"Bitch," June concluded, and I couldn't agree more.

"I don't like this," her brother said.

"What exactly?"

"Everything. What did Amanda get into?"

I was wondering the same about Lucas. And Duane? And Mathilda—she clearly knew more than she was letting on, but she gave up so easily when Nick's mother was mentioned. I wanted to ask him about it, but decided against doing it in front of Mitch and June. He definitely wouldn't open up with them around, fearing their endless questions and suspicions—and rightly so.

We were poking at things around Duane, and then he died.

Then, another desperate thought hit me: Sammy.

We'd talked to him, too.

Chapter Nineteen

September, 2020

MITCHELL WAS TENSE AND VOLATILE, and his frustration, although justified, was spilling over onto everyone, especially June, who bore the brunt of it as they spent the entire morning arguing. She refused to leave without seeing things through, no matter how much he pushed. Nick and I tried stepping in when their voices got too loud, but the backlash was swift, and we backed off, wandering the motel grounds for nearly an hour, making empty conversation, waiting for the siblings to figure things out between themselves.

When we returned, Mitchell was still on edge, but at least calm enough to talk.

"So, what's the plan? Do you want to look for the kid? I'm worried something might happen to him," I said, trying to pull everyone back on track.

"I already have one kid to worry about," Mitchell growled, and June scoffed in response.

"Nellie's right. The boy knows something. Whether or not you care for his well-being, we should find him," said Nick.

Mitchell's head whipped in his direction. "Then why don't you two go look for him if she always knows best what to do?"

I huffed, bristling at his words. Mitchell was taking out his anger on everyone today, but Nick wasn't going to let it slide.

"Let's dial it down a notch, Sergeant," he said, his calm tone making Mitchell's nostrils flare more. I couldn't tell if Nick was trying to diffuse the situation or poke the bear. "We can focus on the boy for today and see if we can get anything useful out of him."

"So, your big plan is to keep running after some kid?"

Nick's demeanor didn't waver for a second. "How about this? Take your sister and head downtown. Nellie and I will recheck the cemetery. If that doesn't work, we'll think about what to do next."

June's wide eyes met mine, and it was clear we were thinking the same thing: Mitchell was dangerously close to losing control again. Without warning, he slammed his open palm onto the table. The impact made the utensils jump and clatter.

"Fine," he barked, standing abruptly. "Let's just hurry the hell up."

We dropped the siblings downtown. June wasn't happy about being left alone with her brother, but there was no way in hell he was letting her out of his sight. Surprisingly, she stayed quiet—probably because Mitchell's last outburst was still fresh in her mind.

I'd hoped that after our conversation, he might reflect on his attitude. But one talk was never enough to change someone. If it were, therapists would be out of work.

At least June was safe with him. Of that, I had no doubt.

"YOU DON'T HAVE to go in if you don't want to. I can go alone."

Nick and I were headed to the cemetery, but my mind kept

drifting back to Mitch, wondering if it was even worth staying, knowing he could snap at any moment. It took me a second to realize Nick was referring to seeing Lucas's grave again.

"I'm okay," I reassured him. "Thanks, though."

My brain was foggy and heavy, soaked with random ideas like a wet sponge. I longed for the moment when these disparate pieces would conflate into something meaningful.

"Penny for your thoughts." Nick glanced at me, one elbow resting on the doorframe. I tried not to get distracted by the trail of ink that looped around his wrist and under his sleeve. I hadn't had a chance to admire any of them.

I offered a weary smile, slightly ashamed by my aloofness. "It's nothing. Just trying to make sense of it all."

"Any ideas?"

"Apart from your cult theory? Not really. I mean, I can come up with a dozen conspiracy theories, but they're based on nothing."

"Humor me."

"Okay," I closed my eyes for a moment to gather my thoughts. "Human trafficking ring, organ harvesting, geographic anomaly, the military conducting experiments on humans, UFOs. Or, like you said," I waved a hand through the air, "a weird cult recruiting members."

A hint of a grin played on Nick's lips. "You've really given it some thought, huh?"

"This trip has been very stimulating. But why do you think it's a cult?"

"Well, the symbols, first. Then, I think Sammy was onto something. I know Sergeant Mitch wants to dismiss it," he sneered the word "Sergeant" with mock emphasis, "but the boy must've stumbled onto some kind of ritual and tried to copy it."

"Doesn't it seem odd that the Reverend is mixed up in this? I mean, he's supposed to be a spiritual leader and all."

"Why not? Christianity is a blood cult if you really think about it."

"How so?"

"Their faith revolves around death. Fearing it. Longing for a good afterlife. Add consuming the flesh and blood of Christ. The rituals, the sacrifice. It all adds up."

"Did you share this with Mitch?" I asked.

"No."

"Why not?" I continued, pulling into the parking lot. The cemetery had been empty the last time we visited, but now, there was a single car parked in a far corner.

"He won't listen to me."

I parked farther away from the only other car, a habitual caution, and reached for the door handle, but Nick grabbed my arm. "Stay inside." He motioned to the other vehicle. "The Reverend's here."

I closed the door and stayed still. For a while, we sat in silence. Nothing had been happening.

"You have an umbrella?"

"In the glove compartment." I leaned over him to get it, that scent of spice warming me anew.

We walked side by side, huddled beneath the umbrella Nick held over our heads. The sky above was a deep, foreboding gray that bled into the ground in a mist that consumed the cemetery. Humidity clung to my skin like a damp kiss, and I shivered under my coat although it wasn't cold. A restless energy stirred low in my stomach, a sense that something was about to happen, heightened by the gothic ambiance.

We halted beside a weathered grave, feigning our respects while carefully observing our surroundings. The caretaker was nowhere to be seen, nor was the Reverend.

The downpour eased its relentless beat, slowing to a sporadic pitter and, finally, to scattered drops.

"I see him. Coming out of the woods."

My breath hitched. That was where Sammy's hiding place was.

Nick slung an arm around my shoulders, probably in case anyone was watching us, a staged show of comfort that doubled as a subtle restraint, even though I hadn't moved, just stood there trembling like a plucked guitar string, tight and on edge.

Minutes ticked by. Behind us, an engine growled to life, and the Reverend sped away.

"He's gone. Let's move." Nick collapsed the umbrella in one swift snap and led the way into the woods.

The forest lay under a damp, gray mist, heavy with the scent of earth and decaying leaves. He held a branch aside, saving me from a cold snap against my face. We pushed through a dense thicket of ferns, but instead of Sammy's familiar hiding spot, I found myself disoriented. The space was different. It was only when Nick stopped in front of me that I understood why. All of Sammy's belongings were gone, just like Sammy himself. The clearing was empty.

"The bark's been cut where the symbol was," Nick squatted by the tree. I approached to see the gash in the trunk, the exposed wood raw and pale as perished fruit.

The forest instantly felt even less welcoming. I started glancing around, uneasy, as if someone might be watching us. The Reverend had found Sammy's hiding spot, and judging by the way he cleared it out, he knew exactly what it was and did not want anyone else to see it.

When we got back to the car, I immediately cranked up the heat and rubbed my hands together, but the shiver I felt wasn't just from my wet boots. Duane's death was no accident, though I'd convinced myself it wasn't our fault, at least not directly. After all, he'd been investigating the disappearances long before we had. Now, the facts stared me in the face: people who knew something were silenced after we'd talked to them.

"Mathilda was right," I gasped, my throat tight. "Duane

didn't paint over his walls. The Reverend did. We need to tell Mitch and June."

"Not yet."

"What? Why?"

"I want to check out that place in the woods. The one Tilly told us about."

"All the more reason to bring Mitch and June! We shouldn't go alone."

"Mitch will shoot it down, like he does with every other reasonable idea we have. I'm tired of him micromanaging us. We should go, just the two of us. Now. And if we find something, great. If not, at least we'll know we tried."

Nick turned to face me, his elbow propped on the seatback. I felt it in my gut—Nick had a point. Mitchell's frustration was clouding his judgment, and as he focused on managing it, time slipped away, fueling his anger. He expected faster results, but each step we took seemed to create more questions. Yet, sneaking off didn't sit right with me. Not for a second time.

"Your shoes are soaked," I said, giving him one last reason not to go. "You'll catch a cold."

"I won't," Nick said, cocking his head as he awaited my response.

I had a pair of running shoes stashed in the trunk. Not ideal, but they'd suffice for a hike through the woods.

"Fine, give me directions."

THE BLACK WATER CREEK TRAIL was the only one on the east side of town. It was pretty far out—about a forty-minute drive—and tucked away in the middle of nowhere, with no signs to mark the turnoff. We almost missed it. From the looks of it, the trail hadn't been maintained in a while. Whether it was the weather or the condition of the path, there weren't any other cars parked nearby. No one else was hiking out there today. Just us.

"Let's start with the trail and see where it takes us," Nick suggested.

I wasn't a hiker. I never understood the appeal or why Lucas loved being in nature so much. Sleeping outside under the sky and looming trees terrified me. He used to say the woods tapped into our primal fears, that they represented the unknown and the uncontrollable, things you couldn't fix by calling the police or flipping a switch. That never comforted me. Quite the opposite.

Aside from the one time I agreed to camp with him up north, we never went together again. I preferred doors and civilization. Maybe it wasn't as reliable as we liked to think, but at least it was familiar.

The forest was shrouded in eerie fog, its tendrils swirling and eddying in the stillness. Rain dripped from the leaves onto me, and I tried to step carefully, avoiding puddles to keep my new shoes dry for as long as possible. Lucas would have scolded me that dry shoes were the most important thing when hiking. Nick, however, didn't seem to care and strolled ahead with a clear direction in mind. But his confidence soon deflated, and he slowed, checking the map on his phone.

Mosquitoes and tiny bugs swarmed around us, flying straight into my eyes and mouth. One bit me on the back of my neck, and it itched so badly I couldn't stop scratching. The high-pitched whine of another zipping past my ear was enough to put me in a foul mood all on its own.

I pulled out my phone as well. The signal was growing weaker, disappearing intermittently. But as long as I could spot the next marker on the tree, I felt reassured that we hadn't strayed from the trail.

"So, what's the story with your mom? Why did she send you away?"

With nothing better to do and to distract ourselves from thinking about Sammy, we chatted about our families.

Nick's face clouded over. "I'm not really sure. It was tough at first, but I got used to it. Oregon felt like home for a while."

"Did you miss her? Your mom?"

"I was just a kid. Of course, I missed my mom."

"And as an adult?"

He said flatly, "We'd grown apart by the time I was older. I spent a lot of time away from her when I was growing up. But it's still weird that she's gone."

We walked in silence for a bit until I mustered the courage to ask something that had been bugging me for a while. "Why did you come with us?"

"What do you mean?"

"You're not looking into your mom's death."

"We *are* looking into it. Among other things"

"No, we're looking into Lucas's and Amanda's disappearances. And now, I guess, into Duane's murder. How do you know they are connected to whatever happened to your mother?

"They have to be. But something weird's going on, and my gut is telling me asking around about another murder might not be the smartest thing to do."

"I guess so," I said with a sigh and rechecked the time, noticing we had no signal.

"How far have we walked?"

"Three miles. You getting tired?"

"No, just don't want to be in the woods after dark."

"We've got time."

We continued on, the leaves rustling and twigs breaking beneath our feet.

"So, you and Lucas, how long had you guys been together?" he asked, changing the subject.

"Almost two years."

"Were you guys happy?" Nick's tone was casual, but the question felt intense.

"Yeah. For the most part." I tried to appear nonchalant, but my eyes darted away, unsure what kind of answer he was looking for.

Nick studied me before asking, "You still love him?"

The question took me by surprise, and for a moment, I wasn't sure how to respond. It had been two years. I wasn't the same person anymore, and if Lucas ever did come back, he probably wasn't either.

I've learned that you can stop loving someone when there is a reason—a shift, a moment, something they do or say, or just the slow, quiet realization that you have moved on. It is a choice, conscious or not, and the feeling fades, dissolving into the past.

But when someone is ripped out of your life without warning, without a goodbye, it doesn't work like that. That kind of love doesn't disappear. It just changes. Shrinks a little, enough to make room for something new. But it stays. I still carried it with me, settled deep, a quiet weight I've learned to live with.

Nick interpreted my silence as me being offended.

"I'm so sorry, I'm not sure why I even asked."

I shook my head. "It's okay. I just don't know what to say."

His face flushed with embarrassment. "It was such an asshole question."

"Honestly, it's fine. And the most asshole question I was asked was whether I murdered him. So, you're good."

A sad chuckle rumbled from Nick's throat as he looked over at me, probing for signs of pain or hurt, but I kept my emotions in check.

The gentle uphill slope warmed me up, and I shed my raincoat and then my hoodie, wrapping them both around my waist, opting for a few mosquito bites over dying of heat stroke. Nick's T-shirt clung to his back, damp from exertion.

We reached a scenic overlook, where the trees gave way to a stunning vista. The hills unfolded before us, fog settling in the hollows and ridges. Nick's gaze immediately locked onto the mountain alignment. "Look," he said, "the three sisters."

"Okay?" I replied, unsure what he was getting at, and then remembered the witch's words. "Oh."

"We should get off the trail here."

"What if we get lost? We don't have food, and I'm the least useful person to be stuck in the woods with!"

Nick's hands settled on my shoulders in a reassuring gesture. The warm pressure poured down my arms like sunlight. "It's going to be okay, I promise. I'm not Mitch, but I know a thing or two about being in the woods."

I hesitated, peering into the trees, as if trying to see if anything dangerous was hiding there.

"I am not sure about this. We can get lost, especially without cell service."

"Whatever we're looking for won't be on the path anyway. Can you wait here, then? I'll be back in a few."

I looked back and forth at the empty trail, weighing my options.

Staying here alone wasn't the best choice either. What if wild animals saw me as easy prey, vulnerable in my solitude? Tilly's ominous warnings flooded my mind, and I let out a nervous whine, quickening my pace to follow him through the dense thicket.

Chapter Twenty

September, 2020

"ARE YOU SCARED?" Nick turned to check on me, and I didn't bother pretending I wasn't exhausted.

I didn't know what prompted his question. I hadn't spoken or made a sound. For the past half hour, I'd been following him like a trusted dog through the woods. We were both tired, and our conversation had long since run its course. We trudged uphill, my legs burning with each step, then descended again. I was adrift, disoriented, and steeped in misery.

Then Nick turned back to the path and froze. Concerned, I stopped dead in my tracks beside him. "What is it?"

A deer stumbled onto the path, its movements stiff and erratic, like a puppet on tangled strings. It halted before us, its glassy eyes fixed in our direction but seemingly unaware.

"Nick," I whispered.

He extended an arm, guiding me to stay close.

The deer's body was grotesquely distorted, as if it had been pieced together by a blind taxidermist. It gasped for breath, its ribs threatening to pierce the paper-thin skin. Its fur was dull and matted, with limbs splayed at unnatural angles. One antler was severed, leaving only a jagged stump. There was no blood, no visible wound. But something truly horrific had happened to it. I could only fathom that it had been ravaged, mangled into a macabre parody of what it had been.

"What the hell is that?" I whispered.

I feared the animal was sick, that it might attack us. But the deer didn't move. It stood rigid, its unblinking gaze trained on us. Then, slowly, it turned its head away. Without a sound, it stumbled back into the woods.

I let out a trembling exhale.

Nick turned to me and I hurried to say, "I'm alright, I'm alright. It's just a deer. They're not aggressive, right?"

"No, they aren't. Do you want to turn back?"

"I don't know."

"Let's walk a little further, and if we don't find anything in the next fifteen minutes, we can go back."

We pressed on, prolonging my suffering. The branches clawed at my head, tugging strands of hair free from my ponytail. Beneath my feet, the root system stretched like a twisted, organic labyrinth, or a swirl of snakes frozen mid-slither. My gaze darted to them again and again as we moved, a cold dread building inside me, waiting for the moment they might begin to writhe.

Nick showed no signs of slowing. He moved with a relentless determination, his focus razor-sharp, his fatigue buried beneath whatever obsession drove him forward.

He led us up the game trail, and I followed closely without protest. I couldn't quite put my finger on why I trusted him. It wasn't as though he claimed to be an expert at navigating the woods. But there was something about him, something in the way he carried himself, his quiet confidence, the way he'd instinctively positioned himself between me and the animal without hesitation. That spoke volumes.

I had just begun to wonder when the fifteen minutes would be up, too tired even to pull out my phone to check the time, when Nick stopped again, his arm shooting back to halt me.

My senses, dulled by depletion, barely registered why we'd stopped. It took a moment to process, and then I reacted with a frightened gasp.

In front of us, sprawled across the game trail like a macabre spectacle, lay the deer. Its lifeless body seemed to stare accusingly into the rain-soaked undergrowth, eyes fixed in a permanent, glassy terror. It was the same deer from before, its missing antler and twisted body a grim sight. But now, its legs were bent at impossible angles, its belly torn open with surgical precision. There was no sign of scavengers. No ragged tears, no feeding marks. Just a dark, empty wound, gaping open as though something had scooped out its insides, leaving behind a hollow shell.

The sight was so ghastly that I was scared to look away, fearful that the deer would suddenly twitch to life.

Nick stepped forward cautiously, his shoe hovering over the deer's flank, before pressing down gently. The body didn't yield. It was stiff, locked in place by rigor mortis. A wave of nausea washed over me.

"It's been dead for a while," Nick announced flatly.

"How is that possible?" My voice was shaky. I wasn't sure of the exact timing, but I knew enough to understand that rigor mortis would take more than a quarter of an hour to set in.

Nick didn't answer. Instead, his gaze shifted upward, fixing on a massive tree, its trunk looming ominously beside the fallen deer.

"Check this out," he said, voice low.

Only then did I see it. The symbol etched into the bark was a circle of twisted lines containing an eye that seemed to watch us with malignant intent. That was the symbol from Amanda's photo, the same one Lucas had tried to sketch on the Post-it note. I was sure of it.

My pulse hammered in my chest. I stared at it, unable to look away, entranced. "Is this—?"

Nick nodded silently, pulling out his phone to snap a picture.

He didn't need to say it. I knew we were on the right path.

We pushed forward, my tiredness fading almost entirely, replaced by a heightened sense of alertness. The game trails twisted and tangled, forcing us to navigate around massive boulders and fallen trees. I spotted a couple of snakes slithering through the leaf litter, but they vanished before the fear could take root. I knew bears roamed these woods, but now, a deeper, more unsettling dread crept in, the thought that we might run into the people who felt at home here. The ones who had left their mark on the tree.

Once again, Nick halted abruptly, and I stumbled into his back.

"What the fuck?"

I peered around him, my heart racing as dizziness set in. We'd been walking in a relatively straight line, or so I thought, but now, before us, lay the dead deer. The same one. Beside it stood the tree with the eye-shaped symbol, its hollow gaze fixed on us.

My mind spun, struggling to make sense of what I was seeing. Had we been walking in circles? How had we ended up back here?

We exchanged a look, and Nick spoke hesitantly, "It's okay. We must've made a full circle without realizing it. It's easy to get lost in the woods."

But his words did nothing to calm my nerves.

"I'd rather we turn back," I said anxiously.

Nick's eyes softened. "I know how to get back from here. Do you trust me?"

I nodded, and he gave my arm a reassuring squeeze before

stepping back onto the path. This time, he made sure we were walking in a straight line. I wished, for a moment, that we had a pocket knife to mark the trees and keep track of where we were. But neither of us had thought to bring one.

The scenery was changing, though the boulders and fallen trees were unrecognizable. Then again, we were deep in the woods. Someone unfamiliar with nature might struggle to tell one tree from another. I was, after all, a city dweller.

"Fucking hell!" Nick swore, and I knew why even before I looked. We'd circled back to the same spot. The deer. The tree. The symbol.

A hollow weight settled in my gut, spreading like a slow, insidious chill through my ribs. "What's going on? How are we ending up in the same spot?"

Nick stood there, hesitant, his eyes scanning the surroundings. "I don't know."

It felt impossible. No, it *was* impossible. Once, maybe, but twice? I was sure we hadn't made a circle, and we were far off the trail, still three miles from the car. The woods grew increasingly uninviting, even dangerous. I felt a persistent, unsettling awareness that our solitude was not as complete as it seemed to be.

"Let's get out of here. Please."

Nick slipped his hand into mine, guiding me toward the trail without a word. His pace didn't falter, his hold steady, leaving me no choice but to follow. No matter how tired I was, I didn't mind pushing through. The feeling of eyes watching our backs kept me moving.

Nick stopped again, his head tilting as he strained to listen. "Do you hear that?"

"Hear what?" I strained to hear, every fiber attuned to the faint sounds around me: the rustle of leaves, the creaking of wooden limbs that seemed to signal the presence of unseen animals nearby. My eyes flicked nervously through the trees, but there was no movement.

"Nothing. Let's go," he said, resuming his pace.

By my calculations, we should have reached the trail by now. But I wasn't sure I trusted my perception of time and distance. Everything was distorted, warped by fear and confusion. Was it getting darker? Or was my frazzled mind playing tricks on me? The overcast sky offered no help, obscuring any sense of time. The woods around us felt alive, filled with presence. I fought to keep panic at bay, steadying my breath and clinging to whatever rationality I had left.

The earth itself seemed to conspire against me, with roots reaching up to trip me, and mud sucking at my feet. But I dared not look down. I couldn't risk losing sight of Nick, even for a second.

Just when I thought I'd shatter, Nick held back a branch, revealing the trail. I gulped in relief, feeling the pressure coming off. Now, at least, we were on the marked path.

"It's okay, we're almost out," he said, helping me onto the trail. "Can you walk?"

I nodded. If I had to, I'd run and not stop until we reached the safety of the car.

"Do you think we were hallucinating?" I asked, still trying to make sense of it. "Maybe it was some kind of fungus or something."

"I thought about that," Nick said. "But if we'd inhaled something that strong, it wouldn't just stop the second we stepped outside. And shared hallucinations are rare."

"But not impossible?"

"No, just unlikely," he said. "And if it were something airborne, we'd probably still feel it—nausea, headaches, at least some disorientation. But we're fine. Physically, anyway. Plus, if there was something in the air, wouldn't the birds or squirrels have been acting weird too? They seemed completely normal."

. . .

THE SUN WAS SETTING, and the world around us started to lose contrast. A heavy cloud from the north threatened more rain. Our hopes of reaching the car before the downpour were dashed. The air grew cooler, and the first raindrops splattered against us, forcing us to pull on our hoodies and raincoats. My second pair of shoes was soaked within minutes.

By the time we reached the parking lot, we were both drenched and miserable. Surprisingly, another car, a lone mud-splattered Jeep, was parked on the opposite side of the lot.

"Who the hell hikes in this weather?" I muttered, shivering.

Exhaustion and cold seeped into my bones, numbing my thoughts. I just craved warmth, dry clothes, and a hot meal, leaving the dark, twisted memories of the woods to unravel like a fraying thread. We got into the van, shaking off as much water as we could. As we settled in, our phones sprang to life.

My screen lit up with notifications. Two texts from June: "Are you dead somewhere?" and "Where the hell are you?" And, of course, a flurry of messages and missed calls from Mitch. Along with that, there was one missed call from my mother, accompanied by a terse text: "What's going on? Where are you?"

"Oh shit!" I gasped, realizing that today was the latest date I'd given my mother for my return home.

"What happened?" Nick asked.

My face flushed. The childish "My mom's gonna kill me!" almost slipped out, but I drew a deep breath and said, "I gotta call my mom." Nick gave a small, understanding smile.

His phone was also overwhelmed with notifications. I let him quickly update Mitch, telling him we were on our way back without going into much detail. He didn't linger on it and started the car right away.

"Where are you?" my mother demanded, skipping the pleasantries.

"Sorry, Mom. I got held up, and my plans got delayed."

Her tone turned suspicious. "What do you mean, 'held up'? What's going on?"

"Something came up."

But she wasn't having it. "What is it? Is this about that boy? For goodness' sake, Nellie, are you still trying to find him?"

I glanced at Nick, who remained focused on the road, but I knew he could hear my mother's loud voice on the phone.

"Can we talk later? I'm driving," I lied.

But she persisted. "Where are you?"

"Bye, Mom!" I hung up and pinched the bridge of my nose.

Nick offered a sympathetic smile. "Sounds like she's not a fan of Lucas."

I shook my head. "She's not a fan of me, period. And anyone I care about gets caught in the crossfire."

He chuckled, and the sound eased some of the tension in my chest.

"I bet she loves you and is just worried."

This was true. My mother did love me, but her love was a suffocating shroud, conditional on my conforming to her expectations. She made me feel guilty for wanting space, for needing my own life, where I could make my own decisions, my own mistakes, and take responsibility for them. I was expected to follow her script.

My right hand twitched toward my left wrist, reaching for the bracelet. I did it without thinking, a habit that kicked in whenever I was nervous or too tired to think straight. But my fingers met only bare skin. I blinked, staring at the empty spot like it might reappear if I waited long enough. It must have fallen off somewhere back in the woods. I couldn't feel anything right away, just this strange buzz under my skin. Another piece of Lucas, gone. Like the closer I got to finding him, the more he slipped away from me.

. . .

MITCHELL AND JUNE were waiting in the hotel room, visibly worried.

"What in tarnation? Where've you been?" Mitchell asked the moment we stepped through the door.

"I convinced her to go search the woods with me," said Nick, taking the blame.

I couldn't bring myself to care about Mitchell's accusations. The most important thing was that something was off in those woods, and we needed to investigate it further, properly equipped.

In the warmth of the hotel room, the scent of the forest clung to my clothes. I shed my coat and sweater, letting them fall to the floor, my body craving a shower to wash it all away. But duty called, and I settled beside Nick on the couch for the debrief.

Nick, too, carried the musky aroma of wet leaves, moss, tree bark, and damp earth. Yet, on him, the scent was oddly fitting, almost like an extension of his natural presence.

I let Nick recount our grim adventures, beginning with the woods and circling back to the cemetery, where the Reverend had allegedly cleared out Sammy's hiding place, and worse.

"What about you? Did you find anything?" he asked in the end.

"Just this." June retrieved a wrinkled piece of paper from the coffee table. Nick took it, flipping it over. Under the bold heading "MISSING CHILD," Sammy's face stared back at us.

Chapter Twenty-One

September, 2020

THE THUNDERSTORM RAGED through the night, promising a grueling hike ahead.

We spent the early hours hunched over the area map. Mitchell traced the lines, trying to make sense of them, while Nick pointed to where he guessed we were. Pinpointing our exact route was nearly impossible. Without a signal, we were navigating blind. Even Nick's expensive watch, with its built-in navigation, came up empty.

Mitchell remained skeptical of our so-called paranormal experiences, convinced we had simply lost our way and were lucky to have made it back.

I flipped through the photos we'd taken from Duane's place, not really looking for anything but unable to stop myself. Deep down, I wanted to catch some detail we'd overlooked.

Sammy's missing child poster lay on the table, staring back at me like an unspoken accusation. *This is your fault.*

"…and the Reverend," I caught the tail end of Mitchell's sentence.

"But why? What's his motive?" June asked.

"For one, he could be one of them," her brother said.

"One of whom?"

"The cult members. It's the only thing that makes sense."

His sudden agreement with Nick startled me. All the same, it was a relief to see his earlier irritability had lifted. Mitch was now on a more productive path. A cult would explain almost everything—the organization, the secrecy, the missing people. Even the connection to the Harvest Moon. The symbols weren't just landmarks. They carried meaning.

"But what's the endgame? And why do they need all these people?" I shook the pack of photos in my hand.

"Recruiting new members or," Nick suggested, "human sacrifice."

"Are we seriously looking for a secret cult that specializes in human sacrifices?" I asked, incredulous.

Mitchell shrugged, his expression confirming the unthinkable.

"It still doesn't explain how people just... vanish," I said.

"Well, we know of at least one Sheriff who covers up crimes," Nick said. "What if they have more?"

"But Sammy didn't go missing on the Harvest Moon," it suddenly occurred to me.

"And that's why there's a chance he's still alive," Nick said.

WHEN I WAS SIXTEEN, my dad taught me how to drive. He used to say, "Stay away from morons on the road," and that advice stuck with me. So, when an old Cherokee caught up with us on the narrow one-lane road, tailgating aggressively, I hugged the road verge to give them space to pass, even though I was driving five above the speed limit. The other car's windows were tinted, obscuring the driver's identity, but instinct whispered it was a man.

We reached a stretch of road where passing in the opposite traffic lane was permitted. The Cherokee suddenly accelerated, cut me off, and then adjusted its speed. I expected it to speed away, but instead it slowed down, and now I found myself tailgating.

Behind us, another car approached, and I was suddenly sandwiched between the two vehicles. I tried to put more distance between me and the Cherokee, but the car behind me nearly rear-ended me.

"Why pass if you're not going to drive, asshole?" I muttered.

The Cherokee began weaving between the left and right sides of the lane, accelerating and decelerating with menace.

"What the heck?" Nick muttered, turning back.

The car in front of us turned on its hazard lights and started moving to the side of the road, giving me space to pass. However, there was no passing lane.

The car behind me signaled aggressively.

"What's wrong with people here?" Taking a leap of faith, I spotted a long enough stretch of road before the next curve and sped up, passing the Cherokee in the opposite lane.

"Nellie, don't!" Nick's warning came too late.

Two things happened.

The Cherokee sped up, not letting me pass, and the car behind it did the same, maintaining a tight distance from the Jeep, making it impossible for me to squeeze back into my lane. I tried to slow down, letting them both go, but they slowed down too. The SUV swerved to the side, side-swiping us. The impact almost shoved us into the gutter along the opposite lane, but I managed to regain control.

"Don't stop, go!" Nick ordered, and I floored it. As I struggled to maneuver back into my lane, the huge 4x4 swiftly pulled up beside me, maintaining our speed and effectively trapping me in the oncoming lane.

"Don't panic," Nick said, his voice oddly composed. "Let's hit the brakes in three, two, one..."

I followed his instructions. The SUV hit the brakes too and turned violently into us, scratching our side. And there we went again, side by side. Only now it also tried to swerve left and bump us again. My hands trembled on the steering wheel as I veered left to escape the clash. The Jeep and the SUV still shadowed our moves.

Up ahead, a car hurtled towards us, careening around the turn at an alarming speed. Its horn pierced the air, but its driver remained oblivious to the full extent of our desperate plight.

"Take a left, now!" Nick's words snapped me out of my panic.

"Where?" I asked, already turning the wheel, blindly heeding his instructions. We were mere feet away from the oncoming car, its relentless signaling piercing the air.

Just as suddenly, the forest road appeared like a lifeline, almost invisible from the main road. It was a close call. We swerved, narrowly missing a tree. I brought the car to a halt and sat stock-still, still clenching the wheel.

"Everyone okay?" Nick asked, looking back. I turned to check on them as well. June's eyes were like saucers, her face pale. Mitch opened the side door and carefully glanced back at the road. Dust motes danced in the air.

"I think they're gone," he said, and I finally released my sweaty grip on the wheel. With stiff fingers, I fumbled to open the door, stepping into the cool air. The adrenaline coursing through my veins left me queasy, but thankfully, the nausea subsided quickly. I pretended to inspect the car, running my hands over the scratches and dents left by the hostile Jeep. The right taillight was broken.

"Fucking hillbillies," Nick said through his teeth, "Can't stage a believable suicide and can't organize a car crash."

"You think they were trying to kill us?" I asked.

"You think that was normal road rage?"

"Probably not," I agreed, still shaking.

This Caravan was a family car. It was intended for long drives to Florida, not for car chases. It didn't deserve to be treated like this, nor did it sign up for such adventures.

"I don't think they are coming for us, but let's wait a few to be sure," said Mitchell.

"Why did they try to make us crash into that other car?" she asked, still doubtful. "Why didn't they just follow us here to finish the job?"

"Maybe they were trying to scare us," Nick offered.

"So we'd leave?" I prayed we would.

"Are we going to?" June asked.

"We'll leave town, for sure," Mitchell said.

"Are we *leaving*-leaving?" June didn't seem ready to throw in the towel just yet.

"No, just leaving. These woods are giving me the heebie-jeebies." Mitchell looked back into the trees as we were loading into the car.

"Can someone else drive, please?" I asked plaintively. The adrenaline had worn off, leaving a heavy, draining sensation in my limbs.

"Sure thing." Mitchell took the driver's seat.

WE RENTED a room at a highway motel, the kind where no one checks IDs and guests come and go so frequently that blending in is effortless. The letters on the "Riverbend Inn" sign hung in tattered strips, and the floors were filthy, but the place had two advantages: its remote location and its cash payments.

Mitch insisted we get food first, so we walked in carrying bags of Chinese takeout. "Gotta fuel up after that adrenaline dump," he said. I didn't know how he could eat after that car chase. I was still shaking, and it felt as though if I put anything in my stomach, it would come right back out.

We squeezed into a tiny room reeking of stale fabric and dust. The bathroom faucet dripped nonstop, but no one complained.

"It's just for one night," Mitchell said, trying to reassure June, who hadn't spoken since we arrived. She didn't even seem to notice the stains on the covers.

"And then what?" Nick asked.

Mitch didn't respond. His eyes had gone glassy, brows drawn tight like he was bracing for something. I half expected him to say we needed to leave before anything else went wrong.

"We should stay," Nick said instead. He glanced at each of us, then added, "Find that place. The one with the trees with eyes, or whatever Duane was talking about. Find the boy."

Mitch looked contemplative, his jaw shifted from side to side. A vertical line formed between his brows. He put his elbows on the table and clasped his hands.

June sat quietly, her gaze flicking between the two men as she held her fork upright, the tines pressed into the plastic plate as if it were a battlefield.

I thought about Nick's mother, Duane, Sammy, Amanda, and Lucas, and what had happened to them, wondering whether there was anything we could still do.

Ahead of me was the option of going back to Ohio, staying with my mother, taking that job, maybe even returning to college. Doing what she always wanted for me. But it all felt distant, like someone else's life. A future that didn't belong to me. I'd spent years following someone else's lead, swinging between doing what others thought was best and doing the opposite, just to spite my mother. I joined the track team because my PE teacher said I should. I was good enough, but I never ran for myself. I chose the University of Minnesota over a closer school mostly to prove I could leave, even if that meant letting go of everything familiar. My life had been shaped by the expectations of others, either trying to meet them or push away from them.

But now, after everything that had happened to us in Black Water, something had shifted. I couldn't go back. Not because it would disappoint my mother, but because I no longer needed her approval to make this choice.

"I'm staying." Everyone's eyes shifted to me. "I'll go into the woods and find that place."

June looked at her brother. "I want to stay too. Even if you're leaving."

Mitch uncrossed his arms, and in that instant, I thought he might push back. But then he stood a little straighter.

"Alright," he said. "That's settled, then."

The plan was to find a safe place to stay for a few days before the full moon and try to locate that strange spot in the woods. But first, we needed to retrieve our belongings from the hotel. I was better off than everyone else, with a few things stashed in the back of my car: some clothes in a box and Lucas's gym bag, untouched since I left Minneapolis. Still, all my essentials were in the Ikea bag back at the resort.

Mitchell and June took my car to pick up everything. He hesitated, debating whether to leave her with me and take Nick instead, but in the end, watching over his sister himself won out.

"We oughta get a rental," Mitchell said. "They've already marked the Dodge, so a different ride might help us keep under the radar."

"Get full coverage, too," I added. "Might need it."

WE WERE STUCK in the grimy room for hours, waiting for the siblings to return. The place was cramped and drab. Stained walls, faded curtains, and a queen-sized bed taking up most of the space. A small coffee table and a sofa sat awkwardly in front of it. The air felt stale, and the only sound was the hum of the old refrigerator in the corner.

"You want one?" Nick offered me a ginger beer from the fridge as I paced the short length of the room. I hadn't even noticed him grabbing them at the gas station. I took the bottle automatically and tried to twist the cap off with the hem of my shirt, but it wouldn't budge. I set it on the coffee table and continued my lengths.

"Quite a day, huh?" Nick lolled on the sofa, mouth hitched in a half-smile that didn't quite reach his eyes.

"That's one way to put it."

"How are you feeling?" He watched me tentatively as he opened my bottle with his keys. The lid fell onto the stained carpet with a sad ping.

I held out my hand, still trembling. "I'm fine."

"Really?" he challenged. He leaned forward, resting his elbows on his thighs. From this angle, the dull overheads flooded his cheekbones in shadows. "You keep pacing."

"Really," I repeated. "It's just my first car chase, you know."

Nick laughed, but there was no amusement in it. "Being so close to death makes you feel alive, huh?"

I took a sip of the ginger beer.

"I thought stuff like this only happened in movies." I rubbed my forehead, still pacing.

"Okay, enough," he said, rising from the couch. In a few strides, he was in front of me. Too close for friendly. His nearness stole the breath from my lungs. I looked up, and for a second, the room narrowed to just us.

"I just can't think about anything else."

"Me neither," he said, voice low. "But I don't think we're thinking about the same thing."

His hand found the side of my neck, gently pulling me closer. His kiss caught me off guard, but the feeling of his lips on mine made me instantly forget the chaos. He pulled back slightly, giving me space to process what was happening. I shifted awkwardly, fisting his shirt. How did that just happen?

Nick's dark brown eyes held a quiet intensity, exploring the contours of my face with a soft, unhurried curiosity. I stood there, still holding onto him, my fingers gently unfastening his buttons.

He kissed me again, deeper and more insistent. The adrenaline still coursing through my veins, I let go of my reservations, ignoring the nagging thoughts of consequences and implications, and Lucas. All that mattered was that Nick was holding me tight, already pulling my shirt off, his touch a slow burn that ignited as his hands made contact with my bare skin. That quiet pull I'd been trying to ignore. I finally recognized it for what it was. I wanted him.

And for once, I didn't care what happened next.

22

Chapter Twenty-Two

September, 2020

THEY'D BEEN GONE TOO LONG. I sat by the window, watching through a hole in the curtain for the familiar sight of the Dodge. Nick was in the kitchen area, but I couldn't bear to look at him. The memory of his toned chest supported above me made a warmth stir low in my belly, and we didn't have time for that again.

One set of headlights followed by another cut through the curtains. Moments later, Mitch and June spilled into the room.

"Everything alright here?" Mitchell asked cautiously, as if he'd expected to walk into a crime scene.

"All good," Nick said. "No problems."

After we got dressed and tried to compose ourselves, the awkwardness had settled in. I didn't know what to do with myself, so I was double-happy to have the siblings back. But deep inside, a sliver of panic twisted in my stomach. *What if they could tell?*

I jerked up from my chair, too fast, too stiff, too sore, and forced a smile. "Sure," I said, my voice a little too bright. "Get everything from the hotel, okay?"

"Yeah, but someone beat us to it," Mitchell said.

Nick joined us by the door, standing beside me so casually that it was as if nothing had happened. "What do you mean?"

I envied his composure.

"Somebody dug through all our stuff," Mitchell explained.

"Is anything missing?" I asked.

"I don't think so. At least, nothing I noticed."

Relief came with knowing that most of my belongings, as well as the papers and photos from Duane's, were safely stored in the car. I'd refused to let them out of my sight, keeping them either in the car or with me, tucked away in a backpack or purse.

The search of our belongings didn't surprise me. In fact, I was convinced it had been their plan all along: scare us, send us running, and buy themselves time to dig through our things. I was sure they were after the photos. There was nothing else of value we had. But how did they even know the images existed in the first place? If they were so important, why hadn't they searched for them at Duane's place? Either way, carrying these photos was putting us in danger. Getting rid of them, however, wouldn't necessarily take the target off our backs.

The hum of anxiety was growing stronger. My movements were jerky, and I kept dropping stuff. The only thing distracting me from it was Nick. I let out a breath, trying to focus, trying to be normal. But my pulse was still off-rhythm, my body betraying me every time I caught the slightest movement from Nick at the edge of my sight. He was too close. Not touching me, not saying anything, but there. And I didn't know what to do with that.

June was surprisingly quiet, going in and out, carrying bags and handing them to me to unload. I'd never seen her like that before. Tense, her lips pressed into a tight line. I got up to help her. Mitchell tossed the last of the grocery bags onto the tiny kitchen table, and June followed with my Ikea bag.

"Oh my, did you guys stock up for a zombie apocalypse?" I asked, pulling out several cans of beans.

"Figured it was best to be ready, just in case." Mitchell nudged another bag with the toe of his boot. "We've also got some fresh veggies and whatnot."

Nick chuckled softly behind me. It was barely a sound, barely a reaction, but it wrecked me. Because he was standing there, completely fine, while I felt like I was about to combust. I needed to pull myself together, so I rummaged through my belongings, trying to determine if anything was missing.

"June, mind getting a pot of coffee going?" Mitchell asked, sinking wearily onto the sofa—the same one where Nick and I had hooked up earlier. I cringed. June, unusually obedient, began fiddling with the ancient coffee maker. It was a bit late for coffee, but Mitchell looked exhausted, and we had a long conversation ahead.

"I'll have a cup too," Nick said.

"Then get off your ass and make it yourself," June retorted without turning around.

"And she's back," Nick said, getting up to help.

WE MOVED the very next day. Nick found a rental cabin on some website, not too far from Black Water, but far enough to keep us hidden. Though tiny from the outside, the cottage's interior was surprisingly spacious. With multiple bedrooms— three upstairs and one just off the living room—we could finally enjoy some much-needed privacy.

"Nice, we can make a fire!" Mitchell eyed the fireplace. A stack of wood sat ready in the backyard, overlooking a neglected pond.

Later, we discussed our options. Going after the Sheriff felt too risky. Digging deeper would only paint a bigger target on our backs. The fact that he'd managed to cover up the disappearances and deaths, including Duane's, for years only proved how powerful and well-connected he was. The Reverend seemed like a more plausible lead, just as unsettling, but slightly more within reach.

Sammy's vanishing had taken a backseat, but I could tell everyone felt guilty about it, including myself. Whenever his name came up in connection with the Reverend, our eyes would dart away, and an uncomfortable silence would fall until someone resumed the discussion.

Nobody said it out loud, but I was sure we all thought it: Sammy was gone for good, and we'd eventually uncover the truth about what had happened to him, along with Lucas, Amanda, and the others.

We owed it to him since talking to us might have sealed his fate.

MITCH AND JUNE set off for Virginia the very next day, planning a day trip to Richmond and back to visit the Reverend's old parish. Thanks to the talkative, albeit odd, woman at the church, we knew exactly where to go.

A long, uneasy day stretched ahead for Nick and me. We didn't talk about what had happened between us, and I was relieved. I wasn't sure how to process it. I liked Nick, but everything had happened so suddenly. It almost felt like it came out of nowhere. Or had it?

It had rained all night and continued through the morning, the steady patter on the cabin's roof creating a backdrop of constant white noise. The temperature had dropped, a clear sign that summer had given way to fall. We stayed indoors, keeping warm.

The cabin's interior looked like a city dweller's Pinterest board come to life: a stone fireplace, wooden signs reading "S'more Memories" and "Life Is Better by the Fire," and carefully placed throw blankets and pillows. Nick added a few more logs to the hearth. We'd found some space heaters, but the fire felt infinitely more inviting.

The room warmed quickly. I settled on the plush rug in front of the hearth, laptop open, and started sorting through the stack of photos and printouts from Duane's place, arranging them in chronological order. I searched each name online, combing through Google and Facebook. Unsurprisingly, people from earlier years had little to no digital footprint.

One name from the more recent dates led me to a Facebook profile of a woman in her thirties who'd allegedly gone missing seven years ago. The photo I held matched the one on her profile. She hadn't posted anything, but her privacy settings were wide open to public viewing. I scrolled through her groups, and one immediately caught my eye.

Nick emerged from the kitchen and placed a plate with a freshly made turkey sandwich beside me on the rug. "Find anything?"

I turned the laptop to face him, avoiding his eyes. "Check this out."

"Safe Space Support: Domestic Violence Survivors," he read aloud. "One of the victims was in this group?"

"Two that we know of. Amanda and her."

"Okay," he said carefully, as if trying not to spook our luck, and sat down beside me on the rug. "Now we've got something."

I clicked the "Join Group" button and completed the questionnaire. I had to bend the truth on a few of the questions since I didn't want to reveal my real reason for joining. Then I sent the request.

"What are you doing?" Nick asked, eyeing the screen.

"Trying to get a look at the member list. Maybe we can connect with the group admin. See if they can provide any insights."

"Okay." He nudged the plate toward me. "Eat something."

Nick was kind. Beneath the grumpy exterior, he was genuinely a good guy. He wasn't the most open, but that didn't change how I felt. I liked him, really liked him.

The problem was that everything about our circumstances made it complicated. I'd never struggled to connect with guys before, but this was different. The timing, the situation, the reasons we'd been thrown together—all of it made things awkward from the start. I did my best to keep a *just-friends-who-work-together* distance, trying not to let my mind wander back to the night before.

To my shame, that was difficult.

The photos of missing people in front of me should've been enough to keep me focused, but they weren't. Nick was too close. His scent clung to the air around me, and I couldn't help but notice the tattoos on his left arm, peeking from beneath the rolled-up sleeve of his shirt. I remembered squeezing them as I came undone, making a mental note to study them properly next time.

Next time?!

I felt very, very stupid. *Concentrate*, I kept telling myself.

The two missing persons posters provided me with the basics: cities, ages, and names. But despite my efforts, I couldn't make any progress. No online records, no news articles, no social media profiles. It was baffling. The few phone numbers listed led only to local police departments, not to any family members or friends. There was no personal connection to follow, no one to talk to. Just a wall of silence.

Lucas wasn't big on social media, but he followed a few local Facebook groups—mostly ones related to Black Water, his school, sports, movies, and bands he liked. No support groups or anything remotely related to disappearances.

Something was missing.

"Was your mom on Facebook?" I asked Nick.

"Just for the store. I helped her set it up. Why?"

"I'm checking if there's anything online connecting all these people. Like a group or something. Did she ever mention anything like that?"

"Not to me." Nick lay on his stomach in front of the fireplace, lazily browsing something on his laptop. He looked so relaxed that he almost seemed like a completely different person. In fact, it was only the second time I'd seen him let his guard down like that. And both times, it had been with me. It was flattering, but it made my heart race and my thoughts scatter.

I rubbed my temples, trying to shake off the unwarranted thoughts, forcing my brain back to the papers scattered in front of me.

The very last name, a disappearance from five years ago, was too common to be found. A multitude of people showed up, but none resembled the photo, nor did they appear to be missing or inactive over the past few years. Some obituaries also appeared, although they were all for someone else. Frustrated, I shut the laptop and lay on the floor.

"It's nice here. Peaceful," Nick said, turning to his side to face me.

And it was, if I could forget the near-death experience, the possible cult, at least two murders, a ghostly deer, a missing child, and the strange symbols carved into trees.

The cabin, isolated off the main road, stood amidst towering trees barely kissed by fall colors, enveloped in a damp, wet fog. It felt as though we were cut off from the world, a comforting yet claustrophobic experience, the fundamental human tug between solitude and connection. Perhaps Nick only liked it here because, unlike at home, he wasn't alone.

"Do you ever feel lonely? At home, I mean?" I asked him.

"Sometimes."

"Why don't you move, then? To a bigger city, for instance?"

He thought for a few seconds. "It's an illusion to think you're not alone just because you're in a crowded city. You're often more isolated, more disconnected, than when you're by yourself."

I "hmmed" indecisively, not sure what to add.

For a few moments, we lay in silence; the only sounds the steady patter of rain on the window and the soft crackle of the fireplace. Then, Nick reciprocated the question.

"Do *you* feel lonely?"

"All the time," I blurted without a second thought. And then, slowly, "Sometimes I wonder if I've ever truly not felt alone, even before... everything."

Nick's hand rested gently on mine, his warmth seeping into me as steady as the fire and the rain into the earth. He looked me straight in the eye.

"Loneliness isn't the absence of people. It's the lack of genuine connection."

I didn't always feel lonely with Lucas, but decided to keep that to myself. Instead, I asked, "Do you think all these people were lonely? And that's why nobody noticed they were gone?"

He propped himself up on one elbow and looked at me.

"I guess."

I sat up, a sudden wave of nerves tightening my chest. Sure, Lucas had a family, friends, and me. But Amanda only had estranged siblings. Nick's mom had just him, and he lived across the country. And the others who'd gone missing didn't seem to have anyone who cared enough to look for them.

"Nobody was really looking for them. Maybe a missing person flyer here and there, but even those felt half-hearted. Maybe it's because they had no one." I paused, letting the realization sink in. "What if that's how they were chosen? Through support groups, or maybe this specific one. We need to talk to the admins."

"Lucas's profile still doesn't fit," Nick said, looking directly at me.

"Right..." I frowned. "But we're onto something. With Lucas,

I just don't know. Maybe he's not connected after all. But how could he not be? What if he and Duane got involved because they were investigating, just like we are? What if this," I gestured to the stack of photos, "is what got them—"

"Killed?" Nick echoed. "Maybe."

I wished we had asked Duane while we still had the chance. But back then, we didn't even know what we were looking for. And now, it was too late.

"We need to find the place in the woods," Nick continued matter-of-factly. "I know we were close. I know it."

For a moment, he seemed far away, as though his mind had already wandered into the trees, walking the trails while his body sat still beside me.

"I really hope we don't have to hike in this rain," I said, my voice pulling him out of his thoughts.

He turned to me again, our faces just inches apart. My breath caught, heart stumbling in my chest.

Then my phone buzzed.

It was a text from June, along with a blurry, poorly lit photo. It looked like it had been taken quickly, probably before anyone noticed. In the background stood a small figure. A little boy. Even with the bad quality, I recognized him immediately.

It was Sammy.

Chapter Twenty-Three

September, 2020

"THE BOY IS ALIVE," Mitch announced from the doorway.

We tried calling the siblings after getting the text, but neither of them answered. Nick and I were left guessing and anxiously waiting for their return.

Mitch rubbed his eyes and sank into the chair. June dropped her bag on the floor and leaned against the wall, spent after too many hours in a car, her blonde hair a mess.

Assuming they'd be hungry, I'd made more cold turkey sandwiches and kept them in the fridge. Now I was glad I had. The siblings immediately dug in, though June first inspected her sandwich with meticulous care, plucking out the tomato slices and giving me a dirty look. I forgot she didn't like them, apparently because the skins were 'too yucky.'

"We spoke to a few people at the parish," her brother said. "Word is, the Reverend got the boot for betting with church money."

"What?"

"They wanted to keep it quiet, so he packed up and moved to Black Water."

I was still trying to make sense of it all. "But what does that have to do with Sammy?" I asked.

Mitch took another bite of his sandwich. We impatiently waited for him to chew and swallow. "From what we were told, the Reverend showed up two days ago with Sammy. Said the kid was in danger. He thought it had something to do with Sammy's family. Claimed he had the paperwork ready. Everything looked official enough."

"This is strange," I said. "Did he kidnap the boy to keep us from talking to him, or was he protecting him from someone else?"

"No idea," June said, then added knowingly, "but the woman at the parish said the Reverend begged them to take Sammy in."

"How did you get them to tell you all that?" Nick asked.

Mitch tapped a finger against the table, faintly smug. "We told them the Reverend sent us to check in on Sammy. You'd be surprised how much people like to talk in a small church like that."

Something still didn't add up.

"If the Reverend was hiding Sammy to keep someone else from finding him," I said, more thinking out loud, "then why would he kill Duane?"

"Can't be sure he did," Mitch said, reaching for his second sandwich.

"But he painted over the symbols in Duane's house."

"I hate to say it," Mitch said around a mouthful of bread, "but perhaps it wasn't the Reverend."

Nick continued, "Or maybe the Reverend knew what was going on and was trying to beat whoever it was to the kid."

"So you think it's the Sheriff?" June asked.

"That's our most likely lead," her brother responded, still

chewing, the words coming out a bit garbled. He'd long since given up trying to swallow whenever it was his cue to talk.

"Richmond isn't far," I said, half to myself. "We followed the Reverend's trail easily enough. What if someone else does too?"

"I doubt that," Nick said. "We knew what we were looking for. Whoever else is out there might not even be after Sammy, let alone know what that boy's uncovered. My guess is it's just a precaution."

"Did you get a chance to talk to him? To Sammy?" I asked.

Mitch shook his head. "No. They got pretty hinky when we started asking questions, so we figured it was time to bail."

I hadn't realized how tense I'd been since Sammy disappeared. But now, the pressure eased from my chest. We hadn't gotten the boy killed with our digging. He was alive, though taken from his family. But after his stories, maybe this was for the best, too.

Now, it was our turn to share the information. I told them about the Facebook group.

"I sent a request to join," I said, expecting at least some recognition.

A flicker of panic crossed Mitch's face. "What? Why would you do that? What if the killer's in the group? What were you thinking?"

My pride deflated instantly, replaced by a wave of embarrassment. Using my real name and account was reckless. I glanced at Nick sheepishly, but he avoided eye contact.

"There are thousands of people—" I trailed off, attempting to justify my actions. But it was too late. Once again, I tried to take the lead, but only made a fool of myself.

THE SHEETS FELT DAMP with restlessness as I tossed again, unable to sleep. The rain had stopped earlier in the evening, giving way to a thick fog that pressed against the windows by midnight.

I scrolled through my phone, checking my dormant social media profiles, which I hadn't updated in two years, as well as the news, sports, and politics. Too dull to read, but not dull enough to lull me to sleep.

My eyes drifted to the blue bag in the corner, the one June had packed. Resting on top was the book she'd *borrowed* from Mathilda's store. I got up, grabbed it, and headed downstairs to make some tea.

The oversized T-shirt I wore barely covered my thighs, and the room felt colder than I'd expected; the fire in the hearth long since dwindled. Curled up on the couch with a mug in hand, I pulled a blanket from the backrest and opened the book—not to read, necessarily, but to flip through the pages until I felt sleepy enough to head to bed.

A single sentence leapt out at me, sending my heart racing, sleep forgotten. I set my tea aside and clutched the book like a life buoy.

"GROWING up in these Appalachian hills, I heard many stories from my grandmother. This one she'd tell me every fall, when it was time for farmers to harvest their crops. She was nearing seventy but still worked tirelessly on her land, growing her own food. Ever since my grandfather's passing, she'd managed alone, her resilience forged in the fire of hardship.

Every time the Harvest Moon was full, she'd sit on the porch, smoke curling from her pipe, and tell me a story about the Harvest Keeper. It had many names, an entity that ensured our land remained fertile and our crops thrived.

Some said it dated back to the early settlers, who learned from the Cherokee to honor the land's dark spirits. Others claimed it was older still, a relic of forgotten civilizations.

"It's a thing that lives in these woods," she'd say. "It wakes on Harvest Moon night, looking for its gifts."

It was said that if you left offerings—corn, cider, or else—the Harvest Keeper would bless your land. But beware: once it knew you had something to offer, it would return, year after year.

"Like bears," old-timers would say. "Once they know you're feeding them, they won't forget."

I never questioned Grandma's tales of the Harvest Keeper, but as I grew older, I started to wonder. Would neglecting the gifts truly bring withered crops and ailing livestock? I'll never know.

What I do remember is this: every year, right before the Harvest Moon, Grandma would mark a chicken with paint, a small, crimson shape on its feathers. She'd carry it deep into the woods, whispering prayers I couldn't understand.

I don't recall if the chicken ever came back."

I SAT FROZEN. It all matched: the Harvest Moon, the disappearances. On paper, the tale seemed innocent enough, but in reality, it was a sinister blueprint. If someone was trying to bring 'gifts' to worship something in the woods, whether it was real or not, it was a motive. No one ever said motives had to make sense to everyone, just to those committing the crimes.

I got up, still clenching the book with both hands, headed to Nick's room without a second thought, and knocked on the door. When there was no response, I waited a bit before knocking again, this time a little louder. I needed to talk to him, and I couldn't wait until morning. Finally, the creak of a bed and the rustle of sheets broke the silence. Footsteps followed. A few seconds later, he opened the door.

"Look at this," I said, turning the open book toward him without apologizing for waking him.

Nick looked like I'd roused him from a deep sleep—weary, disheveled, and vulnerable, his usual composure softened.

"Doesn't it sound familiar?" I asked.

Nick's eyes narrowed as he scanned the lines.

I rushed him, impatient. "What do you think?"

He paused before responding. "This might give us a general idea of what's happening."

I nodded. "It's just like you said. It must be in the woods. If we can pinpoint the location, we can find out who's behind it and stop it."

"Nellie?"

"What?"

"This could also just be a legend."

"But the symbols, the Harvest Moon, the sacrifices? Doesn't it all match?"

"It does," Nick agreed reluctantly, still studying the book.

I exhaled, "So?"

He looked up, and then down, his gaze drifting over my bare feet and legs before meeting my eyes again. "This can wait till tomorrow," he said, his voice low and soothing, as he grasped the hem of my T-shirt and gently pulled me into his room.

The night enveloped us, a shroud of quiet and still. Nick's steady heartbeat pulsed like a metronome, grounding me and anchoring my thoughts as they scattered in every direction. *What was I doing?*

"I should go back to my room," I murmured.

Nick's hand found mine in the darkness, stopping me from pulling away. "Stay," he whispered, his breath warm against my ear. "They won't know."

I hesitated, then relented, leaning into his arms.

THE MORNING CREPT in with a gray reluctance. I drifted in and out of slumber, unaccustomed to sharing a bed with someone. Nick lay beside me, deeply asleep, the gentle rush of air from his exhalations tickling my skin. I didn't want it to end, and it scared me.

Sometime after six, I quietly slid from under his arm, took the abandoned book that brought me here—*maybe just an excuse my brain, hungry for connection, had conjured*—and left, closing the door behind me.

Mitch usually rose early, so it felt like the right time to slip away before any awkward explanations. Not that he would say anything. I doubted he'd dare consider it his business, but some things were best kept private. I didn't want to disrupt the group dynamic, but hand on heart, the guilt was eating me alive. Because, despite everything, it felt like I was betraying the reason I came here in the first place—to search for Lucas.

The next three days were uneventful. I shared my theory about the story in the book. June matched my enthusiasm and read the text several times, while Mitch stayed firmly on Nick's skeptical side.

After sleeping on it, *literally*, I began to doubt the connections I had made. But the more I reread the story, the more convinced I became that I was right. The Harvest Moon, the string of disappearances, and the symbol all fit the sinister pattern we were chasing. Yet everyone carefully avoided saying the word "sacrifice," even though the book spelled it out clearly.

The four of us trekked to the spot Nick and I had discovered off the hiking trail, where the symbol had marred the bark of a tree.

Dread coiled in my stomach with every step. I didn't want to go back, not to the engraved eye, not to the deer's hollowed-out corpse, not to the twisting paths that had almost devoured us last time. My earlier resolve, so firm when we were planning this, dissolved the moment we stepped into the forest. The fear of getting lost again gnawed at me, the thought of wandering in circles, never finding our way out, tightening around my throat like a noose.

But Mitchell's skepticism steadied my nerves. His doubt, his rational explanations, his insistence that there had to be another answer. It kept the fear from fully taking hold. I clung to it, even as unease prickled at the back of my neck.

"Here, we turned here," Nick said, sounding sure, as he veered off the trail into the dense woods. Time ticked by. Minutes, then half an hour.

Nick halted suddenly. "This isn't right."

Mitch glanced at the compass on his watch. "What?"

"We should've found it by now."

"Maybe we got off track?" June suggested.

Nick rubbed the back of his neck. "Maybe."

We retraced our steps to the trail and tried again.

And again.

Nothing.

We couldn't find the tree at all. It felt like déjà vu—the same confusion Nick and I had faced last time—but this time it wasn't surreal. Instead of circling endlessly, we were simply failing to find what we were looking for.

"Are you sure it was there?" Mitch asked.

"Yeah," Nick replied. "I'm certain. I remember this." He gestured toward the scenery, then let his arm drop, his eyes scanning the trees as if willing the symbol to appear.

Mitch turned to me for confirmation. I shrugged. I'd never been good at finding my way in the woods. All trees look the same to me.

After a couple more attempts, we were wet, sweaty, irritated, hangry, and eaten alive by mosquitoes, with no choice but to turn back.

When we finally trudged back to the cabin, drained and defeated, Mitch had another task lined up for Nick and me. He wanted us to dig deeper, find more references to the legend I'd uncovered and look for any potential ties to religious groups or secret societies—*anything that felt hinky*, as he put it. Mitchell himself opted out of the research, claiming he was more of an 'action man,' leaving Nick and me to sift through the details. June, to her disappointment, was told to stay put until further orders. She wandered the cabin like a restless ghost, snapping at everyone.

Nick and I spent hours in the house, poring over articles and old forums on our laptops. The legend, however, seemed frustratingly local. Neither of us could find anything even remotely similar to it.

"It's like it was made up," I said, exasperated.

"Most stuff is," Nick replied.

WHEN WE WORKED, Nick remained focused and composed, fully absorbed in whatever he was reading. But when we could, we would sneak out to fool around.

"Seriously, guys, no more going out after dark," Mitchell admonished, his tone that of a scolding father. "I thought we agreed you'd be doing the research."

"We were just driving around," I said. Being trapped in the cabin had begun to feel oppressive, even with our separate spaces to escape to.

"Find anything?" Mitch asked.

"Nope," Nick said, offering nothing more.

What we eventually found was a good spot to park the car, though maneuvering in the front seats proved tricky. But we managed.

I felt infinitely guilty about our hidden rendezvous with Nick, yet I couldn't bring myself to end it. It had become my little refuge of intimacy.

And to be fair, I was enjoying it way too much—not just the sex, but being with him. Nick would drop random biology facts into conversation, always in some quirky context, and somehow he made even the dorkiest comments seem hot. And most importantly, he made me feel seen, like I mattered—the first time in years.

But was I losing myself in this hookup? Was it even a hookup anymore?

Whatever it was between Nick and me, it was gentle. There was something about his presence that calmed me, quieted all the voices in my head—Lucas's, my mother's, my own. At times, the experience felt almost spiritual. It gave me, more than anything else, peace.

But I didn't let myself think too far in that direction. This wasn't the time or place.

I shut down all the "what ifs" and "what happens after," because no matter how strong our connection felt, our lives were miles apart, literally and figuratively. The age gap was only four or five years, but at this stage, it felt like a canyon. He seemed grounded and established, *like a real adult*. I was still stumbling through the dark, trying to figure out who I was.

Meanwhile, June had grown bored and irritable. She gave me grief for not spending enough time with her and was tired of her brother's constant supervision.

"Weren't we supposed to be buddies?" she'd whine whenever Nick and I slipped away.

The guilt hit hard. My mother was right. I was selfish.

When June asked why we couldn't hang out, just the two of us, I'd say, "You know why. It's safer with Mitchell or Nick. And you don't want to go with Nick."

It was true. But the excuse still made me feel awful.

"Yeah, well, it sucks," June retorted, arms crossed. "You're always with Nick."

All she wanted was a friend. And I was a bad one.

. . .

THE PAST COUPLE of days had been dry and warm, and my body was craving physical activity. I also yearned for some alone time, which seemed impossible in the bustling house.

The contrast between my pre-trip solitude and my current social whirlwind was jarring. I loved being around people, but it also drained me.

"Where you headed?" Mitch asked.

"Just for a jog. I won't go far." I waved him off.

A short, mile-long trail behind the house beckoned. It had been ages since I'd last run, and my muscles ached for the release.

"Where's Nick?" Mitch asked, scanning the living room, where June sat on the couch, glued to her phone.

"I didn't see him."

"He went out," June said.

"Where?"

"I'm not his babysitter."

Mitch glanced out the window and spotted both cars in the driveway. Just then, a figure stepped out from behind the trees.

"Probably making a call," Mitch said, turning back to me. "Want me to come with?"

"Nah, it's just a jog. I won't be long."

He didn't press. Since his outburst, Mitch had been on his best behavior, and we'd all taken advantage of it, sometimes bending the buddy system rules.

The trail led me right to Nick. It wasn't intentional. The path just happened to end where he stood. He didn't see me at first, his back turned, phone pressed to his ear.

"It's best if you do it in person. Please," he said, pacing a short line in the dirt with his boot.

I couldn't hear the reply, but Nick answered, "Just do it. I'll take care of the rest."

I approached from the side and cleared my throat to let him

know I was there. He glanced over and raised a finger, signaling me to wait while he finished.

"Hey," I said softly when he hung up.

He pulled me into a hug, arms around my waist.

"Everything alright?" I asked.

"Yeah." His thumb traced small circles on my shirt. "Just some shipment issues. You know how it is."

I didn't, but I nodded anyway.

"Why are you out here?" he asked.

"Just going for a jog."

He raised a brow. "You sure?" His hands slipped under my T-shirt. "I can think of better things."

"You know they can see us from the house, right?" I laughed, stepping away to maintain some distance. "I'll stop by later."

"You know where to find me."

And that's exactly how the evening unfolded.

THE NEXT MORNING, we settled into our usual routine: breakfast before going for another hike into the woods. A couple of dry days had brought some relief, and we hoped for a less strenuous trek.

The sound of tires crunching over gravel broke through my morning haze. I dropped my half-eaten toast.

"Someone's here!" I blurted, unnecessarily.

We stilled, listening.

The engine hummed, gravel shifted, and then the vehicle stopped just outside.

June rushed to the window. Nick rose silently, moving toward the door.

Mitchell was a picture of calm control, gun in hand. He flicked off the safety with a quick thumb press and checked the chamber.

"Is that—" My voice faltered as Mitchell strode to the window, weapon at his side, posture steely and ready.

"Who is it?" June whispered.

"Can't tell yet," her brother said, voice tight, and then ordered her, "Go back to your room."

June obeyed but lingered on the staircase, peeking through the banister posts.

A knock rang out, playful, almost musical. It landed wrong, like a happy jingle in the middle of a horror movie. Mitchell peeked through the curtain again, muttering, "What the fuck?" just before Nick reached for the door and opened it.

24

Chapter Twenty-Four

September, 2020

TILLY STEPPED IN, immediately filling the space with her voluminous presence. Her perfume, not unpleasant but intense, rushed in with her arrival. I felt somewhat relieved that it was her. She was too open about her presence, and her twisted nature felt too exaggerated to be real. But there was something about her that kept me on edge, and I couldn't quite explain why I disliked her so much. Was it her strange attention to Nick? Even now, her eyes went to him first, as if he were the only one she had come to see.

"What are you doing here?" I asked.

"How'd you find us?" Mitchell interrupted, making it clear he wasn't playing along with the witch's games.

"Oh, like it was hard?" The woman smiled and winked at me. I squinted, unable to contain my disdain. She chuckled and moved into the living room. "A little birdie told me. But no worries, darlings, I ain't meanin' ya no harm." She pointed at the gun in Mitch's hand, "Why, this here ain't no way to greet a lady who comes in peace."

"What are you doing here?" Mitchell repeated my question, still holding his gun up.

"Put that thing down, would ya?" she said, approaching him with ease and gently resting her hand on the weapon as if it were a mere trinket.

Mitchell clicked the safety back on.

"Are you outta your mind?" he retorted, swiftly holstering the gun, his face flushing for some reason, a deep red rushing to his cheeks.

Was Mathilda making him nervous?

"I can ask you the same," she sang in a husky voice, "Aren't you here huntin' ghosts? Chasin' the devil?"

"What do you want?" Nick pushed.

Mathilda gifted him a warm, sultry glance and moved closer, her hand reaching out to rest on his shoulder. "To help you, of course," she declared. "You came to me for help, and here I am."

"What kind of help are we talking about, exactly?" Mitchell asked.

The woman settled into a chair in one fluid, deliberate motion. "I know what you're looking for," she said, a hint of amusement dancing in her eyes, "and I'm here to tell you where it is." She placed her purse on the table.

"That's a pretty big change from what you said last time we talked."

"Let's say my interests–" she paused, glancing at us one by one, as if for effect, "shifted."

June snorted from the staircase. Mathilda drank her in.

"Before, I thought it best you left. For your own safety, of course. But now, why not let the kids play? Right?" She tilted her head toward Nick, eyes twinkling with amusement.

I studied the woman carefully as she sat across from us, taking in her dramatic makeup and ostentatious jewelry. She had a flair for the theatrical, but she wasn't uninteresting. What bothered me was the way she was eyeing Nick, like they shared a secret no one else was privy to.

"What'cha got?" Mitchell asked with skepticism.

"Not so fast, darling," Mathilda turned to him, lifting a hand to stop him. "First, my terms."

"Here we go," Mitchell rolled his eyes, crossing his arms over his chest. "Always gotta be catch."

I weighed the possibilities. Did she want money? Gemstones? Firearms? A drug cartel's cocaine stash? Dirt from the graveyard? Some kind of magical tool?

Four pairs of eyes locked on her, waiting. Mathilda's red lips curled into a satisfied smile.

She had us hooked.

"Nothin' much. Normal stuff," Tilly said with a gentle smile. "Make sure to bring me the grimoire."

"The one from that crazy story?" June asked in disbelief and stepped down a few stairs.

"Just because it sounds crazy don't mean it ain't true," Mathilda replied, her innocent smile undercut by the mischief in her eyes.

Mitchell shook his head and turned away, his whole body shifting in dismissal. The witch sounded out of her mind. Nick was the only one who stayed calm, not even raising an eyebrow at Mathilda's nonsense.

"What if it doesn't exist?" Mitch asked.

She didn't so much as blink. "It does."

"What if it's not where you say it is?"

"Then you keep lookin' until you find it." Her full red lips stayed curled in amusement, but her eyes had hardened. She was serious.

"If it's real," June said carefully, "then why does everyone know about it? Why isn't it a secret?"

The witch turned to her, tilting her head slightly. A trace of condescension colored her voice. "Honey, the best way to keep a secret is to make it sound like a tall tale."

I looked at Mitch, his face turned away from the witch, brows furrowed in thought. He was likely weighing the risks against the potential gain of the grimoire. The truth was, if it was real, we didn't care about it. Having some answers would suffice for me.

Having come to some kind of decision, Mitchell said, "Alright, you got yourself a deal, lady. Now, what have you got for us?"

"I'll tell you how to get there," Mathilda said.

"Get where?" Mitch, June, and I asked in unison. I'd been trying to stay out of the conversation, but curiosity got the better of me.

Nick's "What's there?" came a beat later.

Mathilda's smile remained enigmatic. "You'll have to go and see for yourself."

June rolled her eyes.

Had Mathilda known about our search in the woods? Had she followed us? Or worse, had someone been watching us the entire time? My pulse jumped. I forced myself to take a slow, deliberate breath, trying to calm the sudden rush of fear. It was ironic. Out there, in the woods, the isolation tricked you into feeling safe, like you'd spot anyone lurking behind a tree. But now, I saw how naïve that was. The only ones easy to spot were us. We should have been more careful.

"So?" Nick pressed, finally speaking up.

Mathilda's playfulness faded. When she spoke again, her voice was measured, almost rehearsed.

"Walk with purpose. Don't think about anythin' but the mark. Once you see it, feed it with blood. Walk straight ahead and cross the bridge. On your way out, do not look back. I'll say it again: don't you dare look back, no matter what you hear... or think you hear."

June raised an eyebrow in exaggerated disbelief. I knew exactly what she thought of the witch's cryptic instructions. Mitchell blinked, like he couldn't believe what he'd just heard.

"That's it?" he asked. "Spill some blood, cross the bridge? Fantastic."

"Trust me, that's all you need to know to find it," she cautioned. "But once you do, don't forget what you promised me."

"Well, thanks for your help," Mitch said, moving to the door and opening it for Mathilda. She rose from her seat, her stride confident. Just before she stepped out, she turned back to us.

"And one more thing. If I were you, I wouldn't go flashin' those photos around."

Mitch's gaze narrowed. "Which ones?"

"Any of 'em. Especially the ones with the sigil."

"Si-what?" he shook his head, "Why? What's up with that?"

Mathilda was satisfied with his confusion. "Wouldn't you like to know, handsome?" she teased, then disappeared out the door.

The engine roared to life, followed by the crunch of tires over gravel.

"We gotta spill blood? What the hell?" June said, half-laughing, half-intrigued. "Is this like a ritual or something?"

Nick shrugged.

"Should we write it down?" I asked, though I already knew Mathilda was either crazy or messing with us.

"I remembered it," Mitchell said grimly.

"Are we gonna go there?" June asked, looking as if she was ready to perform a blood rite imminently.

I couldn't blame her for being excited. After days of hitting dead ends, suddenly we had something. Even if it was a little unhinged.

"We definitely should," Nick said and then turned to me, as if seeking validation. "It is worth checking out, right?"

I shrugged. It wasn't just up to me.

"Right," Mitchell said. "But something doesn't feel right about her just showing up and giving us the… instructions."

June hurried us along. "Well, she's nuts, so whatever. Let's just go!"

Mitchell didn't respond. Instead, he crossed the room, grabbed his gun from the counter, and holstered it.

"All this time, you had a gun?" I burst out, finally remembering to confront him. I'd been too scared before, then too distracted by Mathilda's sudden appearance, until now.

Mitchell didn't even flinch. "I'm licensed to carry."

"You could've warned me there was a firearm in my car!"

"Sorry 'bout that," he said, barely looking up.

"Not only did you lie to me, but you didn't tell the Sheriff when he stopped us. What if he'd decided to search us?"

"Hardly ever happens," he muttered, already gathering his stuff like the conversation was over.

I looked at June for support, but she raised her hands in a 'leave-me-out-of-it' motion.

I seethed inwardly, resenting the fact that after everything, he hadn't been upfront with me. That whole "ask forgiveness, not permission" mindset—my dad had it, so did Lucas, and now Mitchell.

But then again, who was I to judge? My own history with honesty wasn't spotless. And neither was Nick's.

So I made a conscious decision to let it go.

Not because I was okay with it, but because, right now, having a gun felt less like a problem and more like a necessity.

AFTER A LONG TRUDGE, we turned at the three peaks, just as we had several times before. I wondered if Nick, lost in his usual quiet focus, was picturing the sigil carved into the tree—the one only we had seen on that first hike—or if he had dismissed the witch's instructions entirely.

I hadn't. I couldn't. The image squirmed and stretched inside my mind, not as a memory but as something alive, something pushing against my thoughts, warping them. The more I tried to focus on anything else, the more it took over, so vivid I sometimes thought I saw it etched into the trees around me. Then it would vanish, only to keep haunting my thoughts.

That's when it appeared.

The tree stood exactly where it had before, its bark split open by those same impossible carvings. Only there were no dead deer at its roots, no scraps of fur, no bones left behind. Either scavengers had stripped it clean, or there'd never been a carcass.

Nick exhaled audibly behind me. No one moved closer.

"This the place?" Mitch broke the silence, and I realized how quiet it had been—no birds, no wind, nothing.

"So..." June said, looking at us each in turn, "who's donating blood?"

If anything, I knew for sure it wasn't going to be me. I was terrified of needles and anything sharp. No one else rushed to volunteer either.

"Let there be blood," Nick muttered resignedly, retrieving a pocket knife from his backpack. After a quick disinfecting ritual with an alcohol wipe, he rolled up the sleeve of his left arm, revealing the pale skin beneath. He positioned the blade over his forearm, where a sliver of skin remained bare from ink, hesitated, then dragged the keen edge across. Blood welled instantly, shiny and thick. It dripped down his arm, pooling in his palm before spilling over his fingers and into the earth. He trembled slightly as he reached up. The symbol, carved into the tree's bark, was high—a stretch for anyone. Nick pressed his blood-slicked palm against the carving, the dark streaks of blood coating the jagged lines of the sigil.

I looked away, nausea rising, but when I turned back, it was done. Nick smeared the last of his blood over the deformed lines as if to seal them in. The mark was vivid and wet, the sigil pulsing with the blood that stained it.

"He's nuts," June gasped, her eyes big and round, but clearly enthralled.

"Hope your tetanus shot is up to date," I murmured.

After Nick tended to his own wound, meticulously cleaning and bandaging it himself using the supplies from Mitchell's first-aid kit, we proceeded further.

We walked for at least half an hour before reaching the bridge Tilly had mentioned, a rickety and worn structure. We crossed it one by one, the creaking and tilting unsettling, but somehow, against all odds, it held.

After a while, June announced, "I gotta pee," and disappeared behind the trees.

"Nell will go with you!" her brother exclaimed, shooting me a look. I'd started to follow, but June spun around.

"No way!" she shouted, taking off faster.

"Don't go too far!" Mitchell warned.

"I'll go wherever I'm comfortable!" she yelled from afar.

We stood waiting, all of us tired.

"This is insane," Mitchell said. "She just sent us off into the woods without any specific details. No coordinates, nothing. 'Take five steps from the tallest tree'—what a fucking jo—"

"AAAH!"

June's scream, high-pitched and prolonged, sliced through the air and then vanished. It wasn't the kind that slips out after tripping over a hidden stone—it was the kind that calls for help.

Mitchell's eyes went wide, and he took off toward the sound. Nick and I followed, but instead of the chaos we'd expected, June stood calmly, her finger jabbed at a tree.

"What the heck is this?" she asked.

The same symbol we'd seen before was carved into the

trunk, relatively high up, and hard to see unless you stood directly beneath it.

"What do you think it means?" June's voice was trembling.

"Means we're close," her brother said, then turned to her with a stern warning. "No more running off. And no unnecessary screaming."

We walked a bit further, carefully checking all the trees, and it wasn't too long before we saw another symbol.

Nick suddenly turned left.

"Where are you going?" Mitchell was perplexed.

"I don't think they're showing us the way. I think they're shielding it."

We all followed him, and he was right. Soon, the trees gave way to a clearing.

"Is this...it?" June asked.

There was a large structure resembling a shed on one side of the clearing, and a massive stone across from it.

"I guess," Mitchell said.

"What's inside?" his sister was already tugging at the door. But it was secured with a metal deadbolt and a padlock.

"No way we're breaking in without leaving a trace," Mitchell asserted.

"Who cares?" June said dismissively.

"We don't know who might care. That's the whole point."

"What if the grimoire is in there?" June asked, pressing her face against the wooden panels to get a glimpse inside.

"I doubt that," Mitch said, but walked along the wall of the shed regardless.

June knocked on the door and listened for a response. None came.

The sudden appearance of a man-made structure in the woods unsettled me, like stumbling upon a witch's house. My whole body tensed, half-expecting someone to step out from behind the trees. Someone who had probably been watching us all along.

June was already by the big stone.

"Looks like an altar," I cringed.

"That's creepy," the girl agreed.

I noticed something on the stone and leaned in to see better. A dull, reddish-brown discoloration nestled in the crease of the facade.

"Is this...blood?" Mitchell leaned over next to me and picked the stain with his nail.

"Now, *that* is creepy," June repeated, drawing out each word like it left a bad taste.

Her brother pulled out a ziplock bag and a knife from his backpack. Like a detective from a movie, he carefully scraped some of the blood into the bag and sealed it. Then, he folded it neatly and tucked it away.

"Okay, well. At least we know the location now. And we can keep an eye on it," I said.

"It's a bit of a walk to keep an eye on it. But we should come back before the full moon and see if anyone else shows up," Mitchell suggested.

We explored further and confirmed that the clearing was indeed surrounded by the carvings in the trees, enclosing the place in a circle.

"You said they were protecting something? What?" Mitch asked Nick.

"I've no idea."

"How did you know that?"

"Just a guess. We should get back. It's going to get dark soon."

But darkness fell earlier than expected, as rain crept in and shrouded the woods. Mitchell rummaged through his backpack and produced a raincoat, handing it to his sister without hesitation. Walking through the woods, trying to outrun the encroaching gloom, felt deeply unsettling. I kept sensing someone's eyes on our backs, and despite Mathilda's warnings, glanced back a few times—only to see the dismal trees looming behind us.

Though the feeling persisted, I kept it to myself, fearing that speaking aloud would only make things worse and that the nightmare inside my head might spill into the world around us.

In the car, June asked, "Do you think Amanda was there? In that shed?"

Mitchell kept his eyes on the road. "I don't know," he said.

"Maybe it was her blood on that stone."

"I don't know, Junie," her brother sighed.

The darkness in my head stretched, whispering that it could have been Lucas's, too.

I closed my eyes and silently pleaded it wasn't.

Chapter Twenty-Five

September, 2020

"I'M STILL TRYING to wrap my head around it." Mitchell, like the rest of us, was struggling to put the pieces together. "So you think it's some kind of cult or something?"

"Possibly," Nick said half-heartedly, his attention riveted to the laptop screen.

We'd gathered in the living room after dinner, wide awake despite the late hour, thanks to Mitch's insistence on a group discussion. June lolled on the couch, her elbow digging into the armrest, her head resting in her hand. I sat opposite her, mirroring her pose, my eyelids heavy with fatigue.

"And they're out there worshipping *something* in the woods?" Her brother paced the room.

Nick grunted a brief, "I guess", still deeply engrossed in his reading.

Mitchell halted in his tracks. "And what's with the blood? Is this some kinda twisted self-hypnosis deal?"

"Maybe it's magic," June said behind a yawn.

Nick shot her a disapproving look over the rim of his laptop.

Mitchell, ever the skeptic, rubbed the back of his neck. His years of military service had occasionally brought him into contact with weird stories. Still, as he said himself, he had never encountered anything that couldn't be explained by logic and reason.

"Let's think about it," he suggested, "If it walks like a duck and quacks like a duck, it must be a duck."

"So?" June said with a heavy sigh. "What kind of fucked up duck is that?"

That was a good question—one I'd been asking myself, too. What would drive people to vanish, make blood rituals effective, and inspire that kind of terror?

"If that's just a cult," I asked, "why was the Reverend scared of the symbol?"

"He wasn't scared of the symbol." Nick closed his laptop, either not finding what he was looking for or giving up altogether. "He was scared of what's behind it."

Mitchell chuckled. "Like what? A demon or something?"

Nick got up without a word, and at first, I thought he was leaving the conversation, fed up with Mitchell's skepticism. But he returned, napkin and pen in hand. He clicked the pen a few times, then drew two perpendicular lines on the crumpled square of paper.

We all watched, holding our collective breath, as if Nick had taken it upon himself to perform magic tricks to convince us.

He held the drawing up and asked, "What do you see?"

June scrutinized the piece. "It's just a cross," she replied dismissively.

"And what does it mean to you?"

The girl shrugged. "I dunno... Jesus?"

"God?" I added.

"We see a symbol and we give it meaning," Nick pointed at the cross on his paper. "Or we have an idea and we give it a form. And then it shapes our thoughts further, gathers power as more people believe it, protect it, kill for it, even."

June was fidgeting uncomfortably.

"Are you talking about crusades?" I asked.

"That's one example," Nick put the paper back on the table. "Symbols help channel belief. Focus intent. If enough people believe in the power of a sigil, it becomes something more."

"It's just a drawing," June winced.

"You're right. And yet, it holds immense power because people believe in it. It represents something greater than itself. Faith, hope, salvation. But also, the Crusades, the Inquisition, the witch hunts—all carried out under the banner of this symbol." Nick tapped the napkin for emphasis.

Mitchell shot a careful look at June before speaking. "It's not the symbol itself that's the problem, it's the people wielding it, right?"

Nick snapped his fingers. "Bingo. People give it power. They believe in it and invest energy in it. But it's just an intermediary. It absorbs this energy and gives it to whoever's behind it."

Mitch rubbed his chin, still skeptical. "I see your point, but—"

Nick cut in, "Think about it: a cross, a swastika, even the golden arches of McDonald's, or any famous brand logo. Aren't they sigils? People invest in them with meaning because they believe in what they represent. They hold power because we give it to them."

"I don't get it." June shook her head. "Are we looking for, like, a demon or a person of flesh and blood?"

"It's just some voodoo crap to scare us off. We're dealing with a person, and we will find him." Mitchell said.

"Or her," his sister interjected. "Women can be killers, too."

"Well, they—he or she—are not a serial killer. They have a plan, a ritual, a tradition. Instructions they follow." Nick said.

I snapped out of my trance, realizing I'd been staring blankly at the napkin without blinking.

June frowned. "So we're supposed to just buy into all this occult crap now?"

"This *occult crap*, as you call it, has cost many people, including your sister, their lives," Nick said in a patronizing tone. "In occultism, there's the concept of the egregore, a collective thought or shared belief that brings something into being. So—"

"Oh, and you're suddenly an expert?" Mitchell scoffed.

"Didn't you tell us to do our research on it?" Nick snapped, his patience wavering.

"I didn't think you'd actually fall for that crap!"

"What do *you* believe in, Mitch?" Nick asked, voice as cold as a tomb. "You think you can take them down with a gun and some tough talk? Risk everyone's life, including June's, just to prove a point?"

June stepped in, cutting off the brewing argument. "What do you think is going on there?" She turned the question on her brother, giving him a chance not just to tear apart Nick's theory but to offer one of his own. It was unexpectedly mature of her.

Mitchell let out a sigh. "I think it's a bunch of crazy serial killers. Like a cult or something, like you said. But I don't buy into all this voodoo crap. Someone, maybe even that so-called witch, is trying to make us believe it's magic. But it's not."

Nick slowly shook his head.

Mitch reddened with frustration. "So how's this magic stuff supposed to work?"

"These people aren't crazy," Nick said calmly, "They have an agenda. They're too organized for this to be random. The question is—what's their endgame? If this is all real, and if that book June grabbed actually means more than meets the eye, then maybe they're getting something in return for these sacrifices."

Mitchell's jaw clenched and unclenched as he shifted his weight from one leg to the other. June and I held our breath, bracing for an outburst. But then, something seemed to click. His face smoothed out, his breathing slowed, and he scratched the back of his head in a deliberate gesture.

"Alright, that's enough guesswork for tonight," he said. "Let's just go to bed and regroup in the morning."

He grabbed his backpack and hastily exited the room, avoiding eye contact with anyone.

As June quietly followed her brother, I turned to Nick. "Are you alright?"

"Yeah." He rubbed the bridge of his nose. "Just need to rest."

I nodded, taking the hint, and headed to my room.

The world seemed to have slipped out of alignment. The image of Nick's blade slicing into his arm, the blood welling up like a dark flower, and the way he smeared it onto the symbol with an unnerving calmness. Did Nick genuinely believe in all these supernatural things?

And what about me? What did I believe in? Growing up without religion, I'd never felt the need to define my own beliefs. Lucas's superstitions and trinkets had seemed like harmless quirks, but now I realized I'd never examined my own convictions. What did I truly stand for, or did I default to the beliefs of others, a mirror reflecting the views of those I gravitated toward?

A WIND-CHIME-LIKE BELL hung from a tree branch by the cabin, its frantic song shuddering through the night like a banshee's cry. The rain had swelled into a raging storm, branches cracking and snapping as the darkness itself seemed to be shifting and moving. I counted the seconds until the window would shatter and something unholy would crawl through. But in the end, exhaustion claimed me before anything else could.

Later, I woke to a strange, lingering anxiety and lay still, straining to pinpoint its source. Gradually, it dawned on me: the absence of sound. The night was eerily quiet. I couldn't recall if previous nights had been so still.

The small porch light cast a faint glow through my window, but it barely pierced the darkness that enveloped the world. I got up and headed out. Sitting on the stairs, I peered into the void, daring the night to show its true face.

The cabin door creaked behind me. It wasn't Nick.

"I saw you from my window," June said, settling beside me on the stairs. She was wrapped in a Halloween-themed hoodie, cheeks puffy with sleep.

"Yeah, couldn't sleep," I replied softly.

We sat in silence until she spoke up.

"I just can't believe Amanda came here of her own free will. Do you think she was tricked or something?"

I shrugged.

"And Lucas? Did he ever mention anything special about this town?"

"Nope."

Lucas had told me many scary stories about Appalachia, but they were just folklore, local legends, and spooky tales meant to thrill children. Yet, he kept secrets—his lies about his whereabouts, his sudden visit to Black Water right before his disappearance.

"It's so quiet here," June murmured, almost to herself. "Spooky. Reminds me of home."

I listened, hesitant to interrupt her.

"It always seemed quieter before he lashed out at us," she continued, "Like, it was in the air. Quiet and dangerous."

"Your father?" I ventured.

June nodded. "He did something bad to Amanda. We all knew. Mom knew. And no one did anything about it."

I waited for her to elaborate, but she remained silent. And then, the pieces fell into place. The abuse, the support group, the isolation, and Amanda's estrangement.

June's voice dropped to a whisper. "And then he killed Mom, too."

I didn't know what to say, so I acted on instinct, reaching out to hold her tight. For once, she didn't resist.

It seemed like Amanda had quite a few secrets of her own, something she never talked to her siblings about.

But then again, secrets were a burden we all carried.

IN THE MORNING, June was back to her usual self, grumbling through her routine, the vulnerability she'd shown the night before nowhere to be seen. Nick still hadn't emerged from his room when the siblings headed out for groceries.

I brewed a fresh pot of coffee and began scrolling through my phone. My mom had texted, asking where I was. I replied vaguely, saying I was still on a trip with friends. We hadn't spoken since our last call, right after Nick and I went into the woods, and now her texts felt suspiciously neutral. But I knew she was holding onto her irritation, saving it for when I walked through the door.

Nick shuffled into the kitchen, bleary-eyed, distracting me from my phone.

"Morning. Coffee?" I asked, holding up a mug.

"Yes, please," he replied, taking stock of the space. "Where's the dynamic duo?"

"Grocery shopping."

I handed him the mug, but instead of taking it, he set it aside and pulled me into a kiss. The suddenness of it stole my breath, though I didn't hesitate. My hands slid up his chest as he stepped closer, his mouth warm, insistent. In one fluid motion, he lifted me onto the counter, fitting himself between my knees, his grip firm at the backs of my thighs, holding me in place.

We pressed into each other, and I kissed him like I meant it. But even then, with his hands on my skin and his lips against mine, something felt off. There was a quiet ache threaded through it, like chasing the shape of a memory that's already slipping away.

"I fucking knew it," June said from the doorway.

I hastily pushed Nick away and jumped off the counter, as if I could undo what had just happened and erase what June had witnessed.

She grabbed her wallet and stormed out without a word.

"Shit," I muttered, pressing the backs of my hands to my burning cheeks.

"They won't care," Nick assured me.

But of course, they would. We'd been searching for my missing boyfriend together, and now I'd hooked up with someone else right under their noses. A part of me tried to justify it—two years was a long time, after all—but it was the way it happened that made it hurtful. We had actively lied about it.

Nick tried to comfort me with a hug, but I pulled away.

"What is it?" he asked.

"It's... everything!" I exclaimed, my voice trembling. "We really messed up. We shouldn't have been sneaking around. We shouldn't have done it at all."

Nick's eyes narrowed. "What are you saying? You regret it?"

I nodded, the word tumbling out before I could soften it. "Yes!"

Nick's expression turned cold. "Good to know," he mumbled before turning and leaving for his room.

"N-Nick, that's not—" I started, but his door closed before I could finish.

"Shit."

And there I was, alone once more.

LUNCH WAS A PRESSURE COOKER, tension crackling like electricity. Mitchell, the only one oblivious to what had happened, was trying to discuss matters as usual. But the rest of us were trapped in an uncomfortable silence. Guilt swirled in my stomach like a snake as I picked at my food, my appetite gone. I prayed to disappear into thin air.

June sulked, her stare pinned to her plate as she ate mechanically, occasionally shooting accusatory glances at Nick and me. Nick, however, refused to meet her eyes—or mine, for that matter. Earlier, he'd exchanged a few words with Mitchell, but he and I hadn't had a chance to talk.

"Pasta's good," Mitchell said to me.

I forced a weak smile. We'd been living off pasta every day because no one had the energy for real cooking.

Mitch let out a heavy sigh and put his fork down.

"Alright, what the hell is going on? Why are you all acting so weird?"

June's gaze darted between Nick and me. I looked down at the cold food on my plate. Finally, unable to contain herself, the girl blurted, "Nellie and Nick were kissing in the kitchen!"

Mitchell paused mid-chew and let out a low, amused chuckle, clearly thinking June was joking. But then our tense silence registered, and his expression faltered as he realized she was serious.

After a beat, he said, "It's none of your business," and went back to eating, seemingly unfazed.

"Whatever," June muttered, rolling her eyes.

A lump formed in my throat. "Excuse me," I choked out, getting up and heading for the door. Once inside my room, I sank onto the bed and let the tears come.

THE NEXT DAY, Nick and I still hadn't talked, and it felt like everything was unraveling. Mitchell tried to give out tasks, pretending nothing had changed, but no one followed through. All I could think of was that my mother was right. I was self-centered and irresponsible, always thinking about my own good. And that's precisely why I was better off alone.

However, despite Mitchell's attempts to smooth things out, the situation only worsened. June was still moody and agitated. She sat straight as a stick in the armchair. Nick was holding a book, as if hiding behind it. I was nervously toying with my phone.

"I've been thinking on what you said," Mitchell threw a careful look at Nick, who lifted his eyes from the book without a hint of surprise, as if he'd always known he was right. "And maybe it's time we broaden our scope a bit."

He checked we were all paying attention, and then continued.

"What about that book June borrowed?" he turned to me. "You find anything else useful in it?"

I cringed internally at his attempt to include me; it was so poorly veiled. He kept trying to diffuse the tension, but it wasn't working.

"No, but I also think we're in over our heads," I replied, unsure where my thoughts were leading. "Maybe we need to step back a bit."

"Easy for you to say," June crossed her arms, her voice pure poison. "You've got your replacement boyfriend there. But I don't think a replacement sister is an option for me."

"Hey!" Nick snapped, slamming his book shut. "Cut it, June."

"You two started it!"

"Enough," Mitchell intervened, rising from his seat to position himself between them. "If this is gonna be a problem, we need to rethink our approach. We're this close," he pinched his thumb and index finger together, "to finding out what happened to Amanda, Lucas, and Nick's Mom."

The mention of Lucas's name hit me like a slap. I had been betraying him all along. I didn't even know if he was actually dead, yet I'd been acting like it didn't matter.

"I'm not staying," I blurted, the words escaping before I could reel them back in. But the thought had been simmering in my head all day. There was no point in staying. I would only make things worse. Thankfully, we still had the rental car, sparing us the awkwardness of a tense ride together.

"Nellie," Mitch called me in a soft voice.

"No. I've thought about it." I stood, resolute. "I found what I was looking for. There's a reason for Lucas's disappearance, but nothing we could take to the police. At some point, we need to accept what's happened and move on."

"If it's about what June said," he hesitated, "then it's nothing. I mean, that's your personal business, and June and I will stay out of it. Right, June?" He gave his sister a stern glance.

"Great," June scoffed. "So, you got yourself a new boyfriend, and now you're done with us. And I'm somehow at fault?"

I stared at her for a few seconds and slowly shook my head. "This isn't about that," I said, trying to keep my frustration in check. "It's about facing reality. I'm sorry about your sister, June, but I'm leaving in the morning. You guys can stay and do what you need to do."

"We're just five days shy of the full moon. You're really planning to take off?" Mitch said, trying to convince me.

"I am. And I'm sorry—for everything."

"Nothing to be sorry about," he threw his hands in an *I give up* gesture, finally letting it go.

It might look like I was running away, and maybe I was. I had backed myself into a corner, and the only way out was to leave. But it wasn't just about escaping the mess I'd made. This discomfort had shown me something I hadn't been ready to admit: I had to stop chasing ghosts. Besides, our search had taken a strange turn. The witches, the sigils, the grimoire, the woods with a life of their own. It was too much to take in and far from what we had expected to uncover.

Maybe it was time. Time to walk away from the search for

Lucas, the mystery that had consumed so much of my life. Time to stop clinging to the idea that finding out what happened to Lucas would finally let me move on. Chasing answers wouldn't change the past, and I couldn't keep risking everything for a chance at them. I had to let go. I had to do it now.

Nick stayed silent, re-immersed in his book, as if he hadn't even heard us.

It was time to close this chapter of my life.

Chapter Twenty-Six

September, 2020

"DROP ME OFF AT THE AIRPORT?"

To my surprise, Nick left with me in the morning. I hugged Mitch and June goodbye, but June was still frosty; her stiff posture and cold shoulder made that clear. We'd only known each other for a couple of weeks, but leaving felt bittersweet all the same.

I expected Mitchell to question why Nick was leaving, but he said nothing, his arms crossed over his chest. Nick definitely wasn't everyone's cup of tea, and he'd grown on me slowly, but Mitch and June had remained neutral to negative towards him. The four of us made a good team.

Until I went and ruined it all.

"Want me to drive?" Nick asked after we loaded our bags into the car.

I handed him the keys.

"I can't believe you're leaving too," I remarked. "You never found out what happened to your mother."

"Probably the same thing that happened to your boyfriend," Nick replied bluntly.

I gave up on trying to make conversation and turned away to look out of the window. I was sick of everyone being mad at me. Was I really such a screw-up? And if he was so upset, why had he tagged along at all?

My phone buzzed, and I jumped at the chance to distract myself. I'd talk to a telemarketer at this point, just to avoid the awkwardness with Nick. But when I saw my Mom's name on the screen, I hesitated before answering.

"You on your way?" her voice came through without a preamble.

"I am."

"What time are you getting in?"

"Around five?" I guessed. "I don't know. Depends on the traffic."

I had nowhere to go except my Mom's, which had been the plan all along. I could clear my head and figure out what to do next with my life. After this emotional rollercoaster, her place didn't seem like such a bad idea. At least with her, I knew what to expect. Stifling as it was, it felt almost comforting.

"Okay, just try to get in by five," she commanded with a note of skepticism, like she didn't believe I was actually on my way.

"What's the rush?" I asked, annoyed.

"I'm going to a birthday party. Diane's."

I had no idea who Diane was, so I guessed, "From work?"

"That's her. She's turning sixty."

"I have keys, so I can just let myself in if you need to leave."

"I want to be there to meet you," she insisted.

"I'll do my best, Mom. You're paying the speeding tickets, right?"

"It's not funny. Drive carefully."

"Sure thing. Hurry up but slow down," I quipped, trying to lighten the mood.

It was the wrong move. Mom hated my jokes, just like she hated Dad's. I had learned early that humor was my lifeline with her, a shield against the criticism she never seemed to run out of. If she insisted on treating me like a child, then that was fine. I would play the part.

"Your mom?" Nick asked after I hung up.

"Yeah, just checking in on me."

"That's good of her."

I bit my lip, tempted to tell him that my mom's niceness could be suffocating at times, but this wasn't the conversation I wanted to have with him right now. Instead, I gave a faint, noncommittal hum. Then, summoning all the courage I had in me, I broached the subject that had been weighing heavily on my mind.

"Hey, about before," I began tentatively. "Not that it matters to you now, but I just panicked. I never had any regrets about us. It was just... a wrong-place, wrong-time kind of situation."

I winced inwardly at how cheesy and lame it sounded, but I had to say something. It was time to start fixing things after ruining them for so long.

Nick threw a glance at me, then looked back at the road. "It's okay. But thanks for saying that."

"Did you?" I blurted out before I could stop myself.

He wavered briefly before shaking his head. "Did I what?"

"Did you have any regrets?"

Nick's response was immediate. "No, of course not."

A tiny weight lifted off my shoulders.

The airport terminal stood as a small, one-story building with low ceilings. As we pulled up to the drop-off lane, only one other car was there, dispatching a family of four with too much luggage.

"When's your flight?" I asked.

"Don't know. I'll buy the ticket now."

We exited the car, and he retrieved his bag from the trunk. We stood facing each other, unsure of what to say.

"Come with me," he said.

I almost thought I'd misheard him. "What?"

"Come with me," he repeated, placing his hands on my shoulders.

"I can't," I said simply, pointing at my car.

It wasn't just that I couldn't leave it here and hop on a plane with him; I had responsibilities to return to.

"Yeah, I've heard it before. *You've got to move on with your life* and all that. But you don't have to go to your mother's for that. You can do it anywhere. You know that, right?"

"I know. But going back to Minnesota feels like a step backward right now. And... I'm just not sure."

"About what?" he pressed.

I stayed silent.

"About me?" he asked.

"We've only just met," I said, though something in me curled back, already regretting it.

Was I making a mistake?

Luckily, common sense broke through.

"You're asking me to take off and move in with you? What if it doesn't work out? Where am I supposed to go then—back to my Mom's, where she'll be even more pissed at me? I need to figure things out on my own first."

He stepped back, fingers raking through his hair in frustration. It seemed like he might shut me out again, turn away and leave, but instead, he reached out, his hands wrapping gently around my elbows. For a fleeting moment, I felt like he was holding me together.

"I understand," he finally said, looking me in the eye, "Can I at least call you sometime?"

"Of course," I said, relieved, though part of me dreaded he meant long-distance.

Mitch once told me that soldiers often struggle to maintain friendships forged during service when they return to civilian life. It's hard to transplant a relationship from one world to another. The truth was, we barely knew each other outside the chaotic situation we'd shared over the past few weeks.

We hugged goodbye, and I watched him walk into the airport before driving off.

The lump in my throat faded soon after.

I ARRIVED home a little after six, setting foot in Cleveland for the first time since Spring. My mother had already left for the party.

I could've made it back earlier, but I stopped for a long lunch at a gas station with picnic tables out front, basking in the late September sun and easing myself back into solitude I hadn't felt in weeks.

Being alone felt strange, like hearing a voice and realizing it was only your own echo. But it was freeing too, the quiet kind of relief that comes with unhooking a too-tight bra after a long day.

Thinking of Nick made it sting a little.

Coming home felt like stepping back in time. Yet, everything seemed just a tad different. The house showed its age in ways I hadn't noticed until now: the faded patches on the upstairs carpet, the door knobs lacking shine. When Dad was alive, he took care of everything, and now that he was gone, Mom was probably struggling to keep up with the house on her own—or maybe she just didn't know how to. But despite all that, it still had a comforting sense of belonging.

The sunset's warm glow painted the faded wallpaper of my childhood bedroom a soft, pink hue. At first glance, everything looked just as I'd left it, but Mom had clearly been tidying up. My school notebooks were rearranged, and my clothes were out of place. I sat down on the bed, the same one I'd slept in a lifetime ago, when Dad was still alive, before Lucas entered the picture, and I still had my whole life ahead of me.

But there I was now: a twenty-three-year-old college dropout, moving back in with my mother, facing the loss of my independence and dreading the uncertainty of what came next.

And that was when it hit me, the same solitude I hadn't known what to do with before, crashing down all at once. It buried me beneath a heavy coat of despair and loss. I had absolutely no one here. My high school friends had drifted apart after we scattered to different colleges. Even though some of them stayed in Cleveland, after Lucas's disappearance, I hadn't been able to bring myself to reach out. Now, reconnecting would feel awkward, like trying to force something that had already slipped away.

I thought about Mitch and June back in West Virginia, tucked away in the cabin, and a wave of warmth filled my heart. What were they doing now?

Then there was Nick. A part of me wanted to reach for my phone and text him, but another part knew it would be pointless. Instead, I cried myself to sleep, silently promising that tomorrow, I would not indulge in self-pity.

I WOKE UP DISORIENTED, momentarily unsure of where I was before it came crashing back to me: my departure, Nick, my childhood room. I lay motionless for a minute, trying to understand how I felt and whether I was ready to tackle the day. After a solid ten hours of sleep, I was surprisingly refreshed, and for the first time in a while, optimistic about my future. Still in my pajamas—a faded teenage relic I'd found in the closet, a worn pair of shorts and a fitted top that seemed ridiculously childish now—I headed downstairs, following the inviting scent of coffee that filled the house. It was quiet, except for the gentle hum of the washer in the laundry room.

Mom was in the kitchen, folding dried clothes on the dining table. We hadn't seen each other the night before. I'd gone to bed early, depleted by the raw, unprocessed emotions and the long drive, and then lulled by the familiarity of my room. She'd probably gotten back home quite late after her friend's birthday party.

"Morning," I greeted her, focusing on the pile in front of her. Beyond the jumble of fabrics, patterns, and colors, I recognized my own clothes.

"Is this my shirt?" I asked, coming closer. "Are these my clothes?"

"I thought you'd like them cleaned," Mom sounded offended, as if I was accusing her of a crime she hadn't committed.

"Did you get them from the car?"

"If I hadn't, you would've been living out of it for another two weeks!"

I scanned the room and saw my suitcase, one of the boxes, and the blue Ikea bag—all emptied out. But the gym bag with Lucas's things was nowhere to be seen.

"Where is it?" I asked, my heart pounding.

She shook her head, disapproving, without saying a word, like my question didn't even warrant a response, like I should've known better than to ask.

"Where is the other bag?!" I demanded louder this time.

She didn't answer, just let out an exasperated sigh. I waited for a few seconds for her to stop ignoring me, then stormed out of the house.

Rushing outside, I was met with my mother's scolding. "Get back inside this instant! The neighbors will think you're crazy, running around half-naked!"

She followed behind me, her measured pace a deliberate display of authority, like a police officer approaching a pulled-over vehicle.

As I reached the end of the driveway, I spotted the bag on top of the garbage can. I grabbed it without hesitation, relieved to find it still there.

"For Pete's sake, stop feeling sorry for yourself! This is embarrassing! That boy walked all over you!" Mom's scathing words cut through the air.

That was it.

"That boy is fucking dead!" I shouted, locking eyes.

A long pause followed. I grabbed the Ikea bag from the floor and hurried upstairs, frantically stuffing my belongings into it.

"Now, what are you doing?" she asked, her voice almost calm. She followed me into my room.

I gave her an icy stare, then turned back to packing, opting for a silent treatment of my own.

"I swear, sometimes I wonder how you make it through the day," she spat behind my back. "If you had an ounce of sense, you'd see he's not worth it."

I spun around, my inner restraint shattering like glass, anger spilling out in every direction. "And if *you* were a better wife, Dad wouldn't have cheated!"

Slap!

And then I was cradling my cheek, and she was frozen with her palm still up in the air. Her eyes blazed, nostrils flaring, as she waited for me to respond, to say something. But I didn't. Instead, I charged past her, still in my pajamas, grabbed the keys from the porch bowl, tossed my bag and Lucas's things into the trunk, and got in the car. My mother stood by the garage door, arms crossed, frowning. I rolled down the window.

"Coming here was a mistake. I'll text you when I get there."

"Get where? Where are you going?" she asked, letting her arms drop to her sides.

Back to where I never should have left in the first place.

. . .

I DIALED Mitchell's number again and again. His phone kept ringing, but no one answered. That went on for two hours straight. Even though Mitchell didn't always pick up right away, I took it as a bad sign, especially when he still hadn't called back.

I tried June next, but got the same result. Each unanswered call tightened my grip on the wheel, my frustration morphing into fear that something terrible had happened.

After another half hour of relentless attempts, I tried Mitchell's number again. To my surprise, someone finally answered.

"Hello?" came a panicked reply.

It wasn't Mitchell.

"Who is this?" I asked, unable to discern their identity.

"Nellie? Thank goodness it's you!" Mathilda's voice trembled like a leaf in an autumn breeze.

I pushed aside my relief and focused on the urgency in her tone. "Tilly, what's going on? Why do you have Mitchell's phone?"

Mathilda's words were high-pitched and frantic. "You gotta get here! They know. They saw me. They'll come for me!"

My heart sank like a stone. "Who's 'they'? Where are June and Mitch?" I asked, but the woman was too hysterical to answer.

"Please, come quick! I'm in the shop!"

"I'm on my way," I promised, trying to sound calmer than I felt. I was still more than an hour away. If Mathilda were in immediate danger, I would be powerless to help her in time.

"Can you call someone? Are you there? Hello?" The phone beeped, signaling that the call had disconnected.

My mind was spiraling, racing through worst-case scenarios faster than I could stop them. I gripped the wheel so hard my knuckles ached, fighting the urge to slam the gas pedal and just go. But somewhere in the back of my head, a small voice broke through the noise, reminding me that if I got into a car accident, I'd be no help to anyone.

Something bad was happening, and I could barely stay calm.

Even though I had promised Mathilda I'd go straight to her shop, I decided to make a detour to the cabin to check if Mitch and June were there. It was almost on my way, and, truthfully, I cared far more about my friends than I did about the witch.

THE SECOND I turned onto the road leading to the cabin, a tight knot of dread twisted in my gut. My heart pounded like a drum during the drive up, a growing sense of foreboding creeping over me. Dark thoughts clouded my mind. What if Mitch and June were...

No, I couldn't let myself think that.

The door was unlocked, which wasn't like Mitchell at all. He was adamant about keeping it secure. I stepped inside, my senses on high alert. With the world around me coming to a halt, I felt the same way I had when walking into Duane's house. I tried to push the morbid thought away, convincing myself that Mitch and June were safe. Mitchell was skilled with weapons; he had a gun and knew how to handle himself.

Our once-cozy refuge lay in shambles: cushions torn apart, drawers emptied, their contents scattered. Books had been thrown off shelves, pages ripped from their bindings. My heart pounded as I scanned the wreckage, hoping against hope that Mitch and June had escaped before whoever did this arrived. The destruction was so methodical, it felt impossible for one person to have done it alone. They must have taken their time, going through every piece of furniture. Even the AC vents had been torn open. I grabbed a kitchen knife from the floor, holding it tightly in front of me, and forced myself to continue searching the rest of the cabin.

I scoured every room, but there was no sign of Mitch or June

—not a forgotten toothbrush, not one of June's horror movie t-shirts left behind, nothing to suggest they'd ever set foot in the place.

This wasn't the first time someone had broken into our place. The same thing happened in that hotel room when we were away. That thought gave me a glimmer of hope. Perhaps the siblings hadn't been there during the break-in. But who had done it and why? Were they looking for the photos? I'd left those with Mitch and June, since they were staying behind to continue the search. Or were they after something else? Something we'd dismissed as mere legend, but that Mathilda had wanted badly enough to risk coming here for?

The grimoire.

The front door creaked, and I jerked rigidly, my heart skipping a beat. Every instinct screamed at me to get out, and fast. I made my way back to the car, my eyes scanning the surroundings with every step. Only when I was back on the road, speeding away from the deserted house, did I relax a little.

The sound came from the front tire on the driver's side. Before I could focus on it, trying to figure out what it was, the rhythmic thrum against the asphalt grew louder and more insistent. The car veered to one side, and I nearly lost control, but managed to bring it to a stop on the grassy verge of the road. I stepped out of the car and circled it in a panic. The tire was completely flat.

"Fuck!" I muttered, on the verge of tears.

Today was a day of reckoning, and I was paying the price.

Chapter Twenty-Seven

September, 2020

OF COURSE, it was a dead zone for cell service. Just to check, I tried dialing AAA, but all I got was the dreaded "network unavailable" tone. It was time to make a choice. I was about ten miles from the cabin and much farther from town, which left me with few options.

I forced myself to stay calm and wait, clinging to the hope that a passing vehicle might come to my rescue. But the road was deserted, hemmed in by dense forest. No power lines overhead, no lamp posts. Nothing. The isolation was debilitating. The kind that made you feel like the world had forgotten you. The possibility that I might be stranded here for hours, with no rescue in sight, was slowly taking shape in my mind.

The sun was already sinking, and darkness would soon fall. I had a flashlight in the car, but what good would that do if no one came? I was too far from anywhere. I wouldn't even make it back to the cabin before nightfall. And after everything, the woods at night were the last place I wanted to be.

I was teetering on the edge when the air vibrated with the low pitch of an approaching vehicle. My heart leapt. The noise grew louder, and I raised my arm to flag down the car. But my arm froze midway as the vehicle came into view. The Sheriff's cruiser was approaching me, fast.

For a brief moment, I considered hiding in the ditch, but he'd already seen me, and there was no running from him without raising suspicions. Besides, how far could I run with no cell service, no coat, and no direction to go? I stood there, unable to move or think, a statue of stupidity and bad luck.

The car slowed to a stop beside me, and the window rolled down.

"What are you doin' here when I clearly told you and your friends to get gone?" the Sheriff asked.

His face was hard to read, but he didn't look angry. If anything, it seemed like he was fighting back a grin, like a card player hiding a winning hand.

The words tangled in my throat, too heavy to leave my mouth. I motioned vaguely, my hands trembling, unsure how to respond—or if he even wanted an answer.

His gaze skimmed over my car and settled on the flat tire. He stepped lazily out of the cruiser and strolled to the front of mine, casually assessing the damage. He clicked his tongue in an exaggerated, almost theatrical way.

He repelled me with a nearly visceral force, and I instinctively took a small step back, quietly calculating whether I could outrun him if it came to that.

"Looks like you've run into a bit of bad luck," he drawled.

"Seems so." I clutched my useless phone a little tighter, stepping even further back.

"Or are you the kinda gal who's just lookin' for trouble?" He moved a little closer, hands resting on his belt, thumbs hooked inside.

I bristled at the condescension in his words, but said nothing.

I was glad I'd changed out of those inappropriately short pajama shorts and that revealing top. The Sheriff was as greasy and repulsive as a slimy pat on the back, in the way he spoke and looked at me. But here, alone on a deserted road, in the middle of the woods, I was utterly at his mercy.

His grin stretched wider, unsettling in a way that sent a shiver down my spine. Maybe he, or someone working with him, had been near the cabin, waiting for a chance to slash my tire. Then they had followed me, just waiting for me to stop so they could make their move. That would explain how he showed up so fast.

If they wanted to kill me, this was the perfect setup. With no one around, the Sheriff could take me wherever he pleased, my car quietly towed and never seen again. Who would stop a Sheriff to check the trunk of his car? No one. The badge was the perfect cover. He could get away with murder. And maybe, just maybe, he already had.

My insides turned to ice as the thought crystallized, my breath catching. It had always been him. And now, there was no escape. I wanted to deny it, to hold on to the hope that it was all just a mistake, that I had just gotten spooked. But every instinct screamed at me to RUN!

He turned and headed back to his car, leaving the door open as an invitation. "You comin'?" he called over his shoulder.

I lingered, torn between the instinct to flee and the grim reality that I had no good options. He had a gun. If I bolted, he could shoot me in the back before I could reach the trees. And even if I managed to hide, what then? These woods stretched for miles. The odds of finding my way out were slim.

So my choices were a slow death—starvation, maybe dehydration if I couldn't find water—or a bullet. And if I got into his car, where would he take me? What would happen then? Would I even get the chance to signal for help if we passed another vehicle? Or would he make sure no one ever saw me again?

He might not even bother driving far. Perhaps he'd knock me out and run me over, just like what happened to Nick's mother.

"I-I'm not sure," I ventured, trying to sound nonchalant despite the rising panic. My voice came out shaky.

The Sheriff sneered. "Listen, missy, I ain't got time for your troubles, but I can give you a lift to town so you can figure out your own business from there. I couldn't care less about you, but you're in my county now, and I'd rather not have to explain why some city slicker got themselves killed on my watch. So do us both a favor and get into the damn car."

The way he spoke made my bones rattle. He wasn't asking, he was commanding. I looked around helplessly, unsure of what I was hoping for, but there was no one else around but us.

"I gotta call my friends," I said, pressing the phone to my chest, hoping to stall for time as my mind raced.

What should I do?

"Can't call from here," he said slowly, his bloodshot eyes locked on mine. "Dead zone. Gotta get closer to town."

I took another step back before I could stop myself, the crunch of gravel under my sneakers sharp and damning in the quiet. My eyes darted up the road, silently begging for headlights —any car, any stranger.

He drummed his fingers on his car's roof, each tap like a warning. "It's getting dark. Soon enough, all kinds of animals will be out. You don't want to be stuck out here alone."

Right. The animals. How could I forget?

I blinked fast, the first sting of tears gathering. Getting into the patrol car was not an option. I was convinced it would be my last mistake.

The Sheriff kept looking at me from under the brim of his hat, his dull, watery blue eyes cold and unyielding, devoid of any glimmer of humanity or compassion. He straightened from his slouch against the car and settled into a more deliberate pose. He was getting suspicious.

I steeled myself, ready to take my chances in the woods. But first, I needed to deceive the Sheriff, to convince him I was complying. I forced a hesitant smile, trying to appear cooperative, as I took a cautious step forward.

"Okay, thank you. Do you mind if I grab my jacket from the car first?"

"Make it quick," he growled, turning back to the cruiser, "I ain't got all night."

I lifted the trunk lid. The jacket lay on top of the chaotic mess; my clothes and toiletries were scattered about like the deer's intestines. I pretended to dig through the pile, my mind scrambling for a plan, but my eyes scanned the trunk with a growing sense of desperation. Then I saw it. My father's baseball bat was tucked away in the corner. My mother hadn't bothered to take it out of the car. It had always belonged in the Dodge, probably because she saw it as something akin to pepper spray— a tool for self-defense. And now, it could be exactly that.

This was my salvation. If I could lure the Sheriff close enough, I could land a solid swing. Even if I didn't knock him out—he seemed like the type who could take a hit, especially with that damn hat—at least it would disorient him long enough for me to make a break for the woods.

"What's takin' so long?" His breath was hot and unexpected against my ear. I shrieked. He was right over my shoulder. "Grab your stuff and let's go."

He yanked my jacket from the van and shoved it into my arms, then grabbed my elbow, hauling me away from the car— and the baseball bat. The trunk slammed shut with a jarring clunk. I twisted, trying to break free, but his grip only tightened, pinning me.

"No!" I protested. "Let me go!"

We both turned at the rumble of an approaching vehicle, and a shaky breath of relief escaped my lips. Maybe this wasn't my final hour, after all. My body tensed, ready to scream, kick, or even throw myself in front of the oncoming vehicle if it meant getting the driver's attention. But just as I prepared to act, the Sheriff's grip on my arm loosened, and he turned to face me, his face flushing with rage.

"Don't you say a fuckin' word," he hissed.

A dark gray pickup truck rumbled to a stop beside us. The passenger-side window slid down with a slow, mechanical whine.

"Evenin', Sheriff," Lucas's father said, his eyes narrowing slightly as he assessed the scene. "What seems to be the trouble here?"

"Oh, hey, Rob. Comin' from the sawmill?" The Sheriff tipped his infernal hat in a casual motion.

"Yeah, I went to check on things," Lucas's dad replied, his tone friendly. "What's goin' on? You folks need help?"

The Sheriff motioned toward my battered minivan. "The girl got a flat. I'm just givin' her a lift to town."

"Can't you fix it, old man?" Rob smirked, stepping out of his truck.

"I don't have the tools. It's no problem. We were just going."

"Well, hold up a second. I'll fix it for you. Just need to grab my wrench and jack stand from the sawmill. It's not far." He turned to me, utterly oblivious to my spitting unease. "You've got a spare, I assume?"

I nodded, though I had no idea if I actually did.

The Sheriff stiffened. "No need to trouble yourself, I'm on it."

"Actually," I interjected, scrounging for an excuse, "I wouldn't want to impose on your time, Sheriff. You must have more pressing matters to attend to."

I turned to Robert, careful to keep my voice steady. I didn't want to alarm him or put him in danger. "Mr. Whitman, if you're heading back to town anyway, could I trouble you for a ride instead?"

I nearly begged, my voice cracking as I fought to hold back a sob. I didn't want to sound too desperate, but I needed Mr. Whitman to understand—we had to get away from the Sheriff. Lucas's dad glanced at me, then back at the Sheriff, whose jaw was clenched tight.

"Of course, Nellie," the old man said, nodding with a kind smile. "No trouble at all. Hop in."

The Sheriff's face tightened. "I can do it. It's no problem," he insisted. "I'm headin' that way myself. You wouldn't want to keep Emily waitin', would you? After all, you're all she has now."

If it had only been a panicked suspicion before, now I was certain: the Sheriff was behind the disappearances. He killed Duane and Nick's mom. He did something to Lucas. He made people vanish without a trace. He was tied to whatever dark secret lingered in these woods, that eerie, dead clearing hidden behind the cryptic symbols.

Who else could have accessed the hotel so easily? Who else had the power to cover up murders for years? But why? Was it really because of that stupid book? Was he coming after me now because of some misguided belief in magic? Because I got too close to figuring it out?

No matter his reasons, his intentions were unmistakable. He was threatening us.

Mr. Whitman didn't flinch. With deliberate slowness, he reached into his pocket, pulled out a handkerchief, and took off his round glasses. He meticulously wiped them, removing every smudge. Once he'd finished, he returned the handkerchief to his pocket and settled his glasses back onto the bridge of his nose. Only then did he break eye contact with the Sheriff to look back at me.

I held my breath, scared he'd get into his truck and drive away.

"Please," I pleaded quietly.

The Sheriff's face twisted into a scowl. "Fine," he spat after a moment that seemed to drag on forever. He turned to me, twitching with malice. "Just tryin' to help."

I nodded, my fingers twitched at my sides. "Much appreciated."

Mr. Whitman gave me a reassuring smile. "That's it, then. Hop on in."

I slipped into the passenger seat of his ageing pickup. The leather was creased and worn, like the lines on Robert's face. A pine-scented air freshener swung from the rearview mirror. Without a word, he turned the key in the ignition, and the engine rumbled back to life.

"Thank you," I whispered.

Robert didn't turn his head. "Nothin' to thank me for."

We pulled away from the side of the road, leaving the Sheriff's imposing figure in the distance. The dense trees blurred past us, their shadows growing long and dark as dusk began to settle over the woods. I glanced repeatedly at the side mirror, dreading the possibility of the Sheriff's cruiser re-emerging.

"Is everythin' alright with you?" Robert asked after I flinched for the tenth time.

"I'm fine," I lied, hesitant to burden him with the truth.

"Where should I drop you off? Where are your friends staying?"

Why did he say 'friends' as if he knew there were more of us? He'd only seen me and Mitchell before.

"They're in town, waiting for me," another lie. "Just drop me off by the town square. I'll find my way around from there. Thanks."

The last rays of sunlight dipped below the horizon. Robert flicked on the headlights, twin beams cutting through the growing gloom. My mind raced, trying to think of my next move. *Where should I go once I arrive in Black Water? Mathilda's?* But what if she was the one who had lured me into the Sheriff's hands? On the phone, she made me swear I'd go straight to her shop. She couldn't have known I'd stopped by the cabin.

"So, you were there when it happened to Lucas?" Robert asked, his voice cutting through my frantic thoughts like a knife.

"What do you mean?"

"When he vanished," Robert pressed. His calmness threw me off. When we arrived at his house, he and Emily had been too shaken to talk about it.

I shifted uncomfortably. "I mean, no one saw what happened."

"Of course, they didn't. No one ever does," Robert muttered in a disconcerting tone.

I sat there, tense and unsure how to respond.

Then, after a long pause, Robert spoke again. "He was everythin' to his mother and me. Our only child. Our boy. His mother is a simple woman. She's not like me. It's much harder for her to understand."

What was he talking about?

"I'm sorry," I said softly, then added, "I loved Lucas, too."

He responded with a gentle smile, his eyes flicking to me. "I know."

"Mind if I open the window?" I suddenly felt short of breath. I needed some fresh air to ease the tightness coiling in my stomach.

"Go ahead."

I longed for the drive to end, to finally be alone, to clear my head and come up with a plan to find Mitch and June.

"Almost there," Robert said, as if he could hear my thoughts. And then, suddenly, he asked, "You have any marks on you?"

"What?"

"Tattoos?"

"No..." I frowned, thrown off.

Why was he asking me that?

"Good. I thought so. Young people love coloring their bodies with all sorts of things."

He turned the car onto a tiny dirt path, barely visible from the main road, and my heart sank. I knew where it led.

To the Black Water Creek trail.

Chapter Twenty-Eight

September, 2020

NO, *no, no, no, no.*

I shot Robert a nervous look.

This had to be a mistake.

"Where are we going?" I asked, trying to sound casual, but my voice came out low and raspy.

"I think you know where."

The truck bounced along the uneven path, branches and twigs snapping beneath the tires, slapping the windows. Long, ominous shadows stretched across the foliage. Night had already taken hold of the woods.

"Let me out," I said carefully. Robert didn't react. "Did you hear me? Stop the car!" I raised my voice and reached for the door, but it was locked.

"Soon. We're not there yet." His tone was soft, almost gentle.

We were barely going thirty miles per hour, but it was still too fast for a loose, uneven road. I yanked the handle again. No luck.

"Let me out!" I lashed out at him in a panic, my hands flying at his face, fingers clawed. He didn't even flinch, just threw out a massive arm, his palm connecting with my throat, and shoved me back against the seat with a force that knocked the breath from my lungs. The ease of it stunned me. Even for a tall, broad man, he was too strong for his age.

The truck came to a stop, and Robert finally released his grip on my neck. Air rasped down my throat. Ahead of us, a cluster of vehicles sat like old wives. Four, maybe five. One of them looked just like the SUV that nearly ran us off the road earlier. I couldn't be sure.

The locks clicked free.

With a trembling hand, I reached for the handle and flung open the door. But before I could run, rough hands tore me from the truck. I was yanked off my feet and slung down like a sack of potatoes.

I landed hard, elbows and knees tearing against gravel. The impact jarred my wrists, sending a sickening jolt up my arms. Before I could gather myself, hands dug under my armpits and wrenched me up in one brutal, snapping motion. My feet scrambled for solid ground, my vision swimming.

I twisted, tried to break free, but then—

A blow to the back of my head.

Sharp. Blinding.

White exploded behind my eyes. My legs buckled.

I would've collapsed, but claws—hands—dug into my arms, holding me up.

When the spinning slowed, when my vision focused, I realized I was pinned between two men in ski masks, their grips like iron.

"Careful there, boys," Robert called over his shoulder, glancing back at us. "Or you'll end up carryin' her."

He was already heading down the trail. The two men holding me dragged me along.

There was no way I was going deeper into that darkness with them.

"No!" I screamed, thrashing and kicking against them. "Let me go!"

"That's enough!" one of them barked. Another man stepped forward, a short one—shorter than me, but stocky and broad. He wore a faded green jacket, and his scarf was pulled up high, hiding most of his face except for his eyes. His gaze was sharp and burning with quiet malice, eyes that wouldn't flinch at killing, and wouldn't lose sleep after.

With quick, practiced hands, he pulled a coil of rope from his pocket and wrapped it around my wrists, binding them tightly. The rope cut into my skin. He yanked it hard, forcing me to stumble forward. My feet slid beneath me, and I almost lost my balance again.

As the last remnants of daylight faded, so did my hope. I shouted for help, but it was pointless. They silenced me with a firm slap to the face, hard enough for me to taste blood in my cheek, but not to knock me out.

A near-perfect circle of the moon, ripe with anticipation, hung low above the trees. There were still three days until the full moon. A chill ran down my spine when I made the connection: Lucas had gone home to Black Water a few days before the Harvest Moon. Had Robert done something to him? Had he killed his own son? But why? And the most horrifying question of all: Was I next?

I moved numbly, astonished and disbelieving, but when we crossed the bridge and the woods fell into an eerie quiet, panic and despair flooded back. I couldn't stop the tears. There was no way to convince them to spare me. I didn't even bother begging.

A familiar wooden plaque loomed ahead, barely visible now: *Private Property. Do Not Enter.* Crossing that last threshold felt like stepping off the edge of the world.

Robert and his followers hadn't used flashlights; somehow,

they had managed to orient themselves in the darkness. But now, they lit up some torches, their flickering yellow flames making the clearing look unholy.

Robert, the only one not wearing a mask, unlocked the shed and ushered us inside. The interior was bare—just a chain hanging from the wall, a shovel, a folded tarp, and a canister with unknown contents. A row of 2-gallon bottles, filled with what I assumed was water, lined the left wall. No altar, no magical trinkets, and nothing that resembled the grimoire Mathilda had mentioned. Three of Robert's companions stayed outside, and two came in with us. One of them retrieved a chair from a dark corner.

"Sit," Robert instructed, pointing to a rickety chair.

The man next to me shoved me onto it, though I didn't resist.

"What do you want from me?" I panted. "I didn't have anything to do with Lucas's disappearance, I swear!"

"I know you didn't, Nellie," Robert said, his voice low and even. He towered above me, a quiet but powerful force seeping from him. The old man I had met at the police station, grief-stricken and vulnerable, was gone. In his place stood someone else, someone who had shed his skin like a snake, revealing who he had been all along.

The killer.

"Then why are you doing this to me?" I sobbed.

He approached me slowly, his hand reaching out. I winced and recoiled, but he brushed his calloused, wrinkled fingers across my left cheek.

"I know all about you," he said softly. "But tell me about your friends, please."

"They're just looking for their sister. She's missing. I don't know anything else."

Robert flicked his eyes toward one of his men. In an instant, a searing pain exploded across my face. My head snapped violently to the side. I thought for a moment my neck had been broken, but then I realized I'd been knocked off the chair entirely.

A punch drove into my stomach before I could react. My breath collapsed inward, and my body folded in half. Nausea churned in my gut as a searing pain tore through my abdomen, blossoming like an evil flower. My diaphragm convulsed, refusing to expand.

Another blow struck. My lungs burned, starving for oxygen.

Then another.

And another.

My world shrank to a single point: agony. I couldn't even scream.

"Enough," Robert's voice came through the blur.

The punches stopped, but the residual pain lingered, a throbbing ache that pulsed through my body. I lay there, whimpering, shaking on the ground.

I felt myself being yanked back into the chair. Robert crouched in front of me, offering a plastic bottle of water. I took a few sips, most of it spilling over my chin and onto my dirty shirt. He stepped back.

"It was you," I croaked, anger searing inside me like a wildfire, no turning back now. "You killed Lucas. You killed your own son."

Robert calmly closed the lid on the bottle and set it aside. Then, he turned to me, his eyes glinting with a cold, calculated menace, and said matter-of-factly, "Don't talk about things you don't know nothin' about."

Another blow landed, less ferocious than the previous ones, but still sending shockwaves of pain through my battered body. I somehow managed to stay in the chair, my vision blurring at the edges.

Robert gave me a few seconds to catch my breath before

asking again, "I need to know where your friends are. And what they know."

"I don't know!" I blurted, catching a glimpse of movement to the left. "Please! I really don't know! I've been trying to reach them all day! I have no idea what happened to them!"

"All three gone?" Robert didn't buy it.

"No, just Mitch and June."

"What about the other one? Tall, dark hair?"

"He went home two days ago."

"Home where?" He pressed, drawing his minions closer with a wag of his fingers.

"Minnesota."

"Minnesota…" he repeated thoughtfully. "And he is…?"

"He was trying to find out what happened to his mother. She died here about a year ago." I deliberately didn't say 'got murdered' to avoid triggering Robert and his lackeys.

"His mother died here?" Something crept into his voice. Disbelief, or perhaps surprise.

"Yes!" I exhaled.

Robert glanced at the wide-open front door, as though calculating his next move. He gave a subtle nod to one of the men, and my phone was handed to him. I hadn't even noticed them take it.

"Give me the passcode."

I didn't hesitate. Any defiance would only bring more pain.

He adjusted his eyeglasses, the frames glinting in the dim light, and measured the comfortable distance between his face and the screen, then scrolled through my contacts with a detached air.

"Is this one of them?" he turned the phone toward me. Mitchell's name was on the screen.

A dark heaviness settled over me, fear and desperation swirling inside like a maelstrom. I nodded. If anything were to happen to Mitch, it would all be my fault.

He continued scrolling, stopping at Nick's name. "And this one?"

I nodded again.

"I believe you," he finally said. "One last question: do you have it?"

"Have what?"

"The grimoire. One of you must have it."

I shook my head, the motion making me dizzy with pain. "I don't know what you're talking about."

Without another word, one of Robert's companions stepped forward, his fists clenched and ready. The blows that followed were relentless, each one like a deadly drumbeat. The chair cracked beneath me, splintering like kindling as I was thrown to the floor, my body shattered, broken.

"I swear, we don't have it!" I spat from bloodied teeth. "She was looking for it, too!"

Robert grabbed a fistful of my hair, yanking my head up with an unforgiving grip. "Who. Is. She?"

"Mathilda!"

Robert released me, and my face slammed back into the floor.

I was sobbing, exhausted, begging for it all to be over. But my prayers weren't heard.

"Alright," Lucas's father said calmly, "It's almost time."

Just then, a man appeared. His heavy boots echoed through the barn. I could barely lift my head before I gasped. The man's face was now concealed by a bizarre mask—a deer skull with antlers.

"No! No!" I screamed again.

Strong hands dragged me out to the clearing. The men now all wore similar stag skulls, their empty sockets staring into my very soul. I shook violently, thrashed in horror. I knew what they were about to do. I was about to find out firsthand exactly what had happened to Lucas and to all those before him.

In the next moment, I was pushed towards the altar, my tied arms forced upwards.

"Please, no!" I cried, choking on my sobs. My body trembled against the cold stone.

The rope above my head tightened, securing my arms in place. Someone approached from behind, and they grabbed and ripped my shirt, the fabric tearing with a harsh sound. Rough hands made contact with my bare skin, and I shuddered with revulsion.

"Stop, please," I yelled, tears blurring my vision. One of the masked men held my head down on the stone, his grip unyielding.

In the fringes of my sight, they moved around me like silent shadows, each step deliberate. They must have done this countless times.

Robert reached into the fire with a gloved hand, pulling out a glowing object that shimmered with a malevolent heat. It looked like a branding iron. My breath caught in my throat.

"No!" I squealed, my body twisting in panic.

Too late.

Pain exploded across my upper back, just below my shoulder blade. The skin sizzled and crackled, the heat so intense I thought I might burn away. The stench of my flesh made me gag. My skin melted under the weight of the iron, the searing heat biting down to bone. My vision blurred as the pain reached its peak, a white-hot fire consuming me from the inside out.

And then, just as suddenly, it was over. The grip on my arms and body loosened, and the world around me felt distant, as though I was floating above it. They stepped back, their presence looming but insignificant now.

I lay there, helpless on the altar, my body twitching with agony, my cries echoing into the emptiness.

Powerless, alone.

It was done.

I managed to lift my head. They stood in line, a few feet away, their stag masks glowing with an eerie life in the flickering flames.

Robert gave a small, almost imperceptible nod. "It's alright. It saw her."

One of the masked men stepped forward, and before I could draw breath, they seized me and hauled me off. My ripped shirt hung in tatters around my arms, my bare back pulsing against the open air. The fire in my chest ignited, and with what little strength I had left, I slammed my elbow into his jaw. The impact was satisfying, but only for a moment. He retaliated instantly with a brutal blow to my head.

But it was enough. I broke free and bolted, spurred by pure adrenaline.

Into the dark, I went.

PANIC SMOTHERED me as I sprinted through the forest, branches lashing at my face like whips, roots leering out to trip me. I had no idea where I was or where I was going, only that I had to keep going. The forest floor exhaled a moist, loamy breath, heavy with decay. The desolate woods stirred with anguish—animals howling and trees groaning. And there was another presence: a vibration, a constant, low-pitched hum, like the earth itself was moaning.

But above it all, the ominous rustle of something massive tearing through the underbrush grew louder, closer.

I dared not look back, fearing what I might see. The presence behind me was relentless in its pursuit, crushing the dense scrub in its path. Low in the sky, hung the round, dull disk of the moon, casting silver light on a world that had been devoured by forest. Heaviness throbbed in my temples. Pain coursed through my entire body. I couldn't go on any longer.

"Nellie."

I stopped.

An unnatural quiet wrapped the forest.

"Lucas?" I sniffled, tears in my voice.

No answer.

And then, again, "Nellie."

Hollow, emotionless, it terrified me.

I whipped around, searching frantically for any sign of movement, trying to figure out where the sound was coming from. It was calling me deeper into the woods, I knew it. And I needed to get away from it, go in the opposite direction.

A branch snapped. And then a heavy step shook the ground beneath me. I yelped and darted off in panic.

Don't stop. Don't stop, I told myself, but then my foot caught on a gnarled root.

The ground rushed up to meet me.

But the impact never came. I kept plummeting into the void, the trees, the moon, and the sky disappearing into an inky blackness that engulfed me in a never-ending abyss.

Darkness above.

Darkness below.

Chapter Twenty-Nine

September, 2020

CONSCIOUSNESS RETURNED LIKE A CRUEL GIFT.

I lay on my stomach, shivering and bruised in my tattered shirt. Each breath was a sharp and sudden stab to the lungs as I twisted onto my back. Blood clung to me like a needy lover, and the branded flesh on my shoulder stung, sensitive to even the slightest brush.

I forced myself upright, head pounding, ears ringing. There was a cold weight on my ankle, and when I jostled it, I winced at the unmistakable clink of metal. They'd chained me.

Blinking back tears, I steadied my breath. *It's okay. It's okay. You're going to be okay.*

Pale daylight filtered through a high, unreachable window in the barn. I strained against the chain, testing its strength, but it held firm. A bottle of water lay nearby, enough to keep me alive for a couple of days. The canisters in the corner were beyond my reach. I clambered for the bottle with trembling hands, taking a few small sips to ease the dryness in my aching throat.

Three days. That's all I had before the woods came for me.

I screamed until my voice gave out.

I DIDN'T KNOW how much time had passed. Outside, it was cloudy and light, early morning or afternoon, I couldn't tell. I drank half the water from the bottle, then sat back, trying to piece together a plan. Wasting energy trying to break free would be pointless. I needed something more innovative. But what? What would Mitch do if he were in my place? After thoroughly scanning the area and stretching as far as the chain allowed, I found nothing.

A dark thought unfurled. There may be a way to end it all, get it all over with.

I shoved it away.

There would be no giving up, not yet. Not until the very end.

Time dragged on, and I sat there like a chained dog, alone, no rescue in sight, no hope.

At first, I thought I was imagining things again. I'd done it before—hallucinated sounds between my desperate screams. My brain conjured footsteps, whispers, anything to keep the silence from pulling me under.

But this time, it was different. These were voices, real and growing louder.

I stilled.

It could've been anything: Robert, his men, or something worse.

A familiar girl's timbre seeped through the cracks in the wall. "It's just weird, is all I'm saying," she said.

"Help!" I croaked, my voice hoarse. "It's me!"

Fast, heavy steps rushed up to the locked door.

Then Mitchell's voice, "Nellie?"

"Yes! I'm in here! Let me out!"

Mitchell's heavy footsteps crunched outside. The lock

creaked and jiggled, and Mitchell's voice, low and authoritative, ordered, "Step back and to the side."

I gladly obeyed, covered my ears and squeezed my eyes shut. Still, I flinched at the deafening boom as he shot the lock; gunpowder stung my nose with its piercing metallic tang. He kicked the door open and stepped inside, backlit by daylight, rifle in hand, like some movie hero. I stumbled toward them, the chain on my ankle rattling. Mitchell's face was a picture of horror.

"Jesus," he muttered, taking in my torn, bloodied state. "What the hell happened to you?"

"Are you okay?" June looked like she wanted to reach for me, but didn't. I guessed I was too beaten to risk touching.

"Can you take it off?" I pointed to the chain.

Mitchell crouched to examine it. "I'll need a bolt cutter."

"Do you have one?"

"No."

"Can you shoot it off like you did with the door?" June asked.

"Of course not. She'll lose her foot."

I was about to say I'd take the risk, but Mitch was already rummaging through his backpack.

"I could try picking it. It's just a padlock."

"Hurry," I said. "I'm scared they'll come back. They might still be close."

"They?" Mitchell looked up from the lock.

"Robert," I said. "Mister Whitman. Lucas's dad! He's the one who made your sister disappear!"

His jaw clenched, muscles flexing under his stubble. "We know," he said grimly. "We checked the sawmill. It's empty. He doesn't run it, doesn't employ anyone. So, he lied. Someone else is paying him to do something else."

"There were other men," the truth tumbled out of me,

jumbled and frantic, as if every second counted. "They wore masks. I couldn't see their faces."

Mitchell didn't lift his head from the padlock he was trying to pick. "Let's get out of here first. We'll sort it out when we're in a safe place."

I closed my eyes. If only he knew—it was way worse than it looked.

The padlock snapped with a crack, and the chain fell to the floor with a final clank. I was free. I let out a slow, shaky exhale and tried to stand, but dizziness hit me instantly.

"Whoa, easy there," Mitch said, catching me before I could fall. Agony bit me, but I welcomed his aid. "Let's get you out of here. June, give me a hand."

"Jesusfuckingchrist," June whispered, sucking in a sharp breath as she approached me, inspecting the area below my right shoulder blade.

Mitchell took off his rain jacket and handed it to me, his eyes avoiding mine as I pulled it around my shoulders to cover myself. My shirt was in pieces, and I wasn't wearing a bra.

They each took an arm and walked me out of the barn. The first few steps were the hardest.

"Why did you come to the clearing? How did you even get in?" I asked when we got back to the trail.

"We tried yesterday," she said, "but kept circling. Even Mr. 'I-can-read-a-paper-map' here couldn't figure it out. It got dark, so we came back in the morning. I just... did what Nick did." She pushed up her sleeve, revealing a bandaged forearm.

"Against my best advice," her brother muttered.

June shot him a look. "But it worked, didn't it?"

"So you didn't know I was there?"

"No. We thought you left."

"I came back. Mathilda tricked me. She answered your phone. And then Robert got me. I was so stupid."

"You're not stupid," Mitchell said firmly. "They're just too cunning."

THE WOODS WERE DEATHLY STILL until we crossed the bridge. All at once, birdsong filled my ears like a rush of water. The hum of insects warmed my cold heart as I stumbled through the mulch and mud. The world felt alive again. But my relief evaporated quickly.

"I'm going to die in three days. It's coming for me next," I blurted.

Mitchell threw a cautious glance over his shoulder. "You don't know that for sure. It's just a story."

"It's not," I replied. "At least they don't think it is. And besides, it happened to Lucas. It happened to Amanda. And they're looking for you. They think either you or Nick has the grimoire."

"The grimoire?" Mitchell echoed. "What the hell is this shit, and why's everyone after it?"

I shrugged, then winced, forgetting how every movement hurt. In movies, the villain often reveals their evil plans to the victim before killing them. Robert didn't waste time on that. He just made me talk.

"So, they're after this grimoire, and that's why they did this to you?" June asked quietly.

I shook my head. "No. At least, I don't think so. They're branding people. And then these people disappear. On the Harvest Moon. It's like a ritual."

"What does the grimoire have to do with it?" Mitch asked, still skeptical.

"I don't know."

I was spent; the words lead weights in my mouth. We still had a long way to go, and my body was on the verge of breaking.

"Maybe they need it for spells or hexes," June mused. "Do you think there's something to reverse whatever they did to you?"

How had I not thought of that?

"Junie, this is not..." Mitch started, faltering, then his eyes met mine, and he said softly, "They're a bunch of crazies. A cult."

"Don't." I waved my hand in front of my face, swatting at a mosquito. "Just... please, call Nick."

"Where is he? We thought you guys left together."

"We didn't *leave* together," I snapped, feeling irrationally angry. "I just gave him a lift to the airport. We need to contact him."

"Why?" His question wasn't meant to provoke, but it sent me over the edge.

"Because Robert is after him, too! And since you don't believe me, I need someone who does. Maybe there's something we can do, because sitting around answering your questions isn't helping."

Mitch fell silent, his face tinged with sadness as he looked at me. Was my state really that bad?

"Sure, we'll call him. I have his number memorized."

Mitch had superpowers, and finally, they were coming in handy, albeit in a situation we'd rather not be in at all.

I took a deep breath, trying to calm down. "Anyway, what happened to you? Where are your phones?"

"Mathilda called us and warned us to get out of the house," Mitch explained. "Ordered us to ditch our phones so no one could track us."

"Can they actually do that?" I asked.

"I don't know. She sounded convincing. Maybe she hypnotized us or something."

Mitch seemed frustrated with himself. He didn't trust Mathilda, and then he suddenly obeyed her, like a soldier reacting to a command without question.

June snorted, "Now, who's stupid?"

Mathilda hadn't been at the ritual, and she had no way of knowing, aside from her self-proclaimed psychic powers, that I'd be heading to the cabin in the first place. It gave me hope she wasn't one of them after all. She could help.

"Did she say anything else about the grimoire? Can you call her?" I asked.

Mitchell tried to reassure me. "Nellie, this is all just smoke and mirrors. We don't know squat about that grimoire. Let's get the hell outta here and get you to a hospital, where you can get some real help."

"Smoke and mirrors?" I snapped, ripping off the jacket he gave me and turning my back to him, forcing him to look at the burn. "Does that look like smoke and mirrors to you?"

His face went grim. "I... I didn't mean..."

I angrily put the coat back on. "Then please, let's do something instead of debating what's real and what isn't. And no hospital. We don't have time for that. *I* don't have time for that."

Mitchell's foot slammed the gas pedal, and the world outside the car blurred into streaks of brown and green. With each bump in the road, I winced.

We pulled up to a rundown motel tucked between a row of trucks. No one said a word. Mitchell got out to call Nick, but his sister stopped me before I could follow.

"Come on, we need to clean you up," June said softly, guiding me toward the bathroom. Her hands shook as she carefully wiped away the grime and dried blood from my skin. She looked at me with a mix of shock and anger, taking in the bruises, broken lip, and seared symbol on my skin.

Mitchell handed me ibuprofen, and I swallowed the pills with a grimace. His assessment was relatively reassuring—maybe one or two broken ribs, but nothing internal, no concussion.

"Easy," he cautioned, guiding June as she tended to the

wound on my shoulder. He'd brought a pile of oversized T-shirts, offering me something more comfortable to wear. A pained "thank you" slipped through my clenched teeth.

Later, I managed to snag a couple of hours of sleep, curled on my left side in an awkward attempt to find comfort. When I woke, the siblings were huddled over the table, studying an arsenal of guns. Mitchell's collection had doubled since I last saw it.

"What's the plan?" I asked, my voice still hoarse.

"First, I'll teach you ladies how to handle these. Then I'm going after the son of a bitch who did this to you. And we're going to find that goddamn book."

One glance at June's offended expression made it clear she wasn't a rookie. Mitch quickly moved on, showing me how to handle both weapons in case it came to that. We couldn't go outside, so it wasn't real practice—mostly theory. This routine gave me a fleeting glimmer of reassurance, making me feel as if we had a plan, even though we didn't.

"You can't go alone," I protested afterward. "There are seven of them—that I counted! And you can't put your sister in danger like that."

"June's staying here with you," Mitchell said firmly, his jaw set.

"No, I'm coming!" June jumped off the bed, as if terrified her brother was leaving right then.

"Going after them by yourself is a suicide mission," I intervened, trying to reason with him before things escalated further. "Come on, you know this! You've said it yourself: never go anywhere alone. What if we talk to that witch first and see what she has to say? After all, she got us into this mess. What if she actually has the book?"

"Why would she be asking us about it then?" Mitch frowned, tapping his fingers against the edge of the table.

"I don't know. To confuse us?"

"We're already plenty confused."

We sat in silence for a few moments, thinking.

"What if Nick's Mom stole it from Robert, and he killed her?" June suddenly suggested. "She was a psychic, right? Maybe she, like Mathilda, wanted the book for her witchy stuff."

As simplistic as June's theory sounded, it was the most plausible explanation, and it accounted for Nick's Mom's involvement.

"Then, shouldn't Nick have it?" Mitch asked carefully, avoiding looking at me.

A firm yet cautious knock cut through our debate, and my heart flipped. Nick burst through the door as soon as Mitch unlocked it, his eyes scanning me from head to toe with an intensity that felt like a searchlight. The next moment, his hands cradled my face, and the tender gesture brought tears to my eyes. The scent of his cologne combined with his worry made me feel exposed and vulnerable.

"Show me," he demanded.

I complied, turning my back to him and lifting my shirt. With everyone in the room having seen me undressed by now, modesty was no longer my concern. June gently peeled back the bandage, revealing the full extent of the injury.

"Holy shit," Nick muttered, snapping a photo with his phone. "Sorry, I just want it for reference. So I don't have to make you uncomfortable again."

I pulled my shirt back down as June finished reapplying the bandage, then turned to face Nick.

Seeing him so concerned broke the last of my composure, and I crumbled into sobs.

"I don't want to die," I whispered through my tears.

"You're not going to," Nick said firmly. "We'll find it."

Mitchell leaned forward, his eyes locked on Nick's. He

cleared his throat, a brief hesitation before his words came out in a low, serious tone.

"We think your mother might have stolen it from Robert. That's why he killed her. That must be it."

Nick's eyes narrowed. "And?"

"She would've been the last one to have it," Mitchell pressed on.

"I already went through all her stuff after she died. I'd have remembered something like that showing up," Nick snapped, his voice taking on a defensive edge. "And if your theory's right, Robert should have it."

"He doesn't," I interjected quickly.

"Are you sure?"

"Pretty sure," I muttered, wincing at the memories. "They beat me up, trying to get me to tell them where it is. If they had it already, they wouldn't have bothered."

"How can we be sure *you* don't have it?" Mitchell interrupted.

Nick's anger flared like a spark. "You think I'd just lie about having it and come here to watch Nell—" He caught himself mid-sentence, his face shifting from indignation to guilt, as if the very thought was too painful to consider.

I knew Nick. He'd always been sincere with me, open in a way that made it impossible to doubt his intentions. If he had the grimoire, he would never keep it from me. There was no reason to question his word now.

The siblings must have reached the same conclusion because June turned to Nick. "Okay, so where do we look?"

Mitchell leaned back, arms crossed. "My plan is to track down Robert and get some answers outta him. Maybe we don't even need that book. I bet these guys know how to reverse this thing."

His unspoken 'if it's even real' lingered in the air like a

challenge. Still, I appreciated that he was willing to entertain the possibility and was on board with the plan.

"I doubt it," Nick countered. "He'd sooner die than talk."

"Why's that?" Mitchell asked.

Nick let out a long sigh, the kind of sigh people give when they're explaining the same thing for the hundredth time, but to an audience that hadn't been paying attention.

"The book June borrowed talks about how people used to make sacrifices to get what they wanted. It's like cellular apoptosis in biology, where the body programs a cell to die for the greater good. The occult works on a similar principle—sacrifice something valuable to gain something beneficial."

June's eyes widened. "So, her death—sorry, Nell," she shot a quick glance my way, "is a good thing?"

Nick's jaw tightened. "No, of course not. But the process is already in motion. If it's reversed, the results could be unpredictable. Dangerous. That's why Robert would never crack. They're using her as a sacrifice so they can get what they want."

"And what do they want?" Mitch asked.

"How should I know?"

"You get how crazy this sounds, right?" Mitch shook his head.

"I do. And yet, here we are." There was a brief silence. "Whatever it is they want from that thing in the woods, someone has to pay for it. Because if it's not paid, they might be putting themselves in danger. And this is why we need to go after the book and not after them."

"How do you know all that?"

"I read a lot," Nick said sarcastically. "You should try it sometime."

"Oh my god, stop!" I buried my face in my hands, exasperated. "We can start with Mathilda. We can either kill her or make her talk. At this point, I don't give a shit."

Nick and Mitchell exchanged a tense glance.

"You're right," Mitch said with a curt dip of his head. "Let's go."

In the car, Mitchell outlined the plan. "We go in, ask our questions, and get out. No drama, no fuss. We can't afford to draw more attention to ourselves."

And, of course, that's exactly how it went.

30

Chapter Thirty

September, 2020

MITCHELL GAVE the second gun to his sister, probably so she could defend herself if things went south. I understood, but it still felt unfair. I was the one in pain, vulnerable, and unarmed.

The "Closed" sign on the locked door didn't stop us when we reached Mathilda's store. Mitchell led us around to the back entrance. Also locked. He pulled out a credit card and started working the latch, but the lock wasn't cooperating.

While he was meddling with it, June spotted a large stone on the ground. Before we all realized what she was doing, she hurled it through the window. Glass shattered with a piercing crash.

"June!" Mitch was aghast, but she ignored him. She climbed in, unlocked the door from the inside, and waved us in like it was nothing.

Nick closed his eyes, exasperated, but said nothing. Mitchell shot June another glare, but she either didn't notice or didn't care. We entered the storage area, off-limits to customers, packed with goods shipped from China, as indicated by the labels on the boxes. So much for "your local vendor."

Mitchell raised a hand, his ears tuned to the house. All was quiet. He signaled us to search. And search we did, leaving no stone unturned and no care for the mess. Within minutes, the room looked like a mini-tornado had ripped through it.

"Trespassin', property dam—" Mathilda's sarcastic remarks were interrupted by a deafening sound as June spun and fired the gun she'd been holding in her hand. A row of delicate figurines exploded, and the bullet lodged deep into the wall. I yelped, my heart hammering, and clamped my hands over my ears. June had done the same, the gun still in her hand, her eyes wide with shock.

Mathilda flinched, but recovered fast. She surveyed the destruction with a slow, disapproving click of her tongue. "You break it, you buy it. And it looks like you're about to buy a lot."

"June, put the fucking gun down!" Mitchell snapped.

She lowered it, shaken.

I stepped forward, my voice trembling with adrenaline-fueled rage. "Tell us everything you know about Robert and the grimoire."

Mathilda's gaze flew to me, her expression softening as she really looked. "What happened to you?" she asked and then paused. Her eyes widened with realization.

"Tell us how to reverse the sigil on her." There was a subtle edge to Nick's voice, a threat barely veiled.

"Why do you think I know how?" Mathilda asked, not even trying to sound convincing. Which, ironically, made it sound true. She played so many games that when she did sound fake, it almost lent her credibility.

I spoke anyway. "Because you and Robert dragged me into this."

Mathilda looked affronted. "I don't work with Robert. I don't work for him. That's not why I called you here."

"Then why?" My voice wavered. She *called me* here.

"Because it has to stop," she said, suddenly serious.

"What has to stop? The disappearances?" Mitchell cut in. "How is her death supposed to fix anything?"

A flicker of sympathy crossed Mathilda's face. "It gives you a reason to act. And fast. The Harvest Moon is in two days."

"Tell us where to find the grimoire and how to use it," I said, desperation leaking into my voice.

"Robert doesn't have it?" Mathilda sounded genuinely surprised.

"No. Apparently, he thought we had it," I said.

I didn't know who to believe anymore. The fragile hope that Mathilda had the grimoire and would hand it over to us vanished into thin air.

"I was sure he had it."

"Why didn't you stop him yourself?"

"Lord, have mercy, are you plumb crazy? You seen him? You got any idea who you're dealin' with? The kind of folks who got his back?" Her voice hardened. "He's been doin' this longer than most folks around here have been breathin'."

"So you let it happen to someone you didn't care about. Great." I bit out.

"You're quick to judge," she retorted. "And you're not just anyone."

"Then at least tell us what we can do," Nick cut in, before I could ask her what she meant by it.

"Find the grimoire," she said coldly. "And get the hell out of my store."

"Yeah?"

I approached June and gently took the gun from her hand. She was so surprised that she didn't even react until it was too late. I glared at Mathilda and clicked the safety off. My finger vibrated on the trigger.

"I told Robert about you. Maybe he or his men in deer skull

masks will come for you tonight. Or maybe I'll just shoot you myself. I've got nothing to lose."

I'd never fired a gun before, but palming it now made me feel almost invincible. Powerful. Like I'd awakened something dark and buried deep, something that had always been there, waiting.

"Nellie, no!" Nick and Mitchell lunged toward me, but I swiftly flicked the safety on. Mitchell carefully pried the gun from my hand.

"You've got plenty to lose," Mathilda said, "So start lookin'. But trust me. It's not here. You're wastin' your time with me."

Her calm never cracked, but the blood had drained from her face when the barrel pointed at her. For a heartbeat, I savored the control, the power. But the taste turned sour, my own bloodlust turning my stomach. Was I really capable of murder?

"Let's get out of here," I said, my gaze holding the witch in place.

Every movement sent a jolt of pain through my body, especially the burn on my shoulder. But for these few seconds, holding Mathilda at gunpoint, I'd felt like I had a grip on something, a fleeting sense of control over my chaotic life. It wasn't the kind of control my mother would've wanted for me, but it was the kind I desperately needed.

Unfortunately, it might be too little, too late.

"ARE you sure the Sheriff wasn't at the ritual?" Mitchell asked for what felt like the tenth time, back at the motel.

"Pretty sure." I collapsed onto the bed, too drained to care. June immediately sat beside me.

"You need a change of bandages," she said, gently tugging the T-shirt off my shoulder.

I didn't resist. She was like a whole new person—helpful, supportive, genuinely concerned about my well-being. Her angsty, guarded teenage attitude had melted entirely the moment they found me in the barn.

Mitchell chewed his lip, then turned to Nick. "And your mother didn't have it? You didn't see anything remotely like an old book at home?"

"I told you," Nick replied, his voice strained. "I went through everything after she died. It. Wasn't. There."

Mitch started pacing the room. "Do you think she could've hidden it somewhere?"

"I don't know."

Their sombre faces seemed to draw the warmth from the room. For the first time since I left the barn, I felt a cold, gripping fear. I *was* going to die.

"I don't dream," I whispered.

Everyone's eyes fell on me.

"Since the ritual... I haven't had dreams. Not even nightmares. Just darkness. Like I'm dead."

Nick opened his mouth to respond, but I cut him off. "Please, help me. I'm scared. I won't even have a grave."

His gaze fell to the floor. The room was silent.

Then he spoke. "The grave."

"What was that?" Mitch asked

"Her grandmother's grave at the cemetery," Nick explained. "What if she hid it there? Think about it. It's the only connection to this place."

Mitchell stood, hesitant. He wasn't convinced. But after a moment, he nodded. "It's worth a shot. Let's go check it out."

June perked up, ready to follow her brother anywhere, even to dig up an old grave.

"Not you," Mitch quickly said. "Nick and I will go. You stay with Nell. Keep the gun close. Don't fire it unless you absolutely have to."

I couldn't decide if Nick truly believed this was a real possibility or if he was just offering a gentle hospice for my sanity, a comforting illusion to ease my fears before I vanished.

The dim glow of the motel room's lamp cast elongated shadows across the walls as June and I huddled over the small table in front of my laptop. We'd been scouring the internet, trying to find information about the sigil. But so far, our efforts had been in vain. We'd seen hundreds of disturbing images— either real or fake—but nothing quite matched the one burned into my skin.

"This is useless." I closed my laptop and pushed it away.

Before June could respond, equally disappointed and frustrated with the state of things, I grabbed my phone and excused myself. I needed to make a crucial call.

The mere thought of my mother never knowing what had happened to me, and being left with memories of our ugly fight, hurt more than the physical pain I was enduring. With trembling hands, I dialed her number on the burner phone Mitch had given me, unsure what kind of response I was hoping for. Either way, it was going to be difficult.

She picked up, and I whimpered, "Mom."

A brief pause hung in the air before my mother responded, "Nellie, what's wrong?" Her voice was tinged with genuine worry, something I hadn't heard often.

I shook my head, trying to stem the tears. "It's... a long story. I'm okay. I love you, Mom. And I'm so sorry," I managed before my voice cracked and tears overtook me again.

"Come home. We'll deal with anything. I promise, everything will be alright. Just come home," she pleaded softly.

I couldn't recall the last time my mother had been so gentle, so concerned.

"I just wanted to tell you I love you," I said, my voice choked with sobs.

"You'll come home right away, right?" she urged.

"Yeah."

"Right away. Wherever you are, just come home."

"Okay."

"I love you."

"I gotta go, Mom. I love you, too."

Hanging up on her was the hardest part, but I had to do it before I broke down completely. I wanted to leave her with something better than our last argument to remember me by.

I stood there for a while, feeling an emptiness inside me, expanding until it filled every corner of me. Something dark and cold was spreading through me, and it was calming in a way that felt wrong. I wiped away my tears and went back to the room.

To my surprise, I found June preparing to go out.

"Oh, good, you're alright," she said with relief. "Want to grab something to eat? There's a taco place nearby."

"Tacos for my special meal? Why not?" I replied, forcing a smile.

"Don't say that," June chided softly.

"I'm sorry."

"I'm not really hungry, to be honest," she admitted, her shoulders slumping.

"Neither am I."

We stayed in.

I PACED THE MOTEL ROOM, nervous energy coiling tighter with every passing minute. It had been hours, and still no word from Mitch or Nick. They'd forbidden us from calling—said they'd check in when they could.

I couldn't shake the fear that something had gone wrong. Maybe they'd run into Robert's men. We had no idea how many were part of his gang. His coven. For all we knew, they might've been patrolling the whole town, maybe even watching the cemetery.

The minutes dragged on, and I checked the clock on the wall

obsessively, willing the hands to move faster. 9:47 PM. 9:52 PM. 9:59 PM.

"Why didn't you leave with Nick? I thought you guys were together or something."

June's words made me pause, and I exhaled, feeling the weight of my recent decisions pressing down on me. "No, I went home. He went back to Minnesota. We're not together."

June's eyes narrowed slightly. "Why?"

I faltered. "Because he has his life, and I have mine. Had. Whatever."

"I'm sorry I outed you guys. It wasn't nice. I was just..." she trailed off, searching for the right word to name her emotions.

I waved a hand to dismiss it. It didn't matter anymore.

June's gaze softened. "Do you still love Lucas? Is that why?"

I winced. She'd hit a nerve. "I don't know. The more I think about our relationship, the less fond I am of the memories. It's like... I was blind to a lot of things, and now I'm starting to see everything for what it was."

June's lips curved downward in a soft, sympathetic frown. "Why? Did he treat you poorly?"

"No, but he kept secrets, apparently. And perhaps that's what killed him. And the entire time, he made me feel like I was the one who was crazy and controlling. But the truth is, I was just never enough."

"I'm sure he loved you," she tried comforting me, but her words only fueled my anger. I didn't need pity, especially not from a nineteen-year-old.

"He lied to me, June. He never told me about any of this. And now, because of him, I'm going to die too. Never forgive a man who lies, and never trust anyone who's lied to you once. They'll do it again."

"You won't die. We'll figure something out. They'll find it. And I'm sure you've had plenty of good things to remember with Lucas."

Lucas's name felt like a curse in my mind. Two years of memories, reduced to a toxic shrine of books and clothes. I'd clung to them, hoping to revive the love we had. But now, they only mocked me. His disappearance left me with nothing but questions and the bitter taste of betrayal. Lucas and his father were equally to blame for my suffering.

Something inside me snapped. I shoved back from the table, my chair scraping loudly against the floor as I shot to my feet. I didn't look at June. I couldn't. I stormed out of the motel room, the door slamming shut behind me, and made a beeline for the car.

I yanked open the trunk, hands trembling as I grabbed the gym bag—the one I'd been too afraid to touch. It held the fragile remnants of Lucas, memories I'd clung to like a relic, desperate to keep him close, terrified to let go. Now, even holding it felt like it was choking me.

"Where are you going?" June called after me, but I didn't answer.

My eyes fell on the dumpster.

With a strangled cry, I hurled the bag at it. The force of my throw was too much, and the zipper ripped open, spilling its contents onto the pavement. Books. Clothes. Old photos. A sound tore from my throat—raw, broken, somewhere between a scream and a sob. It didn't fix anything, but for a moment, it emptied me. My body locked up, chest rising and falling, heart pounding in my ears. Then I started picking up the pieces—his T-shirt, the towel, the textbook, and the concert ticket stub I'd once thought was romantic—and launched them, one by one, into the dumpster.

June stood a few feet away, silently watching.

Books soared through the air, their pages fluttering like wounded birds.

"Nellie, wait!" June's voice was high and shaking.

She crouched in front of a thick textbook, its cover worn and bleached by the sun. As it hit the ground, it flipped open, revealing a hollowed-out core. Every page had been meticulously carved, and nestled in the center was a small, leather-bound book.

It must've been with his things all along, tucked away where no one would think to look. And unknowingly, I'd had it this entire time, too absorbed in my own grief to notice.

June's eyes widened. "Oh my god, Nellie... Is this—?"

I didn't need to open it to know.

THE GRIMOIRE RESTED on the table like something alive, radiating a heavy, electric energy. My fingers trembled as I tried to untie the cord. For a second, I swore the book pulsed in my hands—watching. Waiting.

June's questions came in a rush. "How did it—"

"I don't know," I snapped, cutting her off.

She tried again, "But why does—"

"I said I don't know!"

I finally pried open the small book, its yellowed pages releasing the musty scent of old paper. Hand-drawn illustrations filled the margins—grotesque creatures and arcane symbols that seemed to shift before my eyes, drawing me in.

The motel room door slammed open, and Mitchell and Nick staggered in, their clothes drenched in dirt, looking like they'd just crawled out of a grave. We'd broken our promise and called them, letting them know about our find.

June's face scrunched up in distaste. "Are you sure you dug up just one grave and not the whole cemetery?"

Mitchell shot her a grim look.

June, momentarily distracted from the grimoire, continued her barrage of questions. "Was there a body?"

Mitchell's expression darkened. "We barely scratched the surface."

"Then why are you both so filthy?" June pressed, eyeing their state.

Her brother shrugged. "Caretaker showed up. We hid in a mud pit for over an hour until he left. Didn't find anything. And then you called."

Normally, I would've laughed at the absurdity of it all, but right now, my attention was solely on the grimoire.

"It's on the table," I said.

Nick didn't rush. He first washed and dried his hands thoroughly, and only when they were spotless did he move to the book, approaching it as if it were a relic pulled from a tomb.

Chapter Thirty-One

September, 2020

ALL ATTENTION SHIFTED to the grimoire I'd carried with me this whole time. Nick pulled it closer, carefully flipping through its brittle pages. Without a word, we all deferred to him—he seemed to know more than the rest of us, or at least he acted like he did.

I didn't know what I expected to happen. I hoped he'd find the sigil in the book with a note, "Reversal," and it'd all be done, easy as pressing buttons on a keyboard to undo a command.

My first instinct was to call Mathilda and ask about the grimoire—how to use it, what it meant. But Nick was firmly against it.

"We don't even know if she can help," he said. "And we don't have time for her bullshit."

I was slouched on the edge of the bed, head throbbing in my hands, watching him with a detached indifference. The book disgusted me. It had been from the moment we found it. It had been the root of all our misfortunes. *My misfortunes.*

Mitchell didn't say it aloud, but I knew he still doubted the magic of the sigil. I didn't. I felt it—seeping into my bones, coiling tighter around me with every hour.

Whatever Mitchell thought, he kept it to himself and went along with Nick's search. There were dozens of missing people, and he didn't want me to become one of them. If I hadn't been the one mutilated by these people who had been sacrificing others for decades, I wouldn't believe it either. But here we were, and there was the book.

I still couldn't wrap my mind around the fact that Lucas had it the entire time.

He was superstitious, sure, but so were most people. Everyone had their little beliefs—11:11 on the clock, manifestation nonsense, and all that. It didn't mean any of it was real. But this—this was.

Now that I knew Lucas was gone, I didn't want to hold onto the anger. But being blamed for the mess he'd created and knowing I might be next made my blood boil. He had never trusted me. Had lied to my face. Gaslighted me about where he'd gone on those strange trips. I had thought he might be cheating. For all I knew, he still could've been—like Mitchell said, *cheaters, thieves, and liars.* That had been our relationship in a nutshell.

It was still a mystery why he stole the grimoire from his father and how he intended to use it.

Eventually, Nick withdrew to the second room we'd rented, unable to focus with all the questions and scattered ideas flying around.

"Isn't it weird that Robert never came for you?" Mitch asked.

I raised an eyebrow. "What do you mean?"

"If he thought Lucas gave you the grimoire, why hasn't he come for you?"

I shrugged, exhaustion heavy on my bones. "I don't know, Mitch."

I was so tired of people asking questions, rhetorical or not. I didn't know why Robert hadn't come for the grimoire if he wanted it back so badly. I didn't even know what the grimoire could do, or whether it could do anything at all.

But apparently, Robert believed in the power of it so completely that he hadn't hesitated to kill his own son for it. That explained the grave. They'd known Lucas wasn't coming back. And yet Robert had played the grieving father so convincingly.

Nick's mother, on the other hand, had once again been erased from the equation. Her murder remained a big question mark.

I'd always wondered how many versions of ourselves we carried. I only seemed to have one. Maybe that was my mistake. I was exposed, unprotected. I showed people every vulnerability from the start.

My father had been different. He had a face for work, one for my mother, another for me, and apparently one more for his mistress.

Did Mitch and June have sides of themselves I'd never seen? Did Nick?

The world might've been a better place if we were all just honest. If we couldn't lie. If we didn't know how.

June moved closer, her weight shifting the mattress.

"Do you think… if Nick figures it out, he could bring Amanda and Lucas back too?"

I turned my aching eyes toward her. "I. Don't. Fucking. Know."

Without waiting for a response, I stood and walked to the bathroom, needing to be anywhere else. Her question cracked something open inside me, and I didn't want to feel it.

In the bathroom mirror, I faced a pale ghost of myself. My skin had a sickly green cast, as if something had burrowed in and worn me like a body bag. Freckles blurred. Lips almost white. My eyes were rimmed in red, heavy with deep, hollowed shadows. Purple and yellow blotches ravaged my cheeks, crawled down my arms, and marked my ribs.

I wasn't just tired. I was unraveling, piece by piece.

The front door banged shut, and muffled voices drifted through the thin bathroom door. Mitch, who had gone out to get food, was back. I splashed cold water on my face, stepped out without looking at anyone, and went straight to the bed, curling up with my back to the room.

All I could do was wait. The seconds dragged by in nervous tension. The quiet from the other room was a muted siren's song, tempting my thoughts to dark places. I wanted to barge in, to ask if Nick had found anything, if there was any chance at all. But I knew better. So, I let him work in peace.

The curtains were drawn tight, letting only a sliver of daylight creep through. None of us knew what to do, so we pretended to stay busy. Now, June was in the bathroom, messing with something, the sound of water running on and off faint in the background.

I mindlessly opened my laptop without a clear purpose in mind, then closed it, and opened it again. I logged into Facebook and scrolled down the feed full of meaningless updates. Weddings, kids, dog pictures. Each post felt like it belonged to another world, one that had nothing to do with mine. All these people had no idea what was really going on, trapped in their little bubbles of normalcy. But then again, neither did I. Maybe that's all anyone ever saw—the glitz and glitter of each other's lives.

I pulled up Sarah's profile, my fingers moving on their own. I started typing, but the words weren't right. It wasn't an apology. It was a "Fuck you" message for being a terrible friend. For living the life I couldn't. For her ignorance, for gossiping behind my back. I needed her to know, even if it was the last thing I ever did. What did I have to lose?

I stared at the message, a messy jumble of anger and frustration, then deleted it. It was childish and pointless. A way to vent emotions that wouldn't change a damn thing.

Then I thought about the Facebook group Amanda and the other woman were in. I searched for it, but came up empty. I double-checked the spelling and searched again. Nothing. The group had gone. I checked my pending group requests, hoping for a clue. Nothing.

I turned to Mitch. "It's gone," I said, disbelief creeping in.

"What's gone?" He looked confused.

"The Facebook group."

Mitch's face dropped. "I know," he said, keeping his voice down. "I noticed it a few days back when I checked Amanda's page. I'm sorry I snapped at you about it. It's been bothering me, thinking I should have checked it sooner."

I muttered, "It's okay. You were right to snap at me."

His eyes drop to the floor. "It's not just that. There's a message history with a deleted profile. I could only see Amanda's side of the conversation. They were discussing what had happened to her. She contacted them a few times, but then the messages just stopped. About a month before she visited Black Water."

"What does it mean?"

"You were right. They're finding people online, luring them in somehow. Maybe broken people, like—" He trailed off.

I agreed with him. He should have checked on it earlier. He should have told me about it. And though I knew it probably wouldn't have changed anything, irritation still flickered to life in my chest. He sat there, slouched, his usual military posture and composure gone. I wanted to lash out, say something to make him feel worse, but what good would it do? We were both in the dark, fumbling around.

I closed my laptop with intentional slowness, picked it up and threw it against the wall. The sound of cracking plastic and metal choked the room.

Mitch stayed where he was, his face unreadable.

"What happened?" June burst out of the bathroom, startled by the noise.

I got up and left the room.

NICK SAT on the faded rug, his back hunched, papers and notes scattered around him like a chaotic map of some foreign world. His focus was so intense that it felt like the room could fall away, and he wouldn't even notice.

I set the paper bag on the table. "You must be hungry."

"Hm?" He looked up, blinking slowly as if he were just waking from a long sleep. "Thanks."

I watched him for a few seconds, his eyes already back on the page.

"How's it going?"

"I'm not sure." He ran a hand through his hair, wary of the symbols. "It's like… the book gives you ingredients. We just have to figure out the recipe. It's not nonsense, but it feels like it. It's a language, maybe a cipher. I see things repeating." He pointed to a spot on the page, his finger hovering over the ink as if afraid it might disappear. "Here, and here—the same symbol. And this one—"

I tried not to let frustration creep into my voice, but it still found its way. "So nothing specific?" I leaned against the table. Even if every piece of the puzzle was right in front of him, it would have been like trying to learn Hiragana in a single sitting.

Everyone was worried. Mitchell had retreated into disbelief. June's anxiety was edged with fear. But Nick's concern felt different. It wasn't just concern; it was the kind of desperation that came with the thought of losing someone you couldn't live without. I hated myself for pushing all of that away.

I moved closer, my hands trembling as I cupped his face, brushing my thumbs along the sharp lines of his jaw. I pressed my lips to his. They were dry, warm, and uncertain. And then, he kissed me back, but his touch was delicate, as if he feared he might break me. I didn't mind his tenderness, as long as it came from this place of care. But all too soon, he pulled back.

"I'm sorry," he whispered, his breath warm against my skin. "I don't want to hurt you. And I still haven't figured this out."

"What if you don't?" The words escaped before I could stop them, lingering in the air between us.

"I will."

I nodded, my throat tight.

"Eat something," I said, nudging the paper bag closer to him.

"Nellie, it's there. I promise I'll find it."

I managed a weak smile that didn't quite reach my eyes.

Nick's obsession with the grimoire grew stronger by the hour, filling me with mounting concern. I spent the night beside him, catching a few hours of restless sleep, but he hadn't budged. His eyes took on a wild, anxious gleam. He kept showing me passages, thinking out loud—something he had never done before. His usual calm, distant demeanor had given way to someone consumed by fixation.

He didn't seem like his usual self, and it scared me. At first, I had been hopeful. I believed Nick would figure it out, that he'd find a way to reverse the sigil's power and keep me safe from the thing in the woods and the coven. But as the hours passed and Nick's behavior grew more erratic, the last drops of hope began to dwindle. Desperation, depression, and helplessness weighed me down. I didn't know what to do.

With only a few hours left before midnight, I watched the sun set inexorably, struggling to digest the thought: *This is my last day on earth.*

Mitch knocked and entered our room without waiting for a response. June slipped in after him.

"We need to do something," he said.

"I *am* doing something," Nick muttered, not looking up from the book.

"Let's find Robert. We'll waterboard him if necessary."

They were all scrambling to fix things, but they didn't understand the enemy or the situation.

"No," Nick finally said, lifting his gaze but not his hands from the book.

"What do you mean, 'no'? What do you propose?"

"We'll go to the clearing," Nick said, getting up from the floor.

"Why?" Mitchell asked.

"Robert and the others will be there. They know it's our only chance to change the deal."

"What deal?"

"The deal!" Nick's voice cracked with tired frustration, his words tumbling out in a rush, as if he couldn't believe no one else could understand him. June looked at him like he'd grown a second head. "The deal they made with whatever's in the woods! The one they're sacrificing Nellie to!"

Silence followed. I thought about it, sure, but hearing Nick speak it out loud, so plainly, made the reality colder.

"How can you be sure?" Mitch asked.

"I'm not. But that's all I've got."

"How will you change the terms?" Mitch pressed.

"I'll try something."

"Try something?" Mitchell tilted his head, skeptical.

Nick rubbed his eyes, too tired to argue with him, and turned to face all of us. If there was one thing I'd learned about Nick, it was that he hated explaining his thoughts before he had a plan. And clearly, that was the case now. He was gambling with my life.

"What about the book?" June asked timidly, "Did you find something there?"

The grimoire was now filled with bookmarks. Nick opened it to one of the pages and pointed to a symbol.

"See this? It's part of Nellie's sigil. And this…" He flipped a few more pages, stopping at another symbol. "Is another piece."

"So?" June asked, her brow furrowing.

"Her sigil is a compound one. It's made up of different parts scattered throughout the book, plus some things that aren't even here. And we don't know what else." He looked up, meeting Mitchell's eyes. "Basically, it's like defusing a bomb. You've got a bunch of wires, and you have to figure out which one to cut without setting it off. Our best chance is to go back to the clearing where the sigil was created and try to destroy it there."

June folded her arms. "How do you know Robert will be there?"

Nick hesitated for a moment before answering. "I don't. But if he shows up, it'll confirm my theory that there's a way to cancel this. And he'll try to stop us."

I closed my eyes. What angered me the most was my own inability to do anything. I relied on Nick, Mitchell, and even June to fix things for me. I was a helpless spectator, always waiting to be saved by someone. But what could I do? I was too tired to even feel anger. All my emotions had drained away, leaving me an empty shell. The electronic clock on the nightstand flickered, and its red digits changed, counting down the hours I had left. The monster might as well come and take me now.

"Are you sure about this?" Mitchell asked for what felt like the hundredth time. "Because if we go, and Robert and his men are there, we'd be putting ourselves in even more danger. Shouldn't we just wait?"

"Wait for what?" Nick snapped, his patience at breaking point. "You want to risk it? It's Nellie's life we're talking about."

Once again, I understood Mitchell's doubts, his struggle to believe in something he couldn't see, his desperate need to protect his sister, to keep her safe from harm. Still, it stung, especially since he'd been the one to insist I come with them in the first place.

Nick let out a weary sigh, closed the book, and said, "You know what? If you want to wait, then wait somewhere else. Nell and I will go there alone."

32

Chapter Thirty-Two

September, 2020

FOR THE FEW hours we had left, Nick stayed awake, never dozing off for even a minute. I slept fitfully, tossing and turning, my back throbbing and my ribs aching. It was my life at stake, and I couldn't keep my eyes open, which was painfully ironic. He didn't try to comfort me, and oddly, I was grateful for it. Hollow reassurances would only have made me feel worse.

We drove off in my Dodge, just the two of us, before the sun had fully set, the grimoire buried deep inside his raincoat. A deserted strip mall was our first stop. I waited in the car, staring at the washed-out storefronts while Nick ran his errand. He'd been gone for over half an hour, but I didn't ask what he had been doing there. He wasn't in the mood for questions, and I figured he'd tell me only what he thought I needed to know.

Besides, I was only half-present, reality coming in pieces, shifting and uneven.

I wondered if death row inmates ever truly grasped what was coming. How does anyone comprehend the world without themselves in it? My brain couldn't wrap around the thought. In a few hours, I might be gone. Would I really just... end?

I held on to every shred of control I had, keeping my panic at bay. But as we neared the trailhead, my breathing turned shallow, and my pulse spiked. This was it. We were doing this.

We'd parked farther down the road to keep the car out of sight.

"You okay to walk?" Nick asked, as if I had a choice. I gave a tight nod, and we stepped into the woods.

Veering off the main path at night was dangerous, but remaining on it posed a bigger threat. Robert and his people were probably nearby.

The canopy above absorbed what little daylight remained. We set out while the sun still peered over the mountains, but now the forest had grown murky and still. The humidity clung to me, sticky and suffocating. Sweat slid down my back, but I zipped my raincoat up, trapping the heat inside. I didn't dare take it off. It was the only thing separating me from the world around us.

"Let's not use the flashlights unless we absolutely have to," Nick said.

It seemed like the perfect time to turn one on—I could barely see ten feet in front of me. But he was right—a moving light would give us away, and as long as the sky stayed clear, we had just enough visibility.

Nick checked the route on his watch and moved forward. I stayed close behind.

Every so often, I brushed against rough bark or slipped on rocks, my heart skipping with each stumble. Occasionally, a branch cracked somewhere off the path, probably an animal, but the sounds stayed distant, never drawing closer. I kept reminding myself that if Robert or his men meant to stop us, they would have done so already. We were only two, and unarmed.

But a part of me wasn't afraid anymore.

A part of me was so tired, so hollowed out, it almost wished for the end.

The wind seeped through the leafy expanse above, and the trees creaked out a rasping murmur. They had seen this before, other lives walking toward the same trap. We weren't the first. Just the latest, marching obediently into Robert's snare.

Above us, the moon was a pale disk staring down at me. I stopped walking.

"What is it?" Nick halted, shoulders tense, and followed my gaze. "It's okay. Let's keep moving. We're not far now."

I don't know how he spotted the sigil in the dark, but there it was. Holding the blade in his dominant hand, he hesitated long enough for a tremor to show. He cut right beside his previous offering, now scabbed and healing. Blood trickled down the bark like tears. Nick pulled down his sleeve, and we moved on.

We had to ford the creek, avoiding the weathered bridge. Though the water was shallow, we were soaked up to our knees. I lingered, scanning the area. There was no one around, but the nagging sense of being watched wouldn't leave. Nick grasped my arm and pulled me forward.

"We need to keep moving."

As we crossed, the sounds around us dulled, like they had the first time we came here. Or perhaps it was only my imagination. Only the soft squelch of our soaked shoes against the forest floor broke the stillness. The darkness thickened.

I didn't have the energy to worry about snakes or spiders. My eyes kept drifting skyward. I knew the full moon's technical peak lasted only a moment—a fleeting alignment—but each time that cold, perfect circle broke through the clouds, my stomach dropped.

We trudged through thick underbrush, losing all sense of direction and time. It was like drifting through space, cold, vast, and unending.

Nick's pace quickened, pushing me to my limits. Then,

without warning, he stopped. I stumbled, barely avoiding his back.

"Here we are," he whispered, pointing toward the nearest tree. I couldn't see anything, but maybe his eyes had adjusted better than mine. He shrugged off his backpack and pulled something out. A rugged, heavy-duty knife with a broad blade. Freed from its holster, it caught the moonlight, razor-sharp. I recoiled on instinct.

"What is it?"

"A Ka-Bar," he said, as if the name should explain everything. "Mitch gave it to me."

I wondered why he hadn't used this blade on himself. Maybe it was just too sharp—sharp enough to cut through the darkness —and he was worried that as dusk deepened, he might cut too deep.

He pulled out a sealed antiseptic wipe, opened it, and carefully cleaned the blade. Once it was done, he slid it back into its holster, tucked it into the deep pocket of his raincoat, and turned to face me.

"Listen, we have a slim chance, but I need to cut through the sigil. To change its meaning. Understand?"

My breathing grew shallow. Nick placed his hands on my shoulders.

"You can do this."

I nodded, my throat dry.

"One more thing. Sacrifices must be willing for them to work. Don't go willingly, no matter what."

It could mean a million different things. Consent was supposed to be a clear, unbroken line. But people bent it all the time, saying if you didn't run fast enough, didn't scream loud enough, didn't fight hard enough, maybe you'd allowed it. So, where did it leave me? If I kept resisting, would that be enough to survive the night? Or did I have to claw and crawl and fight every second, never stop, never slip, to prove I still wanted to live? Because if I had faltered, even for a breath, had the darkness already counted me as willing?

"Follow my instructions," Nick said. "If I say run, you run. Don't look back."

"But—"

"No buts. Do you trust me?"

"Do I have a choice?"

"Not really."

Nick had left his backpack in the forest so he wouldn't have to carry it with him, since everything important was already out.

The world tilted. My ears rang louder, time stretched thin, and every step felt like pushing through water. I forced a slow, deliberate breath. *It's just panic,* I told myself.

We moved into the clearing with caution, every sense stretched tight. I expected flames at the edges, figures in masks waiting, but there was nothing. It looked deserted.

The barn door hung crooked, its lock blasted open in the state we'd left it.

Nick's grip tightened around my arm as he led me to the stone altar, the same slab where they'd burned a symbol into my skin only two nights ago. His face stayed calm, but the stiff precision of every measured step betrayed the pressure mounting beneath it.

Movement stirred at the edge of the clearing, where forest shadows bled into open space. Figures emerged slowly, one by one, lighting torches until the clearing glowed with flickering orange light. There were six of them. As before, all but one wore their grotesque stag skull masks.

Only Robert stood unmasked. The coven leader faced us, flame light dancing in the lenses of his glasses.

Nick didn't flinch. He stepped forward, placing himself squarely between me and them.

"A little dramatic, don't you think?" he said, nodding toward the torches.

Robert shook his head. "Feels more genuine to me. Fire's a purifier, after all."

"I doubt it helps."

"Why did you come here?"

"You know why, Robert." Nick's tone stayed even.

Robert tilted his head, smiling faintly as he adjusted his glasses. "Nick Boyd," he intoned the name, as if tasting it carefully on his tongue. "You seem to know me right well. But nobody's rightly sure who you are."

"I like my privacy," Nick replied, eyes locked on his.

That part was true. Nick was the only person I knew with no digital footprint. No social media. No trace.

Robert remained calm. The figures beside him didn't move an inch.

"I reckon you've got the grimoire, seein' as you're here. But I gotta wonder, what makes you think you can use it?"

His gaze shifted, like something had just occurred to him. He looked around slowly.

"Where are the other two? The boy and the girl?"

The masked men turned, checking the tree line as if expecting an ambush. They moved slowly, deliberately, silent figures with horned, skull-like faces, like ghosts caught in ritual. I wondered if they were even real.

Nick cut in. "What did their sister want? Amanda. She came to you willingly, didn't she? You must remember her wish. What did you promise her?"

Robert sighed and held a deliberate pause, glaring at Nick, as though trying to read his mind. When he spoke again, his voice carried new confidence.

"Freedom from it all. From the ghosts in her head, from the hurt, from... her family."

"And you delivered," Nick said, his tone empty.

Robert stepped forward. His people mirrored the motion, closing in.

But Nick didn't flinch. Slowly, he reached into his coat and pulled out the grimoire.

Robert's eyes homed in on the leather-bound book with instant recognition. He stiffened. His followers paused, too, instinctively waiting for his next move.

"So you do have it," Lucas's father breathed. His voice wavered, then steadied. "What'll it take to get it off your hands?"

Nick didn't respond right away. With the same deliberate calm, he handed me the book, then reached into his pocket and drew out a small blowtorch, the kind you'd find in a hardware store.

He guided my hand, still holding the grimoire, and lit the torch with a loud whoosh.

I hadn't known this was his plan. It took everything I had not to recoil from the flame. But I held steady.

"Tell me how to reverse it," Nick said. "Or I'll burn it."

Robert's face dropped its mask of friendliness. His eyes turned cold.

"You can't undo what's been done," he seethed through gritted teeth. "But you can use it for somethin' worthwhile."

"At what cost?"

Robert smirked. "You're young, and to you, it's always black and white. But life's a lot of gray. Sometimes you gotta choose between the lesser of two evils. Helpin' the most folks, even if it means one person gets hurt. You could save a whole lot more that way."

"Yeah, right," Nick shot back. "That's greed dressed up as nobility."

"I ain't doing this for me."

"Then who for?" Nick pushed. "You've got clients, don't you? Politicians? CEOs? Wealthy people clinging to life by their fingernails? You're just another dealer. You could be selling meth for all its worth. Feeding drug lords and calling it business."

Something flickered in Robert's eyes—rage, maybe shame—but he didn't deny it. "What's your price for the book?"

"Why do you even need it?" Nick countered. "You've clearly been running your little operation without it."

"Why don't we just put you down and take what's ours?"

"And risk killing her?" Nick threw a glance my way. "You'd lose everything. One of us dies, the book burns. We made sure of that. So stop bluffing and tell me the truth. Why do you need the grimoire?"

Robert's lips thinned. "We're doin' this 'cause we got no other choice. But maybe there's a way out. If you're givin' it up willingly... maybe we don't have to keep doin' it this way."

I listened quietly, knowing Nick was just buying time. I didn't need to call out Robert's bullshit—Nick saw through it just fine. But the way he held the grimoire at the motel… made every instinct in me recoil. That book radiated something wrong, something toxic, as if it were slick with venom. I hated touching it.

But Nick—Nick looked at it differently. Yes, he wanted to save me, I knew that. But there was something else in his eyes when he studied its pages. Fascination. Obsession. Not with me. With it.

And now I saw the same look in Robert's eyes. Whatever power that book held, it had already begun to work on them both. Robert was drunk on its promise, and I was beginning to wonder how far Nick would go before he was, too.

"Say I give you the book," Nick said, subtly adjusting his stance. "What are you going to do with it?"

"Same as you," Robert said. "I'll hold onto it, keep it from gettin' into the wrong hands, make sure it don't cause no trouble."

"Maybe your hands are the wrong ones."

Robert's response was instant. "My hands are the only ones good enough."

"And what do I get if I give it to you?" Nick asked.

"Anythin'," Robert said. "Everythin'."

Nick didn't reply, but his silence felt like thunderclouds gathering, dense and electric.

Robert went on, smiling softly, like a father gently scolding his children. "It's ours. Only we can rightly handle it. It's always belonged here."

His calmness was far more terrifying than his anger. Behind us, the forest released a cold sigh, like we stood with our backs to a deep well or an open grave. Something was watching—I felt it, though I didn't dare turn around.

"You're wastin' your breath, though," Robert said. "You can't help her now. The deal's been made. We're just here to see it through. But I could show you how to read the book."

He took a slow step back, as if generously giving us space. I could feel Nick coil tighter, his muscles ready to snap.

"We're not bad people, you know. We work for the greater good," Robert continued, mistaking Nick's silence for hesitation.

The scent of damp earth rose from the forest floor, sharp and tangy. Something stirred out in the woods. Robert noticed it too; his eyes flicked behind us for a split second before settling back with practiced calm. He knew something was there. And he was welcoming it.

"A boys' club working for the greater good? Please. We've already had this conversation." Nick's tone was dry, the sarcasm woven so finely into his words that it almost passed for sincerity.

"We don't mess around here, Nick Boyd," Robert replied, removing his glasses. "We're a group of folks who share the same values, workin' to make this world—and this town—a better place for everyone."

"And what a coincidence that all these 'like-minded individuals' happen to be men."

"Women ain't cut out for this kinda power. They're too emotional, too flighty. Men are more level-headed, more rational. We can make the hard calls without gettin' caught up in feelings and personal opinions."

I seethed. His self-righteousness was a stench I couldn't breathe around. He spoke of the greater good, but everything about him reeked of greed and misogyny.

If I had once been consumed by fear, focused only on making it through the night, I now wanted more. I wanted revenge. I wanted him to suffer. To pay.

I wanted him gone.

"Yeah? How tough was the decision to put a price tag on human life?" I snapped. "Your own son's life?"

Robert gave me a condescending smile as he cleaned his lenses, then turned back to Nick.

"Look at your lady friend here," he said. "She's got no idea what she's talkin' about, but she's quick to attack me. The sooner you see she's a problem, not a plus, the sooner you'll be ready for the power I'm offerin'."

A shotgun blast tore through the night. Tree bark splintered near me, exploding outward like someone had taken a bite out of the trunk.

I stood transfixed, watching Mitch move—precise, practiced, deadly. He didn't hesitate. He flowed through their ranks like a blade, clean and terrifyingly efficient.

There were six masked men in total. Three carried guns holstered awkwardly. They were expecting fear, maybe a little resistance. Not this. Not Mitch.

June hovered near the treeline, holding the shotgun steady. One twitch in the wrong direction, and she'd fire. They knew it. Her presence bought Mitch valuable seconds, which he used like gold.

One of Robert's men panicked and fired into the dark. The crack split the air like lightning. Flashlights flickered, casting jerky shadows across the trees. The second shot went wide, hitting one of their own, a man in a grotesque stag skull mask.

He yelped in pain, clutching his shoulder as he staggered back.

The mask fell away, and that was all Mitch needed. He moved fast, delivering a brutal blow to the man's exposed face. There was an audible crunch as he crumpled like a ragdoll.

No one dared fire again, but the fighting kept on. Mitch stood among them, blood on his knuckles, but composed. He looked like he belonged in the chaos.

With one man down, Mitch still struggled with the other five. Even with June watching from the treeline, they had minutes, maybe less.

"Nell, now!" Nick roared, snapping me out of my trance.

The next moment, my raincoat was on the ground. He slashed my T-shirt down the back and yanked the bandage off, no time for finesse. The icy steel touched my tender skin, making me twitch. This was going to hurt.

I leaned against the stone, gripping it tightly, bracing myself against it. Nick began carving into my skin. I tried not to scream, instead letting out a low growl; tears streamed from my eyes. The burning was at least quick. I was terrified I'd faint, but somehow, I managed to stay on my feet, pushing through it.

"Almost done, almost done!" he kept repeating.

June screamed, and another deafening gunshot echoed through the forest.

"Fuck!" she bellowed, followed by, "Watch out!"

But Nick had finished. He scrambled me off the stone, forced the knife, slick with my own blood, and the grimoire, into my hands, and pushed me in the direction of the trees. "Run!"

One of the masked men tackled him from behind, sending him crashing to the ground. I stood there, lightheaded, knife in my hand, hesitating. I could help. But Nick roared again. "Go!"

With all the energy I had in me, I darted into the woods.

The darkness opened like a giant, hungry mouth and swallowed me whole.

33

Chapter Thirty-Three

October, 2020

MY FEET KICKED up rotten leaves as I raced to the bridge. Behind me, heavy boots tore through a tangle of twisted branches and thorny brush. Robert's men were after me. After the grimoire.

But I was faster.

This was muscle memory, years of track meets and laps around the field. My body knew how to run, even as my mind frayed, overflowing with panic and fear.

Two more gunshots cracked in the distance, their echoes dissolving into the night. I didn't look back. I clutched the knife in one hand and the grimoire in the other. The book buzzed faintly beneath my palm. I told myself I was imagining things, though I didn't believe it for a second.

Pain flared in my shoulder as blood soaked through the shredded shirt, tracing my spine like warm fingers. Each breath scraped the inside of my throat. My abdomen clenched, but I didn't slow.

The trees ahead bent unnaturally. In the dark, I didn't see

details, just shapes in the dead moonlight. To the left, I caught a flicker of movement, a shadow of a shadow. It didn't look human.

Two screams—one, then another—sharp and sudden, slicing through the trees behind me. Then, silence.

I pushed harder.

Now, all I could hear was my own ragged breathing and the relentless pounding of blood in my ears. No one was chasing me anymore.

But something else was out there. A presence. Silent. Invisible. A pressure, constant and tightening its grip. It drove me forward, deeper. I forced a swallow, but the bitter sting of bile still crept up my throat.

Something caught my foot, and I went down hard. The knife slipped from my hand as I crashed through the ferns, leaves and branches, landing flat on my stomach. Air rushed out of me in a helpless gasp. For a second, everything went still.

Plastered against the damp earth and trying to catch my breath, I listened carefully. No footsteps. No voices. Just silence pressing in from all sides.

I had lost them.

A sharp ache bloomed across my knees where I'd landed on tree roots. The pain was jarring but survivable. The ground beneath me shifted, almost like it was breathing with me.

I pushed myself up slowly, the grimoire clutched tight to my chest. My free hand fumbled through wet leaves, searching for the knife. But my fingers found something else. Something out of place.

Hard. Rectangular.

Plastic.

I froze.

Leaves and dirt peeled away to reveal a phone, screen cracked and caked in grime. But I knew the case. Even though the old football team logo was barely visible.

Lucas's.

I couldn't move. Couldn't breathe. The woods suddenly felt too close.

I stared at the phone, too stunned to think. My brain couldn't catch up. How had it ended up here, hundreds of miles from where Lucas was last seen? Had it been here the whole time, buried under the leaves, waiting? As if it had been placed there. As if it wanted to be found.

And now I had found it.

This was real. Lucas was gone. Something had dragged him into the dark, and now I had willingly followed it straight into its den.

Overhead, the moon broke through the canopy again, a lifeless eye framed by a mouth full of crooked teeth. My skin prickled.

The silence was so heavy that it felt deliberate, like the woods were holding their breath. I didn't dare move.

Then, a sharp crack.

I spun toward the sound, my heart slamming into my ribs.

A figure drifted between the trees, peeling away from the shadows.

But it wasn't Lucas.

It was my father.

HE STOOD BEFORE ME, wearing the same navy-blue suit and tie he'd been buried in. Now it clung to his mimic's frame, damp at the hem, as if it had just climbed out of the grave. He was barefoot and disheveled. A thin scar ran along his knuckle. But his face—it was unrecognizable, hidden behind a stag skull, the dead sockets glistening.

It stood like him, wore his skin, his suit, his scars, but it wasn't my father, it wasn't the man who had come to my defence so many times, who'd reassured me that nothing was permanent, that someday we'd be happy and unrestricted and free. No, it was a memory someone else had dressed up and sent to mock me. To haunt me. To claim me.

The deity.

I scrambled backward until my spine collided with weathered bark.

The entity took a step forward.

"Why are you afraid?" it asked in a voice that was so much like my father's that its timbre shattered my already weeping heart. It echoed in my head like a thought I hadn't meant to think. It came from nowhere and everywhere. I felt it in the roots of my teeth. In the marrow of my bones. The tree at my back hummed when it spoke.

Another step forward.

"It's not real," I whispered, eyes squeezed shut.

Cold breath on my skin, like leaning over a stone well and feeling the chill rise up from the dark.

"Go away!"

The temperature dropped and a breeze snaked around my ankles. I opened my eyes. In the exact spot where my father had stood, Nick now appeared—barefoot and shirtless, his pale chest exposed. His face was hidden behind the same ghastly stag mask, but I recognized his frame, his body, his tattoos.

He moved closer, each step slow and unnaturally deliberate, as if he were learning to walk in borrowed skin.

The mask's empty sockets seemed to lure me with a magnetic force I couldn't resist. I couldn't look away.

"You came," it said, now in Nick's rich, velvet voice, and my belly warmed, instantly comforted.

The mask leaned in from the darkness, thick and heavy like jelly. The skull hovered inches from my face. At this distance, I should have seen eyes, a glint, a flicker. But there was nothing. Just blackness. Like the mask wasn't hiding anything at all.

Its putrid, sour scent reminded me of death, and I tried not to vomit. I turned away, unable to bear the sight as my tears flowed unchecked.

It's not Nick. It's not Nick. It's not Nick, I repeated over and over, stuttering, desperate to drown out the crushing fear, desperate to wake up, to claw my way back to reality.

Its hand reached out slowly. I watched, transfixed, as it drifted past my face. Only when its fingers touched my back did I feel how cold and inhuman it was.

This was it.

My body trembled violently, my mind shutting down, emptied of everything but the raw, primal terror of dying.

I gasped as the fingers pressed into my shoulder's open wound, where a fresh cut had torn through the burn. It pulsed like it had a heartbeat of its own. My vision blurred and distorted, the world around me trembling, like I was seeing it through shattered, grime-smeared glass.

The hand withdrew, and the creature wearing Nick's likeness rose to its full height, towering over me. I watched as it dragged stained fingers across the mask, smearing my blood in uneven streaks. The fingers moved down its neck and bare chest, marking itself with my pain. Then it went limp.

It wasn't looking at me anymore. It was staring at the grimoire clenched tightly in my hands.

I felt like I'd ingested something toxic, trapped in a psychedelic nightmare.

My thoughts were a tangled mess of what-ifs and maybes. What if I gave it the grimoire? It could spare my life. But what if it didn't? What if this were all just a twisted game?

But then something shifted. A stark, terrible clarity cut through the haze in my mind. I realized I was essentially already dead. There was nothing left to lose. Nothing to go back to.

I lifted my gaze to the deity, still standing before me, waiting. The moon hung high above, an unblinking, cold eye watching everything like an unhelpful God.

"Take it," I said, forcing the words out.

It didn't move.

My feet dragged, but I forced myself to stand and stepped forward all the same.

"Take it," I repeated, this time with more defiance. I wasn't bargaining. I wasn't begging. I just wanted it to end. I held the book out with trembling hands.

The creature seemed to shrink into the shadows. Frozen above us, the moon cast everything in an eerie, unnatural stillness. The black holes of the deity's eyes had changed. They weren't empty anymore. Now, they held a glint, orange and alive, like flames swaying in silence.

"Where's Lucas? Where's Amanda? Where are you taking us all?" I demanded.

I moved closer, no longer feeling fear, but an overwhelming sense of purpose. The deity either sensed my resolve or was simply summoning me deeper, for it took a step back, its eyes flickering like embers.

I didn't care. I followed, agonizing step by agonizing step.

But the closer I got, the more it seemed to fade.

I could see right through it.

The deity wasn't real.

It was never there.

I'd been so foolish. This thing, this spirit, was a projection, a twisted creation born from my grief and desperate need to make sense of everything. It was a figment of my broken mind, a reflection of my fear.

I had longed for it. I had called it into existence with my own terror.

But it had to be real, brought to life by faith and sacrifices. Robert had willed it so in exchange for his wants.

But the figure refused to hold its form, dissolving into the night. Only the orange orbs of its eyes were an indication of its presence.

"No, wait!" I pleaded, but the flames had already snuffed out.

I ran without direction, desperate to bring it back, to make it obey, to reverse it all.

The little flames kept drifting farther away, teasing me, disappearing and reappearing again in the distance.

Only when I drew closer did I realize what I was looking at.

I BURST INTO THE CLEARING, uncertain how I'd circled back. Two torches, the ones I had mistaken for the eyes, still burned, but the others lay on the ground, knocked out by either Robert's men or Mitchell.

My hands were full—the grimoire in one, the knife in the other.

Wait.

I turned the cold steel over in my palm, tracing the killer edge like a fever dream. I thought I'd lost it in the woods when I tripped and fell. Was I hallucinating then, or was I hallucinating now? How long had I been gone? It felt like forever, yet not much had changed.

Robert, another man, and Nick were fighting nearby. Mitch was shouting something at June, who was trapped against a tree by a figure in black, his mask gone, too. She held the shotgun uselessly, having spent all the shells. She was too far away for me to reach. The men who had chased me for the grimoire were gone. I didn't know if they'd run, gotten lost, or something worse had happened.

"You?" Robert's eyes widened as he stumbled backward, clearly not expecting to see me. Then he looked up at the moon. It looked ordinary now—no flare of death, no omen in the sky. "You've ruined everything, you stupid bitch. If he doesn't get what he wants, we're all going to..."

He didn't clarify who "he" was: one of his clients, or the monster lurking in the shadows.

I raised the knife, but Robert only smirked.

"Get the grimoire!" he barked, noticing the book in my other hand.

Two of his men lunged toward me, and reality snapped back into focus. At the same time, everything seemed to slow down, like time itself had been stretched thin.

"Give it to them!" Nick shouted when he saw me.

I stalled. They'd been after the book all along, and Nick's order to just hand it over was strange. But I had promised him I wouldn't question his orders.

With all the force I had, I twisted and hurled the book into the trees so hard that it almost felt like my arm was going with it.

One of Robert's men gave chase, but it made no difference. We were still outnumbered and outgunned.

The other tackled me to the ground, winding me. The knife flew from my grip again, but my hand instinctively closed around a nearby stone. I swung it blindly, catching my attacker in the shoulder. The hit wasn't clean, but it was enough to throw him off.

The masked figure reappeared from the trees, the grimoire held tentatively in his muddied fingers. He presented it to Robert, who accepted it for the sacred relic he believed it to be. They now had the book, and our chances of escape hadn't improved.

Robert scanned the pages, his expression twisted.

"What the hell is this?" he bellowed, flipping through the pages faster, each movement more frantic than the last.

His distraction rippled outward.

A thump, and Nick had managed to throw his attacker off his back. I took the opportunity to wrench myself free, scrambling up from the dirt like a reanimated corpse. Robert remained distracted, wholly absorbed in whatever was wrong with the pages.

He didn't see me coming.

I charged, the stone still in hand, and swung at his head. But Robert didn't fall. He blitzed like a storm, lashing out with an outstretched arm. I tasted leather and musty pages. He'd hit me with the grimoire. Pain shot through my skull as I hit the ground, weak and spent, blood trailing from my lips.

He stormed toward me, his footsteps breaking the earth with the weight of an avalanche. I tried to squirm away.

"You bitch," he spat again, and then, all at once, he stilled, choking on a guttural roar.

Just a few paces from me, he began clawing at his back in withering despair. I didn't understand until his knees buckled and he crashed onto his stomach.

My knife jutted from his back, and Nick stood over him.

A LOW, foreboding rumble shook the clearing. It wasn't quite an earthquake. It was deeper, stranger. A humming sound that grew louder with each passing second. I covered my ears, holding my breath until it stopped.

When I finally dared to look up, Nick was staring at me, the same shock scarred on his features. The man who had been attacking him was gone.

I turned toward Mitch and June. Robert's men were fleeing into the woods that had refused to take me.

The grimoire lay by my feet. I picked it up.

Its cover fell away in my hands, revealing a plain notepad underneath. The pages were the same size, but lined like an ordinary journal, mass-produced and modern. I blinked down at it, stunned.

June caught my eye. "Did it work? Is he dead?" she asked, her voice shaking. She was still hiding behind a tree, as if trying to decide whether it was safe to come out.

Robert lay on his side, his body slack in a way that left no doubt.

It seemed impossibly mundane. Anticlimactic.

After everything, it wasn't a curse or a monster that ended him. Just a knife.

A man like him, undone by something so ordinary.

NICK HAD SWAPPED the grimoire for a fake. I didn't know why he hadn't warned me, but I assumed he had his reasons. My best guess was that he wanted me to believe I was carrying the real thing. Maybe that's why the deity hadn't taken it—if it ever wanted it in the first place. At least the fake had done what it needed to: distracted Robert long enough for Nick to end it.

We didn't go after Robert's men, though June wanted to, still riding the adrenaline, but Mitchell stopped her. Judging by how Robert had carried himself and the way the others had followed him, it felt safe to assume he'd been the one holding it all together. The one with real power. They wouldn't survive without him, and without the grimoire.

I sat down, covered in blood, and stared blankly into space. After two years of being accused of murder, directly and indirectly, I had somewhat lived up to my reputation. We'd killed a man. I was an accomplice, and I would have to live with that for the rest of my days. But no matter how hard I tried to wrap my head around it—to feel guilt or remorse or anything at all—it wouldn't come. We killed a man to stop him from killing others, to save ourselves. When I found Duane's body, I went into shock. Now, after seeing someone die, I felt a hollow calm. June and Mitch acted like it was nothing. But we still had a dead body on our hands.

Mitchell came back first, carrying a stuffed backpack and a shovel.

"Where did you get the shovel?" I asked, my brain too tired to process anything else.

"We packed it up, just in case. Grabbed some other stuff, too. Snacks and whatnot." He tossed a protein bar at me, but I didn't catch it. It softly hit my chest and landed on my lap.

"Sorry," he winced. "Eat it. You'll need the energy."

"He made me carry his stupid backpack," June whined. "It was so heavy!"

I buried my face in my hands and laughed wearily. Hearing her complain again felt like a breath of fresh air.

NICK WAS PUTTING the real grimoire back into its cover, wrapping it with fabric before tucking it into his backpack. He'd stashed it in the woods near the clearing, keeping it hidden the entire time.

"They probably searched the motel room, too," he said. "Didn't want to risk leaving it there."

"Can't we just leave it here? Or destroy it?" I begged.

"No," he said abruptly. "We don't know if it'll calm it down, set it free, or piss it off. Let's not risk it."

No one had the energy to argue. We all looked like we'd been through the wringer. Nick's eyes were sunken, his skin pale and clammy, and his clothes were torn and stained. Mitch had a nasty gash above his eyebrow, and his lip was swollen and bruised. June's hair was matted and tangled, her clothes ripped and filthy. She didn't have any visible wounds, but she was limping slightly. I probably didn't look any better. My shirt was torn, and I was splattered with forest mud and blood, the bruises from before still in bloom on my face.

On the bright side, I was so tired that the pain barely registered.

"Wait here," Mitch said, nodding at the corpse on the other side of the clearing. "We'll take care of him."

They hadn't come back for two hours. During that time, June kept retelling how they fought and how she'd almost shot a guy. I asked how long I'd been gone, and she said,

"Like, five minutes? Maybe less?"

To me, it had felt like forever.

As we were leaving, she picked up the abandoned stag mask. "What happens to them?" she asked of the men who'd fled. "Are they going to die?"

Nick gave a slight raise of his shoulders, as if he didn't care. And maybe he really didn't.

I wasn't sure I did either.

34

Chapter Thirty-Four

October, 2020

I DIDN'T KNOW where they buried Robert, and I had no intention of finding out. The less I knew, the better. No one even mentioned calling the police. When June asked what would happen if someone found the grave, Nick's reply was a curt "They won't."

I clung to the hope that he was right.

Dawn had already broken by the time we left the clearing. Our procession was a grim sight: bloodstained, dirt-smeared, and silent. Bone-deep weariness numbed our senses, leaving only a dull resolve to press on.

Mitch took his knife back, wiped it clean, and tossed it into the river as we crossed the bridge. We agreed not to ditch all the weapons in one place, so we kept the guns. Even though we hadn't killed anyone with them, there were still bullets scattered about. We didn't want to risk leaving a trail.

We dropped off the rental car and crammed into the van, which Nick and Mitch had fixed up, the donut tire a temporary fix for the flat. Mitch was driving, and I tried to get comfortable in the back, but leaning against the seat was impossible. I kept twisting and turning, every part of my battered body aching. Luckily, I didn't need stitches, or at least it didn't seem that way. Nick and June took turns tending to me. It felt nice to be cared for, although I'd have much preferred not to be injured at all.

I was glad to leave Black Water as soon as we could, but we had one more stop to make.

Mitchell argued with Nick that we didn't owe Mathilda anything, since she hadn't directly helped us and had almost gotten me killed, even if it wasn't intentional. To my surprise, Nick stood firm, and Mitchell reluctantly conceded.

The siblings stayed in the idling car, keeping a watchful eye on the square. It looked deserted, as though everyone had gone into hiding.

Nick wanted me to wait in the car, too, but I refused. I wanted to look the witch in the eye. I wanted her to see what she'd put us through.

"Please don't attack her. At least not right away." Nick squeezed my hand, grounding me, making sure I could hold back.

I gave a complicit nod. A crushing heaviness and bruises kept me in check; otherwise, I might've gone for her throat and made her feel the terror she'd let me suffer. But holding my tongue was one thing. Hiding my expression was another. I didn't have the energy to fake a neutral face.

Mathilda had been waiting—I could tell. The moment the doorbell chimed, she emerged from the back of her store. Her stilettos and perfume were back, robin-red lipstick on her mouth, every curl flawless and in place.

The witch's eerily calm, almost cheerful countenance made me seethe. It was like nothing had happened. She knew everything, and yet she'd chosen to stay on the sidelines, sending us off to die for her own hidden motives.

She raised a perfectly arched brow, her mouth curling into a subtle, knowing smile. Somehow, she already knew it was over.

"Where's the other half of your cheerful quartet?" she asked.

"Here. For all your troubles. Now, we're even." Nick ignored her question, skipping the small talk, and handed her a folded piece of paper with the symbol he'd copied from my back. The hand-drawn replica wasn't perfect, but it closely resembled the original—and the one seared into my skin—minus the lacerations.

She took it, scanned the page, and looked at us with a flicker of disappointment.

"That's it? Ain't exactly what I was hoping for."

Nick gave a slight, firm shake of his head. "It's what you get. And it's already quite a lot."

"So, you found it?" she asked, folding her arms, her tone flat and unsurprised. "Where's it at?"

"It's safe," Nick replied. "And it's staying that way. No harm will come from it."

"Books don't cause harm," Mathilda said, eyes narrowing. "People do."

And that was the only thing I could agree with her on. Whether their deity was real or not, it didn't matter. People were the ones who orchestrated violence.

"Tell us why they were doing it. Why did they need the ritual? And what did they need the grimoire for?" Nick asked.

"They need a ritual to get what they're after. And that grimoire—my guess is, it's 'cause it ain't quite right," Mathilda gave me a rueful smile, "and they need the book to tweak it some more. Or to do something else."

"And he wouldn't let you in on the game? Is that why you wanted him gone? Is that why you want the grimoire now?" I asked, remembering Robert's words, how women couldn't be trusted with magic.

The irony of it. Taking witchcraft away from women.

Mathilda's arms tightened around her body. "I wanted it stopped, period. No amount of money or power's worth killin' people for. And what makes you think you're entitled to that grimoire? You think you can handle it better than me?"

The last words were addressed to Nick.

"Yes," he said in a way that left no room for argument.

She went quiet, studying him, as if deciding whether to push back or let it go. Then she waved her hand dismissively, as if saying, *To hell with you. If you get yourself killed because of it, it won't be my fault.*

She turned to me, her gaze lingering on my battered face. "You look like death, girl."

"Thanks to you," I shot back, no longer bothering to hide my resentment.

The witch chuckled, low and throaty. "You best be grateful. If it wasn't for me, this'd still be draggin' on, and you'd be in a whole lot worse shape."

"Why? Can you tell us anything at all?"

Mathilda folded her arms tightly. "That's all I know. They figured out how to summon the deity, tradin' favors for lives. And that's all I'm tellin' you. Leave it be."

"Do we need to worry about the rest of the coven?" Nick asked.

She shook her head. "They're probably hidin', shakin' in their boots. I'll handle them if they ever work up the nerve to show their faces."

I wondered what it was about Robert she couldn't handle when she wasn't afraid of six men. Either way, I didn't care. If they came for her, that was her problem. What mattered was that they didn't come for us.

"What about Robert's clients?"

Mathilda chewed her lip. "Don't know who they are. And best you be careful, too. Don't go digging too deep."

I interjected, "You almost got me killed. *Now* you're telling us to be careful?"

"How was I supposed to know they'd take aim at you? And I figured your beau here would've had your back. I'm a psychic, not a mind reader."

"But you knew!" I spat. "You knew it was Robert this entire time. You've been screwing us over."

Mathilda's laughter rang through the room, a light, tinkling sound, as she turned away to rummage through her shelves. "Trust me, sugar, I ain't been lyin' to nobody. If anythin', I've been the only one tellin' it like it is around here."

She approached me slowly, her presence wrapping around me like a net. Despite being much shorter, she radiated a power that unsettled me up close. I couldn't look away from her, hypnotized. Her fingers grazed the bruise on my cheek.

"I've been lookin' out for y'all since the day I knew you were in town," she murmured softly and gave Nick a smile. "And hey, all's well that ends well, right? Even if some secrets are best left unspoken."

Nick, tense throughout the conversation, gently pulled me away from her.

She stepped back and reached for a shelf behind her, then presented me with a small pouch. "Here. Take this. It'll help you heal."

I eyed her warily, trying to figure out what her game was this time, but she seemed genuine.

"Just some herbs from my patch for your tea," she said.

I instinctively reached for the pouch, only for Nick to catch my wrist.

Mathilda tossed the pouch onto the table. "Suit yourselves. Just tryin' to help."

"Let's get out of here," Nick said, and I followed him, my anger draining, leaving me limp and hollow.

The witch called after us with a sarcastic, "Don't be

strangers," just as the doorbell chimed and the door clicked shut behind us.

Finally, we were done with her.

THE EARLY MORNING sun spilled a pale, cold light over the landscape as we rolled out of Black Water. The town felt changed somehow—less put together, as if a strange weight had been lifted, leaving behind a fragile emptiness. It was now just like any other neglected small American town, weathered and worn. On the church steps, the Reverend swept in slow, deliberate strokes. He caught sight of our car but quickly looked away.

We hadn't stopped to properly clean up; just changed out of the bloodied clothes to avoid drawing attention, but we had meticulously wiped down the weapons before hitting the main road. We dumped them into a local river, where they sank slowly into the murky depths.

Once we passed the sign that read 'You are now leaving Black Water,' I exhaled, trying to expel some of the tension from my chest. We were still a reasonable distance from the highway, crawling along a narrow, empty back road where it would've been far too easy for someone to intercept us. I kept glancing behind us, checking for any sign of pursuit.

Nothing. Just the hollow stretch of asphalt.

Mitch drove with June beside him in the passenger seat, staring silently out the window. Nick sat next to me, eyes closed, breathing steadily.

"Why did Robert say you couldn't use it?" June asked, snapping out of her reverie and turning to us.

"Hm?" Nick opened his eyes, squinting against the bright light.

"The book. Why did he think you couldn't use it?"

"No idea. He was crazy. Just wanted the grimoire back."

That answer seemed to satisfy June, and she settled back into her seat. But only moments later, she turned to face us again.

"We never learned why he killed your mom."

Nick let out a frustrated breath. "It's not like we can ask now." His eyes fluttered closed.

The mystery of why Robert had killed Nick's mother bothered me, too. Had she crossed paths with him, interfered with his plans, or perhaps sought the grimoire for herself? Was this why Mathilda preferred to stay away?

"You think the others will come for us? The ones that ran away?" June pressed on, ignoring the cue to let Nick rest.

"I doubt it," Nick replied with a sigh.

June asked, "You think they'll come for the grimoire?"

"Shouldn't we just destroy it?" I cut in, my thoughts racing back to all the insanity and death this book had caused.

"No one will come for it. But if they do—well, that's even more reason to hold on to it. Now, can you please let me rest a little? I've got a long drive ahead."

June persisted. "But what about that thing in the woods?"

"June, stop," Mitchell interrupted, his voice weary.

"Why? What if that monster goes on a killing spree now that we've set it free?"

"There was nothing in the woods," Mitchell cut her off firmly. "Just a bunch of crazies who kidnapped and killed people."

Nick didn't even bother engaging, letting Mitchell hold on to his version of events. June pouted and angrily slumped back in her seat.

The truth was, I didn't see anything in the woods. I was scared and hurt. Even Lucas's phone could have been a hallucination. I regretted leaving it behind. It would've proven something. But maybe it was better that I didn't bring it back with me. Admitting it was real was just as terrifying.

I looked back one more time. A white car was approaching us quickly. My heart started racing.

"There's someone," I whispered in a tight voice.

Before Nick or the others could react, the car drew closer, its overhead lights flashing and the siren honking briefly. The Sheriff.

Nick stayed motionless, slumped in his seat with his arms crossed, but his posture stiffened.

"Are we in trouble? We should've kept the guns!" June panicked, but her brother gestured for her to be quiet.

The Sheriff leaned into the open window, his piercing eyes scanning each of us.

"All four of y'all made it out? No casualties?" he asked, his tone slightly amused, but it was hard to tell if it was genuine or sarcastic. No one answered; it was clearly a rhetorical question.

"Where is he?" the Sheriff demanded gruffly.

For a heartbeat, I wasn't sure who he meant. But it became clear: Robert.

"Gone," Nick replied from the back seat.

The Sheriff's gaze narrowed. "Is he dead?"

Nick sat rigid, jaw clenched. "We weren't exactly in the mood to check his pulse."

The Sheriff's lip curled. "Where's the body, funny guy?"

"Gone," Nick repeated flatly.

The Sheriff's eyes darkened, his stare like a threat. "Any chance someone might stumble upon him?" he asked, voice low.

Nick shook his head.

The Sheriff exhaled with a hiss. "I'll take it from here when his wife notices he's missing."

"Why are you doing this?" Nick asked.

"Because I have to."

"Then why were you covering for Robert?"

"Cause I didn't have a choice. Now, get on outta here and lay low. Pray nobody comes lookin' for ya. Big folks are gonna be upset."

"Maybe throw us a bone so we know what to expect? Mafia? The government?" Nick asked, and I couldn't tell if he was teasing the Sheriff or being serious.

The Sheriff didn't respond, just clicked his tongue, turned his back, and got into his car.

Mitchell waited until the Sheriff made a U-turn and drove off in the opposite direction. Then he started the car, and we kept moving. Whatever it was, we'd just been let off with a warning.

WE GAVE Mitchell and June a ride to the terminal. Saying goodbye felt strange.

But wrapping my mind around the reality of what had happened was even harder. It already felt like a distant, fading dream. We each had our own perspective on the events of that night, and while they listened to my account with concern, Mitchell never wavered in his belief. He was convinced that Robert had been part of a cult, that the disappearances had been meticulously orchestrated. But the inexplicable earthquake tremor remained a mystery, and despite scouring the internet for news of a local seismic activity, we found nothing. The same went for whoever was covering for Robert. Somehow, he managed to instill fear in so many people, convincing them he was performing magic favors, and they drank his Kool-Aid without question.

June hugged both Nick and me goodbye, holding on to me a little longer, whispering, "We'll still text, okay? Maybe meet up sometime?"

"Of course," I said, and I meant it. I had grown attached to her.

Mitchell wrapped his arms around me, mindful not to touch my back, then exchanged a firm handshake with Nick.

In the end, it didn't matter much who believed what. What mattered was that we had faced some bad people and managed to stop them. We got the answers to what had happened to Lucas and Amanda, and to many others who had disappeared before them, even if those answers weren't entirely clear.

Still, uncertainty lingered about the people the Sheriff had hinted at—their reach, their influence. Were they a secret society, a religion, weaving a web of power? It sounded like the plot of a thriller, but the world had seen stranger things. In the end, we had no choice but to leave it at that.

As soon as we crossed state lines, we stopped at a motel next to an auto shop—we couldn't go much farther on the donut. While we waited, we used the time to get some much-needed rest.

Lying in bed, I turned to him.

"I saw you in the woods," I whispered, as if saying it aloud would make it more real.

I hadn't said anything before. Everyone had been too caught up in other things, and honestly, I was so disoriented and confused that I doubted what happened, and it was hard to put it into words. When I tried to tell them about it, only a mumble of disjointed, half-spoken sentences came out. But now that I had time to process it, I needed to let it out. Even though I wasn't sure it had really happened, it scared me to death.

"What do you mean?"

"When I was there alone... I saw something. First, it was my dad. Just like I remember him from the funeral. But he was wearing this mask, like Robert's men. Then it changed, and I saw you wearing the same mask."

Nick looked at me for a few moments, tentative, mulling over what I'd said.

"I was at the clearing the entire time."

The image of Nick with that mask on was so vivid. "Do you think I'm crazy?" I asked.

"Of course not. Whatever you saw—it's legit. Whether it was real or not. It probably just took the shape of whatever was on your mind."

"Which means it wasn't real?"

"I guess," he said, and reached out to gently tuck a strand of my hair behind my ear.

I wondered why I hadn't seen Lucas in the woods. Maybe because, while the guilt I felt over him consumed me, he slipped out of my mind and heart completely.

THE TRIP to Duluth took almost three full days because I couldn't drive, and we both needed rest. It felt like a spontaneous decision, but it also seemed like the only reasonable thing to do. I couldn't show up at my mother's house in the state I was in, with the car dented and too many questions waiting for answers. Nick didn't push me, but his offer to go to his place and stay there for a while made sense. And deep down, I was starting to feel excited about it. My guilt was slowly lifting, and I no longer felt the urge to run from him. He had been right all along: running away doesn't fix anything.

Nick seemed worried, though he didn't voice his concerns. He avoided highways, opting instead for quieter country roads, which added even more time to our journey.

Every night, I was haunted by nightmares. I kept waking up in a cold sweat, shaking, sometimes bleeding from the wound on my shoulder. In my dreams, I was back in the woods, running from something I could never quite see, something always just behind me. But I found comfort in the fact that I was dreaming again, after days of nothing but a black void every time I closed my eyes.

Sometimes, my thoughts drifted to Lucas. I wondered whether he had known what would happen, or if he genuinely believed his wish would be granted. I leaned toward the latter.

He had trusted his own father, and in return, he had been betrayed and murdered. Sacrificed.

The thought sent chills through me every time.

35

Chapter Thirty-Five

LIVING with Nick was strange initially. We no longer had to sneak around, but it still felt odd without Mitch and June. I had only ever known Nick in relation to the siblings, as a contrast to Mitch, and the target of June's sarcasm and complaints. And now, suddenly, he was just himself.

I wasn't sure how to feel about living with a guy I'd only known for a few weeks. I'd never lived with a lover before, and something told me this wasn't how people usually did it—moving in after less than a month, with no plan and no clear future. But then again, our situation wasn't exactly typical. And despite all my doubts and fears, it wasn't bad at all. Quite the opposite.

Nick was sensible and kind, and he never put any expectations on me. He made sure I was comfortable and gave me space while still staying close. He never asked what I planned to do, and whenever I tried to reassure him I'd find a job to help with the bills, he brushed it off and asked me to focus on getting better and making myself at home.

My burns and lacerations were healing well, and Nick took meticulous care of them, changing the bandages each day. Though he never flinched, I still felt self-conscious exposing the raw, unsightly marks on my skin, even with his constant reassurance that they didn't diminish my appearance or attractiveness.

On the outside, my body was gradually mending. Inside, however, the darkness remained. The nightmares persisted. Every night, I was back in the woods—running, scared, and hurt. Sometimes, something was out there with me. Other times, I was alone beneath a black sky and tangled branches. I wasn't sure which was worse. Each nightmare ended with me bolting upright, drenched in cold sweat. Nick never asked what they were about. He simply offered his closeness.

The Sheriff's warning to lie low still echoed in our minds. We kept an eye on the news, unsure if anyone was looking for us. But everything remained quiet. There were only a few strange events that might have been coincidences: unexpected political shifts, bursts of social unrest, and unusual fluctuations in the corporate world and stock market.

The world outside felt both suspicious and ordinary, leaving us suspended in a state of uncertainty.

AFTER BLACK WATER, the feeling of being watched lingered, clinging to me like a shadow. It made me glance over my shoulder whenever we stepped outside and strain my ears at every passing car. One time, during my second week in Duluth, someone used Nick's driveway to make a U-turn. Nick wasn't home, and I panicked. I grabbed a kitchen knife and hid in the closet, crying and praying they wouldn't come for me. That's how Nick found me, and it took a long time for me to calm down.

But over time, distance and our quiet routine began to

envelop us like fog, softening my paranoia and distorting my memories into something dreamlike.

Part of me, the rational part, was wary of the influential people the Sheriff had hinted at, the ones who might come for us or for the grimoire Nick kept in his office. But beneath that lay a more profound, less logical fear: that the deity in the woods had been real, and it wasn't finished with me yet. I worried it might still find a way back, or worse, that I'd brought some piece of it with me. Maybe I'd inhaled too much of its air, let it into my blood and bones. Perhaps I hadn't walked away untouched.

It sounded ridiculous when said out loud, like something from one of those possession films I'd watched too many times, but the fear didn't care about logic.

One night, after waking from a nightmare, I broke down. Through sobs, I told Nick that I was terrified I carried something from the woods inside me. I begged him to get rid of the grimoire, convinced it was drawing something to us and that nothing good would ever come from keeping it.

Nick didn't mock or minimize. He pulled me into his arms and promised that I would be okay. That he'd never use the grimoire for summoning forest demons or causing any kind of havoc. He joked that if I ever started showing signs of possession, he'd haul me to church and dunk me in holy water without hesitation. I laughed through tears, and eventually the panic ebbed.

By morning, the anxiety seemed distant, the breakdown embarrassing in the way nightmares often are after the sun comes up. But when I apologized, Nick only shook his head and said he'd do whatever it took—even go to church every Sunday —if it made me feel safe.

He was more at ease in his own space, talking more, smiling more, and even cracking jokes.

During the day, while he worked—packaging and mailing orders, managing inventory, and maintaining the website—I explored the house's dark rooms, creaky floors, hidden corners, and cozy nooks. Like a cautious cat in unfamiliar territory, I started by pacing through the indoors but eventually ventured outside, prowling the neighborhood streets and even making solo store runs.

I was still nervous about driving the van, afraid someone might recognize it, so I used Nick's truck instead, hiding behind Minnesota plates and pretending to be local.

The Dodge sat quietly in the backyard, dented and frost-dusted, untouched since our arrival from Black Water. Winter had come early here, far harsher than I was used to, so I made a habit of starting the engine periodically to ensure it hadn't given up entirely.

As I regained strength and could move without worrying about reopening wounds, I started cleaning and rearranging things. Nick didn't mind. He said if nesting helped me feel better or more at home, I could do whatever I liked. While it didn't necessarily make me feel at home, it gave me something to focus on, a way to occupy my jittery hands.

I avoided the old storefront, though. Partly because I didn't want to interfere with the way Nick had arranged things in there, and partly because it reminded me too much of Mathilda and everything tangled up in that memory. The place made my stomach turn.

IN DECEMBER, we celebrated Nick's birthday, just the two of us. Although he had friends in the area, he opted for a low-key night out. We went out for tacos, had a few margaritas, and ended up getting kicked out of a bar for making out a little too passionately. We laughed the whole way home.

Fridays became our quiet tradition. Nick handled the bookkeeping, and I kept him company. He'd build a fire, pour me a glass of wine or hard apple cider, and we'd settle by the fireplace. With his laptop open and balance sheets on his screen, he'd work while I chatted and flirted, pretending to distract him. I knew he liked it.

I tried going for runs, but January's cold and wind quickly killed that motivation. Around the same time, I took on a part-time job at a community center, where I helped with senior events twice a week. I also volunteered to drop off Nick's store orders at the post office, taking any excuse to get out and feel useful.

Sometimes, my mom would call.

At first, she was furious. She accused me of worrying her with a cryptic call and then disappearing. She tried her usual manipulation tactics, but they no longer had the desired effect. Surviving a deranged group masquerading as a witch coven led by my ex-boyfriend's father had recalibrated my tolerance for emotional drama. My mother's tricks no longer registered. I was done being led through the darkness by anyone else's hand. I had to find my own way, free from guilt and emotional strings.

I tried to explain it gently, but she sulked for weeks, clearly hoping to provoke me. When I didn't react, she eventually gave up. I think part of her was just relieved I'd left Minneapolis, where the whole Lucas mess had taken place, and was slowly accepting that she no longer had full control over my life.

I told her a carefully crafted story: that I'd planned to visit Lucas's parents in West Virginia before coming home, but ended up having an emotional breakdown that made me realize I couldn't go back to living with her.

She asked if I was on drugs. I reassured her I wasn't.

I didn't mention Nick. It felt too personal, too drastic an update to share over the phone. If things worked out, I decided to ease her into it eventually. But she guessed anyway; she kept asking if I was with someone.

Maybe I owed her more of an explanation. But to give one, I'd have to lie more, and I didn't want to do that. Over time, she started speaking to me with a little more respect, likely because I stood my ground with quiet resolve—something I should have done a long time ago.

We never spoke of my dad again, and I was glad. Some memories were best left untouched, not resurrected and dissected.

ONE THING that truly unsettled me was Nick's obsession with the grimoire.

He didn't study it constantly, but when he did, it was with an intensity that sent a cold ripple through me. Sometimes he'd sit hunched over it for hours, taking notes, eyes flicking across the pages like they were whispering to him. When I asked what he was looking for, he said, "I just want to know what's in it, why they thought it was so important."

And maybe that was true. But beneath it, something else stirred. Nick wasn't just curious. He was hooked. Mesmerized.

And that terrified me.

Some nights, he stayed up late reading, then slipped into bed with cold hands and wild eyes, waking me with his nervous energy. He'd touch me absentmindedly, his mind clearly still tangled up in whatever he'd read. I pretended to be asleep.

I wanted nothing to do with the book. If it were up to me, I'd burn it and bury the ashes deep.

THEN SOMETHING HAPPENED that I couldn't confess to Nick.

One afternoon, while he was out, I went into his office to print shipping labels. The grimoire was on the desk, open. I didn't mean to touch it, but my hand moved before I could think. I flipped through the pages, trying to see what Nick found so fascinating, but it was only brittle paper and nonsense symbols.

I snapped a few pictures with my phone, hoping to run a reverse image search or find a cipher tool online. But the photos came out warped and blurred, with nothing identifiable. At first, I thought it was the dim light, so I turned on the lamp and even stood near the window, but nothing helped. I tried again, and again, with the same result—the ink seemed to melt or shift the moment I hit the button. I attempted to make a video, but that didn't work either.

Nick's truck rumbled into the driveway, and I scrambled, suddenly aware I was invading his privacy. I dropped the book, bolted from the office, and forgot all about the labels. My heart was still hammering when he called up to ask what I wanted for dinner.

I deleted the photos and never went near the book again, not because I was afraid Nick would find out, but because I feared that if I kept digging, I might uncover something I wasn't ready to face.

After that, life returned to its strange version of normal. But beneath it all, there was a quiet tension, like something waiting just out of sight. Some days, it felt as though I couldn't breathe, as if the walls were inching closer.

I kept telling myself it was only paranoia.

JUNE and I texted now and then, but we never called each other. Most of her messages were complaints about her brother's overprotectiveness or questions about how to move away and start over. Then, one afternoon, while I was making dinner and riding the high of a sudden burst of culinary inspiration, my phone rang. Mitchell's name lit up the screen.

"Hey, Foster. How's it hanging?"

I told him I was doing well. "Anything exciting on your end? Did you start the police academy yet?" I tossed the steaks onto the cast iron, and the sizzle was louder than I expected. I jumped away so hot oil wouldn't splatter on me.

"I, uh..." He hesitated. "I'm in firefighter training now. Trying to get certified."

He said it like a confession.

"Really? That's a change. What made you switch?" I reached for a dish towel to wipe up a spill, half-distracted.

"Kinda got disillusioned with the whole police thing," he said. "Figure helping people directly might be more my speed than just filling quotas."

I was taken aback by how honest he sounded. "That actually makes a lot of sense. I bet you'll be great at it." I dropped the knife, and it nearly hit my foot. "Shit."

"You alright? Need me to call back some other time?"

"No, it's fine. I'm just on a cooking mission. But I'm good at multitasking," I said, brushing it off and reaching for the salt, only to knock over a jar of spices. "So, what's up? Is June okay?"

"Yeah, she's fine. Still got her heart set on moving to New York, chasing that art dream."

"What kind of art does she do?" I asked, crouching to gather the spilled spices.

"She doesn't do any art," he said with a deep sigh.

I snickered.

"Listen, Foster..." he began, then went quiet.

"Yeah?" I prompted, only half-focused as I moved around the kitchen.

"I... well... you know..." His voice dropped, barely audible.

Outside, the rumble of a car engine grew louder. "Hold on, Nick's home. Want to say hi?"

"Nick? Our Nick?" He sounded surprised, like it hadn't even occurred to him. "You guys are together?"

I realized then I'd never updated either of them. As far as they knew, Nick and I had gone our separate ways.

"Yeah, kind of," I said, keeping it vague.

"Kind of?" his voice faltered, like he was caught off guard.

"I'm staying with him right now," I said, suddenly feeling awkward. My mind flashed back to the day June had walked in on us, caught in a less-than-appropriate moment in the kitchen of that cabin.

"I see." Mitchell's pause hung in the air.

"You want to talk to him?" I offered.

"It's okay. I gotta go," he said abruptly.

"Wait, didn't you want to tell me something?" I asked. I could feel him holding something back.

"No, it's nothing. Just wanted to check in." His tone had gone flat, like a door quietly shutting.

"Well... alright then," I was puzzled by his reaction. Why would it matter to him if I were with Nick?

"Yeah. Take care, Foster," he said, then hung up.

Nick stepped into the kitchen, bringing a swirl of winter air that briefly cut through the warmth.

"Cold out, huh?" I asked, though I already knew the answer. February rarely surprised.

"Very," he said, shedding his winter coat as he took a deep breath. "Smells amazing. I didn't know you cooked."

"I don't," I admitted. "Just wanted to do something nice for you. So, eat at your own risk." I peered at him. "Mitchell called earlier."

Nick's expression shifted. "What did he say?"

"Not much. He hung up out of nowhere. Now I'm wondering if something's going on."

Nick smirked. "Perhaps he was about to confess his undying love for you and got cold feet."

I laughed. "Yeah, sure." But my smile faded. "What if someone was bothering him, and he was trying to warn us?"

"Then why didn't he?"

"I don't know. Maybe he thought we'd be safer not knowing. Mitch has always been protective."

Nick nodded slowly. "That sounds like Sergeant Mitch."

A STORM RAGED OUTSIDE, the tempest's unrelenting wail jolted me awake. I turned over, reaching out for Nick's warmth, but his side of the bed was empty. I got up and wandered into the room he used as an office. He was hunched over the table, surrounded by books and papers, the grimoire open before him.

"Still trying to summon the devil?" I asked, half-teasing.

Nick jumped. "You almost gave me a heart attack," he said with a shaky laugh. "Why are you up?"

I pulled the blanket tighter around my shoulders. "Couldn't sleep."

He beckoned me over, and I curled into his lap. We sat quietly for a while, the wind rattling the windows as the storm battered the house. Nick held me close, steady and calm.

"Sometimes it feels like this will never end," I murmured.

"Hm?" His breath was warm against my ear.

"Like we're stuck in limbo. Like the storm will go on and on, and we'll just be here forever."

Nick's arms tightened around me. "You feel stuck here? With me?"

I let out a quiet laugh, suddenly self-conscious. "No... not like that. I just meant—"

"I know what you meant," he said gently. "I feel it too. But honestly? I kind of like it. It's like the rest of the world disappeared."

I thought of my mom, how far away she seemed, as though she was living on a different planet. Was she thinking of me, too?

Nick gave my hip a light tap, pulling me back from the spiral. "Come on," he said. "Let's go to bed."

36

Chapter Thirty-Six

March, 2021

AT THE BEGINNING OF MARCH, the weather was bitter, forcing us to venture out only when absolutely necessary. We huddled indoors, where Nick coaxed warmth from the fireplace almost every night; the central heating wheezed and groaned, struggling to hold back the cold.

Now, nearly five months after our trip to Black Water, we still hadn't heard anything. It was like nothing had ever happened there. I occasionally Googled the area to see if there was any news, looking for posts about Robert's death. I wanted to be prepared, just in case. And I was worried the investigation, if the Sheriff had started one, would circle back to me, dragging up questions about my involvement in both Lucas's and his father's disappearances. But days turned into weeks, and weeks into months, and still, nothing.

Curiously enough, I was finally left alone. No one contacted me for interviews or tried to push me for answers anymore. I didn't think it was a miracle, just the natural passage of time. My story had gone stale, and people had moved on.

Even as the drama surrounding me died down, none of my former friends from Minneapolis ever followed up with me. My social media accounts were still active, although I hadn't posted in ages, and my phone number hadn't changed; yet, nobody reached out. To be fair, neither did I.

My phone stayed silent, except for the occasional spam call about my car's extended warranty. Those were easy to ignore. Since my number was registered in Ohio, most of them came from the same area code.

But not this one.

The screen lit up with "Unknown Number." I hesitated, still wary of unfamiliar callers, then decided to take the risk.

"Miss Foster, this is Officer Jenkins from the Minneapolis Police Department," a woman's voice said. "I'm calling regarding your recent inquiry about Lucas Whitman."

I almost fainted. *This is it,* I thought. *They found Robert. They're investigating. We're done.*

It took me a few seconds to remember the officer and my visit to the station in September, nearly half a year ago, before our trip to Black Water.

The woman continued, "This is a courtesy call to inform you that we did look into the links between the individuals you brought to our attention. Are you still there?"

"Yes?" I croaked.

"While I can't disclose specifics, a small connection between Lucas Whitman and the car accident victim Erin Boyd was discovered. Both lived in the same region—"

"Black Water?" I interrupted, too shaken to hold my tongue.

She paused. "Yes. But our investigation suggests that was an isolated coincidence. Erin Boyd died in a car accident. Lucas Whitman is still considered missing."

Relief washed over me, slow and staggering. "Okay." But as her words sank in, a cold dread began to seep into my veins. "Wait. Erin Boyd? Not Mary Flynn?"

"Yes. That was the legal name of the woman."

"And she died in a car accident? She wasn't murdered?"

"Like I said, Miss Foster. A car accident." Her tone cooled. "If that's all—"

"Hold on!" I cut in, panicked she might hang up. "You said Mary—or Erin—lived in Black Water? Please. This might be important."

"Is there something you're not telling me, Miss Foster?"

"No... I'm just trying to understand. Lucas's disappearance ruined my life."

"I can't share that information." Another pause, like she was weighing what she could say. Then a sigh. "The estate now belongs to her surviving relatives. You may be able to find public records online, but I advise you to leave them alone and find other ways to rebuild your life."

"I didn't know she had property in Black Water. I thought she moved years ago," I murmured, barely registering her warning. "So... does that mean it belongs to her son now?"

"I'll repeat myself, Miss Foster: stay out of this. If you come across new information, contact me. Otherwise... good day."

And with that, the line went dead.

This couldn't be right.

I SAT IN STUNNED SILENCE, my heart racing like a jackhammer, trying to piece together the fragments. The puzzle we'd been trying to assemble and make sense of had been upside down all along.

However, without revealing much, the officer provided me with enough information to go on. It hadn't dawned on us that the land deep in the woods could be privately owned. We thought the private property signs were just there to scare off tourists.

That single detail changed everything. If Nick's mother had

property there, then he must have known about it. Why hadn't he mentioned it?

What he told us was that his mother had suddenly gone to Black Water for reasons unknown to him and was murdered there.

I started thinking back. Nick often opted out of things, subtly redirecting us without ever making it obvious. He made it seem like it was my idea, or Mitch's. He said his mother's death wasn't relevant and might get us off track. But did he really believe that, or was it just a convenient excuse?

He was intelligent, inquisitive, and always seeking the truth. He was the one who made most of the connections in the case. Or had he been guiding us the whole time? Nudging us in specific directions while keeping himself in the background? But why? What was he trying to achieve?

The grimoire.

The thought snapped me back to the present. Was I seriously entertaining the idea that Nick, *my Nick*, had orchestrated all of this just to get the damn book? That he'd planned it from the beginning? But we were the ones who'd shown up at his door. Besides, it was Mathilda who gave us the coordinates to the place.

That couldn't be right. He couldn't have known.

I got up and went upstairs to grab my laptop. It wasn't hard to narrow down the approximate location of the clearing—we'd been there enough times. I searched for the parcel number and eventually found the deed and property records. My mind kept racing with a silent, steady *no, no, no*. And then I saw it.

The owner's name:

Nick Boyd.

My heart sank. Everything inside me dropped away.

I stormed into Nick's office, hands trembling, fury and confusion flooding my body. I tore through the shelves, yanking out books and files, looking for anything—an explanation, something to prove it was all a mistake—but instead, I found a folder with a letter from a lawyer confirming the inheritance. Property transfer papers. There it was, in plain black and white. Dates. Signatures. Legal stamps.

I reached for my phone to call Nick, who was out running errands, but stopped myself. One part of me wanted to scream at him, burn the book, throw everything into the fireplace and watch it curl to ash. Another part whispered to stay quiet. To forget I ever found this. To go on like nothing happened. To stay here, in this calm and quiet life we'd built.

Or maybe this wasn't a haven at all. Maybe it was a limbo. A place where you're locked alone with your thoughts and fears, forever spinning in circles, simmering in your own self-loathing.

I had stayed with Lucas, even after the way he treated me. I convinced myself it was love, that I just needed to wait things out.

But that got me nowhere.

It was only a matter of time before the same—or worse— would happen with Nick.

BY THE TIME Nick got home, his entire office was in disarray. Amid the chaos of scattered books and papers I never bothered to pick up, the damning documents lay neatly arranged on the floor, like evidence at a crime scene.

He called out from downstairs. I didn't respond. I was afraid that if I used my voice, I'd start screaming and wouldn't stop until my vocal cords tore into a bloody mess.

Still calling my name, he came upstairs. When he reached the doorway and saw the mess, he stopped short. His eyes scanned the room, then locked onto the papers. Recognition flared in his expression, which then shifted to a sheepish, caught-in-the-act look—the kind of look a husband gets when he's just been found messaging another woman. He took a step forward but froze when I raised a hand, warning him not to come any closer.

"Nell... It's not—" he began, cautiously.

"Do you think I'm stupid?" But maybe I was. It was right there in front of me, and I never cared to check.

"Let me—" he tried again.

"Oh, *now* you want to explain? Now that I've pieced it all together myself?"

"I swear, I had nothing to do with it. I just... didn't know how to tell you," Nick said, stepping toward me again before hesitating. "Nell..." he started, but I sucked in a sharp, furious breath—and that was enough. He stopped, lowering his head just a touch, shoulders falling.

"Okay," I said. "Then tell me. Tell me the whole truth. Right now."

He turned away, ran his hand over his face, and then turned back to me. Finally, he spoke, "My mother was born in Black Water. She got the grimoire from her great-grandmother. The story about the coven is partly true—only the grimoire never disappeared. It's been in my family for generations. Maybe longer. I don't really know."

He lifted his eyes to mine and continued.

"She met Robert when she was very young. Apparently, together they managed to decipher parts of the grimoire and create sigils that actually worked. At some point, she didn't feel safe around him anymore. You've seen him. He was insane. That kind of power... it didn't do him any good."

"What does Lucas have to do with it?"

"He stole the grimoire from her. She didn't see it coming. She didn't even know Robert's son knew anything about it. Robert kept his wife in the dark, so it's weird he told Lucas that much. But he did. Then Lucas forced her to grant his wish. Something ridiculous. Like to be a star athlete. Like getting into some hall of fame or whatever." Nick said, starting to roll his eyes.

That explained why Lucas had the grimoire. He didn't steal it from his father. He stole it from the real coven leader—Nick's mother. Robert didn't kill his son.

But Lucas had come back different. So full of himself. So confident. No talismans, none of the usual gear he'd bring to a game. Just blind arrogance.

"And she sacrificed him instead? He didn't even know?"

Nick nodded, eyes cast downward.

"How did you get us to come to you?"

"I didn't. I wasn't expecting you at all. But… I recognized you. After what my mother had done, I kept an eye on the story."

Silence stretched between us. He kept glancing from me to the floor.

"You believe all of this?"

"Don't you?" he asked quietly. "You've seen it. With your own eyes."

"You made me think it was just my imagination."

"What did you want me to say? That it was all real? You were already barely sleeping. You looked like a ghost. How could I do that to you?"

"You did so much worse," I said, my voice low, soaked in contempt.

"I never wanted any of this to happen to you."

"But it was worth it in the end, wasn't it?" I said, the venom in my tone reminding me of my mother during her fights with Dad. "You got what you came for. In fact, I handed it to you."

"The grimoire's been in my family for centuries. I can't let it be out there for anyone to figure out. I just wanted to keep it safe."

But he was lying to me and himself. I could see it already beginning to consume him. That same glossed-over look in his eyes I'd seen in Robert's. Even if he meant to keep it safe, there was no guarantee he wouldn't go down the same path. Just like his mother. Just like Robert.

How could he hold me, care for me, be with me every night and lie to me so completely? The betrayal burned so deep I thought it might split me in two. But I held onto the anger. Clung to it. Because anger is easier than heartbreak. Easier than shattering into pieces right in front of him.

"What about Mathilda? What's her deal? She knew you, didn't she?"

"She knew my mother. But I swear, I didn't lie to you. I had no idea who she was. She said my mother helped her years ago, and Mathilda felt grateful. Attached. That's why I asked her to be the one to lead us to the clearing."

The clearing, nestled in the woods his mother once owned, now his. A place where people came willingly, hoping for their wishes to be granted, only to be sacrificed and vanish without a trace.

"Why am I here?" I asked quietly. "Keeping me close just so you could watch me? Make sure I didn't find out?"

"I didn't bring you here to trap you. I brought you here because I didn't know how else to keep you safe," Nick said. "Because when I'm with you, I don't feel like I'm drowning in all the crap my mother left behind. Because you're the only thing that feels real in all this mess."

He stepped forward carefully and placed his hands around me, touching me ever so slightly. I pulled away.

He wasn't the Prince Charming, saving me from the dragon. He was the wicked wizard, condemning me to the tower.

"Nell—" he began, but I cut him off.

"You're a coward, hiding behind our backs."

Nick tried to speak, but I interrupted him again.

"I have one more question."

"Ask away," he said, hopelessly. He didn't bother denying

the accusations. He knew they were true. He held my gaze, finally owning up to it.

"Did you know your mother planned to kill Lucas?"

Nick's jaw clenched in anguish. His face twisted in a struggle to find words, but none came. I closed my eyes, fighting back tears.

"I do care about you. I looked out for Mitch and June, too. I never meant to lie. I just didn't know how to explain without being the bad guy. They wouldn't believe me."

He skirted the question, but in doing so, revealed the truth.

"You're not just the bad guy, Nick," I hissed, "You're the villain."

"I'm not! I wanted the grimoire to stop Robert's harm."

I shook my head. "I have no idea why you wanted the grimoire, but stopping Robert was just an excuse. Ironically, if you'd told us earlier, we would've taken you at your word. Now, no one will believe you. But it doesn't matter, does it? You've got your precious grimoire."

"Do you know what your problem is?" Nick snapped, shifting from forced calm to full attack mode. He uncrossed his arms and stepped forward, making me instinctively retreat.

"Your problem is that you live in an idealistic delusion where good is absolute," he continued, tossing his hands in the air. "But the world isn't black and white. Good needs fists and weapons to fight back—and sometimes to strike first."

He sounded uncannily like Robert, rationalizing every choice he'd made.

"You're right, the world isn't black and white," I agreed. "But I won't let you—or anyone else—dictate my morals. You lied to us from the start. It almost got me killed. How can I believe you now?"

"Would you have believed me then? All you, Mitch, and June did was suspect me!" He was losing his patience, edging on desperate.

"All I did was defend you and find excuses for you!" I sobbed, hastily wiping tears away with the back of my hand.

His chest rose and fell with a slow breath. "I'll do anything to prove you can trust me."

"Then do it," I said, "Destroy the grimoire."

He went still. "I can't."

"Are you going to use it for a summoning again?"

"What? No!"

"Then destroy it! Prove that I can trust you."

His gaze dropped again, and he repeated, "I can't."

And that was what I feared most. Something I had been bracing myself to hear. He, like Robert, cared about the book more than anything else. Drawn to the idea of such power. He might not realize it yet or simply wasn't willing to admit it, but at its core, that's what it was all about.

I suddenly felt awakened, resolute, as if someone had dumped a bucket of ice water over me. After the initial shock of accepting the truth, I was ready to take the necessary steps.

"Please don't leave," Nick pleaded. "I never meant to hurt you."

"Then you should've thought ahead," I seethed, and in that moment, I noticed a haunting resemblance to Robert. The same hairline. The same height. Perhaps Nick's mother and Robert had shared more than just coven ties.

I forced myself to walk around him, down the stairs, and out the front door to the Dodge, fighting the urge to look back, to see if he was watching. Leaving was the only right decision.

Tears threatened as I drove away, but it wasn't until his house vanished from the rearview mirror that I let myself cry. I still managed to pull out the SIM card and toss it so he couldn't reach me. Now, I had to focus on my own disappearance. In case he came for me.

I didn't doubt he could let me go. But I was certain he'd still come for the grimoire—safely tucked under layers of clothes in my blue Ikea bag.

Epilogue

MY FINGERS WERE DRUMMING a staccato beat on the table when Mitchell finally walked into the coffee shop. I'd only been waiting for five minutes, but I kept mistaking every blonde man for him, afraid I'd forgotten what he looked like. I hadn't seen him since we left Black Water.

He gave me a long hug, and we exchanged warm greetings. It felt surreal to see him in Brooklyn, still sporting the same haircut and wide smile I remembered.

It had been nearly six months since I left Duluth, and I had only recently told him the truth and asked for his help. Instead of answering, he changed the subject and shared some surprising news: his sister was moving to the city too.

We settled in, and I clutched my iced latte, afraid the glass might start rattling in my nervous hands. He glanced around the cozy coffee shop in Cobble Hill, taking in the mismatched chairs, the plants, and the worn-out bookshelves. I could tell from the look on his face that he was a Starbucks guy.

"How's June?" I asked.

"Fine. Excited," he replied. "Dropped her off at her place. She's unpacking still. Told her I needed some fresh air and to stretch my legs."

August was sweltering and oppressive, so his excuse for preferring the scorching streets to the comfort of an air-conditioned apartment felt flimsy, but if his sister didn't object, it wasn't my place to judge. We had agreed to meet without her.

"I'm still shocked she's actually doing this. And you're helping her!"

"Yeah, well," Mitch rubbed the back of his neck, "time for her to fly solo, make her own mistakes."

In the Winter, Mitch had been skeptical about June moving, and neither of us thought she was serious. But shortly after I left Minnesota, she applied to an RN training program and got accepted. Her fall semester was about to start. She hadn't said anything to either of us until she received the official news, and though Mitch had his reservations—we'd talked about it a few times—he was proud of her. I was, too.

"Anyway, I'm glad to see you. And thrilled about June's move. Maybe you'll be around more, too?" I said, trying to keep my nerves from showing.

"Nah, East Coast ain't my style. Too much chaos. Besides, I gotta get back home by Monday."

"When's your training over? Can you officially call yourself a firefighter now?" I asked, shifting the subject.

"Already done. Been working for a month now. Just here for the weekend," he said, looking down with a modest smile.

"Congrats! Too bad you have to leave so soon. But if June needs anything, I'll be around."

"Thanks for looking out for her," he said.

"Sure thing. Alcohol, weed, and sex dungeon passes. Whatever she needs!" I teased.

Mitchell gave a wry laugh, shaking his head in mock disapproval. Then his face turned serious.

"So, you hear from—" he started to ask.

I cut him off. "No."

"That's good, I suppose." Mitchell rubbed the back of his neck again.

The coffee shop was bustling with people coming and going, with a line forming at the counter. The smell of fresh pastries almost seduced me, even in this heat. We were lucky to have snagged a table by the window. Here, amidst the chaos of the big city, I felt safer than anywhere else. And for the first time since we'd left Black Water, I could finally talk about it.

"Is that why you called me back in Winter? To tell me?"

We hadn't spoken about Nick since. I'd briefly told Mitch what happened, and he'd acknowledged it without surprise. I gave him everything I knew, including that I'd stolen the grimoire.

Mitch gave a curt tilt of his head, his eyes avoiding mine.

"How did you find out?" I asked.

A heavy pause hung in the air before he spoke. "Remember that private property sign? It kept bugging me, so I did some digging. Turns out it belonged to... well, you know who. Rest was easy to piece together. Figured he knew all along and was after the book himself. So I thought I'd let you know."

Mitch must have gone down the same path I had, only he'd connected the dots himself.

"Why didn't you?"

His shoulders rose in a shrug. "You seemed happy, safe. Didn't want to go ruining it for you."

We fell silent for a moment. I kept looking into my coffee, unsure how to feel about it. Always the one to tell others what to do, Mitch hadn't wanted to ruin my happiness, even if it meant leaving me in the dark.

While I tried to decide whether it was noble or deceitful, he continued. "Sorry it didn't work out, but I'm glad you know the truth now. Didn't want to be the one to hurt you, that's all. If it's any consolation, I think he really did care about you, all that crazy stuff aside. Maybe you were the one thing that kept him grounded, you know?"

A weight lifted off my shoulders. Hearing that from someone else felt strangely reassuring. I didn't know what Nick had been up to or what choices he'd been making, and I wasn't sure I could have changed any of them. He may have tried to be the best version of himself for me. But in the end, I had to face the truth: Nick was a manipulator and a liar. There was no reason for me to keep sacrificing my life, holding my love like a burning candle for him, hoping he wouldn't go off the rails.

"You've got nothing to apologize for. And thank you," I said.

"For what?" Mitchell looked genuinely surprised.

I looked at him and saw a different person from the one I'd met last fall. This new Mitchell had learned to let go, even when it hurt, and to prioritize others' feelings over his own sense of righteousness.

"For being a good friend. Speaking of which..." I opened my tote and pulled out a large edition of a popular fantasy book, a little pun I couldn't resist.

Mitchell's eyes widened in surprise.

"Is this...?" he started to ask.

"Uh-huh," I said, smiling. "How do you like the makeover I gave it?"

Mitchell raised an eyebrow. "Disturbing. I'll take care of it. It'll be—"

"I don't want to know," I interrupted, shaking my head. "Just make sure it's somewhere safe, where no one will find it."

"Why didn't you burn it like you wanted?"

"I thought about it," I confessed, "but I was scared it'd do more harm than good. After all, we really don't know what this is. I left Nick because he lied and put us in danger over it. But I'm not a crazy book burner."

Mitchell slid the grimoire into his backpack, and I breathed a sigh of relief. Even though I'd spared the book, having it with me again felt heavy with malevolent energy, especially after unknowingly holding onto it for so long. People had died over it.

Mitch suddenly leaned in, "I got a buddy to dig into Robert's finances, his sawmill and all," he said, his voice low and cautious.

I stilled. "What did you find?"

"They wired large chunks of cash to him a few times. Couple times from real people. He wouldn't name them, and I didn't push it, didn't want to put my buddy in a tight spot. But a few times, bigger sums came from offshore companies that got dissolved right after."

"Did your friend find out who was behind those?"

Mitch shook his head. "Nah. And he told me to back off, not to dig any deeper. Said if we start sniffing around them, they might start sniffing around us. So we just let it go. It just... ain't right. Amanda's life—and others'—were thrown away so some rich folks could get richer."

"So the people behind it were... powerful?" I asked, watching him closely. He had to know more than he was saying.

He gave a slow nod.

"How powerful?"

His voice dropped.

"Very."

Goosebumps rose on my arms despite the heat. The coven actually had some serious clients. Getting confirmation of that was too spooky for my liking.

Mitch gave me a serious look. "Let's keep June out of this. She's been through enough."

"Sure."

He glanced around the coffee shop, where people were typing away on their laptops or chatting in small groups. Just as Nick had once said, lots of faces, but no one really cares about you. To me, that anonymity was comforting. I was a drop of water in the vast ocean.

"It's tough, letting her go. And so far away," Mitch admitted suddenly.

"She'll still be your little sister. And trust me, she'll feel closer to you now than ever before."

Mitch looked away for a moment, clearly struggling to contain his emotions. He took a deep breath before continuing. "You know, I've always known I got my temper from my dad. Always figured there'd come a day when I'd turn out just like him. That's why I had to get out of the military. Got into a scrap. I was scared to death back in Black Water that I'd mess everything up, that she'd get hurt on account of me."

I reached out and placed a reassuring hand on his arm. "You are not your father, Mitch. And you didn't ruin anything. You saved us all."

Mitch's gaze faltered. "I don't know about that."

I squeezed his arm gently. "I've lived with you for several weeks, Mitch. You're a good person. An amazing big brother and friend. And I would never be scared of you, because I know you. You were always there when we needed you."

Mitch nodded again, his eyes still cast downward. He squeezed his mug of untouched coffee. "Thanks," he said, "You're a good kid, Foster."

I smiled inwardly at him calling me kid, even though he was only a couple of years older than me, and hoped he knew I meant every word I'd said.

"You like it here?" Mitchell asked.

I beamed in agreement. "I do."

Here, I was in my element. Finishing my degree, working, and living in the city I had grown to adore made me feel in control of my life. The ridiculous rent a relatively small price to pay for the sense of self I had found.

The Lucas ordeal was finally behind me, and although

memories of Nick still lingered, they no longer felt like an open wound. I was moving on, healing like the scar on my back.

Nick had been right about one thing: we needed to move toward a purpose, not just run away from things. Sometimes, that meant making hard choices.

And so far, I've been happy with the ones I've made.